A GOVERNESS OF GREAT TALENTS

The Governess Bureau, Book 2

Emily E K Murdoch

ARE YOU SIGNED UP FOR DRAGONBLADE'S BLOG?

You'll get the latest news and information on exclusive giveaways, exclusive excerpts, coming releases, sales, free books, cover reveals and more.

Check out our complete list of authors, too!

No spam, no junk. That's a promise!

Sign Up Here

www.dragonbladepublishing.com

Dearest Reader;

Thank you for your support of a small press. At Dragonblade Publishing, we strive to bring you the highest quality Historical Romance from the some of the best authors in the business. Without your support, there is no 'us', so we sincerely hope you adore these stories and find some new favorite authors along the way.

Happy Reading!

CEO, Dragonblade Publishing

Additional Dragonblade books by Author Emily E K Murdoch

The Governess Bureau Series
A Governess of Great Talents (Book 1)
A Governess of Discretion (Book 2)

Never The Bride Series
Always the Bridesmaid (Book 1)
Always the Chaperone (Book 2)
Always the Courtesan (Book 3)
Always the Best Friend (Book 4)
Always the Wallflower (Book 5)
Always the Bluestocking (Book 6)
Always the Rival (Book 7)
Always the Matchmaker (Book 8)
Always the Widow (Book 9)
Always the Rebel (Book 10)
Always the Mistress (Book 11)
Always the Second Choice (Book 12)

The Lyon's Den Connected World
Always the Lyon Tamer

Welcome to the Governess Bureau

You are most welcome, sir or madam.

When the nobility and gentility of England are at their wits end, they send a discrete note to Miss Vivienne Clarke's Governess Bureau. Only accepting the very best clients, their governesses are coveted by minor royalty, with every governess following three rules:

1. *You must have an impeccable record.*
2. *You must bring a special skill to the table.*
3. *You must never fall in love...*

CHAPTER ONE

October 30, 1812

I T WAS ALMOST certainly her. Miss Anne Gilbert had only had the pleasure of her acquaintance for a few days, that was true, but there was no mistaking that look, something more than smug, more than happy. It was almost…incandescent joy.

"Hallo, Meredith—I thought you were up north with some duke?"

Anne grinned at the woman dressed in far finer furs than she had ever seen her in before. She turned—it *was* Meredith. Miss Meredith Hubert, fellow governess of the Governess Bureau. But if the rumors were to be believed, then the gentleman beside her, all dark brooding and serious, was the man she had been posted to.

The man she had broken all rules for…and married.

Anne could not help herself. "Goodness, are you it?"

She stepped forward to get a better look, no self-consciousness at all. It was what her mother had always scolded her for, but at almost five and twenty, Anne was past caring what her mother said.

Most of the time.

In any case, the gentleman did not appear to mind. A smile

broke out on his face as he looked at Meredith. The sunlight poured down into the alley which housed the governess' entrance to the Bureau, which Anne had been making for, and a chilly wind ruffled his hair.

"Why yes," he laughed ruefully. "I am it."

"The gossip is true then!" Anne launched herself at Meredith, pulling her into an embrace. "You really did marry him?"

"She really did," said what must be the Duke of Rochdale. "Goodness, don't strangle my wife, Miss."

Anne released her with an apologetic grin. She was always wont to allow her emotions get the better of her; it was the red hair. At least, that was what she blamed, which was easier than actually admitting that one's emotions, unlike what they should be in a refined young lady, were always just below the surface.

"Well, I don't mind saying how pleased I am, Meredith, I really don't," Anne said, meaning every word. *There were plenty of opportunities for ladies in 1812*, she thought, *as long as they were brave enough to take them.* "I'm heading in now to find out my next charge. Apparently the master's just arrived!"

"Ah, you'll be for the Earl of Clarcton, then," said Meredith with a knowing smile.

How did she know whom she was to be placed with next? It was a matter of prestige; the grander the title of your master, the more impressed the proprietress was with you.

Anne swallowed. She had just completed her assignment at the Earl of Allun; not an easy job, and it was a slight relief to be rid of him and his brood. *But no one knew about that*, she reminded herself. The secret had stayed with her and always would.

Meredith was watching her, and Anne realized she had not responded.

"Oh, another earl!" She nodded. "Well, you know more than I do, then. Better dash, Miss Clarke is a stickler for punctuality, as you know. Good luck!"

Her heart was thumping as she bid the new duchess adieu and stepped through the governess door into the side passage.

Another earl. Well, she had certainly earned it, Anne thought as she walked lightly along the corridor she knew so well. First a baronet, then another, then an earl, which had quite taken all her resources to manage.

The corridor was quiet. Anne could well remember a few applicants to the place being rejected merely for the heaviness of their steps.

And now an earl. If Meredith was correct, of course, though Anne saw no reason why she would offer the information if merely guessing.

"Being a member of the Governess Bureau is an honor."

That was what Miss Clarke had said the day of her first assignment. She took the staircase that spiraled down to the waiting room. She was right. There was no other place a nobleman would dare consider sourcing a governess from. They were the best.

Anne took a deep breath as she reached the waiting room door and paused.

The moment she walked in, she would be scrutinized, judged, and measured—and that was by the other governesses. She respected Miss Clarke, naturally, but she was rather a gorgon.

Besides, it was coming up to Christmas. Anne had never been one for ceremony, but Christmas had always been a time for family—though she knew precisely what would happen.

A smile crept over her face. As the governess, her mother would swiftly enlist her to care for her many nieces and nephews. Anne had nothing against children; most governesses did not. But with four siblings, each of whom had at least three children…

Anne grasped the door of the waiting room firmly. No. She was ready for her next assignment. This Christmas would be spent with another family, not hers.

The waiting room was half full as she stepped inside and looked for a seat. A few governesses of more advanced years, their gowns in yesteryear's fashions and their hair streaked with silver, sat in a corner muttering. There was a girl who looked half in need of a governess herself, a nervous look on her face. Two ladies Anne recognized as Miss Helena Patrick and Miss Rachel White sat together in silence, each reading a book.

Anne grinned at those who glanced at her and took a seat opposite Miss Clarke's office.

Curiosity was a virtue—or a failure—she had been born with, and she looked around now. Yes, it would be December in just over four weeks, which was always a busy time for the Governess Bureau.

It had surprised her when she had first joined the ranks. Christmas was a time for family; that was what her father had always said. Why would a nobleman wish to introduce a stranger into the home at such a time?

"Because," Miss Clarke had informed her when she had unwisely asked such an unguarded question, *"a nobleman will wish to enjoy the season, and that is simply impossible without a governess."*

Anne had not quite believed her until her first posting. Sir Moses of Wandorne had been a pleasant enough gentleman; that was, he was kind to his wife and children, and Anne had seen no ill of him.

But when December appeared, she had not seen him for almost six weeks. Every evening, an engagement in town, a ball, a house party, a dinner at the Hall…

It was a wonder, Anne had thought at the time, he remembered he had any children.

"Good…good morning," said a young lady nervously.

Anne smiled. *Poor thing.* First time being given a posting, if she was any judge, and with that sort of reticence, Miss Clarke may not be impressed. There were many a lady who joined the Governess Bureau only to be disappointed and never receive an assignment.

The families that came to the Governess Bureau, after all, were looking for something…well, a little different.

"Good morning," she replied with a smile, receiving a glare from one of the reading ladies, as though she had interrupted the sacred silence of a library.

Anne caught the nervous-looking girl's eye and grinned. "I am Anne Gilbert."

"Elizabeth Fletcher," came the shy reply. "Beth."

Anne smiled but said no more. Miss Fletcher's cheeks had flamed, and her gaze became downcast. The memory of Miss Fletcher was returning now, a sweet thing, rather scarred by a boisterous set of twins in France, wasn't it? She would be back for her second assignment then, still relatively green.

Sighing and leaning back in the chair, Anne mused over what Meredith had said.

"Ah, you'll be for the Earl of Clarcton, then."

The Earl of Clarcton. It rang a bell, though Anne could not precisely remember why. Most titles were mentioned in the great drawing rooms of society, and it was entirely possible she had heard him mentioned while serving the Earl of Allun—or Sir Moses, for that matter.

Clarcton. It was north of here. But the gentleman himself, his family…no, Anne could recall nothing.

Except—wasn't there some sort of scandal? Not scandal exactly, but intrigue? Anne could recall seeing the name in newsprint, though what the story was had quite disappeared from her mind—and if what had been written about the Earl of Allun's daughter was anything to go by, newspapers rarely had the whole truth anyway.

"Who are you getting?"

Anne started. Miss Fletcher had moved closer, smiling nervously.

"The Earl of Clarcton," said Anne softly, glancing quickly around, "I think, but I am not certain. I am sure Miss Clarke will inform me."

Miss Fletcher's eyes widened. "An earl! You are most fortunate—or at least, I should say, you have evidently worked hard. Your previous master must have been impressed."

Anne worked hard not to smile. It was not ladylike, and it was certainly unbecoming of a governess to take pride in her work. She should not crow. Preening was not something to be praised, and she had worked hard for the dues she was hoping to receive. Being arrogant was an unflattering look.

"I did what I could for his lordship," she said softly.

Miss Fletcher looked amused. "I have found earls and dukes far more grateful, in my experience. Especially with those as many children as the Earl of Allun."

Anne blinked. *Earls and dukes?* She had taken the woman before her as more girl, assumed she had not yet taken the plunge, and cared for children as a governess yet.

But the way she spoke…

"Do not worry, you are not the only one to assume I am younger than I am," said Miss Fletcher with a shy smile. "'Tis something of an advantage, in truth. Specializing in twins means traveling, and wherever I go, I am assumed not to have reached my majority."

"Twins!" said Anne, allowing her voice to rise and receiving a *look* from one of the older governesses. "Twins," she repeated quietly. "I would not even know where to start!"

"It is not for the fainthearted," said Miss Fletcher with a soft laugh. "But then, nothing in the Governess Bureau is ever easy. And the Earl of Clarcton…well. After all the rumors."

Anne nodded, cheeks flushing at the hint which she did not understand. *The rumors.* There was evidently something interesting about the Earl of Clarcton, yet she would feel a fool asking, now she had already made herself a fool assuming Miss Fletcher was inexperienced.

The rumor…what was it? Why was her memory failing her at this critical junction?

"Yes, the rumors," she said carefully. "Well, I suppose I am not even certain that the Clarctons will be my next posting. I will have to see whether Miss Clarke gives him to me."

A dark crimson covered her cheeks. *What phrasing to utter aloud—and in public, too!*

She could hear a mutter from one of the older governesses, and felt the flush deepen down her neck. *Blast!* She was usually so careful with her words! Trust her, when Miss Clarke was hopefully about to give her the next assignment, to speak so carelessly!

"I know what you meant," said Miss Fletcher kindly, only increasing Anne's shame. "I must admit, I am hopeful for a duke, myself. What an honor to be given such a charge."

Anne smiled. *What was it that made dukes, earls, all those other impressive sounding titles…well, impressive?*

The world had always been so, as Miss Clarke once said. But no earl was any more well-educated than her own father had been, and he had been a gentleman and no more.

Even governesses at the Bureau were liable to fall into such thinking. Anne could remember their initial training, designed to inoculate the ladies against fear of grandeur.

"You will always be respectful," Miss Clarke had said, glaring as *though daring them to consider otherwise, "but you'll never be afraid. Governess Bureau ladies are afraid of nothing."*

Anne had almost laughed at the time. Now she was three postings from that moment, she could see the truth in it. If she had been easily cowed, she would not have been so vital to the Earl of Allun. As it was…

Well, Anne had never met someone with a title that she could not respect, but beyond that, what was there to crow about? Being a duchess or a countess, what difference did it really make to your life?

"If you ask me, he did it."

Anne blinked. Miss Fletcher had a knowing look on her face, her voice low.

"Did it?" Anne repeated.

Miss Fletcher nodded. "I cannot imagine that she has truly—"

"Miss Gilbert."

Anne rose, curtseying to Miss Clarke, who had emerged from her office.

The owner and founder of the Governess Bureau. Somewhat of a legend in the drawing rooms of London, the woman mamas contact when truly at their wits' end.

Anne found her heart beating uncomfortably fast. If Miss Clarke had heard the last few exchanges between herself and Miss Fletcher—it was well known she had no tolerance for gossip.

"Come on in, then," said Miss Clarke sharply. "We do not have all day."

"Good luck," whispered Miss Fletcher as Anne strode forward.

It had been a little while since she had been within Miss Clarke's study. Her assignment with the Earl of Allun had been for two years. It had not changed much in that time. The paintings were the same, gorgeous landscapes of mountains and lakes, which made her think of Lady Maria's descriptions of Switzerland.

There was the small harpsichord, and Anne had never seen one so delicate, with sheet music scattered across the top, as though Miss Clarke had been searching for a particular piece.

And there—there was a new painting. At least, Anne had not noticed it before. It was a portrait, one of a lady with a somber look on her face. The gown she wore was at least twenty years out of date, and her eyes…

Her eyes were sad. Anne could just make out *Miss Evangeline Jones* inscribed on the bottom.

One's décor, she had always thought, told one much about a person's character. Whoever Miss Evangeline Jones was, she had evidently been important to Miss Clarke. *A cousin? A friend?*

"You are quiet, Miss Gilbert."

Anne did not jump, precisely, but she was startled. It was easy, in the quiet comfort of the study, to forget why she was here. Turning to look at Miss Clarke, if Anne did not know better, she would have said the proprietress of the Governess Bureau was…*rattled*.

A smile crept over her face, but Anne quickly quashed it.

What was it the Duke of Rochdale had said, not fifteen minutes ago?

"The gossip is true then! You really did marry him?"

"She really did."

A great betrayal, at least in Miss Clarke's books. No wonder she looked unsettled, as though a part of her steady and organized life had been utterly upended.

A governess had married her master. Anne had never heard of such a thing occurring, and it was, of course, directly against rule three of the Governess Bureau.

You must never fall in love.

Anne had not batted an eyelash when she had been asked to agree to them when she had first joined. The idea that she would marry at all was ridiculous. Her siblings had, and she had to work. That was that.

Yet, there was something rather wonderful and joyful about the whole thing. Meredith Hubert—or the Duchess of Rochdale, as she was now—had certainly looked happy. Happier than Anne had ever seen her.

When they had trained together, Anne had seen no ill of her. She was not the sort of hussy to go after a duke, so the entire thing must have happened most spectacularly.

"Miss Gilbert?"

"Yes?" Anne recollected herself and smiled wanly at her employer. "Yes, I am quiet, Miss Clarke. Is anything the matter?"

Her innocent question was not answered. "Sit down."

Anne obeyed, an action more likely to keep the peace than if she answered back. However, her teasing nature could not quite help itself. "Are you well, Miss Clarke?"

Miss Clarke, *a woman in the prime of her life, as she would probably consider it,* thought Anne wryly, glared.

There was no other response. Anne swallowed and found her warm demeanor quelled rather quickly in the presence of Miss Clarke. She was formidable. All governesses thought so. Any woman who could create a business like this, against all the odds, against all those gentlemen in society who had laughed at the idea...

Well, she had shown them. But by grit, not warmth.

Miss Clarke took her seat on the other side of the impressive mahogany desk, and her gaze slipped past Anne, over her shoulder, and toward the door. It remained there for almost a minute until Anne coughed gently.

Well, really. It was a little rude, Miss Clarke showing quite clearly that her mind was already on another appointment.

"Ah, yes. Miss Gilbert," said Miss Clarke, her gaze finally focusing on the woman before her. "Yes. Tell me about your previous assignment."

This was a rather strange question, considering Anne could see a letter on the desk between them with the seal of the house of Allun.

"Of course, Miss Clarke," she said aloud. "I was engaged two years ago by the Earl of Allun to care for his three children. Lady Maria Grantchester is now seventeen, Lord Grantchester is fifteen and departed three years ago to Eton, and the Right Honorable Gordon is eleven and followed suit last week. All three children have been educated to a high standard, and Lady Maria will enter society this Season—at Almack's in two weeks, I believe. No unusual circumstances. A happy family."

It was a concise summary, and one she had rehearsed in the carriage ride back to London. The earl had been very good about that. *Well. He did owe her a favor.*

Anne had expected Miss Clarke to speak, to agree with her summary, ask a question, anything. But the older woman just sat there, staring.

The silence elongated to such an extent Anne started to feel the prickle of nerves creeping down her spine. *Why wasn't Miss Clarke saying anything? Was there a chance the report from the earl, clearly sitting between them, said anything different?*

She swallowed, tasting fear. When one joined a household, you trusted your master and mistress with your reputation just as they trusted you with their child. The grander the title, the higher the expectations. That was natural. But she had always given her best. There was nothing in her memory that suggested she had ever done something indiscrete. *Had she?*

Miss Clarke's glare had raised the temperature of the room by several degrees, but after what felt like an eternity, she picked up the letter with the earl's seal.

"It says here," said the proprietress after another minute's silence, "that you are a governess of discretion."

It was evidently not a question, so Anne waited.

"And why would the Earl of Allun say such a thing?"

It was not like Anne to hesitate, but this was a... A delicate situation.

At the end of the day, she had not intended to do it. She had not planned to walk into that bedchamber on the hunt for Lady Maria's blue spring bonnet, and she had therefore not intended to walk in on the earl making love to his mistress.

She had quickly departed and endured a rather uncomfortable conversation afterward.

Anne knew Miss Clarke was waiting for her response, but what was she supposed to say? That the earl had offered her money for her silence—money!—which had offended her conscience far more than the indiscretion.

"I am a member of the Governess Bureau," she had said coldly. *"My master's secrets are as closely guarded as my own."*

"I am waiting," said Miss Clarke, her voice cutting into Anne's thoughts.

Anne took a deep breath. "I really could not say what he means."

There was a laugh but not from Miss Clarke. The voice was low, mischievous—masculine.

Anne whirled around and saw, to her surprise, a gentleman, tall and with closely cut chestnut hair, was standing by the door. She had not heard him come in, which meant...

Which meant he had been there when she herself had entered the room, but she simply had not noticed!

Cheeks flushed, Anne quickly recounted all she had said. *No, there was nothing there she was ashamed of.*

"My God, look at you," the man breathed.

Anne's stomach twisted. *Now, what could he mean by that?*

"You do not know what he means?" Miss Clarke persisted, and Anne turned to face her. "You refuse to tell me?"

This was not how it was supposed to go at all. Anne had not expected wild and extravagant praise, exactly, but she had worked hard for the Alluns and had hoped for a similarly impressive station next.

"I said," she uttered clearly, "I do not know what he means."

The gentleman behind her snorted. "A governess of discretion indeed!"

Whoever this man was, Anne thought irritably, *he was most rude not to introduce himself and listen to her conversation with Miss Clarke.*

Besides, she had given her word to the Earl of Allun. Even if that promise had not precluded ensuring that her mistress, the Countess of Allun, had discovered the presence of her husband's mistress accidently...

She had not told anyone.

Anne smiled. *Just because she had discretion, that did not mean that she did not have a moral center.*

"She's perfect." The gentleman stepped forward and dropped lazily into the chair beside her. "I'll take her."

"B-But you have only just—don't you want to see others?" spluttered Miss Clarke. "There are plenty of governesses currently on my books who—"

"No, I have seen all I need," said the gentleman with a grin.

His gaze scanned over Anne. If she had known she was to be judged by a future master, she would have done something more with her hair and certainly given a longer report of her time with the Alluns.

As Miss Clarke spluttered on about the variety of different expertise available to him within the Governess Bureau, Anne took the liberty of examining what appeared to be her future employer.

He was young, younger than she had expected if he was indeed the Earl of Clarcton. For some reason, she always pictured earls as elderly gentlemen, doddery, and stuck in their ways.

Most earls were not as attractive as this one, either. His jaw always seemed to be held at a jaunty angle. His eyes were sharp, a dark blue, and uncompromising in their view.

Yet if Anne had passed him on the street, she would not have taken him for an earl. Though well dressed, his waistcoat was barely embroidered at all, his cuffs frayed.

An earl was supposed to be...well, more dashing, Anne mused. He appeared subdued.

The gentleman's gaze caught her own, and he chuckled, his eyes teasing her as though she had been a maid caught in the act of sitting on the mistress' bed.

Anne looked away.

"No," he said with a grin. "This is the one."

Anne looked at Miss Clarke, who sighed.

"So be it. Miss Anne Gilbert, Timothy Lexington, Earl of Clarcton. My lord, Miss Gilbert has just finished an assignment, and before her next, she is due a certain amount of rest and—"

"I'll take her now."

This man was really starting to irritate her now. She was not some sort of parcel that could be wrapped and immediately sent!

Miss Clarke was evidently thinking the same way. "My ladies are not so easily delivered, as though merely dropped onto a mail coach!" she snapped. "Please do not forget, my lord, that you are not ordering from a catalog!"

"Could have fooled me," he said easily. "At least, that's what the Duke of Rochdale told me."

It was Anne's contrary nature that made her smile at this. *The Duke of Rochdale had just wed one of Miss Clarke's precious ladies, making him probably the least favorite person of the proprietress at this moment.*

"See, Miss Gilbert is all for it."

It was not in Anne to allow that to pass. "I said nothing, my lord."

"You did not need to," he countered, rising to his feet. "You will take the position?"

Anne swallowed. He was a strange man, not like the previous earl she had served at all. But there was something about him...something enticing. And there was that rumor she could not remember and the whispers from Miss Fletcher.

"If you ask me, he did it."

"I will," she found herself saying.

Their eyes met for a moment, then in a flash, he looked away. "Excellent. Miss Gilbert, meet me at the George Inn, Southwark, in an hour. We leave at once."

With that, he strode out of the room and slammed the door behind him.

Anne's mouth dropped open. *Well, of all the rude, arrogant, impulsive—*

"His lordship is seeking a governess of discretion," said Miss Clarke quietly.

"Why?"

Miss Clarke stared for a moment as though considering how to respond. "I suppose you will eventually find out."

CHAPTER TWO

November 2, 1812

T HE SHARP PAIN in his shoulder was jolted once more against the side of the carriage.

"Blasted roads!" Timothy Lexington, Earl of Clarcton, muttered. "You would think, all the tax I am paying, that the damned roads would be better!"

As the curse words poured off his tongue, he felt immediately better, the heat of his rage cooled by his words.

It was only when he looked up and saw his companion in the carriage that he collected himself.

Damn and blast. If only he had remembered himself sooner, he would have saved the trouble of having to apologize. It was a shame that as he opened his mouth to do so, the carriage jolted again across what was presumably a stone in the road, tipping him once more into the carriage and causing another stream of oaths to pour from his mouth.

"Damnit!"

Timothy tried to stem the tide, but it was no use. That was what two years of being alone did to you—alone other than his gentlemen friends, who cursed far worse than he did.

But he was not with them. He was in his carriage, rattling back to Clarcton and doing its best to deliver him there black and blue, in the company of the new governess.

Timothy sighed heavily. *Blast it indeed.* It was most unfortunate she was to see such a poor side of his character, but if there was one thing he could be depended upon to complain about, it was the roads.

"You always complain about the roads," she had said all those years ago, that smirk on her face. "Why don't you do something about it?"

Pain. Pain in his hands. Timothy looked down and saw he had clenched his fists so tight his fingernails were digging into his palm. On his left, there were marks. On his right, he was bleeding.

Putting thoughts of *her* far from his mind and wiping his hand on his breeches, Timothy looked up to see if the governess had noticed the curses or self-inflicted injuries.

It appeared not. At least, he could not exactly tell. Miss Anne Gilbert did not appear offended by the way he had spoken nor shocked at the anger he had turned on himself.

She did not appear interested in him at all. From what Timothy could see, she was far more interested in the book behind which she had disappeared within five minutes of entering the carriage.

Timothy shuffled in his seat, but the movement did not gain her attention.

Not that he was attempting to. That would be pathetic. Though it was jarring to sit in such elongated silence, day after day. People usually hung on his every word.

Tension grew in his shoulders, partly due to the bumping carriage, partly due to his own damned pride. *This was foolish. Who was he to impress a governess?* It was supposed to be the other way around. *She* would need to demonstrate her worth.

It wasn't as though he knew much of her, anyway. All that could be seen of the delectable—*no,* Timothy immediately halted himself. No, he was not going to fall into that trap which presumably most masters tipped over into whenever they had a new female servant enter the home.

He did not select his servants for their looks, though it had been rather a shock to see her in old Clarke's office. *The resemblance, it was startling.*

"My God, look at you."

It was beyond anything that he could have imagined. Even if he had sought the mirror image of her, he would not have found a better one. Except the hair, of course. Red, not blonde.

But other than that, they could have been sisters. If he was not absolutely sure they were not the same person, he would start to wonder...

Timothy cleared his throat, an uncomfortably guttural sound in the empty carriage. *God in his Heaven, he was bored.* He hadn't thought to bring any entertainment for the journey, preferring to spend it asleep.

That was no option now, not with a lady in the carriage. He supposed she expected conversation, but on the few occasions when the book descended, and Timothy could look directly into her eyes, he had...

Said nothing. *What was there to say?* He was desperate for conversation, connection. He had been at Clarcton Castle too long. *He had been alone too long...*

But whenever those blue eyes met his own, it was too much. *Too much like her.*

The coincidence, for coincidence it must be, was disconcerting. Timothy had almost mentioned it when he had first heard her give her little report to Miss Clarke. It had been on the tip of the tongue.

"You are the spitting image of..."

Timothy coughed. His mouth had gone dry at the very thought.

But there was no chance—Louise had no sisters, he knew that. *Or at least,* he thought wryly, *that was what she had always told him.* Now he was not entirely sure what to believe.

His gaze raked over the little he could see of the woman seated opposite. A simple gown, covered by a thick pelisse. A muffler laid beside her as delicate fingers turned a page. He could not see her face. He did not need to; he had its every curve memorized, every inch was known to him.

The hair, a brilliant red, almost scarlet, peeped out over the leather tome that was so absorbing. Timothy's mind rebelled, expecting to see the blonde he had loved on Louise.

A pox on this silence. *He had to break it!*

"Miss Gilbert…" he began quietly.

He had expected her to speak. To jump at the chance for conversation, to put the book down and smile.

Miss Gilbert merely turned another page.

A flicker of irritation curled around his heart. He had not expected such reticence. Who was she to be reticent about speaking to him?

The Governess Bureau. It was Rochdale's damn fault. He'd said the place had the best reputation, and it was not as though Timothy was an expert in the field. It had been many years since he had needed a governess.

And he had asked around, as any caring parent would… Rochdale was not entirely wrong; even princes from the Continent had availed themselves of a governess from the Bureau.

Miss Anne Gilbert, if he remembered her name correctly, had already proved herself a governess of discretion, and that was what he required.

Clarcton didn't need an educator. It needed a guardian, someone who knew to keep their mouth shut.

Timothy shifted uncomfortably. *Blast, these long carriage rides would be the death of him. If only someone could be convinced to do something about these accursed roads!* That was the problem with Rochdale; he never did anything in government.

He was not a cruel man. He did not consider himself such, at least. But he was a clever man, and he saw opportunities where others just saw problems.

He was looking at Miss Gilbert now, and she was an opportunity.

He had not planned this. He was no mastermind, and Miss Gilbert had just fallen—well, not into his lap, worse luck, but still. *Close enough.*

Timothy smiled at the thought. *She would be part of the Clarcton household, and so like Louise...*

An idea was forming in his mind, and there was no doubt it was a wild one. It would never work, and even if it did, she would never agree to it. She was a governess of discretion, which was what he had wanted, but that did not mean she was willing to do the ridiculous.

Another page turned. Timothy tilted his head to make out the title.

The New Critique of Reason.

He sat back in his seat. *God's teeth, that anyone, let alone a woman, could bear to read such a thing—and with apparent enjoyment, if her silence meant anything!*

No, his was a foolish idea. Timothy should not have permitted it to cross his mind. There was no chance Miss Gilbert, prim and proper, corseted up with the decorum of society and the prestige of the Governess Bureau weighing on her, would consent to such a wild scheme.

Timothy almost laughed at the thought. *No, why would she agree?* She did not know him, had no loyalty like the other Clarcton servants. She had no reason to trust him, no reason to see how the whole thing could be so simple. He wasn't about to bribe a woman for such a task. Not yet. He wasn't nearly desperate enough.

The carriage swerved, the wind getting up as it whistled past them, and Timothy swore quietly under his breath as he was once again thrown into the side.

"Damned roads," he muttered.

Even he could hear how petulant he sounded. *Christ and all his saints, he was better than this!*

It appeared that particular curse was sufficient to interrupt the governess.

Her book lowered to her lap, and Timothy was for the first time in hours able to look directly into the eyes of the woman he had secured as governess for the child. She was looking rather more directly than he was accustomed to, and her tone—frank, direct, with no servility to speak of—was another surprise.

"What would you like to talk about, my lord?"

Timothy blinked. *Well, that was rather unexpected.* Miss Gilbert spoke as though she was speaking to a butcher: ordering and expecting a response.

It was so odd, he found himself self-conscious under the focus of her gaze.

Or was it that she was so similar to Louise?

"I don't know what you mean," he said sternly.

Miss Gilbert looked unfazed. "Really? Because you have complained about the roads twenty-six times over the last three days."

Timothy's mouth fell open. The woman had been counting how many times he had complained—and nary once had she bothered to respond or engage in conversation!

"That suggests to me you wish to talk but are unsure precisely which topic to raise," Miss Gilbert continued smoothly, her eyes never wavering. "Am I correct?"

Timothy closed his mouth hurriedly. *Here he was, an earl, a Clarcton, and he was making himself look a complete fool before a governess!*

This was not what he expected. The governesses from his youth, from what he could remember, were vague, floaty things who drew flowers on their days off and got upset when he refused to complete his sums.

He laughed, despite himself. *Well, a change was as good as a rest, wasn't that what they said?* "You are very direct, Miss Gilbert."

"I like to be," she said with a brief smile that disappeared.

"Were you expecting someone a little more demure?"

It was on the tip of his tongue to say that he had. Someone quiet, willing to do whatever he ordered merely because he was her master. *Wasn't that how servants worked?*

Timothy could not remember the last time he had actually earned someone's trust. Beyond his parents, and even then, that was debatable. Mrs. Seton, maybe? Dewey had never questioned him.

Miss Gilbert cleared her throat. It could not be more obvious she was waiting for his reply. *It was damned rude, damned forward.*

"I have no wish to speak about anything," he snapped.

And that was the end of it. Or at least, it would have been with anyone else. Anyone else would have heard the tone in his voice, seen the warning signs Timothy was all too self-conscious of, the flared nostrils, the way he immediately folded his arms across his chest.

But Miss Gilbert did not know them—that, or she simply refused to see them.

"Are you sure?" she asked lightly. "There appears to be much on your mind, my lord, if you do not mind me saying so. Sometimes a conversation, even with a stranger, is the best way to get it out."

"You are very sure of yourself, speaking to me like that," said Timothy. He had not intended to berate her so directly, but really. *Who spoke to an earl like that!*

Miss Gilbert smiled. It was only then he noticed a difference between her and Louise. No dimple on the left cheek.

"Perhaps I am," came the reply. It was not radical, not rude, but it was clear and unwavering, with no embarrassment. Miss Gilbert's smile grew. "I am a naturally curious person, and I speak as I find. You will have to become accustomed to me, my lord, as I grow accustomed to you."

A curl of doubt crept around Timothy's heart. *Discretion was what he wanted, what he had hired her for.* There had been several other governesses in that Bureau of Clarke's, but Miss Gilbert had been his choice for her self-declared and quite evident discretion.

"I said, I do not know what he means."

He had almost laughed himself silly when she had said that. Do not know what he means? Everyone knew about the earl and his mistress, everyone. Why she had bothered to hide it, he did not know.

But she had, and that was the point.

Now to discover a streak of curiosity within her…well, that could be a disaster. Clarcton Castle held many secrets, some of them even he did not know. The last thing he needed was someone worming their way in, discovering all that could disgrace him.

Timothy examined her more critically. She had a sensible head, or she would not be a governess. He just had to hope she knew when to leave well alone, or…

It would be a disaster. She certainly wouldn't be permitted to stay.

Silence fell between them as Timothy sought for the right response to her words. How could he impress upon her the necessity for discretion? Nay, for her curiosity to be left in this carriage when they arrived at the castle, for it would do her no good in her new home?

All his carefully worded phrases were lost, however, as the carriage rumbled over a bump in the road.

"What rattle-headed, pocked-marked fool built this road!"

Miss Gilbert had not yet returned her book to her hands, and so this time, Timothy was privy to the expression on her face when he cursed. It almost made him swear again.

"I…I must apologize," he said, discomfort stirring in his stomach, forcing the apology. "I am unaccustomed to a lady's presence."

Which was a damned foolish thing to say, he thought in hindsight. *Why not just tell her the whole damn secret now?*

But Miss Gilbert did not look offended; she laughed. "Oh, my lord, please do not concern yourself! My father used to swear like a trooper, and though it surprises me from a gentleman such as yourself, it does not offend me."

This was an intriguing statement indeed. "I suppose he was in the army then, or the navy? 'Tis difficult to tell which is the more ill-tongued."

"Neither," she said cheerfully. "No, my father was a gentleman."

This was becoming a far more interesting conversation than expected. Timothy knew many gentlemen, even considered a few of them his friends. None of them swore to the extent Miss Gilbert was suggesting.

"Yes, well, you may wonder," said Miss Gilbert, reading his mind. "He liked florid language, I suppose, there was very little anger in it. It made my brother absolutely awful to live with when he reached his majority, I can tell you."

Timothy nodded. This was starting to seep into chatter, a type of conversation he loathed. Chatter was only found where a lady was present, and it managed to communicate almost nothing in triple the number of syllables actually required.

Besides, he could not trust her. *Not yet.* Conversing in this fashion would lead to him speaking openly before her, and that would not bode well.

He had to trust her. He had to know she was trustworthy. It did not take long to ascertain whether a person was worthy of his confidence, and he had only been wrong once.

"I suppose I should inquire about my charge or charges."

Miss Gilbert's voice cut through his thoughts, and Timothy looked in surprise. "Did your Miss Clarke not tell you?"

"I am sure she would have done," said Miss Gilbert serenely, pleasant despite the stiffness of his tone. "But unfortunately, I was instructed to leave town immediately and had little time for the typical briefing that I would have expected."

She spoke with no hint of accusation or censure, a smile dancing on her lips as though she had told a joke only they two would understand.

Timothy did not smile. Yes, he had hurried her out of London; but he had good reason for it. The last thing he needed was for her to stay in that place any longer. It was only a matter of time before the rumors would reach her ears, and if they had, there was a real chance she would have rescinded her agreement.

"I suppose that is my fault," he said testily.

"You were the cause, certainly," Miss Gilbert countered with no heat in her voice, "but I would not term it a fault."

Timothy nodded, despite himself. It was well said. He had not imagined a governess of her age—or any governess, in truth—to be that quick.

A little of the ice around his heart melted. She did not think ill of him, then, for his desire to quickly leave London. It was quite marvelous how a person's refusal to dislike one person could endear them to the other.

Yet he must remain aloof, taciturn, even. There had to be distance between them, not merely due to their stations, but because that would protect her. *Protect himself.*

"You'll know all you need to know when you meet her," he said stiffly.

Miss Gilbert did not appear convinced. "I am not so sure. I now know there is a singular charge and that she is a girl, but I need to know her age, interests, previous schooling."

Timothy raised an eyebrow as the carriage rattled along. "You do, do you?"

"I do," said Miss Gilbert, her gaze meeting his. "It is vital information that will permit me to do what is best for my charge. I am sure you understand that, my lord. I am sure you want what is best for her."

There was something about the way she spoke, something reassuring and yet threatening. As though Miss Gilbert, young as she was, naïve as she certainly had to be in the ways of the world, already knew the damage that could be wielded against a young woman.

Timothy's jaw tightened. *Frances had already suffered so much.*

More than she knew. The last thing he would ever want for her is to suffer again.

He sighed heavily, looking out of the window at the gloomy skies rather than at the woman who had bested him once again.

She was right; but still, it was most irritating to be so spoken to by a woman he only met a few days ago and had spent the rest of the time in relative silence.

It was only because he was tired, Timothy told himself. It was because he had not slept well since...

Since that night.

But that was hardly Miss Gilbert's fault. If he was going to maintain the façade that everything was quite well at Clarcton Castle, he would need to put in a little more effort.

Timothy sighed. *Short and sweet.* "I have one daughter. Frances."

Why was it impossible to speak her name without his heart breaking?

"Frances," repeated Miss Gilbert. "A pretty name."

"A pretty child," he said. "She has just turned four years of age, and I now require someone more competent to take care of her, to see to her education and manners. She has grown beyond a nursemaid."

Miss Gilbert nodded, and Timothy saw with interest that there was no jesting look in her eyes or smile dancing around her lips. She was genuinely interested.

"Bold or shy?"

Timothy blinked. "Shy? I suppose."

He heard the uncertainty in his voice and hated it. He should know his charge better, but since...it had been difficult, spending time with her. *She was so much Louise's daughter.*

"And does Lady Frances know her numbers, her letters, that sort of thing?"

Miss Gilbert's tone was brisk rather than accusatory, but Timothy could not help but hear the implied criticism within.

"I really don't know," he said as airily as he could. "I...I have not spent as much time with her as I ought. As I intend."

It was a statement that would invite judgment, but Miss Gilbert merely nodded.

Perhaps she was used to this, he thought. *Perhaps most fathers have either little interest or little time with their daughters.*

"And the rest of the household," continued Miss Gilbert, as though running through a list of questions in her mind. "You have a large one, I assume?"

"Oh, the normal array of servants," said Timothy dismissively. "Watch out for Mrs. Seton, I doubt she will like you."

The words were out of his mouth before he realized, and warmth spread across his chest. *Blast it.* Everyone knew Mrs. Seton was not looking forward to having 'another woman in the house,' as she put it, but really!

"I just mean she does not like anyone," he added hastily.

He would undoubtedly pay for it later, Timothy thought ruefully. The worst thing was he knew the most important facts had been entirely left out.

His wife.

He should tell her. He knew that, yet his desire to keep the secret just a few more days overwhelmed him. He could not go back now, would not. If the wild idea that had seeded itself in his mind could work, if it was even close to that...

"You have neglected to tell me more about your family," said Miss Gilbert pleasantly.

Timothy examined her. *She was clever. He would have to be careful.* "Yes, I have."

She waited as though expecting him to continue, but the earl just stared until she picked up her book and disappeared behind it. It was clear that their interview, for want of a better word, was over.

Timothy closed his eyes. Well, the guilt of keeping the secret for another day would weigh heavily on him, but he knew the burden of telling her would have been far worse.

Not today. Not yet.

CHAPTER THREE

November 3, 1812

A NNE HAD NEVER been particularly accomplished at hiding a yawn.

Her mother, always desperately attempting to raise the family back to where they should have been if her husband had not...well...had always pointed this out as her particular failure.

"Keep your mouth shut," she would say, usually with a screaming child in one hand. "Please, Anne, for goodness' sake!"

And she had tried. She had tried as a child, and she tried now as an adult, sitting in the swaying carriage that felt more ship than coach, on the last day of their journey to Clarcton.

Raising a hand elegantly, she hoped, as she turned a page of her book, she delicately hid the tremendous yawn that simply would not be forced down.

Ye gods, this was tiring.

The Earldom of Clarcton was not far from London. In the summer, it was probably only a day's ride.

Now, however, in chilly, muddy November, it was difficult going. The driver, a pleasant enough young man, had been good enough to attempt to keep Anne's leather shoes out of as much mud as possible, but he was no miracle worker.

Her feet ached. *How could her feet ache?* She had barely taken more than one hundred steps the last few days, yet every muscle in her feet and shoulders cried out for relief.

His lordship had paid for the best rooms at the inns where they had stopped, she could not begrudge him that, but there was something about sleeping in a bed which had been occupied by another the night before...

Anne curled up her nose at the very thought. She was more than ready to arrive.

Another yawn threatened to surface, and Anne turned another page, despite the fact her eyes had not yet reached the bottom, to cover her rudeness. She had completed this book twice on this journey alone, and she knew what was going to happen in each chapter.

Anne's gaze slipped past the edge of the book and affixed on her companion.

Timothy Lexington, Earl of Clarcton.

There was a power in that name. The longer she spent with him, the more she saw it, coiled like a spring within him. He did not use it, chose to keep it deep within himself, as though he was afeard of its power.

Despite his limited conversation, it could not be clearer that the man had little time for governesses in general, and herself in particular.

Anne smiled and returned to the page. *Well, she was not here to be liked.* It was irritating, true, but that was not her purpose. She was here to care for a child; one who, by the sounds of it, had little attention and no devotion.

Her heart panged for the girl. *Four years old, and her father did not even know whether she knew her numbers and letters?*

The carriage jolted.

"Curses to all men who build roads!"

Anne smiled again. *Thirty-six. The poor man really needed to find a hobby.*

She considered asking the earl just how much longer he believed they would be on the road. Her heart sank at the thought of another night at an inn, but he had made it perfectly clear over the last few days that she had but two roles during this journey.

To remain quiet and not to ask questions.

Anne turned a page, more for something to do than anything else. Questions; that was something the earl was quite nervous about, she could tell. No mention of the household, really, besides the tidbit that the housekeeper would not like her—*charming!*—and no reference to his wife whatsoever.

It was a sad state of affairs, but not a unique one. Anne had met plenty of gentlemen while in the charge of the Earl of Allun, who could not accurately name all of their children, let alone give insight into their characters.

Gentlemen, society said, just had to father them. Once sired, the children were the province of the mother.

Anne could see the logic in this, at least at first. Whether wetnurse or mother, it was a feminine domain. But once the child was weaned, surely there was a role for the father?

"And does Lady Frances know her numbers, her letters, that sort of thing?"

"I really don't know. I...I have not spent as much time with her as I ought. As I intend."

What that could do to a child, Anne did not know, but certainly not something good.

At least the earl had the good sense to be embarrassed when he revealed his ignorance. Something had occurred, Anne was sure, between him and his wife. There was a disconnect there, almost the taste of an estrangement.

It was a story oft-told in the upper echelons of society, Anne knew. Now she thought on it, in all her dealings with the family, friends, and acquaintances of the Alluns, she could not recall a single couple just as in love as when they had met. If they had ever loved at all.

The Countess of Clarcton. Anne found her thoughts meandered to her as the carriage brought them ever closer to her.

What was she like? Was she tall, short, loud, inquisitive? Would she be authoritarian with her first governess, hover over her as Anne had seen before, prevent her from teaching Lady Frances anything of use?

Anne sighed as the carriage jostled her to the left, and the pitter-patter of gentle raindrops started their rhythm on the roof. *November weather.* It was a wonder anyone bothered to go to town for the Season, if they had to travel in this.

The Countess of Clarcton would remain a mystery until she arrived at her destination, and then Anne would be able to observe her. She hoped she was close to the child. Perhaps that was why she had decided to remain at home with her child, yet it was just as likely the opposite was true. What child deserved such unloving—

"Finally!"

The earl's explosive syllables made Anne jump, but she covered her surprise well and genteelly lowered her book to her lap.

"Finally?" she repeated in a calm voice.

The gentleman glared. "Yes, finally."

His gaze shifted immediately to the window, and Anne followed suit, just in time to see some impressive wrought iron gates open slowly to admit them, past a lodge house made of dark grey stone. The carriage immediately smoothed out onto a drive.

Anne tried to hide a smile. *The earl's driveway, of course, was elegantly cared for.* It could not be more apparent where his priorities were—driveway, not daughter.

"Clarcton Castle," the earl said with some relief.

Placing her book in her reticule and shifting closer to the window, Anne looked for her first glimpse of her new home for what could be years, with her charge being so young.

The drive was indeed well cared for, with oak saplings every few yards on either side.

"My father took some advice from old Capability Brown," said the earl with a great degree of satisfaction. "One day, there will be a magnificent avenue here."

It was rather difficult to imagine, in the gray and miserable drizzle currently seeping from the overcast sky.

"Yes," she said, her voice croaky for lack of use. "But it will be at least one hundred years, surely, before anyone will enjoy such an avenue?"

There was a chuckle, and Anne looked over to see a genuine smile on his face.

"My dear Miss Gilbert, I am an earl," he said. "The decisions I make are not for myself. I will not see the outcome of most of them in my lifetime. No, I make them for descendants. A future Earl of Clarcton will find blessed relief from the sun and the joy of the greenery, and it will be because last year, I planted saplings."

It was difficult not to be impressed by such a statement, but Anne said nothing and merely turned back to the window, which was still full of views of saplings.

Being an earl must be a rather wonderful and yet terrifying thing, she mused. He was right; his decisions could change the way an estate was managed for generations to come.

While the carriage glided smoothly over the carefully managed drive, Anne found her eye drawn not to the saplings, but to the man who had order their planting.

He took his responsibilities to the estate seriously, which made it all the more strange he had evidently little interest in giving his daughter the upbringing she deserved as Lady Frances Lexington.

The further along the drive they moved, she watched him visibly relax. The tension dissipated from his shoulders and his arms.

It was not so very surprising, thought Anne. Most gentlemen preferred to be at home in the country rather than in town. What was odd was just how long it was taking them to arrive. The driveway had swept along, and the oak saplings had disappeared, bowing out to their natural successor, the parkland with wide oak trees and beeches in the distance. What appeared to be a river came into view, cutting through it like blue stitching across green cloth.

A movement—deer. A smile broke across her face. She would have many pleasant evenings walking in this parkland, she was sure—if she was able to reach it from the house, that is. Still, the carriage rumbled onward, and they appeared to be no closer than when they…

Anne gasped. They had turned another corner, and a house had appeared as though by magic, hidden by the slope of the hill before it—and what a house.

House was not entirely the right word for it. Castle, perhaps, though it did not appear to be the sort of medieval castle she had seen in her picture books when a child.

She had never seen anything like it. The carriage slowed, giving her the chance to take a closer look at the huge building that was still yet unfurling itself, growing larger and larger the closer they came.

It was awe-inspiring. More manor than house, more castle than manor, it was surrounded by gardens of the latest fashion, all clipped box and delicate stumps, which Anne assumed would, in the summer, reveal themselves to be roses. For now, they were all covered by a gentle dusting of wintery frost, even this late in the afternoon as the sun began to set behind the castle.

There was a fountain—two fountains, either side of the rear of the house, neither of which were flowing in this cold temperature. There were benches, and what were probably two majestic greenhouses in the distance, one of which appeared to have an orangery within.

The castle had four towers with two grouped together, as though the place had not been built but grown. What once could have been a moat encircled it, and the windows were mullioned, shimmering red in the dying sun.

As the carriage came around and slowed, Anne gasped again at the impressive façade. She swallowed, hands clasped in her lap and heart now racing.

It would be easy to become overwhelmed at such grandeur, she told herself, *but she was not so foolish.* It was natural that an earl would live in a place like this. It befits his title, and it would soon become as homely to her as any other place.

She had considered this Earl of Clarcton to be much on the same footing in society as her previous master. They had, after all, the same title.

But this *was* different. The Earldom of Clarcton was ancient, far older, and more noble. This was an assignment far more impressive than she had been led to believe in her hurried conversation with Miss Clarke.

"Clarcton Castle," said the earl into the silence as the carriage came to a halt.

Anne nodded, rather than trust her voice. The place was magnificent, and the dying sunlight only emphasized the extraordinary stonework and elegant masonry.

It had all been theoretical over the last few days when this carriage ride appeared never to end, and she was stuck in the awkward silence that this gentleman seemed to prefer.

But now? Now she had to face reality. She, Miss Anne Gilbert, was the governess here, of Clarcton Castle. That meant she had a responsibility to represent the house and family as best she could, giving her privileged access few in the town could dream of. Within weeks, the corridors of this place would become as familiar to her as they were now to its owner.

She would need to win over the housekeeper, that was true.

"Watch out for Mrs. Seton, I doubt she will like you."

Anne smiled. It sounded a hard task, and even the earl seemed to be aware that he had transgressed one of the basic codes of servanthood, which was never to tell one what the other thought of them.

But after the housekeeper, the butler, the rest of the household, which now she saw the size of the property would be numerous indeed, and then...

The mistress.

Anne swallowed again. It was always more challenging to win the hearts and minds of the women of a household, Miss Clarke had always warned them.

"You are entering their domain," she had emphasized during a particularly long lecture. *"Remember, you are the interloper here. It is their home, their right to consider you an outsider. You have to earn their respect, for you will not be given it."*

Miss Clarke had been proven right at each of Anne's assignments. The mistress of a home always considered a new governess to be a threat, and it was during her second posting that Anne had realized why. *Naïve, innocent that she had been then.*

No danger of that here, though. Anne glanced at her master, the gruff, rude, and taciturn gentleman, who whined about roads and knew nothing about his daughter. *No, she was unlikely to be tempted there!*

"Right," he said, opening the door on his side and stepping out of the carriage.

Anne waited for a moment, but instead of moving around the carriage and opening her door, or even waiting for a servant to perform the task, the earl did neither. Without a backward glance, he strode toward the house.

Anne sighed. *She should not have been surprised, not really.*

Struggling with the catch on the door, it opened suddenly, and Anne saw the driver, a young Mr. Holt, standing outside the carriage.

"Don't mind him," he said with no preamble. "He's like that, but he's a good master. Good wages."

Anne nodded but did not respond. It was unladylike to speak of money, her mother had always told her. *Even when it was the only thing preoccupying one's mind.*

"Here, let me." Holt held out a hand, and Anne took it gratefully and stepped onto the gravel drive.

"Thank you," she said, a little self-consciously. It was uppermost in her mind that though perfectly respectable, she was technically alone with a man she did not really know.

He grinned. "Oh, it's nothing. Let me get your luggage."

Holt stepped away and gave Anne the chance to take in her surroundings. The wind was freezing, far colder than she was accustomed to—but still, she had made it, and if Holt was anything to go by, there were servants here who were friendly. That would be important during the long winter evenings she would otherwise spend alone.

A grunt caught her attention, and she turned to see Holt struggling with her trunk.

"Oh, do you want a hand with that?"

Holt looked offended. "No, I know where your room will be, and I am perfectly capable, thank you. I'll take it up."

Anne hid a smile. Even the suggestion a man may not be strong enough, and you would soon see the fire in their eyes. Well, she offered to help. It would give her time to—

"Miss Gilbert!" The earl appeared in the doorway. "Do you intend to enter my home or make yourself comfortable in the gardens?"

Anne bit down the retort she would have liked to give and said, "Thank you, my lord."

Of all the arrogant, gruff, and discourteous men, she thought as she stepped forward with a bland smile, *this man topped the lot.*

It was difficult to feel irritable, however, when she stepped over the threshold and into the hallway, which was vast and twice as high as she had imagined.

"My goodness," she murmured.

It was like stepping back in time—at least, to a time that once must have existed but seemed to be more dreams of England than what England had ever been. It was a Great Hall.

A minstrel's gallery ran around the edges of the room high above her, the walls adorned with swords, knives, even a stag's head! As Anne's gaze moved lower, suits of armor appeared along with paintings of hunting scenes that looked as though they had been painted from life in the parkland she had just passed through.

Anne swallowed, and tried to keep her face as unimpressed as possible. This was an entirely new level of nobility. *The Earl of Allun had rented his country home!*

What on earth had she managed to get herself into?

"You must be tired." The earl was being divested of his great-coat by a man who could only be the butler.

"I am," she said honestly. "Very tired. If I may—"

"Mrs. Seton!" the earl bellowed.

Anne took a step backward unconsciously, his voice was so loud. *Goodness, this could not be the way the man managed a household, could it? It was barbaric!*

Yet, that appeared to be the norm. The butler had not blanched. A door slammed somewhere in the depths of the castle, and footsteps echoed until a woman with graying hair and a scowl entered.

Anne thought her first words and tone were rather unnecessary.

"This her, is it?"

Anne could not help but bristle. *Really!*

Yet losing her temper was not liking to endear her to anyone, least of all her new employer and the housekeeper. She curtseyed low and said nothing.

Mrs. Seton snorted. "None of us here are impressed with your fine ways."

"Mrs. Seton," the earl said in a warning tone.

Anne looked between them and watched as the housekeeper sniffed and drew herself up, as though holding in all the things she clearly wished to say.

"I suppose you want to see where your room is, then?"

Anne took a deep breath before saying, "Yes, please, Mrs. Seton."

Without saying another word, the housekeeper turned and walked through the door she had come through. It could not be more evident she expected the governess to follow her.

Anne looked at the earl for guidance, but he was gone. It

appeared she was to be left to the mercy of Mrs. Seton, worse luck, and she caught up with the older woman at the base of a wide staircase.

"It is lovely to meet you, Mrs. Seton," she said quietly. The castle had a rather bizarre way of making any speech echo in a most disobliging way. "I've heard great things about you."

The housekeeper said nothing, merely stamping up the stairs in silence.

Anne tried again. "I have been told little about my charge, Lady Frances, and I am eager to meet her. When will I have the chance to meet the rest of the family—to meet the countess?"

It was not an unusual question, Anne thought, and yet the housekeeper treated it as though she had asked the secret combination of the master's safe.

"'Tis none of your business, I would say," she snapped. "I would not dwell much on the family, just focus on the girl."

The girl? Anne's heart sank. The child was ignored or even disliked by most around her.

"It is my business," Anne said calmly as they reached the top of the stairs and started down a corridor. "I am here as the governess. It is vital that I—"

"I said, it's none of your business," said Mrs. Seton with a fierce look.

Anne did not speak immediately. It was bad the housekeeper was so disobliging, but she was attempting to remember the route they were taking so she could find it again. *Up the stairs and left along the corridor, round the corner to the left again, but take a right...*

"So the countess is not here, then?" Anne tried again.

Mrs. Seton glared, but seeming to find it was impossible not to at least answer this one, snapped, "Not at the moment."

It was very strange indeed. As they turned another corner and started up a flight of stairs which looked as though it had been added there as an afterthought, Anne wondered where on earth the countess could be, if not here and not in town—*perhaps visiting someone else in the neighborhood?*

"What a shame, I would have liked to see her. I always think it most interesting to see the mother, to see what the daughter will become," said Anne, trying to inject warmth in her tones as they reached the top of this staircase and took a right. "I suppose there is a portrait of the countess somewhere?"

At those words, Mrs. Seton halted abruptly and turned on her. "What have you heard? What rumors got to you?"

Anne was so astonished, she could not think what to say. *Rumors?* She had heard nothing, if one did not count that whisper of Beth Fletcher's, and she certainly didn't.

"If you ask me, he did it."

What a strange reaction from a housekeeper about a woman that Anne had never met.

The earl had mentioned nothing of note about his wife in their carriage ride, and it was only now Anne realized just how strange that was. *Almost forty complaints about the state of the roads, and yet not a single mention or allusion to his wife?*

"Nothing," she said.

Mrs. Seton's gaze narrowed. "Are you quite sure, Miss Gilbert?"

Anne could not think possibly what had come over the woman—unless…

Ah, perhaps that was it. Was it possible they were divorced, secretly, and that was why she was not here? The countess had been sent away, and the pain of potential scandal was still raw, even in the household staff?

It was not impossible and would be scandalous if true. The earl would want to keep that quiet. Yet the housekeeper had said 'not at the moment.' Was she visiting relatives?

"I am merely curious, nothing more," Anne said aloud to the waiting housekeeper. "As I said to his lordship in the carriage, I like to know about the people I am working for. That was all."

The hackles on the back of Mrs. Seton seemed to lessen, and she looked uncomfortable that her temper had gotten the better of her.

"Right, well," she said awkwardly. "No more talk about that portrait. Come on, now."

She started walking again, and Anne mirrored her, curiosity piqued.

That portrait, Mrs. Seton had said. Not *a* portrait. There was one, then, or else the housekeeper would not have become so upset about it. Where could it be?

Before Anne could think, the servant stopped and opened a door. "Here you go."

Her mouth fell open, a seemingly common occurrence at Clarcton Castle.

"You must be mistaken," she said in a strangled voice. "This cannot be my room."

It was magnificent. The rooms Anne were accustomed to were usually a little larger than a maid's room; if she was fortunate, large enough for a bed, chest of drawers, and wardrobe, a chair, and a desk. If she was lucky.

But this...this was on a main corridor and appeared to be a guest room. Silk hangings around the four-poster bed, a large bay window with a view that overlooked the formal gardens, there was a rug on the floor that could even have been an Axminster!

"You...you're quite sure this is my room?"

"If I had my way, you'd be up in the attics, not this close to the family. But that's his lordship's orders. Close to Lady Frances."

She turned to leave as Anne stood in the middle of the room looking around in wonder, but she was prevented from doing so by a man holding a trunk.

"Out of the way, Holt," she grumbled as she stepped around him.

"Sorry, Mrs. Seton," said the man apologetically, but she was already gone. "Found it all right, then?"

Anne smiled. *A familiar face.* "There must have been a mistake, his lordship cannot possibly think I need a room like this?"

Holt heaved the trunk onto the floor beside a stunning chest of drawers, and drew himself up. "I don't know, the master always is very good to us," he said, trying to mask his breathlessness. "So. Miss Gilbert. Where were you before this?"

Anne could sense his desire for conversation, but she had never been less talkative in her life. After such a journey and such a welcome, all she wished to do was be left to her own devices to unpack and unwind.

"Thank you for bringing up my luggage," she said instead. "I will unpack now, I think. Good day, Holt."

"Right you are," he said, nodding and closing the door behind him.

Anne heaved a sigh into the silence of the room. *She would have to be careful.* The last thing she needed just as she arrived was to be accused of having a gentleman follower. That would almost be as bad as trying it on with the master!

She laughed in the silence at the very thought. She could not think of anything less likely.

The room—*her room*—only appeared more beautiful and luxurious the more she looked at it. She had come a long way to be here, both figuratively and literally, and though Anne was not entirely sure she deserved such luxury, she was hardly one to turn her nose up at it when offered.

The peace of her own company was to be her reward, and she would need that rest before the biggest challenge still ahead: meeting Lady Frances and her mother, the Countess of Clarcton.

Just as Anne reached out to unfasten her luggage, a heavy noise reverberated around the room. A dinner gong.

"Miss Gilbert!"

The voice echoed, but it was clearly her master. Anne opened the door.

"Dinner, Miss Gilbert, and your presence is required!"

Anne's mouth fell open, a habit that she was going to have to curtail if she was going to live here for more than a day. She had not been given the gift of even five minutes to herself, but there was nothing for it. She would have to go downstairs and see that cantankerous man again.

CHAPTER FOUR

T HE DOOR OPENED, and Timothy looked up, only to be immediately disappointed. The frown that covered his face was not personal; he would have defended that to the hilt. But surely, she knew the basics of etiquette? *She was a governess, for crying out loud!*

"You haven't changed," he barked across the room.

Miss Gilbert closed the door quietly and faced him. The dining table was between them, long and formal. Timothy could not remember the last time he had dined here.

Christmas past, perhaps? The obligatory visit from the Reverend Critchley?

"Changed?" Miss Gilbert's face was blank. "In the last five minutes?"

Timothy did not intend to glare, but it was an instinctual reaction that bore more relation to her own looks than her actions.

God's teeth, but it was strange having her here. Timothy had never been one for throwing open the doors of his home and inviting guests. The customary balls were hosted out of duty more than anything else.

But it was more than that. *It was her. Miss Gilbert.* Now he saw her in better light than that of a traveling carriage in winter, it was clear she was not an exact replica of Louise. There was softness around the cheeks. A gentleness in the eyes Louise had lacked. Moreover, the hair was entirely different.

But not different enough. Timothy took a deep breath as though that would change the frantic beating of his heart.

No, she was not Louise, yet there was enough similarity to throw even him. It was as though a person had painted Louise from the verbal description of another.

"Yes, changed," said Timothy, suddenly aware the conversation would struggle if he did not respond. "For dinner."

It was not as though his request was surprising. All society changed for dinner. Why, when last in town, forced to attend a few card parties in the evenings with undiscerning hosts, he had even spotted a few tradesmen and their families following the practice.

She was a governess, for goodness' sake. Surely she knew that?

Miss Gilbert was looking at her day gown. It was mud-splattered at the hem and appeared very much worse for wear.

"Change for dinner?" she said lightly. "And you believe you gave me sufficient time to do so? I note you have only changed your jacket."

Timothy felt the hackles on the back of his neck rise. "That's as may be, this is my house, and if I choose to keep the same waistcoat and—I don't have to explain myself to you!"

These last words were barked rather than spoken.

Miss Gilbert smiled. "As I do not need to explain myself to you. I have not yet had sufficient time to unpack my trunks, and I believed a prompt arrival for dinner was more important than my apparel. Where would you like me?"

The impudence! Timothy could hardly believe it. She had been the governess for another earl; surely he was asking no more than her previous employer—and yet she spoke to him like...*like a child, who needed correcting!*

"Here," he said, pointing at the seat to his left. He had no patience to chastise her now, and knowing his temper, he was liable to say something he would undoubtedly regret.

Better to suffer through this dinner then return to his own chambers to sleep properly for the first time in...God knew how long.

"Thank you, my lord," came the smooth reply from the governess as she stepped lightly across the room and sank elegantly into her seat.

Timothy nodded. *By God, this was going to be an ordeal—but he knew what was due her rank, even if she had no care to recognize his own.*

A governess was...well, a sort of will o'the wisp, when it came to hierarchy in a house, he was vaguely aware. Servant yes, but not servant. Not merely a part of the household, but part of the driving force. Like Mrs. Seton, or Dewey—the people who mattered.

"What a delightful dining room," said Miss Gilbert cheerfully. "I can imagine you hosted many a fine dinner here, with friends and neighbors."

"Not often," said Timothy, finding his curt response left his mouth before he could think of anything polite. "Not if I can help it."

Silence fell after this pronouncement.

Ye gods, this was a punishment. Timothy had known, from the moment Louise had stepped into his life, that he would be unable to stay away from her, and that she would be his ruin.

And he had been right on both counts.

He cleared this throat. "This won't be something we do every day."

Miss Gilbert raised an eyebrow.

"Dine together," Timothy clarified. "I would not wish to intrude on your solitude, and I am a solitary creature myself. Just on Sundays. You can tell me how Frances is doing."

The last thing he needed was a lovesick governess mooning about the place, thinking he was inviting her to dine because he liked her. *God forbid!*

No, this was strictly to ensure everyone, the household, the world, knew he was doing what was right by Frances. She should not have to suffer for her parents' ills.

"Sundays is an excellent choice," said Miss Gilbert.

Relief, sweet relief spread down Timothy's shoulders and released the tension in his chest, which he had not realized he was holding. He did not go out of his way to offend; it was just something that occurred naturally when he opened his mouth around other people.

He had several reasons for wanting to keep the governess at arm's length, at least for now. If the idea brewing in his mind could work, he would need to ascertain whether he was absolutely mad for conceiving it and whether this Miss Gilbert would be amenable to his terms.

Blood and bones, if the scheme could work—if he could make this entire thing work to his advantage...

"Sundays was the arrangement I had at my previous posting," continued the governess. "I think it will do well here, too. Thank you, my lord."

Timothy nodded. "Yes, the Alluns. I think their eldest daughter is about to come out into society, is that right?"

It was not intended to be an interview. That work had already been done, back in London, in the Governess Bureau. Miss Clarke had been surprised at his insistence on discretion, perhaps even offended.

"All my ladies are discreet, my lord," she had said with a sharp look.

And he had explained...*well. Enough.*

"Yes, Lady Maria will attend her first ball at Almack's this very week, I believe," said Miss Gilbert. Her voice was a little wistful.

"And you wish you could be there?"

The governess caught his eye. "Now, wouldn't that be a scandal? A governess at Almack's? I know my place, and it is certainly not in the company of the great and the good."

There was a sparkle in her eyes, and Timothy found to his surprise, he was smiling.

"I did not intend the remark as a trap," he said mildly.

"I am sure you did not," came the arch reply. "But what a good thing I stepped around it, for both our sakes."

Timothy laughed, then halted quickly. *They were not friends; they were master and governess.*

"The two younger children, of course, are now at school," she said. "They were good boys but in need of school by that age. Young people of a similar age to them, the chance to shift their horizons."

"I am not sure I had my horizons much shifted at school," Timothy said as a door opened behind him, and food was brought out by a footman.

Miss Gilbert examined him. "I don't suppose you did."

Her nonchalance made him bristle. *What the devil did she mean by that?* He had been to one of the best schools in the country, and his parents had always ensured that—

"Oh, tomato soup, my favorite," said Miss Gilbert, smiling her thanks at the footman who had brought their bowls.

Timothy nodded. *Dear God, she did something to him, this governess.* There was something about her, something about the cheerful and open way she spoke, about the curiosity she gladly owned and did nothing to hide.

It was as unlike Louise, unlike the life he had lived for the last five years as could be.

Miss Gilbert was not a breath of fresh air, more a hurricane that threatened to upend the way he saw himself and his entire world.

A world he had to protect.

"When you were at the Alluns, you had a reason to be discreet," he said abruptly as Miss Gilbert took her first genteel mouthful of piping hot soup. "What was it?"

Those blue eyes met his and held his gaze far longer than he was comfortable with. Timothy refused, however, to break it. It was her responsibility, not his, to speak.

"I really don't know what you mean," she said finally with an honest expression.

"So, you keep your master's secrets?"

Once again, Miss Gilbert did not reply immediately. Instead, she gently laid down her soup spoon, licked clean in a rather enticing way. Timothy attempted not to notice and she leaned back in her chair with her palms in her lap, examining him.

"Yes," she said finally, no hint of mischief on her face. "I keep my master's secrets. That is what discretion means."

"I am not here for a lesson on definitions," said Timothy sharply. "I wish to understand why you display such loyalty for a gentleman who is no longer your master. *I am*. And I am asking."

Miss Gilbert was not cowed by his tone. "That does not make his secrets any less secret. I would do him, and myself, a disservice if I considered my vows of discretion dissolved merely because he no longer paid my wages—as I would expect to keep any secrets shared with me in this house to remain secret, even after I left."

It was a long speech in the quiet room, and it was well made. Timothy found his respect for the woman increasing, despite himself.

It was not as though he had been given many positive examples of women in his life to date. His mother was well-meaning but a gossip to the bone, no sisters or cousins, and he had been too intoxicated with Louise to realize she was…

He had become accustomed to thinking of women as those who could not keep their mouths shut, who could not keep to their word—who did not really understand what keeping their word meant.

It appeared Miss Gilbert was a rarity. Thank God. If she stayed more than a week, she would need that skill.

"Your own tomatoes, I presume?"

Timothy blinked. "What?"

Miss Gilbert indicated her soup. "Your own tomatoes? From

your kitchen gardens?"

It was such a change in topic that for a moment, Timothy's mind struggled to keep up. "Kitchen—yes, our own tomatoes," he said hastily. "Yes, Nelson, my head gardener, and Cook are very accomplished, very good indeed."

"I quite agree," said Miss Gilbert, raising her spoon and taking another mouthful.

She appeared to be utterly unfazed by his questioning, which was all to the good. Timothy had no time for women who threw hysterics to get their own way, or found fault in those around them or took offense at simple questions.

All lessons he had learned from one woman.

"I must admit, I just assume the food will be good," he said gruffly. "It has always been so here at Clarcton Castle, and I keep the same high standards my father expected. All who serve me know that."

Miss Gilbert did not reply, and Timothy found himself piqued. *Was he a substandard conversationalist?* Had he really been alone for so long that he was unable to keep a woman's interest for more than five minutes?

He ate his own soup in silence, calling down a curse on all women everywhere. *God's teeth, but if only Frances had been a boy.* He could have found a perfectly decent tutor, and there would have been none of this female nonsense for him to deal with.

The footman, Holt, stepped forward and removed their bowls—but not before a look of recognition and pleasant surprise on Miss Gilbert's face, and a wink from Holt.

The damned cheek! Timothy could hardly believe what he was seeing right before his eyes. If that was not bad enough, a flush spread across Miss Gilbert's cheeks!

Well, he was going to put a stop to that immediately. He would have none of that in his household.

A stern glare was enough to make the man drop his gaze and scurry out of the room.

"Do not," Timothy said darkly, "permit men to take liberties,

Miss Gilbert."

The words had not been intended as censure, more as warning, but there was an answering force in Miss Gilbert's face he had not expected.

"You can rest assured, my lord, that I do not require advice on that front," she said coldly. "It was pleasant to see a friendly face, that is all. I am sure you can understand, as I am miles from anyone else I know."

There was censure in her voice, and Timothy found himself feeling guilty for the heavy-handed way he had expressed himself. For all he knew, governesses and footmen socialized in the kitchens and servants' hall. Perhaps some matches were made once in a while.

Still. Miss Gilbert was not here to make friends. She was here to make Frances a lady.

As though the governess had read his mind, she said quietly, "And when will I have the pleasure of first meeting your daughter?"

"Frances," corrected Timothy, despite himself. *Ye gods, he needed to get himself out of that habit if he was going to ensure no rumors ever left this house.* "Yes, Mrs. Seton will bring her in for a few moments."

There was a look of genuine confusion on Miss Gilbert's face as she asked, "Not your wife? I had assumed the countess would be here soon, even if she were visiting friends in the neighborhood."

It was such an innocent question, asked with no guile. No, she spoke as she found. *How could he explain it all?* She had barely been here five minutes, and already she was asking the pertinent questions he absolutely would not answer.

Not yet. Not until he knew he could trust her.

True, Miss Gilbert had betrayed no faults that would encourage him to return her to London. She was polite, genteel, and genuinely discreet, which was a miracle.

But it was too soon for her to hear the whole sorry tale—or at least, to hear the portion of the truth that he would have to, eventually, tell her.

"You do not have anything to fear from me."

Timothy looked at Miss Gilbert, who had spoken softly but with real warmth. How did she do it? How did she intuit precisely what his concern was at any given moment?

"I can keep my silence, if required," she said softly, "but it is always easier to lie when one knows the truth."

Timothy could not help but laugh dryly. *Well, may she say that, in her ignorance.* Ignorance was a state he was determined to keep her in for now.

"The countess is not here," he said, trotting out the lie that all the household had agreed, even Mrs. Seton, and that had taken some persuading. "She is away. For her health."

It was not the best lie. Timothy was aware of that. If he had had any sense, he would have created a more complex falsehood that would have stood up to questioning. But he was reluctant to create worthless drivel merely to appease the curiosity of a stranger.

Miss Gilbert surprised him. The curiosity he had been expecting never came.

Instead, she nodded. "Thank you for telling me."

Relief surged through his heart. Another obstacle overcome, and though it was with a lie, it was a cleverly chosen one.

Away for her health. It was vague enough not to require proof but personal enough that anyone with good breeding would not dare to ask any more questions.

Clearly, Miss Gilbert was one such well-bred lady, for she did not appear to have any questions to follow.

Timothy fiddled with the fork beside his plate. *Damn this silence, damn this waiting!* He had found himself a lady, that was true—didn't she mention at one point in the journey here that her father had been a gentleman?—but still, there was nothing more awkward than sitting in silence with a person one did not know.

Her father a gentleman, and yet here she was, a servant in another person's home? The family must have fallen on hard times if a daughter of the house was working for her keep.

What could have happened?

Though tempted to ask, Timothy held back. That was a dangerous path. As soon as he asked a question, it would surely give her the right to ask more questions.

Questions he would not answer.

Besides, she was just a governess, nothing more.

The door behind him opened once again, to Timothy's relief, bringing in not just the next course of their meal but—

"Papa!"

Timothy beamed. There she was, the one creature in the world he could look at without hatred or irritation.

Frances. She was hand in hand with Mrs. Seton but quickly released her grip to rush toward him, giggling wildly.

"Come here, you little rascal!" Timothy could feel his heart practically bursting with affection. The one person who looked at him and smiled, who would never betray him. "And what do you think you're doing?"

Frances squealed with delight as she was pulled into his lap. "Papa!"

Her little arms threw themselves around his neck, and Timothy swallowed to prevent tears from creeping into the corners of his eyes.

Christ, he would never understand it. How could a small person like this utterly claim his heart while asking for nothing in return?

"And what have you been up to, you rascal?" he said aloud, conscious of Miss Gilbert's gaze. "Nonsense, I'll be bound!"

"I was a tiger today, Papa," said Frances with no preamble. "A tiger in a jungle!"

"Were you indeed?" said Timothy seriously. "And did you eat anything?"

"Lions, and a rabbit, and a man!" said Frances, oblivious to the entertainment she was giving. "And…"

She babbled away, as serious about her day as anyone, and Timothy interjected with questions and exclamations, as her rattling tongue would allow.

He drank it all in. Frances, the daughter of Louise. She was precious to him in a way he had never been able to describe. He spent little time with her, shameful he knew, but every time he saw that blonde hair…

Miss Gilbert was still watching him closely, though it was hardly a secret he had great affection for the child.

"—then stopped being a tiger but, Papa?" Frances looked up with big, open eyes. "Papa, who's the lady?"

Timothy glanced at Miss Gilbert, who was smiling. If Frances did not take to Miss Gilbert, it would not matter how accomplished or discreet the governess was.

She would be back in his carriage on the road to London the next morning.

"This," he said impressively, tightening his arms around the child, "is Miss Gilbert. She is your new governess and has come all the way from *London*."

Frances's eyes widened, though she had no real comprehension of what London was.

"And…and what is a governess?"

Miss Gilbert smiled. "Someone who can teach you about the world and show you what you are capable of."

Timothy had to admit this sounded very impressive, but Frances was a daughter of the house of Clarcton, not a son. He was not seeking a radical upbringing.

"And will help you grow up to be a *young lady* worthy of your name," he added, catching the eye of the governess meaningfully, "to help you when you get married and create a household of your own."

He did not want to belabor the point, but it had to be made. Frances was a lady, but there was no knowing what she could be. A countess, as her mother was? Perhaps a duchess.

Miss Gilbert seemed to understand his meaning. "Yes, it is

very important you understand what is expected of you when you are older, Lady Frances, and that is what I am here to do. And be your friend if you ever need one."

Now it was her turn to give Timothy a meaningful look, and he nodded.

Well, she was not wrong. Frances was alone most of the time, and when she wasn't, she was surrounded by footmen with proper jobs to do, Dewey who was typically preoccupied, or the dreaded Mrs. Seton.

It would do Frances good to have someone dedicated to her and no one else.

"I think…" said Frances slowly, nestled into Timothy's arms and looking at the governess carefully, "I think I like you."

"I think I like you, too," said Miss Gilbert just as seriously, "but I will have to get to know you properly first. You could be a pickle as well as a tiger!"

Frances giggled at the very idea, and Timothy tightened his grip around her as he saw the growing rapport between governess and charge.

Thank God. There were few people who ever saw Frances, and fewer had any time for her. It was crucial that Miss Gilbert, or any other future governess, wished to understand her.

But this had been going on long enough. Timothy caught the eye of Mrs. Seton, who immediately stepped forward.

"Come on now, Lady Frances," she said roughly, "time for bed."

Frances sagged with disappointment, but she slipped from his lap to the floor with no argument.

"Buh-bye, governess," she said, attempting a very poor curtsey, then reaching up to take Mrs. Seton's hand.

Timothy saw Miss Gilbert was touched by the gesture, and as the door closed, he leaned forward to eat, his stomach churning.

"What a charming daughter you have," said Miss Gilbert into the silence. "I am utterly delighted."

"Thank you. I must say I am biased, of course, but I consider her one of the most delightful children I have ever encountered. Why, when she was born, I said..."

He swallowed. *Damn and blast—trust him to become so unguarded!* It always happened when it came to Frances. She was his one weakness, and he forced himself away from her for just such a reason.

He cleared his throat. "She is my pride and joy."

"I can see why," said Miss Gilbert smoothly. "She is truly charming."

"I would do anything for her," Timothy said, determined to make sure the governess understood. "Anything—if I thought she was in danger..."

The smile disappeared from Miss Gilbert's face. "Has that happened? Has she been in danger before?"

Timothy looked at his food. *Damnit, he needed to have better control than this if Miss Gilbert was going to become a permanent member of his household.* The last thing he needed was to give her reasons to wonder.

"No," he said curtly. "No, of course not."

He could taste the lie in his mouth and took a bite of the roasted chicken to cover it. How many lies would he end up telling during the course of this dinner?

"I see," said Miss Gilbert, who clearly did not. "And is Lady Frances like her mother?"

"Nothing like," snapped Timothy. His cheeks had darkened at the mere suggestion of that woman, but he tried to brush it off. "Isn't it funny how that happens?"

The governess did not appear to see anything funny in it whatsoever. That look of curiosity he was starting to know well had appeared again.

He had to do something. "As you can probably tell, I am concerned about my wife. She is...her health has not been..."

His voice trailed away without anything meaningful said. He had never been a liar.

"Liars and Lexingtons do not go together," his father had always

said. *"We Lexingtons never lie."*

It had been a founding part of himself, even when he had—well, it was his own fault. When Timothy had met Louise, become infatuated so quickly, what had she said?

"Oh, my dear man, I will always lie to you," she had giggled, twirling that wine glass between her fingers in that transfixing way. *"I will never tell you the truth."*

"Please," he said, his voice slightly strangled. "Let us talk about other things."

"Of course, my lord," came the gentle reply. "Tell me about the castle. It appears to have been here a long time, perhaps centuries?"

Timothy took a deep breath and shifted into his automatic spiel about the place. He had given it so often, his mind was not required to become involved—a perfect topic.

Well, it could have been much worse. In the course of a dinner, he had ascertained she was truly a governess of discretion, introduced her to Frances, and discovered she had a curiosity far outstripping that which was comfortable.

He would know soon enough: either she was not trustworthy enough and would have to go, or she was trustworthy and could be invited to play the part in the scheme of a lifetime.

CHAPTER FIVE

November 18, 1812

T HERE IS A strange sort of energy in a household, a balance
achieved through mutual understanding between everyone
who lives there.

Anne knew this. She also knew that when a new person, an
interloper in the eyes of many, joins that household, then the
balance is upset. If that person is to stay, and become part of it,
then it would take time.

How much time would depend on the welcome they received there.

Her first day at Clarcton Castle had not boded well. The
strange way Mrs. Seton had become so very agitated over the
mention of a portrait of the Countess of Clarcton; the overly-
friendly Holt, sometime driver, sometime footman; the impene-
trable earl, along with the sweet child who seemed to have no
idea there were secrets in every nook and cranny of the place.

No, it was with a heavy heart Anne had returned to her room
after dinner that night and curled up in the large, ornate bed,
mind exhausted and heart unprepared for what lay ahead.

Yet fourteen days later, it was with a smile that Anne stepped down the wide staircase, a sense of peace in her soul.

She had done it.

Well, not entirely. Mrs. Seton was just as unwilling to befriend the governess as she had been to speak to her. Each day had brought fresh opportunities for the two of them to grow closer, yet the housekeeper had kept Anne at arm's length.

But the rest of the household had, eventually, welcomed her with open arms. The flow of the household had eddied around her, but now she was taken up with the current, just as much part of the place as any of them.

"Good morning, Smythe," Anne said as a housemaid scurried past her, late in her duties to light the fires in the East Wing.

"Morning, Miss Anne," came the hurried response.

Anne smiled as she reached the bottom of the stairs and curved around the servants' hall to take a corridor toward the west side of the house. The hustle and bustle of a house waking up was something akin to nothing else.

She imagined it was rather like a ship. All hands on deck when required, but most of the time, the huge edifice seemed to continue on without much input from anyone. The small, everyday tasks of many kept the old thing moving along.

As she stepped along the corridor, warmth from fireplaces already lit hit her through open doors, a brief relief from the freezing corridors Anne was still getting used to. It was not unusual to see two or three shawls around the shoulders of Mrs. Seton as she passed.

Anne had shivered grievously the first few days she had meandered around the place until a housemaid had taken pity on her and lent her one of her own shawls.

She had it around her now. A dark blue, heavy wool, something that was made with love and had been worn over and over again.

"No, you take it," the housemaid had said with a smile against Anne's protestations. "'Tis only a shawl, and my mother will happily weave another for me."

It had been worth its weight in gold. The Clarcton lands were only a little further north than Anne had been, but it made all the difference in these wintery months. Besides, she was not entirely convinced the castle had been built for warmth.

It did not appear to have been built for anything; its rambling corridors took twists and turns against all reason, and there were several rooms one could only enter by going through another. There were small staircases that only went from one floor to the next, refusing to go all the way up, and more than once, Anne was at a dead-end, utterly lost.

But it was with a smile that she stepped along the corridor today. *Two weeks.* That was quite an achievement, considering, far above the master's expectations, Anne could tell.

Timothy Lexington, Earl of Clarcton.

She had hardly seen him. Twice, for dinner, which they had spent in relative silence. Once, when he had been leaving a room, and she had happened to be in the Great Hall, when he had nodded but said nothing. And that was all.

Her new master's inattention aside, however, Anne was finding Clarcton Castle was a place she could be happy. The food was good, her bedchamber more than sufficient for leisure and rest, and Frances an absolute delight.

Frances's drawing room, as it had been called, was at the end of this corridor.

"Drawing room?" Anne had said in bewilderment on the second day at the castle. "She is but a child, four years old. Does she really have a need for her own drawing room?"

And Mrs. Seton had glared. "You think the heiress of Clarcton does not deserve her own room?"

"That is not what I meant," was the hasty response Anne had given. "I just meant—"

"Her bedchamber and nursery are above, and her drawing room is here, below," Mrs. Seton had said, interrupting her. "You will see to it that she spends a little more time in the drawing room every day. The nursery is no place for her."

On that, at least, she and Mrs. Seton could agree. Two mere weeks in the company of the child had told Anne she was tired of being molly-coddled and was far more advanced for her age than anyone seemed to credit her for.

"Miss Anne," curtseyed a housemaid that she passed.

Anne could not help but smile as she inclined her head and continued on her way. *Two weeks.* It was heartening, in a way, that it had been a fortnight until she had not only gained the respect of those in the household but had slipped into the routine of the place.

Finally, she was starting to feel as though she belonged here. As though this household now contained her as a vital part, a cog in a wheel that could no longer be summarily removed.

Well. At least she had not got lost the last two days in a row, which considering the small and narrow corridors winding their way around the house and the several doors she had discovered that had since been boarded up…

She had not spoken the thought aloud—she still had no one within the household with whom she could truly confide.

"Watch out, careful now!"

Anne stepped to the side as a pair of footmen rattled along the corridor carrying coals for the fireplaces.

"Sorry, Miss Anne!"

She could not help but laugh as they rushed past her.

It was your role as interloper, she knew, to fit into the pattern which had already been laid out. It was the biggest challenge a governess had to face.

Miss Clarke had been clear on that. "You think the children you care for will be the challenge? Oh no, ladies. 'Tis the household itself, the behemoth beast you join, which will decide whether to welcome you in or spit you out."

Anne had been horrified at this remark when she had first heard it, but then, as always, Miss Clarke had been proven right.

Every household she joined, Anne found the children—if not willing, then at least accepting—yet the household itself was usually resistant.

The corridor opened out into the Great Hall, and Anne slowed. It was always an experience, the Great Hall. Larger than her mother's house, her gaze drifted upward at the swords and muskets which adorned the walls.

The Clarcton family was an old one, that much she had known before she had received the posting, and now she could see that it was an impressive one.

Every battle that England had waged over the last five hundred years had been attended by a Clarcton. Every victory gained a banner for this room. Every defeat left a space in the portrait gallery for a man who did not return.

Anne shivered. It was a strange feeling, the sense that history had been shaped and yet had, in its turn, molded the fortunes of one family.

Her own parentage was good, well-respected, honorable, but it was nothing to this. Few families could compare to the nobility of the Clarctons when it was expected one would know the names of one's great, great, great grandparents.

Anne smiled as her gaze caught one of the suits of armor, one she had nicknamed 'Teddy' in the solitude of her mind, due to the remarkable bear wrought in iron on its helmet. The more she explored this house, the more strange and intriguing she found its current master.

All this history, all this weight of expectation. It was surely too much for one person to bear, at least alone.

Her heart skipped a beat. In all her wandering, all her exploration, and that one time she got lost and had to cry out for someone to rescue her...she had never seen a painting of a woman who could have been the Countess of Clarcton.

Reaching the other side of the Great Hall, Anne took the western corridor and smiled as Dewey appeared in her view.

"Ah, Miss Anne," he said genially.

Anne curtseyed, as was due. "Dewey. Good morning."

The butler smiled. He had been one of the first servants to

think well of her, and his acceptance, she had no doubt, had played a large part of the rest of the household's.

"How are you this morning, Miss Anne?"

"Quite well, I thank you, though I believe it will rain later, which will be a pity. I had hoped for a long walk in the park after my duties had been discharged."

"Rain?" The butler snorted and shook his head. "You will be fortunate if it is not snow, Miss Anne, in these temperatures!"

Anne's heart sank. "You think so?"

"I know so," said Dewey, pointing at his knees darkly. "The old arthritis never lies."

And with that, he continued on his way, evidently eager not to lose much time for his morning routine.

Anne continued along the corridor, spotting Smythe frantically lighting a fire in the morning room as she passed. She was so attentive to the sights in the rooms she passed, however, that she walked almost directly into someone.

"Oh, I do beg your pardon!"

Holt grinned, brushing down his waistcoat. "No harm done, I'm sure, Miss Anne. And where are you off to this fine morning?"

Anne smiled weakly. It would have been friendly, even charming perhaps if it was not the same old tired routine they had fallen into.

"Along to Lady Frances's drawing room," she said helplessly. "As you know."

The gentle rebuke did not seem to register in the footman's mind as he smiled eagerly. "And after your duties today, what will you do?"

Anne was utterly lost at what to say. There appeared to be no actual harm in Holt, from what she could see. She had heard only good about him from the other servants, and he had not attempted anything she would have considered inappropriate.

Still. He was an eager man and appeared quite taken with her. If he was a butcher's son, or from a farming family, Anne would not have taken it quite so awkwardly, but they resided in the same property. *This could not continue, not like this.*

"More chores, I am afraid," she said cheerfully. "There is much to prepare for Lady Frances's future schooling, as you can imagine. You will have to excuse—"

"But in your free time," said Holt, stepping across the corridor to bar her way. "What do you do?"

Anne laughed. "I must admit, I do not have much free time. Good day, I must—"

"No free time? 'Tis a scandal of the first degree!" the footman said, stepping to block her way once again with a smile he obviously thought was charming. "The master cannot expect you to work all the time. All of us deserve a little...leisure."

Anne did not know what to say. The questions in themselves were not harmful, neither rude nor inflammatory, she could find no fault with them.

The fact he was a good-looking man, all sandy hair and freckled cheeks, was neither here nor there. Anne was not here to find a gentleman follower. She was here to care for Lady Frances.

Besides, if she was interested in any gentleman...

The image of her master flashed through her mind, and Anne flushed, her cheeks hot, and Holt's smile broadened.

This was not the time to lose her head! She should not be thinking of the master like that, not at all, and it would only serve to give the footman false hope.

Anne Gilbert was not in the market for any man.

"I really must be going," she said, finally getting around the footman and walking down the corridor faster than she would naturally.

Quickening her pace seemed to be the only way to escape him, and Holt did not try to follow her. *Thank goodness.* The last thing she needed was for gossip to spring up from a perfectly innocent conversation.

Well. Innocent from her side, at least.

Frances's drawing room appeared as she turned a corner, and Anne halted outside it to catch her breath.

The first two weeks in any new posting were the most intense. She knew that; anyone worth their salt from the Governess Bureau knew that.

She was fortunate indeed to have a charge both obliging and pleasant. Now she had overcome the first fourteen days, she could settle into a routine of her own, carve out her own niche within the household, and be happy for...

How long? With a child this young, she could feasibly be a part of Clarcton Castle for ten years, maybe more.

Anne tried to slow her breathing, taking in slow and measured breaths. Ten years here would certainly be an honor, but it could also start to feel like a prison. All she had to do was take each day as it comes. All she had to know was *keep going*.

A smile, bittersweet, crept over her face. *Just keep going.* A favorite phrase of her mother's.

Just keep going.

Taking a deep breath and throwing back her shoulders as though heading into battle, Anne opened the door and stepped inside.

"Miss Anne!" Frances's face lit up, and though this was charming in itself, it did cause a little pain to sear through Anne's heart.

That a child should be so happy to see what was a relative stranger was symptomatic indeed of a lonely life. *Where was her mother?*

She had not been here for some time. Smythe had been here almost a year, and she had admitted in a quiet corner of the servants' hall just four days ago that she had never seen the mistress.

A sickness severe indeed to take her away from her child for a quarter of her life.

Anne's heart broke as the little girl rushed toward her, babbling away about a toy she held in her hand. She scooped her up, pulling her into her arms as nature intended. A child in a pair of loving arms. It did not matter whether they were a parent's.

What this child needed more than anything was love.

"—over the top of the hill and back down again!" Frances said, bright-eyed.

"Goodness, what an adventure to be had!" said Anne brightly. "Come now, show me."

The child wriggled out of her arms, which was all to the good for Anne kept forgetting how heavy a four-year-old was, and scampered over to the window where the Grand Old Duke of York was waiting to go up and down the hill, or pile of cushions, of Frances's making.

Anne dropped to her knees, no concerns about standing on ceremony here. She was starting to become a part of Frances's world. It would be impossible to teach a child of any age, let alone only four, if you were not already accepted into their world.

"Can you make me go over a hill?"

Anne blinked. "I beg your pardon, Frances?"

Frances was smiling wistfully. "It's what Papa used to do, ages ago. He whirled me around and around!"

Her face had lit up at the memory. Every daughter had a memory of being whirled around by her father. Anne certainly did.

"I am not sure I am strong enough," she said ruefully. "But let's have a go. Up you get!"

Frances jumped to her feet, eagerness spread across her face and offered out her hands. Anne found to her surprise that she was strong enough, the child whirling around with shouts of joy and giggles overflowing, and a rush of joy filled her own heart.

This was what she was here for. To make Frances feel joy, to show she was loved and wanted. It met a need so deep in Anne that she had no idea from whence it came. To feel wanted, to feel needed by someone so desperately that—

"Put my daughter down."

It was fortunate indeed Anne was slowing down anyway, for the sudden voice behind her may well have caused her grip to slip and the child to fall.

As it was, she slowed enough for Frances's feet to touch the floor and, once she was certain she was not so dizzy that she could not hold herself, Anne turned around.

The earl was standing behind her, arms crossed, and thunder across his face.

The flush that seared her cheeks was natural, and Anne could not stop it. She had done nothing wrong, but it was clear she had transgressed some sort of line as yet unmarked.

"Papa!"

Frances, unaware of the icy tension between the two adults, ran toward her father. "Papa, we were playing going up hills! Look, look at the hill I made with the cushions!"

The earl glanced at the pitiful two cushions stacked one on top of the other and immediately looked away and returned his gaze to the governess.

A spark of irritation flared in Anne's own heart. Here he was, a gentleman with a spirited young daughter, and he ignored her. Frances was so desperate for attention that she quickly embraced a stranger, and her father did not think it worth attending to her?

The memory of her first meeting with Frances replayed in her mind, and she bit her lip as though that would prevent the censure she felt for the father from pouring from her mouth.

There was warmth there. She had seen it; she was not mistaken. But it had disappeared as quickly as a winter sun once a cloud covered the sky, and it confused her most heartily.

Why would the earl not permit himself to love his daughter?

"Come with me, Miss Gilbert," said the earl coldly before leaving the room.

Anne swallowed. This could not be good, and yet there was no censure specifically in his words, nor tone. Just a general sense he was not to be crossed.

Taking Frances by the hand, for she could hardly leave her alone in the drawing room set aside for her own personal use, Anne stepped into the corridor just in time to see the earl step into the next room along. It was unknown to her, like many of the rooms in the castle.

"Hurry up!" said Frances with all the eagerness of a child.

Anne obeyed, entering the room and seeing to her surprise that it was laid out in much the same manner: a drawing room, with pianoforte, armchairs, sofas, and a roaring fire that was a relief to her toes, which were unprepared for northern climes.

"Now, Frances, come here."

The child released Anne's hand at once as she scampered over to her father, who was holding out—

"A dolly!"

It was indeed a doll, finely made, with blonde hair and a delicate gown of silk. Frances's squeals of delight were enough to tell Anne this was evidently a particularly favorite style of gift.

"Thank you, Papa, thank—"

"Yes, yes," said the earl distractedly, pointing to the other side of the room. "Go and play with her by the pianoforte, child. Your Miss Anne and I need to discuss something."

Anne sat obediently in the armchair that he pointed to opposite his own. Had she done anything wrong? Had Mrs. Seton complained about her, invented some small slight to whine about—or worse, had she noticed Holt's rather persistent attentions and sought to bring them to their master's attention as soon as possible?

She smoothed her skirts with nervous hands as the earl said nothing.

If she did not know any better, she would have said this was a second interview. Looking to him for insight was useless; the earl sat blankly, his face impassive, the only movement his eyes as they raked over her.

Anne swallowed. She had done nothing wrong. Until she was accused of mishandling the education of her charge, or anything else, she would do as her mother had always told her.

Just keep going.

"Miss Anne Gilbert," said the earl finally, as the happy chatter from Frances grew.

He said no more, and Anne found a little of her red-headed defiance.

"Timothy Lexington," she said calmly, meeting his gaze.

He smiled. "You have done well these two weeks, Miss Gilbert. Very well indeed."

The tension which had built in her immediately dissipated—so he was not upset about anything she had done? The personal opinions of masters had never really mattered much. Nor had those of her mistresses, in truth; it was the views of the children that she cared about, and as long as Anne had the trust of her employers, she was typically permitted to get on with her duties to complete them quite happily.

But if she did not have that trust…well, she knew what would happen. It had never happened to her, not yet, but there were plenty of ladies in the Governess Bureau who were quietly dropped from the books if one was found wanting by two or three postings in a row.

"It is an honor to serve," she said quietly, conscious Frances was in the room, "and a pleasure to get to know my charge."

The earl glanced at her, a shadow passing across his face as he took in the small child.

It was there only for a moment. If Anne had not been examining his expression at that very moment, she would have missed it. It was almost as though seeing his child not only brought him joy but unhappiness, too.

Could it be something to do with his wife, Anne wondered. *Did the child look like her mother?* Had there been some tragedy—had the birth rendered the countess so unwell?

"You must have wondered about my wife."

Anne jumped, startled at the strange sensation the gentleman had read her mind.

Still, it would be uncouth to deny it. "I have, my lord."

The earl sighed. In that moment, he appeared to age almost ten years. "Yes, I thought you would. I had no wish to tell you immediately. It was important I knew I could trust you. Two weeks has been sufficient to see you are dedicated to your charge and to her care, and that is sufficient for me. You deserve the truth."

Anne leaned forward, despite herself. *Was she finally about to understand why a child was here motherless, a man stuck in his castle without his wife?*

"My wife," said the earl heavily, "has no wish to be here. She left me, the child, this place almost two years ago now. She has no wish to return, and so I do not require it."

It was such a banal response Anne waited for the rest of the story. When it became clear that there was no more forthcoming, she leaned back in almost disappointment.

"Left?" she repeated. "Left. So why is the truth hidden?"

It was the wrong thing to say.

The earl snorted. "You think there would be no scandal if it was discovered that the Countess of Clarcton disliked her husband so utterly that she would abandon her child?"

Anne swallowed. It was a foolish thing to say, in hindsight. Yet her curiosity was heightened rather than abated. To leave a child, so young as Frances must have been—something must have occurred between the husband and wife to precipitate such an event.

What had happened? What had the earl done to frighten away his wife?

"And that leads us to the favor I must ask of you."

Anne looked up from her palms, carefully folded in her lap. "A favor?"

Why was it that the earl looked so discomforted? "Yes, a favor, and I speak advisedly. This is a request, and you must feel perfectly able to reject it if you do not believe yourself up to the task."

Up to the task. That competitive streak her brothers had trained into her rose.

"Ask, my lord," she said lightly. "The worst I can say is no."

He looked far more concerned than she would have expected. *What sort of favor did an earl have to ask a mere governess?*

Out of a pocket, the gentleman pulled a sheaf of envelopes. "Do you know what these are?"

Anne blinked. "How on earth would I know that, my lord?"

Timothy laughed dryly. "I suppose that would be too much to ask, even of a governess of the Bureau."

Anne's smile was brief. She did not consider the Bureau a laughing matter. She had worked hard to earn her place there, and she would do nothing to risk it.

The earl opened up one of the envelopes. *"My dear Earl of Clarcton, I would be honored if you would delight my daughter with your presence at dinner this evening.* A very pretty invitation from the Merriweathers."

Anne waited for more as the earl met her gaze, as though she should understand something important.

"Nice family," he said nonchalantly. "Or how about this one? *To the Earl of Clarcton, please consider this your invitation to this summer's house party, there will be several young ladies in attendance with whom I am sure I can secure an introduction."*

Anne did not understand. Introduction to ladies? The earl was married though, wasn't he?

"It was this one which upset me the most," said the earl, pulling out a letter that appeared scented, if Anne was any judge. "Miss Theodosia Ashbrooke. A matchmaker, perhaps you have heard of her?"

Finally, Anne was able to rejoin the conversation. "Miss Maria had already requested to her mother, the Countess of Allun, that Miss Ashbrooke would be a useful connection in case…well. Her Season did not go to plan."

The earl barked a laugh. "Yes, quite. Well, Miss Gilbert, this handful of letters is just a smattering of missives I receive on a weekly business—to say nothing of the in-person nonsense I must suffer."

He looked at her expectantly, but Anne was entirely at a loss. "It must be distressing I suppose, but I am sure more upsetting for your wife. The countess."

Timothy's eyes met hers, and Anne almost gasped aloud. There was such intensity there, such ferocity. A coldness, like a lake that might be warm if welcomed in.

"The Clarcton Christmas ball. I am forced to host it once again," he said heavily. "I need...I need you to pretend to be my wife."

Anne laughed, but her laughter became uncomfortable as the earl stared, unsmiling.

She halted quickly. "I am sorry, could you repeat that?"

"I need you to pretend to be my wife," said the earl. "To attend, as my wife. To dress as my wife would. To dance with me, as my wife. In short, to present yourself as the Countess of Clarcton for the world to see."

The words individually made sense, but Anne could not take in the meaning.

Was he mad? She, a mere lady and that only due to the good fortune of her birth, pretend in a new place, a new neighborhood...to be a countess?

"Why on earth would you make such a request of me?" she asked slowly.

Why was there such hesitation on his face? "As to that, I cannot say."

Anne examined him. It was perhaps the first opportunity she had to do so without the risk of attracting condemnation for being so forward.

He was a handsome man. She had been correct in that assumption when she had first met him in Miss Clarke's office. He did not appear to be an evil man. He was not cruel. She had seen no evidence of malice or wickedness.

He did not attend church, to be sure, but Anne could not count on two hands the number of gentlemen who attended purely to satisfy the demands of their wives.

Pretend to be his wife. Attend a ball, as the countess? It was a test. A trick. Perhaps even a trial. Why would an earl require someone to pretend to be his wife?

"So...so you want me to lie at a ball, pretend to be your wife?"

It sounded ridiculous now she said it aloud, but the earl did not appear amused.

"Yes," he said calmly.

Anne had to laugh. "What on earth for? Forgive my bluntness, my lord, but it seems like such a foolish idea. Why not just say your wife is still away? Better still, tell the truth, and share that you do not know when she is coming back?"

It was harshly spoken, but someone needed to shock the earl from his radical thinking, make him see that what he was asking of her was not only impossible but downright ludicrous!

But the earl smiled. "Miss Gilbert, I do not believe you can comprehend what it is like to be a gentleman in my position."

Anne looked around the luscious drawing room—the third she was aware of. "No," she said. "I suppose not."

"It is assumed by many that I have divorced my wife and that I am therefore free to marry," continued the earl as if she had not spoken. "I am tired of being chased by matchmakers, tired of avoiding young misses who wish to catch me. If everyone knew my wife was—I mean, she has been away for such a long time, it is natural what everyone assumes."

Anne swallowed. It was on the tip of her tongue to ask whether the earl had indeed divorced his wife before he sent her away—for that was the only reasonable answer to this riddle, was it not?

His suggestion was a wild idea, a foolish one—and yet her sense of adventure was rising within her.

To be a countess. *To pretend to be a countess*, she corrected silently. What a scheme! Being a governess was all very well, but it gave little occasion for merriment.

To attend a ball, *properly* attend, nay, to host it with the earl at her side...

"You have thought about this carefully, haven't you?" she

asked quietly.

The earl nodded. "I would not ask if I did not think it would work. You have...a passing likeness, shall we say. Few here met her, and that was a long time ago."

Anne hesitated. There was a secret here. The patter of child-ish play continued to her left, and she glanced at Frances.

Poor, motherless child. Did she not deserve to know what happened to her mother?

Perhaps, if she stayed, if she took on this ridiculous role the earl proposed...perhaps then, she would discover the truth. Maybe even find the countess. *Bring her back.*

"I...I will do it."

"You will?"

Anne laughed dryly. "You sound surprised, my lord. Are you accustomed to refusals of your requests?"

"You do not wish for a reward, some sort of additional pay-ment?"

She shook her head. "I am a governess of discretion, and that means if that is what you need, I will help you."

At her words, the earl smiled broadly—and that was when Anne's heart lurched painfully. Painfully, and yet with a sweet-ness that she had never felt before.

His smile did something to her, something she knew instinc-tively would lead to trouble. It was going to be interesting, pretending to be Timothy Lexington's wife.

CHAPTER SIX

November 20, 1812

"**A**ND SHE WILL arrive…?"

"Within the hour, my lord," said Dewey smoothly.

Timothy nodded. *Within the hour.* Fewer than sixty minutes to get his damn nerves under control, make sure he could speak like an adult, let alone a gentleman, and tell Miss Gilbert what was expected.

No easy task when his heart was racing as though he had just finished a hunt.

"And you have told her?"

The butler turned to face his master, seated at the breakfast table. "I have informed Madame Griffon that the countess requires a new gown for the Christmas ball. That is all. She was most…intrigued, is I think the word I would use."

Yes, I bet she was, thought Timothy wryly. "Thank you, Dewey."

The butler bowed and turned to the sideboard. Every item had to be straightened, inspected, ensured it had been polished adequately. Woe betide any footman who found himself on the receiving end of Mr. Dewey's wrath.

Timothy leaned back and looked at his breakfast. The remnants of his toast, the eggs gone, leaving nothing but a yellow stain across his plate.

His eyes were unseeing; however, his mind occupied on what would be accomplished in the next hour.

The first visit to the castle of a person outside the household who would meet...*the countess.*

It was up to her, the governess, the woman who had been chosen for her discretion and yet presented quite an opportunity with that resemblance to his wife, to impress the dressmaker and all his guests with her wit and charm.

She was the one who should be nervous. She should be the one waking up in the night in a cold sweat, wondering whether she had made a terrible mistake in accepting this role.

Yet he was the one who had it all to lose.

"More eggs, my lord?"

Timothy jumped. "What?"

Dewey was standing to his right with the platter of fried eggs in one hand and a serving tong in the other. "Eggs?"

"No," said Timothy shortly. "No, thank you."

The butler inclined his head and returned the platter to the sideboard.

It was foolish to be this jumpy, the earl told himself. As he attempted to force down emotions rushing through his mind, the faster they soared, reminding him of the dangers he undertook by even considering this rash charade.

If it was rash. If he succeeded, if he could stop, once and for all, all these petty flirtations because society believed he was available for matrimony...

Timothy breathed out slowly as the butler moved quietly around the room. All he had to do was hold his nerve. Easier said than done. As the butler moved another platter with a slight noise, Timothy found his temper unable to be denied.

"For God's sake, Dewey, can you not leave them?" he snapped.

Dewey looked at his master with some surprise. "Of course, my lord. I will see to this later. Good morning."

With a deep bow, the butler left the earl in silence. Timothy took great pleasure in swearing.

Well, he may as well get it out of his system before he saw Miss Gilbert again. Christ alive, he was taking a risk, asking the dressmaker to come so far in advance of the ball?

But she had to be tested at some point. Miss Gilbert would need practice, and an old dressmaker who had never met Louise was a good enough test to see how much training she really needed.

Timothy picked up a teaspoon idly and twirled it. The metal caught the candlelight, spinning its beam of light around the room.

Was he getting himself into the most awful trouble? Was he setting himself up for failure—worse, for scandal, by offering his governess the chance to play at being a countess for a night?

His jaw tightened. He was, and worse, he was almost certain that attending that ball would be the gentleman for whom Louise had betrayed him.

He was certainly local. She had seen him frequently, he was sure, and the knowledge he had been cuckolded by someone he knew tormented him for God knew how long.

Since the moment she had laughed in his face.

"You really think you have been the only one?"

The teaspoon dropped to the table with a clatter. There would be one person at the Christmas ball who would *know* Miss Gilbert was not the Countess of Clarcton.

"I...I will do it."

A dry smile crept over his face. No matter the consequences, it appeared the governess was game. *Brave, really.* She had no idea what she was getting herself into, and she wouldn't for some time, if at all.

It was the resemblance to Louise that had done it. He had not been auditioning for false wives when he had journeyed to

London; it was a governess he had sought, and he had gone to the best place to find them.

What a shock he had received when she had turned around, that piercing blue stare affixed on him as he was so accustomed to.

Louise. Anne. *Coincidence, surely?*

Timothy rose, feet unable to stay still any longer, moving around the room like a caged animal, unable to rest.

How would he react to her, convince everyone she was, indeed, his wife? How could he be that close to her for so long? How would they convince the world, for they would need to, that they were in love?

He laughed in the silent room. *What was he thinking?* His mind had grown wild and tangled the longer he had remained here. Worrying whether acquaintances would be convinced of his *affections* for his wife?

What nonsense. He could not think of a single gentleman who had any real feelings for his spouse.

No, it was marriage they were feigning, not sentiment. They were rarely the same.

The heavy, jangling noise of the front doorbell echoed through the room. Timothy winced. It had been his father who had insisted the entire place rattle with that noise.

Still, it gave him sufficient forewarning, and never before had that time been more prescient. That must be the dressmaker. He would have to hurry. Miss Gilbert would need to be briefed before she encountered the dressmaker.

If they were to succeed, the dressmaker had to be convinced she was in the presence not of a mere woman plucked out of obscurity, but a countess, born and bred to nobility.

It was too much to hope she could be left to her own devices.

Striding out of the breakfast room, waiting for the first catastrophe, Timothy took a left rather than a right toward the Great Hall to avoid meeting the dressmaker.

Instead, he took the largely forgotten backstairs, slipped

through the Japanese room that had been closed up when his mother had died, and opened a door into the main corridor.

He did not hesitate. He did not knock. Timothy opened the door unceremoniously to the governess's bedchamber and found her half-dressed.

"Get out of—my lord!"

"I-I-I did not mean…" spluttered Timothy, absolutely unable to take his eyes from the vision of beauty before him, knowing with every frantic heartbeat that what he was doing was wrong.

Yet so right.

"Please, go away!" said Miss Gilbert, cheeks scarlet as she stood in her petticoat and corset but not much else, gown now held over her breasts. "My lord!"

"Right. Right!" said the earl hastily, backing out of the room and closing the door.

He had not wanted to. Everything in him had cried out to stay and take in more of the delectable sight he had only glimpsed.

Christ and all the saints above, but she was beautiful. More, she was tantalizing. Who could have guessed underneath all that starch and linen there was such a goddess beneath?

He leaned against the wall, wiping sweat off his forehead.

It would do no good to lose his head now. Yes, there was an attraction there. He would be a fool to deny it. Any man would find himself stirring at that sight of a woman.

Timothy remembered the sharp look Miss Gilbert had just given him and smiled. *Well, they always said there was something about governesses, didn't they?* Something formidable, something about a woman giving orders.

This was daft, he told himself. It was his monk-like existence that was giving him this strong reaction. He had not permitted himself to go near a woman for over two years.

After all the palaver Louise had brought to his door, after all the pain she had caused, the nightmare she had left him with…

No woman had seemed worth it, after that, and who could

blame him?

But now...

"Don't you knock?" came the irate voice of Miss Gilbert through the door.

Timothy stifled a laugh. *Well, it was funny, and he rarely had any occasion to smile as it was.* "I have never needed to. This is my home, Miss Gilbert."

"Well, you need to now," was the response, "or there will be hell to pay, bargain or no bargain!"

He did not attempt to stifle his laugh now. *Oh, it did his heart good to have some sort of merriment in his life.* Why had he crept away from joy, allowed it to leave his life?

"I need to talk to you," he said quietly. "Now."

"And you will do so when I am properly dressed!"

There was no point arguing. He could open that door and tell her he had no interest in seeing her because he had come to prepare her for the first stage of the agreed façade.

And yet that declaration would be a lie, wouldn't it?

Timothy swallowed. By God, he did want to see more. More of Miss Gilbert promised to be quite a sight indeed.

The door opened to reveal a governess with scarlet cheeks and a fierce expression.

"You will have to get used to that," he said mildly, hoping she could not see how flustered the encounter had made him in turn. "We are husband and wife, after all."

There was a gentle teasing in his tone, which he had hoped would make her laugh, break the tension between them.

It did nothing of the sort.

"Pretending to be your wife does not give you access to my bedchamber," said Miss Gilbert with a ferocious glare.

Timothy almost took a physical step back. Of course, that was what she must have thought when he had stormed into her bedchamber with no regard for her privacy.

God damnit, he was no cad! Was that what she had thought when he had made the suggestion? Did she believe he was making such a demand?

"You do not wish for a reward, some sort of additional payment?"

It had not been further from his mind at the time, but now in hindsight, he could see how she could take it in such a manner. *But she had said yes.* Did that mean she had opened herself to the possibility he could bed her as part of this façade? She was ripe for the plucking, and he could easily put off the dressmaker for twenty minutes while they…

No. Timothy forced his mind away from such desire, counseling himself silently as the governess stood waiting for his reply.

No. He was not that sort of man or master. Though she was beautiful and surely sweet to the touch, he would not take her due to her sense of obligation.

No, if he kissed Miss Anne Gilbert, it would be because she wanted it.

"Well?" she said, cutting through his thoughts. "I await your reason, my lord, as to why it was so necessary to barge into my bedchamber this early in the morning?"

Timothy swallowed. *Control, that was what he needed. He had to take control.*

"It was for no such nefarious deeds, I can assure you," he said as coldly as possible. "I have a dressmaker arriving for you, and even now, I believe she is below."

Miss Gilbert's fierce look disappeared immediately. "Below? Now?"

Timothy nodded. "I have asked Dewey to keep her downstairs for at least thirty minutes from her arrival, but that was five minutes ago, and we have not a moment to lose."

There was fear on her face now, all the bravado gone. "But she is here, now? I had not believed I would be pretending to…to be your wife so suddenly."

"I thought it best not to worry you ahead of time," lied Timothy. *Well, he was hardly going to admit that he had forgotten to forewarn her, was he?* "We can consider this a practice. I am sure you will be perfectly—"

"What is my name?" Miss Gilbert said urgently—not an unfair question, Timothy had to admit. "What is my excuse for being out of sight of everyone for years?"

A flash of memory resurfaced in Timothy's mind, despite all his efforts. A face, blonde hair swept around it, tear strained or rain dampened, he could not tell. *The screams...*

"You have been away for your health," he said more firmly than he felt. "Ill health. Ladies are famously delicate."

"I am not ready," said Miss Gilbert, her voice strained, eyes wide. "We have made no preparations. I have not considered—"

"Practice," said Timothy firmly. "Come, I will show you our bedchamber."

Taking her arm in his hand, he started down the corridor.

"Our bedchamber?"

Timothy's jaw tightened. "Yes, well...a matter of speech. They are two interconnected rooms. We will need to get into the habit of speaking of our home, our daughter, that sort of thing, but...but that does not mean you will be sleeping here."

It was fortunate indeed Miss Gilbert's attention was focused on the imminent arrival of the dressmaker, for the mere thought of her in his bed was making Timothy distracted.

It would never do for her to see the effect she was having on him. *On parts of him.*

"What is my name? What is your wife's name?"

Timothy hesitated as they turned a corner. He had, so far, managed to avoid naming his wife in the governess's presence. A strange sense of foreboding always overcame him when he mentioned it. His gut told him keeping it from her a little while longer would do him good.

The little she really knew about Louise, the better.

"You will be known as the countess, and that is good enough," he said aloud. "There will be no need for names. Fewer opportunities to make mistakes."

He expected Miss Gilbert to challenge this. Surely this would raise her suspicions beyond what she could reasonably expect to bear.

Yet she nodded as they stopped outside a pair of double doors. "Do all the servants know—the household, are they aware of the...the subterfuge?"

Timothy nodded. "I trust them all with my life—no, no more time for questions. Here we are."

Releasing her arm, he opened the pair of doors to reveal his bedchamber.

It was gaudy, he knew, but something in him wished Miss Gilbert to be impressed. To find this most secret and private part of his life as wonderful as he found it.

By the look on her face, his wish was granted.

"My goodness," Miss Gilbert breathed as she stepped inside.

Timothy followed her, shutting the doors behind them. It was easy to forget sometimes, when one lived in the same environs day after day, that one lived in splendor.

Designed by a renowned artist over fifty years ago, there was more velvet than was necessary, a painted ceiling cleverly picked out with gold, and furniture even a duke would be envious of.

"My lord..." breathed the governess.

"Yes, yes, it's all very pretty," said Timothy hastily. "Look, you need to familiarize yourself with the place, or Madame Griffon—"

"Who?" asked Miss Gilbert as she picked up a hairbrush from the dressing table.

"The dressmaker," Timothy said. *Why couldn't the woman focus on what was important?* "Look, it's a hairbrush, not an enigma. Your gowns are here, jewels here..."

He could not help but feel the governess was not really paying attention to what he was saying. Her gaze moved from the gold earrings to the string of pearls to the diamonds, a look of wonderment on her face.

"My lord," said a voice.

Timothy turned. His valet, Cecil, came out of his dressing room with a rather confused expression.

"I was not expecting," he began, his gaze drifting to Anne.

"I know," said Timothy hastily. *Dear Lord, the last thing he needed was for the dressmaker and the valet to come to blows.* "'Tis a simple enough thing, I am more than capable – yes, thank you, Cecil…"

He was able to get the valet out of the door, but he had left Anne alone, and she was looking vaguely around.

Timothy took a deep breath. "A short history of the jewels. Over here…"

There was so much to tell her, so much she had to take in. Was it possible for one person to absorb so much?

"It's a great deal of information to take in," he said pointedly. "If you cannot take it all in now, then—"

"Pearls from your grandmother, earrings from you, diamond ring from…from the jewelers in London you frequent every year," rattled off Miss Gilbert.

Timothy worked hard not to look impressed. "I am expecting a lot from you."

"So you should," she said curtly, turning to face him with a sharp expression. "I am from the Governess Bureau. You only get the best from us."

He smiled, despite the wild pulse roaring through his veins. Well, the plot begins. Who knew how it would go? But they had to start somewhere.

"Ah, my lord."

Timothy turned to see Dewey opening one of the double doors and ushering in a woman who looked just as impressed as Miss Gilbert had not five minutes before, holding two large bags and a trunk.

"Madame Griffon, my lord," said the butler by way of introduction. "His lordship."

The dressmaker placed her wares down before dipping into a low curtsey. "My lord."

"And…" Dewey licked his lips before continuing with, "my lady."

Timothy's gaze flickered to the governess. How would she respond to this first introduction as a countess?

She was majestic. As the dressmaker sank into an even deeper curtsey, Miss Gilbert gave the woman a cursory glance, nodded, and turned back to the jewelry on the table. She was haughty. She was dismissive.

She was everything Louise had been.

A chill passed through him. The two women had never met, the former never described to the latter. And yet Miss Gilbert had her mannerisms perfectly. How?

"My lady, 'tis an honor to be dressing you," said the dressmaker respectfully.

Miss Gilbert smiled briefly. "Yes, I suppose it is."

Timothy almost laughed. It was like walking onto the stage of a most excellent play, knowing the swindle was going to unravel perfectly. *How did she do it?*

"I-I have a number of patterns here, many of which are—"

"Any from Paris?" interrupted Miss Gilbert, finally looking at the dressmaker. "I must be dressed with the best."

The woman did not need his guidance on how to speak down to someone, Timothy realized as he took a seat in an armchair by the window. She was a natural. If he had not known better, he would have assumed she had been born to the title.

All he had to do was be quiet and let her get on with it. The two women chattered away, one eager, the other cold. Where did she get this skill from? How was it possible to step into the shoes of another and be so convincing?

Even he was starting to wonder whether she was truly Louise with her hair dyed with the clever inks that he had seen ladies use for their wigs before.

But it couldn't be. Even Louise could not come back from the d—

"With permission, your lordship, we will start right away?"

Jerked from his reverie, Timothy looked up to see the dressmaker peering at him. Clearly, she required confirmation from the pocketbook before she started to flog her wares.

"Oh, yes," said Timothy lazily waving a hand. "Go ahead. Whatever she wants."

Madame Griffon beamed. "Now, if you will kindly remove your gown, my lady, so I can measure you..."

She bustled to her bags, and Miss Gilbert turned wide eyes to him.

Timothy almost laughed. *By God, she was going to have to undress—and of course, it would cause no comment for a husband to see the gowns his wife was thinking of purchasing.*

It was scandalous. If the dressmaker had any idea they were not married...

"I am sure my husband will not want to be bored with patterns and cuts," said Miss Gilbert in a clear voice. "He can wait for—"

"Do not mind me," said Timothy pleasantly. "I'll just sit here and enjoy the view."

If Madame Griffon had noticed the daggers his "wife" was shooting him, she would undoubtedly question whether there was some love lost between them.

As it was, she was far too interested in rummaging through her belongings.

"That's right," she said distractedly. "His lordship can just sit and admire."

Miss Gilbert had a choice to make, and Timothy was delighted to see that though still glaring as if she wished to skin him alive—which really was no material difference from how Louise had looked at him—she did start to unbutton her gown.

Timothy crossed his legs. *By God, but she was a beautiful woman.* Dressed plainly, as all servants were, as the gown descended, leaving only petticoats, her beauty was revealed.

"Now, my lady, if you would just raise your arm as so to— that's it. Goodness, I can't remember the last time you were in the neighborhood," chatted away Madame Griffon as she started to measure the woman she knew as the countess. "Where have you been all this time?"

Timothy leaned forward, but he need not have worried.

"That is none of your concern," said Miss Gilbert imperiously. "I was under the impression you were here to dress me, not quiz me."

Madame Griffon flushed, and Timothy could not help but feel a little sorry for her. It was unfortunate she was caught in the crosshairs of their plan.

The following twenty minutes were full of fascination for Timothy. It had been a long time, it felt, since he had seen the female form—even longer since he had been permitted to be this close to it.

Something was stirring within him, something darkly physical, which had to be ignored. Miss Gilbert was not a chit of a thing he could buy for coin and enjoy. She was his servant, in charge of the child he was raising.

And yet…

"There," said Madame Griffon triumphantly. "I have all measurements and preferences noted, my lady, and I will have the gown for the ball ready three days beforehand."

Miss Gilbert nodded, and Timothy rose. She was clearly fatigued, and no wonder. It was onerous to pretend to be something one was not.

He would know.

"Thank you, Madame Griffon," he said courteously, ringing the bell by the fireplace. "I am grateful for you taking on the commissionon such short notice."

"And I am honored," she said with a low curtsey. "If I can ever—oh, dear!"

"Get out! Get out, right now!"

Damn, he had entirely forgotten Miss Gilbert was still in a state of undress. The door had been opened by Holt, of all people, and his astonished look to see the woman standing in naught but her petticoats had caused a crimson flush to seep across the governess's face.

"I had better," began the dressmaker hastily.

"Out!" bellowed Timothy, though this was aimed at the footman.

Madame Griffon half ran, half fell out of the doorway with the shocked footman, and Timothy slammed the door behind them both, leaning against it to take in the view which had so shocked his servant.

It was shocking that such splendor could be hidden under all that poise.

"Timothy Lexington," said Miss Gilbert in a stern voice. "If this plan is nothing to do with your wife and entirely focused around...around seducing me, then you are entirely mistaken about my character."

A flush seared his cheeks. "'Tis nothing of the sort, and never has been. I did not—I had not remembered you were still undressed."

The governess raised an eyebrow. "Well, that proves it, at least."

It was not entirely the truth, but he could not have this plan fail.

"Please, I require your help in this," he said. "I will not be so...so foolish again."

She was well within her right to storm out of the place and leave for London.

Timothy stepped across the room, picked up her gown, and approached her. "Please. Accept my apologies for my rashness."

Miss Gilbert reached out for the gown. Their fingers touched but for a brief moment, but it was enough. Heat flared between them, a heat that singed, a heat he had not expected and yet drew him toward her like a moth to a flame.

"Anne..." he said.

Miss Gilbert stepped back, icy coldness once more. "Thank you for my gown. You may leave the room while I dress."

Timothy nodded, not trusting his voice, and did not take another breath until he had left the room and leaned against the wall.

Hell's bells. What did all that mean?

CHAPTER SEVEN

November 22, 1812

"—THOUGH I HAVE never concerned myself much for his opinion, it is vital we converse with him for at least ten minutes. It is expected, though it will bring me no pleasure," said the earl, coming to a halt.

Anne nodded. "I see."

She did see. It appeared the poor Reverend of Clarcton, like vicars everywhere, was respected enough to be invited to the ball but not liked enough to be listened to.

It was a shame, but Anne was far more concerned with her own ability to be listened to. "You know, my lord, I think we have discussed the guestlist for your ball—"

"Our ball," interrupted the earl with a stern look.

Anne took in a deep breath. "Yes, our ball. The guestlist for our ball has surely been discussed sufficiently?"

"Not in the slightest. We have much to review," he said dismissively, leaning back in his armchair. "Now, if you consider the Marnmouths…"

Anne sank back into the sofa in the west drawing room and sighed heavily. It was a rather bold thing to let him see her displeasure so openly, but it did not seem to matter. He did not seem to notice.

They had been here—what, two hours? Frances, the delightful child that she was, had found a few cushions and had made them into a fort, playing quite happily.

At least she was entertained. Anne could not believe it possible for one person to talk on and on about people he did not like, yet the earl had managed it. So absorbed in recounting the guestlist and the minutiae of their lives, he seemed quite unaware that if he continued much longer, he would be doing so to a sleeping audience.

"His wife, on the other hand, is a complete brute," said the earl matter-of-factly, as if it was totally normal to describe a lady in such a way. "I would not go near her for anything."

Anne blinked. "The Countess of Marnmouth? A brute?"

The glare she received was scorching and unforgiving. "No, the Right Honorable—have you been listening to a word I have been saying?"

"Almost all, yes, but you must admit, my lord, that—"

"No. No, that won't do."

It was most infuriating. "And what, may I ask, won't do?" Anne inquired icily.

Her gaze met the earl's. Warmth blossomed in her chest whenever he looked at her like that. There was something in the eyes, in the way his gaze looked through her.

Through her clothes, at the very least.

"You cannot call me your lordship," the earl said lazily, waving a hand. "No, my wife would never do that. It would be first names, naturally."

Heat spread to her cheeks. "I...I cannot call you Timothy."

He smiled. "My dear Anne, you are going to have to."

What was it about the way he said her name that made her shiver? So few people called her that, and it was intimate.

And he had not earned that right. *Not yet.*

"I am your countess, and that...that means you may call me

'my dear,'" she said coldly, as though granting him a great favor.

He did not appear cowed by her remark, more entertained. "Oh, that is how it is going to work, is it? And pray, what are you to call me? My dear?"

Anne shivered. She had thought the nameless moniker would somehow lose its power, but the idea of wandering around a *castle* calling the Earl of Clarcton 'my dear'…

"Clarcton," she said hastily. "'Tis your title, and undoubtedly what many of your friends call you. It is personal, but not…not intimate."

He held her gaze for just a moment longer than was comfortable. If only he was not so…so…

Anne could not articulate, even within the privacy of her own mind, just what the Earl of Clarcton did to her.

It was all his fault. It had all started with this game he was playing, pretending to be his wife, indeed. There was probably some sort of stupid bet he had with a friend to see whether he could get a servant to dress herself up like a fool and prance about the place, pretending to be a countess.

If it had been anyone else, she would have refused such mockery and stormed away, perhaps as far as London. But as it was…

Timothy Lexington, the Earl of Clarcton. Anne had a rather worrying feeling she would not be able to deny the man anything. When the dressmaker had departed and Timothy—and the *earl* had handed over her gown…

She could not have been mistaken. Surely, he had felt it, too, the sudden rush of heat, the connection, the desire to move forward and—

Anne cleared her throat. She was losing her head like the fool of a chit he undoubtedly thought she was.

It had been scandalous, standing there in the earl's bedchamber in naught but her petticoats, his hand on hers, and her heart racing at breakneck speed. It was scandalous, seeing the spark of attraction in him.

Had she deluded herself? She had felt rather than seen the effect she had on him. It had been intoxicating, the knowledge she could cause such vulnerability and yet such desire in any man, let alone an earl.

"Clarcton?"

Anne jumped. "I beg your pardon?"

The earl had a rather strange look on his face. "You wish to call me Clarcton?"

This was what they had been talking about before she had become lost in reverie.

"Yes," she said decisively. "I think that appropriate. I know several titled husbands who are referred to as such by their wives."

"Perhaps in company," said the earl mildly. "Surely not in private. In private, they would go by their first names. Far more intimate, don't you think?"

He is teasing you, Anne told herself fiercely as her heart quickened. *Teasing. He does not mean it.*

"And as we will be in public for most of this charade," she said sweetly, "I can see no better time to start practicing than the present. Clarcton."

Anne had never considered herself forward. Her mother might have disagreed. Anne, her sisters, and cousins were always getting into mischief when younger, and nine times out of ten, it was her mother who had rescued them.

"You will always have your way," she would sigh, wiping the mud from Anne's face or washing strawberries from her gown or whatever trouble she had got into. *"You do not always have to be right, you know."*

And yet she did. It was imperative she had her own way in this regard, too, or else there was a very real chance this earl would utterly overwhelm her. *Where would that lead?*

"Clarcton," he said with a teasing smile. "Well, my dear, where were we? Ah, the Reverend Critchley. We will have to be careful, I'm afraid, for he did meet my wife at least twice, and there is a small chance he will wonder…"

And they were back to where they were twenty minutes ago, Anne thought dully. Really, all this preparation: those she had to smile at, those she must ignore, those she should present with a cutting remark…

It was all so false. A woman would not be so calculating, would she? Anne had never met such a person, and as Clarcton's monologue continued, it became clear she had no wish to.

Her gaze drifted over to Frances. The child had been left entirely to her own devices for at least two hours yet showed no signs of requiring attention.

Anne's heart broke. It was a truly lonely child if, at the age of four, they were so easily diverted.

"—but the Merriweathers are safe, they never met my wife," continued Clarcton, voice dull as though reading from a list. "Their daughter is one of those shameless ladies who has attempted to make it clear just what an interesting match we would be. The cheek! Last time I saw her…"

Anne nodded, though she could not see what poor Miss Merriweather had done that was so dreadful. After all, her father was a baronet, and he was an earl. Surely there was a potential match if he had indeed been single?

"—you understand?"

Anne blinked. "Yes."

Clarcton nodded. "Excellent. Well, those are the notables of the area, though there are a few others you should be made aware of. The local mayor, a nice man, terrible manners, will probably wish to dance with you at least once."

Anne's eyes glazed over. Goodness, he was not expecting her to memorize all of this, was he? No person could be expected to know all of this; it was impossible!

Why could she not just rely on her wits? She had adorned herself with the scorn of a countess with the dressmaker. Had not Madame Griffon been utterly taken in?

The door opened, and the butler stepped in soundlessly. Anne caught his eye.

"...admit I quite like the father, but the mother!" Clarcton shook his head with a dry laugh. "No, you must avoid her at all costs. She is far too inquisitive and will assuredly ask more questions than you are comfortable with. The son, however..."

Anne smiled briefly at the butler, who rolled his eyes. She had to stifle a laugh. It was pleasant if only for a short moment, to feel herself connected to another while preparing for this rather wild scheme.

The agreement had changed things. Of course it had, she had been foolish to assume it would not. The isolation she had felt on the first day she had arrived at Clarcton Castle had started to thaw, and now it had returned.

Still, it was painful. The distance between herself and the others had somehow opened into a gaping chasm, now she was to be introduced to the world at the ball as their mistress.

"Are you listening, *my dear*?"

Anne smiled but did not turn to the earl. "I am indeed, Clarcton. Please do continue telling me about Master Hastings and why he is more palatable than his mother."

She would not permit herself the pleasure of seeing how impressed he was with her ability to both pay complete attention to his words and consider other things.

Well, really. She was a governess! More, she was from the Governess Bureau. Did he really think she could not do two things at once?

"Right," came the rather surprised reply. "Yes. Yes, the son is charming and yet innocent in his own way, so I would not concern yourself with him..."

Anne's gaze meandered over to her charge. Frances had finally, it appeared, reached boredom. Instead of playing with the cushions, she was lying on her back, staring at the ceiling.

The poor child was evidently accustomed to being bored out of her mind, and yet she did not cry, complain, or criticize. She did not even speak.

And that meant, Anne knew, she was accustomed to no one listening.

She was here, first and foremost, not as a countess but as a governess!

"—though when I last saw him—"

"I am sorry, Clarcton," said Anne with a bright smile. "I am afraid my countess classes will have to wait. I am needed."

Clarcton blinked. "Needed? Needed by whom? I am the one who requires you to—"

"I may be your countess for one evening, but my purpose here was to be a governess," said Anne. She nodded toward the child, who was motionless and silent on the floor.

Clarcton shrugged. "I find children can usually entertain themselves. See, Frances is not unhappy."

It was all Anne could do to hold her temper, but her pulse was starting to pound in her ears, and her hands were warm.

How could he say such a thing—how could he mean it? He had evidently spent so little time with his daughter, he had no idea of her boredom. Worse, had he completely forgotten what it was to be a child?

"Timothy Lexington," she said aloud, her governess voice perfectly pitched. "Was that what you did when you were young? Entertain yourself, all alone?"

His gaze met hers with just as much steel as her voice. "Why, yes."

"And how did you like it?" She held his gaze for what felt like an entire minute, and then he blinked.

"Not in the slightest, as a matter of fact," he said, a smile across his lips. "Goodness, *my dear.* Perceptive, aren't you?"

"Yes, but then that is part of my stock and trade. If I cannot perceive what a child needs, no matter the age of the child, then I am not worth my salt."

For a moment, she thought she had gone too far. The Earl of Clarcton was not a gentleman to be trifled with, and though he had asked her to partake in this ruse, she was not foolish enough to think this put them on an equal setting.

"You know, Anne Gilbert, I think I like you," Clarcton said softly. "You're not bad at all, are you?"

Anne's heart skipped a beat. "I do not think so, but then I am biased."

He laughed, the tension breaking. This was a gentleman who perhaps if he had been a friend of her brothers', she may have liked.

May have loved.

Anne forced away the thought. He may play at being equals, but she should never forget there was a chasm of difference between them. The Earl of Clarcton and a governess? *Preposterous!*

"So, what is your remedy?" asked Clarcton. "I assume you have one?"

"I do indeed," said Anne, who had no plan but was hardly about to admit it. "I suggest a walk."

They both looked over at the windows, where thin, watery sunlight was managing to make its way into the room.

"A walk? It's November, Miss—my dear," corrected Clarcton, raising an eyebrow.

"Nothing like a brisk stroll in wintery sunshine," said Anne bracingly. Anything to be out of this drawing room where he would drone on and on about people she would soon meet.

Clarcton did not look convinced. "You just want to escape listening to me."

"I can think of more exciting things to do, yes," said Anne, honestly. "Do not think I am ungrateful for the advice, but if we took a walk, I can look around and be entertained while you...monologue."

It was the most audacious speech she had spoken to him, but instead of being offended, the earl looked pleased.

"You know, I have forgotten how refreshing it is to have honesty spoken to me," he said lightly. "You really think you'd prefer to be outside?"

"I can listen to you just as well outside as inside," said Anne. "And Frances would benefit from the exercise."

She watched him glance over at his daughter, and once again, there was that shadow she did not quite understand.

What had gone wrong between Timothy—between the earl and his family? Wife missing, for all intents and purposes, daughter almost entirely unknown to him…

Was it a wonder he was so lonely?

"Fine," he said heavily with a mocking air. "Off we go then."

It took but five minutes for Anne to find a coat and scarf that would fit Frances. They appeared to have been designed for young gentlemen rather than young ladies, and Clarcton laughed heartily as they stepped into the Great Hall.

"Dear Lord," he said. "It's been almost twenty years since I saw those."

"They are yours, then?"

"Mine, my father's before me—if there's one thing that will never go out of fashion, 'tis well-made gentlemen's coats," he said with a laugh. "Are you warm enough, little one?"

Frances's eyes shone as she looked up at her father. "I don't think I've ever gone for a walk with you before, Papa."

Anne felt his embarrassment rather than saw it. He did not permit his face to alter in any way, but the discomfort in the atmosphere increased.

"Well, I think it's about time we changed that, don't you?" said Clarcton with an impudent smile. "Come on."

Anne watched as the man offered his hand to the child, who took it eagerly.

In all this subterfuge and strange feelings that Timothy stirred, she really must remember to prioritize the relationship that really mattered here.

That between father and daughter.

It was a crime they were so distant. Perhaps, in time, she could help him see what a treasure he had, even with his wife gone.

"Are you to join us, Anne?"

Anne blinked at the pair waiting by the door. "I am indeed."

She stepped forward and braced herself for the freezing temperatures. Thank goodness she had seen fit to pack both scarf and muffler in her trunk in that hasty one-hour window between being selected for this assignment and leaving with her new master.

Clarcton laughed as he opened the door, and a freezing gust of wind blew in, making Frances squeal and Anne gasp.

"Come now, I thought you were the one who wanted to go outside," he said, stepping forward with Frances's hand in his. "Keep up, Anne!"

She could not help but laugh. There was something about him that drew her to him even when he was being his most irritable, his most irascible.

It was attractiveness, but not as she knew it. A handsome man had always been, she had thought, someone whose features were pleasing to the eye. Though the earl fit that description, there was something more beyond how he looked.

Anne shivered as she followed them into the cold air. That memory of Timothy—of *Clarcton* handing her the gown had surfaced once again in her memory.

Why did it keep coming into her mind?

"Goodness, it is cold," said Anne as the cold wind worked its way through her pelisse.

Clarcton raised a knowing eyebrow. "Did I, or did I not, say that you would be cold?"

Anne was not about to let that go unchallenged. "What you said, Clarcton, was it was November—something I never contested. Frances, which direction would you like to go?"

The child looked almost overwhelmed and looked around her with wide eyes.

"Any direction you want," said her father with a smile. "You just tell us."

Frances smiled, all adoration. "This way!"

They set off toward, as far as Anne could make out, parkland. It truly was a beautiful estate, and if she had arrived at the beginning of spring rather than winter, she would have explored a great deal more.

As it was—

"Now, I had not started listing the families with which the Clarctons have friendly relations," said Clarcton, "and those who are only invited because otherwise, it would be a great scandal. In the first group, there is—"

"Clarcton," said Anne, "do you not want to know anything about me?"

She had meant it in jest, and was pleased to see him utterly shocked at her suggestion.

"You?"

Anne nodded. "Yes, me."

Clarcton stared over Frances's head. "Why would I want to know about you?"

It was spoken so honestly, with so little guile, that Anne could only laugh.

"Because," she said, as they stepped along the path, "I am about to pretend to be your W-I-F-E!"

She spelled out the word, suddenly conscious of her master's daughter between them, but the child did not look at them. She was far too preoccupied with looking around.

"Acorns!"

She ran off and picked up a handful of the things before turning back to the two adults and grinning.

"Can you find me five acorns that all look alike, Frances?" asked Anne.

The child nodded, looking carefully at those in her hand.

Anne came to a halt with Clarcton beside her, the wind rustling the last few oak leaves not yet on the ground.

"We are about to have a house full of guests," she said under her voice, watching Frances. "Do you not wish to know if I can dance, what music I like, whether I can play the pianoforte?"

Only then did she look at him and saw his panic.

"I did not think of that," he admitted.

Power rushed through Anne. He may be the earl, the one with the money, the power, the title—but it was she, and she alone who could make this ploy a success.

Or failure.

"I do not know why this scheme you've got up means so much to you," she said lightly, "but if you want to make it work, you have got to put in the effort."

Frances squealed with delight as they watched.

Eventually, he spoke in a low voice. "I thought all the effort would be yours."

Anne smiled. "Not entirely. But then, you are a gentleman, Clarcton. You should have no difficulty extracting those details from me through conversation. You may even enjoy it."

Why had she said that? It was a flirtatious thing to even think, let alone say! Anne felt her stomach twist, but the earl did not look embarrassed.

"So, tell me," he said, "and pretend we are in one of the best salons in London. Do you have any siblings, Miss Gilbert?"

"Two brothers and a handful of sisters," said Anne. "Our father died when we were young, so my brothers and I had to work, a great disappointment to our mother. Her sister lived in the neighboring town, and our cousins were almost like siblings, though I admit I did not care for all of them."

Perhaps she had spoken too much. The last thing Clarcton probably wanted was old family gossip.

"Not all of them?" he asked curiously.

Anne shook her head. *By God, it was years since she had last thought about her.* "No, one of them—"

A scream, high pitched and gut-wrenching, cut through the air.

"Frances!"

The name was uttered quickly by them both, but as they turned, Anne saw she was happy and well, examining the acorns in her hand, leaf mulch staining her cheek.

"What the devil—" Clarcton looked around them hastily as another scream wrenched the air.

Could this be something to do with the missing wife? Such a scream, such terror or pain within it…

And then her eyes caught sight of the culprit. "There—look!"

Her heart was pounding. Further down the path, three gardeners were surrounding the trunk of an old oak tree. It had died on one side, and Anne could see they were attempting to saw off part of it. One of the gardeners was trapped underneath it, and his piteous moans were terrible to hear.

"The poor man!" Anne filled with panic. From the shouts she could hear, the man was badly injured. *What could she do?*

Clarcton, however, had no such question. He just acted, rushing over to the gardeners, desperately attempting to move the heavy wood from the man's leg.

Another cry, this time of an entirely different pitch—Frances. Anne saw the child sobbing and rushed over to pull the child into her arms.

"There now," she said comfortingly, kneeling on the lawn to embrace Frances tightly. "Everything will be well."

Even as she spoke, she looked over the child's shoulders at the man still entrapped below the oak branch. It was a dangerous world, even with the security of a castle. Clarcton may treat his servants well, but there was always something that could go wrong.

"Together men, after three," shouted the earl, trying to get his shoulder underneath one part of the heavy branch. "One, two, three!"

They heaved together, and Anne could not help but stare in awe.

A warmth curled around her heart. No matter the mystery of his wife, and the rather gruff way he spoke, Timothy Lexington was a good man. His wife, wherever she was, was fortunate to have him.

With groans of effort, the oak branch was shifted.

"Right, coats, everyone," said Clarcton quickly. "Hold them out—make a stretcher, it will have to do, we must get him into the house."

He was pulling off his own greatcoat as he spoke.

"It'll just take two of us," said one of the gardeners, face red and eyes concerned. "Can I go get doctor? Five more minutes could—"

"Yes, go, do what you think is best," said Clarcton, not looking at him, eyes only for the patient. "It's John, isn't it? How do you feel, John? Stay awake for me."

Anne could do nothing but watch as two of the gardeners stepped away from the man. The one who had voiced the desire to seek a doctor—a wise thought—ran toward the house, and the other approached her.

"Sorry you had to see that, Miss," he said, taking his hat off and twisting it in his hands. "And the child, too."

Anne nodded. No words seemed adequate.

"Isn't master a brick?" he said, and Anne could hear the admiration. "I was fortunate to get this position, my mum in the village was hopeful, but there are only a few vacancies every generation."

This seemed so incongruous with the vast numbers of servants Anne had already met that she frowned as she straightened up.

"Really?" she said. "I would have thought there would be ample opportunities here."

The gardener shook his head, hat still twisting between his fingers. "A job here is a job for life, always has been. No Earl of Clarcton has ever sacked a man, nor woman neither."

Anne frowned. "What, not ever?"

"I can't think of no one who has ever been asked to leave," shrugged the gardener, eyes still fixed on the injured man. "If you get sick or old, there's always a house in the village for you."

The more she heard of Timothy, the more impressed she became. What sort of master was he, that he could, on the one hand, rush toward danger at the drop of a hat, and on the other side, request that his daughter's governess pretend to be his wife?

"He always seems to know what to do in every situation."

The gardener snorted at that. "Not he. When the mistress ran—"

Anne turned to him. "I beg your pardon?"

The gardener flushed and carefully returned his hat to his head. "I had better go, Miss, you understand."

He was gone before she could ask any questions.

His wife ran—ran what? Ran to where? Where was this countess whose presence hovered, almost ghostlike, above them all?

"Is Frances frightened?"

Anne turned to see Timothy standing in the freezing wintery air with no greatcoat.

"You—you were so brave," breathed Anne.

"Gaskell will call on the doctor now, which is all to the good," Timothy said, not questioning her response.

"Well, yes, but how will the poor man afford it?"

It was as though she had suggested the stupidest thing in the world. "Afford it? My dear Miss Gilbert, you cannot think that I would allow a man like John to pay his own doctor's bill? After being injured on my land, serving on my staff? Dear God, the bill comes to me."

"That is…well. Unusual," she remarked, unable to help herself.

She shivered as his gaze met hers. The air was cold, the breeze getting up, and yet she was warm—warming up the more they stood here in conversation. There was something about him. Something she could not help but admire.

"I would never stand by and do nothing," he said, shrugging.

"And yet," said Anne, taking Frances's hand in hers and nodding at the house to indicate her intention, "many earls, many gentlemen, would take that course."

Timothy laughed at this as they made their way back to the path, Frances still sniffing, acorns clutched tightly in her hands.

"I suppose so," he said genially, "but I am not like most earls."

CHAPTER EIGHT

November 23, 1812

NOTHING BUT A good gallop cleared Timothy's head. It had always been. Whenever he had needed to escape the castle, leave Louise behind, all her bitterness…

He came here.

Timothy looked over the parkland, which had been his home for as long as he lived. The tell-tale signs of deer rutting could be seen on the base of the trees, the bark stripped away by the buck's antlers, marking their territory.

The sun attempted to shine, but it was doing a poor job. Timothy's riding coat was warm, but his hands were still cold in his leather gloves.

Despite the chill in the air, he had been unable to stay away. His horse, Admiral, had not been exercised for days, and once again, the castle had become some sort of hothouse—though for an entirely different reason.

Damn, thought Timothy. *He was thinking of her again.* Anne Gilbert. The governess would save him from the marital schemes of the neighborhood if she was as good as she appeared.

His stomach turned. Anne standing in his bedchamber in

naught but her petticoats.

He should have looked away. He should have controlled himself, should have known he would have been unable to prevent his body from reacting to such sweet perfection.

And just yesterday…

Timothy's jaw tightened, and he slowed Admiral to a trot as he approached the trees. John would recover, which was a miracle. He must remember to pay a visit to Dr. Ensoll at some point.

But his heroic rush, his actions…could he honestly say he would have acted so if he did not have the beautiful and charming governess watching him?

Timothy sighed. And that was precisely why he was out here, rather than in there, in Anne's presence.

Clearing his head. He did not appear to be doing a very good job of that, not as his thoughts continuously meandered back to her whenever allowed free reign.

"Because I am about to pretend to be your W-I-F-E!"

Anne Gilbert.

By God, she was starting to infiltrate his dreams and his waking moments. Timothy breathed in the deep pine of the forest that curled around this southern side of the park and tried to put her out of his mind, but it was impossible.

Everywhere he went in that house, there she was. No way around it, of course; he needed to teach her everything she would need to know before this damned ball.

It was a foolish scheme, and he was a fool to attempt it—but Anne was *perfect.* He could have scoured the streets of London for a hundred years and would never have found anyone with such a resemblance to his wife.

Nor that glint in her eyes, that boldness which made his breath catch in his throat.

"Damned nonsense," Timothy muttered aloud.

Admiral snorted at the unwelcome noise, and his rider patted his neck.

"I know," he said quietly. "I'm a fool. I'm a fool for even putting this scheme together."

Now he'd started on this wild path toward the Christmas ball, where she would either be heralded as a triumph—as the countess—or instead unmasked as an imposter, Timothy did not know how to stop. And if he thought his reputation was shaky now...

"But I am not like most earls."

The woods opened up to a beautiful view across the wetlands. Birds fed eagerly in the winter scarcity. As he nudged Admiral closer, some rose in unhappy surprise.

Timothy shook his head. It was his own fault for marrying Louise. He had known, then, what she was. What she would become. He had wed her just to possess her.

And now here he was, with a governess in the house who seemed all too eager to please. Despite his determination to remain aloof, to use her for what he needed and then to return her to London with a large bonus and a warning to stay quiet...

His jaw tightened as he recalled how Frances had clung to the governess after that terrible accident. The child he was raising trusted her, and she had been here but three weeks.

"Clarcton, do you not want to know anything about me?"

"Why would I want to know about you?"

He laughed, and a swarm of birds rose in a wave, disquieted by the noise.

He had not expected to actually like her.

The wetlands became a lake further along the path, and as Timothy grew closer, he found the tension tying his stomach in knots was disappearing. It always happened when he rode out here. It was difficult to worry about social niceties expected in the drawing rooms of society when one was here, breathing in the very essence of nature.

Timothy pulled Admiral to a stop. He was right on the border of his own land here, where it simply became common land. He had come here often when she...when Louise had betrayed him.

For whom, he had never ascertained.

The fact she had needed to find affection in the arms of another had been anathema to him. He had been unable to consider it without rage in those hot, heady days when the news had been fresh.

Timothy sighed, watching his breath blow out in steamy whorls. *Why could she not have been happy with him? He had offered her everything, given her everything she wanted. Why had it all gone so wrong, so quickly?*

He had been alone at Clarcton Castle—alone other than Frances, and a child did not count—for two years. *Far too long.*

Perhaps that was why he was finding the governess's company so diverting. Perhaps compared to the loneliness he had endured before, any chit of a thing off the streets of London could entertain him.

The memory of last Sunday's dinner seeped into his mind. She had been so charming, so witty, he had quite forgotten to ask a single question about Frances.

And so had she.

Timothy swallowed. She was a gentleman's daughter, but that made her no match for a gentleman of his standing. If he ever wished to marry her, he would—

"Marry her?" Timothy spoke the words aloud, they were so strange.

How had such a thought even entered his mind? He had no desire to marry, no ability to do so. He was, in the eyes of the world, married to Louise.

Besides, Anne—*Miss Gilbert, damn it*—was a governess. She was here under his protection, that which all servants gained when entering his household, and he was hardly about to do something so foolish.

Something caught his eye, closer to the trees. A figure—no, two figures.

A soft smile crept over his face. Anne, with Frances beside her, arms no doubt full of pinecones. There was a collector's nature in that child; even he had started to notice it.

Without thought, Timothy turned Admiral so he could watch them. They were moving slowly back toward the house; evidently, one of those long walks Anne had spoken of, designed to tire the little girl out before lunch and a nap.

The sun broke through the clouds, and a glimmer of red hair glinted.

Timothy's stomach lurched. Whenever he believed himself reconciled to her presence, something reminded him of her sensual poise designed to tempt him.

He had almost forgotten last evening when they had sat in his drawing room and laughed about the nonsense of London society, that she was *Anne*. Twice he had almost called her Louise. It was as though she had returned, hair a different color, true, but the same woman.

The spark died in his eyes as his brow furrowed. But she would never come back.

The temptation to ride over there, to accidently intercept them and spend time with Anne was great, but Timothy managed to resist.

It was not normal, he knew, for any master to spend so much time with a governess. Even with their scheme racing forward at full pace, he could not justify adding to the many hours he had already spent in her company.

The last thing he needed was for his heart to be truly touched.

"What is happening to you, man?" he asked under his breath. Admiral whinnied in response, making him grin. "I don't know either, old boy. You've never tied yourself in knots for a mare, have you?"

The horse snorted, and Timothy laughed. He was being foolish, he knew. Like a green boy of eighteen who had spotted his first debutante. But he had been almost a hermit for the last two years.

What harm could it do to ride over and talk? Besides, Timothy argued silently, *he would see Frances, too.* That was something he knew he should do more of. He would ride over, and—

"Oh, hello, my lord!"

Timothy groaned, but changed it to a cough so the speaker would not be offended. *Damnit, he should have known he was riding too close to the Merriweathers' estate.*

"My lord!"

Her voice was excited, eager, and Timothy knew she would not leave him alone until he spoke to her.

Well, he had brought this upon himself, he thought with a sinking heart. All he could hope was that the conversation, painful as it would be, would be a short one.

"Miss Merriweather," he said, smiling briefly at the woman riding a white mare. "How are you?"

"Perfectly well, I thank you," said Miss Merriweather, nudging her horse closer. "And you?"

Timothy knew it would be the height of bad manners to allow Admiral to retreat, keeping the distance between them. There was nothing *wrong* with Miss Merriweather. Compared to many of his acquaintance, she was pleasant company.

There was that small matter of her tears at his wedding…

Well, everyone had expected it, Mrs. Seton had told him sternly years later, as though he should have already known. Miss Merriweather and the Earl of Clarcton? Neighbors? Their fathers such fast friends?

All had expected it, Miss Merriweather, more than most.

"I am well," he said. If he was brief, their conversation would be over before—

"And what are you doing on this side of the lake, may I ask?" said Miss Merriweather, evidently thinking she was smiling coquettishly, while looking as though she had swallowed a lemon. "Hoping to run into me, were you?"

Timothy smiled painfully. "Just enjoying the view, Miss Merriweather."

As soon as the words were out of his mouth, he saw his mistake. Miss Merriweather preened, smirking at the great compliment he had paid her—*and in a way*, he thought ruefully, *he had.*

"La, my lord, you do say such things," she said, raising an elegant hand to move a strand of hair from her eyes. "And here you are, out all alone. I imagine you want company."

Timothy forced his face to remain impassive. He would not smile for fear of giving her quite the wrong impression, but he could not show his irritation either. That would be a mistake.

He may be a fool of an earl, tricked by his wife and eventually despised by her, but he was not a cruel man. He had no wish to hurt Miss Merriweather's feelings.

"I have all the company I need," he said stiffly.

Miss Merriweather, however, did not take the hint. "But I could give you so much more, Timothy. You know that. I think, in a way, you have always known that."

This was far too close to dangerous territory, and Timothy knew it. *Poor thing.* There were so few opportunities for ladies to express their desires, even if that desire was a husband with a title and a good name.

Miss Merriweather had all the social graces one could wish for but no establishment of her own, and Clarcton Castle was indeed the best place for miles around.

"I am married, Miss Merriweather," he said softly. "I have no wish to offend you or to read into your words further than you must have intended."

Had he gone too far? Even suggesting a high-born lady such as Miss Merriweather could have been offering herself to him ...

But it appeared the hint had entirely passed her by.

"Well, I have not seen the countess," she said blithely. "Many in the neighborhood are not even sure whether you are still married. My mama says—"

"You will have the pleasure of seeing my wife at the Christmas Ball," interrupted Timothy, unable to take this much longer. "I hope you will enjoy her company as much as you evidently enjoy mine."

It was a little on the nose, even he had to admit, but really! The woman had to be put in her place. *One simply could not make eyes at a married earl and expect him to come running!*

"Oh," said Miss Merriweather, face falling. "She...she will be there, then?"

Timothy crossed his fingers beneath the reins. *She would be ready.* "Yes."

Miss Merriweather examined him, then smiled. "You cannot fool me, my lord, I can hear the longing in your voice, 'tis no secret between us. Well, you are married, for now. If that ever changes…"

Allowing her voice to trail away in what she clearly thought was an enticing manner, Miss Merriweather turned her horse and trotted away, riding habit streaming behind her.

Timothy sighed heavily. It could not be more obvious Miss Merriweather believed she was wooing him, despite his 'marriage' to Louise.

He shivered. *My mama says…*

Yes, Lady Merriweather had been quite as blatant as her daughter in their hopes of securing him. Even after he had wed Louise, after Frances had arrived and all had celebrated, and those who despised him pitied him for it being a daughter…

Timothy's jaw tightened. Even then, the Merriweathers had treated him like a piece of meat, to be salivated over or auctioned off to the highest bidder.

With Louise unseen for two years now, the rumors were natural. He had heard a few of them himself, through Dewey.

The Countess of Clarcton was missing. The Countess of Clarcton was dead. The Countess of Clarcton was divorced.

The truth did not matter. Whatever the fate of his wife, the Earl of Clarcton was back on the marriage market.

There was only one person who could prevent the Christmas ball and every other social engagement for the rest of his life being unbearable, and that was if Anne could convince them all that the countess had returned, if only for a while.

Digging his heels into Admiral, Timothy made for home. He had been out too long. There was a myriad of things he needed to attend to, and if he was careful...

Yes, he had been right. Choosing his path carefully toward the pine forest and around the house, Timothy 'stumbled' across...

"Papa!" said Frances in joyful surprise, dropping her armful of pinecones and running to him.

Timothy's heart skipped a beat. Admiral was a gentle creature, but even he may act strangely as a small child shrieked and rushed at him.

Anne was quick, grabbing Frances and halting her exuberant footsteps.

"Careful, now," she said softly, crouching by Frances and pointing up at the large beast. "That's your Papa's horse, and I do not think you have been properly introduced yet."

Timothy's heart softened as he watched the governess, who was starting to become dearer to him with each passing day, gently teach Frances.

Louise had been a mistake, and she had brought much misery to his door—but she had also given him Frances. Her greatest gift. His pride and joy.

"Good day, Anne," he said. *Damn and blast it, why was his throat scratchy?* "Miss Gilbert, I mean."

The governess glanced up, but her attention was all for the child between her arms. It was impressive, to be sure, but Timothy could not help but feel piqued by the inattention.

"Are you enjoying your ride, Clarcton?" she asked stiffly. "No, Frances, stay here. Your father's horse may not like strangers."

One word stuck in Timothy's mind, sharp and painful—but she was not to know. No one was. He had been careful not a rumor of his suspicions ever reached a living soul.

"My ride has been pleasant," he said. *Christ, this small talk would be the death of him.* "I met Miss Merriweather earlier by the lake, and managed to escape—I mean…"

His voice trailed away, unable to continue due to the merriment he saw dancing in Anne's eyes. *She never misses a thing, that woman.* Whether it was her governess training or just something innate in her character, he would certainly have to be careful.

"Escaped?" Anne arched an eyebrow, straightening up now Frances had a hold of her impulses. "I would not have thought an earl would retreat from such a conversation."

"Then you have not met Miss Merriweather," said Timothy, tongue unguarded. "She is desperate to be the second Countess of Clarcton, and no matter what I say, she will not believe my wife is alive and well."

"And is she?"

"My wife is no concern of yours, and you would do well to remember that, in just a few short weeks, you will *be* her," Timothy said as coldly as he could as heat seared his veins. *In another light, that sentence could be seen very differently.*

Anne did not appear unsettled. "She is a bold one, then, to be actively seeking your hand when she knows it to be taken."

Timothy snorted, making Frances giggle. "She is not the only one! I am tired and beleaguered with women attempting to discover whether I have secretly divorced my wife, always assuming I am the market once again."

"And that is where I come in, I suppose?"

He held her gaze for longer than was strictly necessary. "Yes, Anne. I look forward to the Christmas ball, where you can prove to them I am unavailable."

She did not look away from his stare. "Yes. Unavailable."

The simple word only increased the fire in his chest, and Timothy's fingers itched to dismount and move toward her. But he could not be so foolish.

"Good day, Anne," he said, and without waiting for a reply, nudged Admiral toward the stables.

It took ten minutes of hard riding, which, thankfully, took his mind off the delectable governess he had just left behind, until

Timothy reached the stables. After dismounting and handing the reins over to a stable hand, he entered the side door of the castle. Mrs. Seton would surely skin him alive if he came through the Great Hall in his muddy riding boots.

It was therefore when he was coming down the main staircase after changing that he almost ran into Anne.

"Anne, where are you—where is Frances?"

His mind moved to her immediately, the surge of panic rising in his chest threatening to overwhelm his tongue. Anne had only been a part of his household four weeks, and yet he was accustomed to seeing the pair of them together.

"She is asleep," said Anne quietly. "She had a large breakfast and was so tired, I did not think it important to make her eat lunch before she rested."

Timothy felt the hackles on his neck flatten. "Of course. Her nap."

"Though if you ask me, Frances is almost of the age to outgrow naps and start in the schoolroom," said Anne. "At some point, we should discuss—"

"Anne, what are you doing at this moment?" Timothy had not intended to interrupt, but the thought had occurred so quickly, the words poured out.

The governess blinked. "Why, standing halfway up a staircase and conversing with you, Clarcton."

Timothy almost swore out of frustration but then saw the twinkle in her eye. "You are jesting with me."

She laughed. "I am. Apologies, my lord, 'tis my nature. What did you need from me?"

More than you would ever be willing to give. This was not the time to ostracize the woman vital in his plan to herd off expectant mamas. He craved time with her, each hour of separation only heightening his desire for her.

For her company, that was.

"If you have time, I would be grateful of your company," he said, attempting that suave turn of phrase he had heard Rochdale use a thousand times before.

Apparently, he had not used it as cleverly.

"Time?" said Anne hesitantly. "Now?"

It would have been easy to be offended, but thankfully Timothy's brain caught up with his senses. As governess to a young child, Anne could not have much time to herself. It appeared she would rather spend it alone.

"I quite understand," he said, inclining his head and continuing down the stairs.

"You...you would not order me to come with you?"

Timothy turned to see her rather bemused expression. "You are a governess of discretion indeed, Anne. You had no wish to sit and hear me talk on, and yet you said nothing."

There was a lilting playfulness in his tone, and his stomach lurched as she smiled.

"And because of that, I would gladly spend some time with you, my lor—Clarcton."

The drawing room at the front of the house received the most sunlight during the day, and it was there he went with her by his side.

"I must say," he said, opening the door, "I am impressed with your care of Frances."

"Knowing you, that is a compliment," said Anne with a smile, sitting by the window.

Timothy sat opposite her. Was he truly such a hard taskmaster that any praise from him was considered unusual?

There was such a mischievous look on her face that Timothy was overcome with the desire to lean forward and do something that would truly surprise her. Like kiss her. Like pull her into his arms and show her just what, as her husband, he would do if—

"I am sure there are many things still to discuss before the ball."

"Wh-What?" Timothy leaned back hastily.

"Before the ball. We have discussed the guests, but I am sure there is more you would wish to review before you consider me ready to…to be your wife."

It was the way she said it, suddenly self-conscious. It made Timothy feel…*well*. Not what one should feel about one's staff.

"Yes," he said, determined to bring the conversation back onto an even footing. "Yes, I have a list of things we need to complete before the ball."

"Well, we only have a few weeks," said Anne, tucking one foot behind the other in a most distracting manner. "What did you have in mind?"

Many of the things currently on Timothy's mind did not bear speaking of. "Just three things, I think. Dining, music, and dancing."

She laughed, and Timothy's brow furrowed. He had not intended to be amusing.

"My dear Clarcton—"

"Timothy." He did not know what made him say it. All he knew was that to be on first name terms with this woman would be an honor indeed—an honor he coveted.

The air seemed to electrify, a sudden tension within the atmosphere. Anne was looking at him carefully, as though attempting to understand a foreign language.

"Timothy?" she said softly.

He nodded. "Yes. It is my name, after all."

She opened her mouth to argue, then obviously thought better of it. "Timothy…I believe you are overzealous. I am not some village fool who needs to be taught what a fork is."

Hearing his name on her lips…it was better than cigars, better than the fieriest whisky. "Ah, but when you dine at the ball, you'll need six forks. Do you know what they all do?"

Ah, the confidence was gone now. "But it's a ball, cannot we just focus on dancing? I have my duties with Frances to consider, I cannot just—"

"A few hours a day," Timothy found himself saying. "That is all I need to bring you up to the standard of a countess. You'll have at least one hour when the girl naps."

An hour a day with Miss Anne Gilbert. What was he getting himself into?

"You did promise to help me, Anne."

"I know," she said. "But I can always take that back if I choose."

It was a heart-stopping moment. The invitations had gone out, and Mrs. Seton had rallied the staff. The world expected a Countess of Clarcton, and that is precisely what they would get.

But Anne was right. He could not force her.

"You have that right, I suppose. I will not oblige you," he said. "I know you to be a governess of discretion. I know you would not tell anyone of our...of my plan."

"Of course not!" Her words echoed around the room. Her voice dropped. "I would never do that."

Timothy did not think. Leaning forward, he took her hand in his. "Thank you. I am in your debt."

The contact between them was unlike anything he had experienced. It connected them deeper than mere touch; something from the very roots of who they were bonded in a tantalizing way that made Timothy's very skin tingle.

"Why is it I find I cannot refuse you?" Anne whispered.

Timothy swallowed. It was on the tip of his tongue to say he wished that was true, but this was dangerous ground. Much as it would hurt him, he needed to break the connection.

Releasing her hand and leaning back, he cleared his throat. "We are agreed then."

"I suppose we are," she said softly. "Where do we start?"

Timothy attempted to think. "I cannot ask Cook to create the complexity of dishes required tonight. Let us do dinner in a few days, dancing tomorrow, and the piano now. Conversation we can practice continually."

He glanced at the pianoforte. It had been her pride and joy, Louise. She had loved it. Far more than she had loved him.

"Ah, well, that should be easy," said Anne with a smile, rising and walking over to sit at the instrument. "I was taught the pianoforte and practiced at my aunt's house after my father's passing. I just hope I am not too rusty."

She spread out her fingers over the keys, took a deep breath, and started to play.

Every muscle in Timothy's body froze. It was the same, the very piece Louise would always play when looking to impress.

It was too much of a coincidence. Was this a trick? Did she know Louise somehow? If it wasn't for the different hair color, he would assume they were the same person. Now this?

A stumble, a jarring discord, and Anne placed her hands back in her lap and laughed.

"I never was very good," she said lightly, "but as my mother says, just keep going."

Timothy gripped the arms of his chair. *Just keep going.* Were those not the very words that Louise would always say to him?

"Just keep going. That's what I always say," she had said with a bitter laugh. *"Even if I am trapped with you here, Timothy. Just keep going."*

"Let me try again," said Anne, and she began the piece a few bars before her mistake.

Though his heart was pounding painfully, Timothy started unclenching his fingers.

No. Despite the similarities, despite coincidences that twisted his stomach, that woman was not Louise nor like her. Not after making a mistake and continuing without concern.

Louise had flown into a temper every time it was revealed she was not perfect.

"You know, you are not listening," said Anne, finishing the piece with a flourish. "I can tell, even if I cannot see you."

Timothy smiled weakly. "I do apologize. I was thinking of...here, there is sheet music you can practice from."

He stepped across the room quickly and was careful to ensure his fingers did not brush against hers as he handed over the music. She was not Louise, and for that, he was glad, but he could not consider her a replacement, either.

Anne Gilbert would be his wife in the eyes of the world, but he needed to keep his distance. Before he did something he would regret.

CHAPTER NINE

November 24, 1812

W HEN ANNE SAW the resplendent bed hangings above her, a smile drifted across her sleepy face.

It was starting to become a regular occurrence. She had not been unhappy exactly with the Earl of Allun. She had felt almost welcome at times, a part of the family. She was treated with respect and kindness, more than most servants could boast, and she had the distinction of three pupils who actually wished to learn.

But she had not been *happy*. Happiness had been discovered here, in Clarcton Castle.

Contentedness was not a guarantee in the governess trade, she thought ruefully, as she stretched her legs in the warm linen bedsheets. One could end up in any house, with any sort of master and mistress—and the children!

Some of the horror stories she had heard from other governesses in the Bureau...she had been fortunate indeed with her charges.

Frances was a dear, and her father...

Anne pulled the bedclothes tight around her. Timothy Lexington, Earl of Clarcton. He was having more of an impact than she should permit. It was most scandalous to think of him—it was rather wicked for a lady to think of any man that way—yet she could not help it.

"I must say, I am impressed with your care of Frances."

There was no higher compliment.

It had felt good to have keys of a pianoforte under her fingertips once again, but that sensation had been incomparable to having him close to her, watching her play.

It was a wonder she only made small mistakes. With his gaze on her, her body tingling with the anticipation of him coming closer to turn the page—it had almost been too much.

"You are fooling yourself, Anne Gilbert," she whispered. "Making yourself a fool."

And yet it had been he who had suggested the wild scheme that was now overtaking many of her waking thoughts and almost all her sleeping ones.

For a day, for one evening only, she would be a countess. His countess.

This was madness. Miss Clarke must certainly never hear of it, or she would be dismissed not just from this position but from the Bureau—and rightly so.

It was wrong. She could feel it in her bones, knew waltzing around pretending to be a countess was wrong. There was no law against it, but there did not have to be.

She knew it as deeply as she knew murder was a crime.

Yet that wrongness had not yet made its way to her heart. When she was preparing for such a ruse, no hint of concern touched her conscience. It felt right, being with him, talking with him.

When he had pulled a chair to the pianoforte, sitting beside her to turn the pages, leaning forward, so his breath warmed her skin...

Anne swallowed. She was playing a dangerous game here, and it had nothing—or at least, very little—to do with the façade they were creating.

No, it was him. *Timothy*. When he was close, every part of her tingled, and she wanted to—*well*. She was no fool. She knew the ways of love, but as she considered matrimony to be unlikely in her future, she had not given it much thought.

Soon the world would look at her and see a married woman. Married to the earl.

"If this plan is nothing to do with your wife and entirely focused around…around seducing me, then you are entirely mistaken about my character."

Anne bit her lip. In a strange way, her thoughts and feelings were altering since she had spoken those words. A small but growing part of her wondered whether making the bargain so complete would be the end of the world.

Her cheeks streaked scarlet, even alone, with the thoughts unspoken.

It was a brazen thing to think! To lose her innocence, to give herself up to a man who was not only her master but was married?

No, it could not be done. It would not be done.

She was hereto care for his daughter and provide a…a favor for one evening. She would pretend to be his wife to keep away potential mamas who were desperate to marry off their daughters, and that would be the end of it.

Anne sat up, pulling one of the spare pillows behind her, so she was propped up in bed. The morning was still early, the sun not quite yet risen, and the room was dark. Nonetheless, she could still make out the beautiful furniture and a glimpse of the painted ceiling.

Such luxury as this was almost worthy of a countess, and yet she was the one enjoying it. Where was the real Countess of Clarcton?

Anne had not noticed any portrait in the castle which could be Timothy's wife, but surely if the mistress of this place returned—worse, if she appeared on the night of the ball—and found an imposter in her place, what on earth would she think?

Why did she stay away? A disagreement between herself and her husband Anne could understand, at least in theory, but to abandon her child for this long? Two years?

Someone knew the truth, Anne thought darkly. Someone in this house knew where the countess was and why she did not return—or why she could not.

It was a highly suspicious affair, and if it had been anyone else, she would immediately suspect the husband. That was what happened, wasn't it? Strange affairs between a married couple, the wife disappearing…it could only be the husband.

Yet, there was no sense of danger here. Anne considered carefully and found that in her entire time at Clarcton Castle, she had felt in no peril.

All of the servants had been welcoming, to greater or lesser degrees. Dewey was polite, the maids were respectful, and Holt was perhaps a little too eager to ingratiate himself. Mrs. Seton was the only one who had kept her distance, but she was hardly threatening.

Of course, that left…

Anne sighed. "Timothy."

She could no sooner imagine Timothy harming his wife than him taking flight to the moon, but there was no one else. It was his idea to dress her up and parade her around as his countess, he who seemed to know where his wife was and why she was not here.

Perhaps he just did not like her. It was perfectly possible, Anne supposed, they had merely agreed to live apart. If the countess wished for divorce, would the earl give it to her?

Her scattered thoughts were interrupted by a clanging sound and her bedchamber door flying open.

"Wh-What—Mrs. Seton!" Anne had pulled the bedcovers up protectively, as though they would shield her from an intruder, but she had not expected to see the housekeeper with a tray in her hands and a glare on her face.

"Miss Gilbert," said Mrs. Seton bad-tempered as she shut the door with her foot.

Anne gaped, utterly astonished. "May I ask what...is that a breakfast tray?"

The housekeeper frowned. "What does it look like?"

It certainly did look like a breakfast tray—or at least, the trays which Anne had seen taken up from the kitchens to the Countess of Allun. A teapot in the same pattern as the teacup and saucer beside it, milk jug, sugar cubes, slices of toast, a pad of butter, some sort of jam...

"Well," said Anne uncomfortably, conscious she was in her night things. "Yes, it does look like a breakfast tray. What an honor, I...thank you, Mrs. Seton."

It was such a strange thing for the housekeeper to do, Anne could not help but stare.

"Hmmph," said Mrs. Seton, striding over and dropping the tray none too carefully beside the governess. "I wouldn't have done it if I hadn't been ordered to, you can be sure of that."

That could not be more apparent. "Why do you dislike me, Mrs. Seton?"

The housekeeper blinked. Her eyes narrowed as she beheld the governess. "'Tis not about like or dislike," she said eventually.

Anne sat up, careful not to knock over the teapot. "It isn't?"

Mrs. Seton cleared her throat. "No, 'tis...'tis more about you taking her place."

"Her—oh, you mean the mistress? The countess?" Anne could not help her curiosity. It appeared Mrs. Seton was a loyalist to the woman who had not been seen for over two years.

What was it about this woman who had such a hold on a curmudgeonly servant like Mrs. Seton? Anne would have assumed it would take a lot to earn the housekeeper's loyalty, and yet the gardener she had spoken to was dismissive when speaking about his mistress.

"What is she like, Mrs. Seton?" asked Anne curiously. "I have not heard anyone speak of her, and I would like to know more about—"

"So you can ape her at this coming ball?" snapped the housekeeper.

Anne hesitated. "No, actually. I am genuinely interested. She is Frances's mother, after all, and Timothy's—and his lordship's wife." *Blast, she would have to keep a more careful eye on her tongue.* "And of course you knew her, and so I wondered—"

"It's not to be talked about," said Mrs. Seton stiffly.

If she had thought this would lessen Anne's interest, she was much mistaken. *Not to be talked about? What wasn't? What had happened here?*

"I understand you are loyal," Anne said carefully, watching the older woman. "I have no wish to pry, I simply wondered—"

"No, you cannot convince me to speak of her," said the housekeeper. "Master could not stop me if I wanted to, o'course, but I don't want to. Not to you. Not to anyone."

Anne saw to her surprise that the woman looked genuinely distressed, and immediately dismissed any thought of asking again. *Something had happened, something awful. Something to do with the countess who had been—what? Hurt? Abducted? Forced out of the earl's home?*

The Countess of Clarcton was an absolute mystery; she had no idea what she looked like, what her character was, her likes and dislikes. Whenever she was spoken of, it was in hushed tones, restrained pain, or a tone of such dismissal it was as though she had never existed.

But she must have done, Anne reasoned. *Where else had Frances come from?*

"I do apologize, Mrs. Seton," she said awkwardly. "I...I had no wish to distress you. I will not ask you anymore, and thank you for bringing up my breakfast."

Mrs. Seton sniffed. "As I said, I only did it because I was ordered to. When you're ready, the master says bring Lady Frances down to the ballroom, quick as you like."

The door had slammed behind the housekeeper before Anne

could say another word, which was probably for the best. Not only was the woman evidently unwilling to spend any time longer than necessary with her, but her tea was getting cold.

It took five minutes to eat the hot buttered toast and gulp down her tea. The sooner she was ready, the sooner she could descend to the ballroom, another unexplored room, and...

And dance with Timothy.

A shiver ran down her spine at the thought. Dancing was something she indulged in on rare occasions, but it was not that which made her heart flutter. It was dancing with him. *Timothy.* Their hands would touch, and his arm would be around her side, and—

Anne caught herself just in time. This was not the time to lose her head and forget that she was doing this because she had a bargain with the man.

One night to be a countess, and then she would return to her normal life—a life of hard work and taking care of other people's children.

It was the jolt to reality she needed. Pulling off her night-clothes and getting dressed hurriedly in the cold, Anne took a quick glance in her looking glass as she pinned up her hair.

All she had to do was remember her place. She was a servant. A governess, yes, which meant she had far more education than most servants—but she was a servant, nonetheless. It would not do to forget that.

When she entered the nursery, a room quickly being out-grown by its occupant, Anne smiled at the child playing with her dolls in one corner.

She was such a pretty child, blonde hair, blue eyes. She was good-natured, everything one would want in a child. Why did Timothy find it impossible to spend time with her?

"Good morning, Frances," she said aloud.

Frances dropped the doll in her hand unceremoniously and beamed. "Good morning."

"I know you are playing with Maryanne," said Anne, self-conscious at the name Frances had given her latest toy. "But your father has asked for us, and we should not delay."

Frances stood obediently, eyes shining. "Papa wants to see me?"

Anne's heart twisted. *Why was it this child should be so surprised to hear her own father wished to see her?*

"Yes, he would like to see you," Anne said decisively. "He wants to see both of us in the ballroom!"

"B-But I'm not allowed in there," stammered Frances as they walked out of the nursery and into the corridor hand in hand. "Miss Anne, I'm not allowed."

"You are if you have been invited," said Anne kindly, nodding at a maid who paused in the corridor and curtseyed as the daughter of the house passed. "And your father has invited us, so it is all right—but yes, if you are told not to go somewhere, you must always obey that."

Frances nodded solemnly, and Anne hid a smile. Everything was so much simpler when four years old. Sometimes she wished to return to that stage of innocence again.

Like in situations like this. Anne tried not to look too irritated as Holt appeared before her, beaming as though they had made this assignation purposefully.

"Ah, Miss Anne," he said cheerfully, stepping to the side of the corridor. "How lovely to see you again—I was going to ask you, when you next have a day—"

"Apologies, Holt, the master has asked for us," said Anne breezily, not pausing.

She did not look back either, though she could feel his gaze on the back of her neck. Dear Lord, she would have to be firm with the man; this simply could not continue. She dreaded going to the servants' hall now, for he seemed always to be there, waiting.

Did the man have no work to do?

"I think that man likes you," said Frances solemnly. "He wants to be your friend."

Anne hid a smile. "He was very polite, wasn't he? It is always good to be polite, Frances. Especially to servants and those who are of a lower rank than you."

The child nodded thoughtfully, though Anne thought she had gone a little overboard. The child was young, and she may not entirely understand the difference of rank which she would inhabit for all her life.

Still, no better time than the present to start learning. She would have servants tending to her every need for most of her life, if Timothy had his way with her marriage. She needed to begin lessons. If she could notice Holt's interest in her, it was time for formal education.

"I do not have a mother, you know."

Anne stopped. The corridor was empty save for themselves, and Frances looked up in wide-eyed innocence.

"Yes, you do," said Anne, out of her depth. "It is just that she is not here."

"Why?" asked Frances.

Anne was at a total loss. No one had thought to inform her about the real reason the countess was not at her husband's side, and this made things rather complicated.

She would not lie. The last thing a child like Frances needed was to believe a falsehood about such an important thing.

"I..." said Anne helplessly. "You will have to ask your father that question."

Well, he clearly knew, she thought. Perhaps an innocent question from his daughter would be the push he needed to actually tell someone.

Frances seemed to be thinking carefully, then said, "So...can I call you Mama?"

Anne swallowed. It was such a lovely thing to say, such an innocent thought—and in a small way, she wished it was possible. It would give Frances some sort of grounding, a woman in her life that she could turn to, no matter what.

"Only if you are very good."

Anne whirled around. There stood Timothy, a teasing smile on his lips and arms crossed.

"And I thought I told you to bring my daughter to the ballroom," he said mildly. "Though I suppose we could attempt to dance in the corridor, 'tis certainly not unheard of."

Anne understood every word, but she was unable to respond. Not now her heart had leapt, her stomach twisted, and her very soul realized that the man before her was...

The man she loved.

It was a disaster. Pulse pounding in her ears, Anne knew it was impossible. She should not consider her master like that, even though her body shivered when but feet from him.

How had this happened?

Perhaps it was inevitable. Perhaps from the moment he had asked her to be his countess for a day, she had started to see herself by his side, loyal, trusted...beloved.

She wanted to be his. He was married. Though the countess was not before her, that did not prevent her existence.

"Papa!" Frances had not noticed her governess had frozen in shock at the emotions which had flooded through her and rushed to her father.

"Frances Lexington, I do declare you are almost too grown up to be picked up like this!" he said cheerfully, pulling her into his arms. "You will be able to pick me up soon!"

Frances chortled at her father's foolishness. "No, I'm not! You will always be able to pick me up, Papa, won't you?"

"Of course," he said genially, turning and walking down the corridor to the ballroom.

Anne followed, and her heart jolted as he turned to smile briefly at her.

Oh, goodness. The sooner this ball came and went, the better. This intrigue was too much, now she knew Timothy—*the earl, she should at least try to remember how far above her he was*—had entirely stolen her heart.

As they walked to the ballroom, Anne found her gaze drawn

to the portraits on the walls.

"Here we are," said Timothy impressively, opening the double doors.

Anne gasped. It was like walking into a palace. She had no idea there was such a room in the castle, although by now she shouldn't be so surprised.

Glass and gold were everywhere. All along the walls were looking glasses, reflecting back an infinite number of musicians. Candelabras and chandeliers festooned the place—it would surely be a haze of light when they were all lit. The floor was polished brightly, and the place echoed as they stepped across it.

"Right chit, I'm putting you down."

Frances sighed heavily at losing the connection with her father, but her interest was immediately caught by the gaggle of people within the ballroom. "Who are they?"

"They," said Timothy catching Anne's eye, "are the musicians. I thought I would bring them over for practice."

Anne nodded. It was clear what he intended then: music, dancing. She could endure that without falling even more in love with him, she was sure. Almost certain.

"Look, Frances, let us go and see the different instruments," said Anne, determined to make this at least partially educational. "Look, two violins, can you see the strings?"

But they had only stepped a few feet from the earl before his voice rang out.

"I didn't actually do this for a lesson for Frances."

Anne smiled, despite herself. "Useful though, don't you think?"

Why was it her heart skipped a beat every time she made him smile?

"Frances, sit by the musicians and be quiet," he said. "Anne, come here."

It took all Anne's self-restraint not to walk into his arms as she approached. Instead, she managed to stop a few feet away.

"You can dance, I take it?"

Anne hesitated. This, like the pianoforte, was a proficiency one could not lie about. "Yes, but mostly country dancing, which is what I enjoyed when I was young. Some of the more formal dances are beyond me, though I have seen them, of course."

There was no point pretending she had greater skill; he would soon find out.

Timothy nodded. "Well, they aren't that difficult. Play…play *La Boulangere*."

One of the musicians nodded and turned to his fellows. Within seconds, music was echoing around the ballroom, and Anne found her nerves had returned.

"Now, watch me," said Timothy, as though she could do anything else.

Anne watched. He was right, the steps were simple and repeated in a pattern. If only the person giving her the lesson was not so handsome. The earl was wearing a shirt and waistcoat only, and Anne found herself longing to take his hand and—

"Understand?"

Anne jolted from her reverie. "What? Oh, yes. Yes, I follow."

"I want to try!" Frances's voice had just a little petulance thrown in.

"Please, Frances, just sit there," said Anne hurriedly. "I will come over and—"

"Come on then, you rascal, come here," Timothy laughed.

Anne stared as the child rose to her feet and scampered over to her father.

"Now, put your feet on mine—no, the other way around," said Timothy. "Now, here we go!"

Holding her hands carefully, Timothy repeated the steps of the dance he had been showing Anne but with Frances standing on his feet.

"Faster, faster!" she giggled, her laughter becoming more high-pitched as Timothy increased the pace while making wild faces.

If only this was their everyday life, Anne thought. There was so much potential for joy here, so much potential wasted.

"Now, we have to stop," said Timothy eventually, breathing heavily. "No, no complaints chit, your Miss Anne and I have to practice."

Frances appeared too pleased with her dancing to argue, and as she retreated to her seat by the musicians, Timothy extended a hand to Anne.

"Ready?"

Anne had never felt less ready, but it would be churlish to say so. She stepped forward and curtseyed.

They began to dance. Anne had studied well and managed to keep up, though none too elegantly. The first time their hands met, heat seared through her fingertips.

Did he feel it, too? There was such a look of gravity on his face, Anne found she could not tell. Did his heart leap as hers did when she turned and found him there, ready and waiting? When his arm came around her, and she felt his strength, the certainty of his body, did he feel her softness, her warmth?

Or was this all in her own mind? Anne could barely tell, but thankfully thoughts became less hurried as the dance quickened, and all she could do was feel the rhythm of the movement, feel the tug of his presence as they grew closer, and—

Her foot stumbled, and Timothy paused, which caused the musicians to stop.

"I...I will never learn this," she said self-consciously.

Timothy did not seem concerned. "You will have to practice. Besides, we only have dining left to cover in your education, other than formal conversation."

Anne tried to smile. "You are not worried I will be discovered?"

His eyes searched hers before he replied, "No. No, I trust you, Anne."

Hearing her name on his lips made her all the more desperate to—to what, she was not sure. But she wanted more than this, whatever this was.

"One more time," he said bracingly. "From the top."

Anne really did try to concentrate, but her emotions swept her away far quicker than her mind could concentrate. She found her hands entwined with Timothy's, and this time they both slowed until they stood there, unmoving, hands clasped together and eyes locked.

There was some strange sort of magnetism occurring, something Anne did not understand. All she knew was that she was growing closer to Timothy, her gaze on his lips.

A kiss. *What harm could it do?*

"Timothy," she breathed.

It was a mistake. He dropped her hands as though they had burned him.

"Yes, well, that's probably enough dance practice for one day," he said, speaking to the musicians. "Right, Frances, let's away to your drawing room. Miss Anne needs to practice her guestlist."

Anne swallowed. He must have seen it, too, the desire in her eyes—and he had not wanted it.

And that was quite right, of course. Earls did not go around kissing governesses.

CHAPTER TEN

November 25, 1812

"Hmm." Timothy was careful to ensure his careful consideration was audible. That was the best way to ensure the next time he inspected something, the thing was perfect.

But his servants knew him well. There was no concern on the footman's face as the earl leaned closer to the table, looking to see if a single fork was out of line.

"Interesting," he said quietly, stepping around the table. "Very interesting."

There it was—a flicker of uncertainty.

"If there was one thing about this table you would change, man," he said abruptly, "what would it be?"

The dining table was laid as though for a banquet, just as Timothy had asked. With the ball mere days away, it was imperative every single member of staff knew what was expected. Though the Earl of Clarcton did not entertain much, when he did, he expected the place to be absolutely spotless.

The footman looked along the table with a nervous air. "Anything, my lord?"

Timothy smiled. "One thing."

All his servants had to meet his high expectations, scullery maid to head gardener, though it was not the fear of dismissal that he held above them, like a wild despot.

The idea a man could simply release a servant from their service was not the Clarcton way. But there was more than one way to reward someone.

"I think I would place the flowers on the table," said the footman hesitantly. "The cutlery, the crockery, the place settings...all are perfect. But there is no decoration. I assumed you would not wish to waste such decorations, but now…"

Timothy decided to put the poor man out of his misery. "Exactly right. Can't be having all those flowers about the place days before our guests are here, yet they are the one thing the table is without. Well done."

And there it was, that swell of pride.

He was not a man who praised easily nor quickly. It took great care by a person to reach a standard that the Earl of Clarcton would praise.

Timothy smiled wryly. He had learned that from his father, and undoubtedly the man had learned the habit from his own father.

It was a Clarcton thing. It was a strange feeling, knowing one could inspire such fear and yet such gratitude. Perhaps that was why the first Earl of Clarcton took up the tradition to give anyone who joined the household a place for life.

The place itself could change. As far as he could remember, Mrs. Seton had begun her service as a kitchen maid.

But the opportunity to rise and grow, and earn good wages in safe lodgings was there to anyone fortunate enough to join the Clarcton household.

A job for life. Timothy had always smiled at that when lectured by his father.

"We have a job for life, don't we, my boy?" he had always said. *"Earl of Clarcton, that is not a role that one can simply lay aside. So*

why not for our servants, eh?"

And the old boy had been right. Timothy had never seen greater loyalty or better work than from servants who knew they were safe.

On the rare occasions when he had paid house visits, he had seen just what service one received from underpaid and barely appreciated servants, and it had made him all the more thankful the Clarcton house was run differently.

"You are confident in your cutlery, then?" he said aloud, conscious that he had been silent too long.

The footman nodded. "Yes, my lord."

"Hmm."

Timothy walked down the table and picked up a spoon at random, holding it up to his eyes and examining it.

A nervous cough behind him made the earl smile. It was perfect, just as the footman, whatever his name, had said. He had been right to have such confidence.

"It is all perfect, and you are to be congratulated," he said, placing the spoon in precisely the same spot he had removed it from.

The footman's shoulders sagged with relief. "Thank you, my lord."

"Now, be off with you," said Timothy easily. "I am sure there is something Cook has taken her eye off for more than two minutes that you can snap up. Go on."

The footman bowed and hastily retreated, leaving the earl alone in the dining room.

Timothy's eyes scanned the table once again. Yes, this was almost exactly how it would look when the Christmas ball came around, save for the flowers. He would have to tell Mrs. Seton—it was surely impossible she had forgotten such a detail, but it was a little while since the house of Clarcton had hosted anything like this. The first time in years it would be presided over by not just himself but also a woman. His countess. For want of a better term.

The silver gleamed. It was all far more ostentatious than he would ever have, but he had his title to think of. An earl simply could not host an occasion like this without some sort of ridiculous show of wealth and power.

"Ah, my lord."

Timothy turned. He had not heard Dewey come in, but then that was the sign of an excellent servant, wasn't it? You barely saw them.

"You have everything you need, my lord?" asked the butler.

Timothy nodded. "Yes, I think so. Please congratulate…I cannot remember his name for the life of me, you know who I mean."

"Holt, my lord," said Dewey smoothly. "Do not concern yourself. There are so many I do not often concern myself with learning their names until they become first footmen."

Timothy hid a smile. He was sure there had been a time, once, when Dewey himself had been a mere footman, but he was not foolish enough to remark on it.

"I must say, it is rather unusual for us to have a rehearsal of this magnitude," said Dewey with some hesitancy. "I assume there is a purpose to it?"

There were few people Timothy would permit to speak to him in such a way, but thankfully for the butler, he was one of them.

"It is essential Anne—Miss Gilbert is fully trained on the correct etiquette for such a thing. The last thing we need is for someone to notice her using a salad fork during the fish course."

He had not considered his words inflammatory, but the servant looked uncomfortable.

"Yes," he said delicately, "but even so…I cannot help but feel we are going far beyond what is necessary. If you do not mind me saying so, my lord."

Beyond what was necessary? Well, he supposed he was, in a way. He cast his gaze along the table that could seat twenty. The last ball—the last one with Louise attending—they had only laid the table for three when he had perused it to ensure his standards were kept.

Twenty sets of knives, forks, and spoons glittered under the candlelight.

Perhaps it was a little much.

Timothy swallowed. *What had possessed him to do order a thing?* Was this a desperate attempt to…well, impress the governess?

He must not think of her as Anne. That was a habit he had slipped into, desiring to hear his own name on her lips, but he had to force himself away from that.

If he had needed a sign, he was considering Miss Gilbert with anything more than masterly reserve, then the dancing in the ballroom had been the perfect wake-up call.

He had been mere seconds away from kissing her. Timothy had wondered, late at night, tossing and turning in his bed attempting to find elusive sleep, whether he should have.

Perhaps one kiss with the delectable Miss Anne Gilbert would rid him of this desire.

It was crippling, this heat he felt whenever he was in her presence. It prevented him from thinking, removing conscious thought and leaving him with nothing but yearning.

"My lord?"

But she was just a governess. The thought had occurred to him several times, but each time it had been pushed away by the very presence of the woman.

Just a governess? No, she was far more than that. She was a lady, her father had been a gentleman. She was no typical servant, and her curiosity made her an interesting woman.

And that form; the way her lips pursed whenever she was thinking…

Dear God, it was enough to drive a man to distraction.

Timothy could no longer deny it, even if he was the only one who knew it. But he was finding himself daydreaming about the damned woman far more than he would like.

And yet she was the mirror image of Louise. Christ, it was all tangled in a most discomforting way. How was he ever to concentrate on the ruse if endlessly distracted by—

"My lord, can you hear me?"

Timothy jumped. The butler was waving his hands before his eyes, evidently concerned he had utterly lost all grip on his senses.

Hell, Anne. She was not even here, and still, she was having a damnable effect on him.

"Yes, yes, I was just thinking," he snapped. "Can't a man think for a minute? Must he always be speaking?"

It was a return to his typical gruffness, and it seemed that was what gave the butler the confidence to step back and nod.

Timothy slowly walked around the table, looking to all the world as though he was carefully examining the placement of the crockery.

Anne would be here any moment if she had taken his request to heart and bothered to dress for dinner. He would seat her…

No, not there. Timothy's jaw tightened. It could have been only yesterday when he had last seen Louise seated there, face laughing at his outrage at what she had just revealed.

"You really thought otherwise?" she had said, giggling. *"Goodness me, Clarcton, you really do have a way of deluding yourself. But you know what they say, just keep going!"*

A muscle spasmed by his temple.

No, while Anne and Louise may look similar, a trick of nature, there was nothing of the nature of one in the other. The pain of Louise's betrayal, so sharp though two years had elapsed, had not yet been eclipsed by the joy Anne had brought him.

But it was not far off.

"Excellent plates," he said aloud, conscious that the butler was still watching him. "Which service will we use on the night?"

"Oh, I thought the Clarcton star," said Dewey impressively. "Yes, I don't think we have used that service for a while, and it is most impressive, the light blue with the gold. I remember when we first used it, I thought…"

Timothy let the man carry on. His mind was still consumed

with the pain of her betrayal.

How would he ever forget it? He was not entirely sure he ever would. *Still, if he was ever to find the blaggard…*

"…so that would be my choice," finished the butler.

Timothy nodded. "We'll need footmen for Anne—for Miss Gilbert to practice."

Dewey nodded. "They do have other duties, my lord, but I can spare you a pair if that would be useful?"

"Perfect. Send them in."

It was only after the door had closed behind the butler that Timothy breathed out. He had to concentrate on what was important, the fact that in just a few days, a woman who had probably never seen this many forks was about to be presented to the world as his countess.

His wife.

Yet he was not entirely ignorant of the secret reason he had insisted on these countess classes, as Anne called them: all in the name of spending more time with the woman.

Timothy smiled. Yes, it was true; and the way she was with Frances made it worse. If she had taken a dislike to the child, he would have found it far easier to…

To what? He was not in love, he was no fool. So what was this? Pure desire?

"Ah, good evening, my lady." The voice came from outside the door, in the corridor. A footman.

"Pardon?" That was Anne's voice, then she realized her mistake. "Oh, yes. Thank you. Good evening."

Timothy shook his head. She was going to have to do much better than that if she was to convince the neighborhood that she really was his countess.

The dining room door opened, and the footman and Anne stepped into the room. But it was an Anne he had never seen before. One of the gowns Madame Griffon had already made arrived—Timothy had ended up ordering several—had changed her.

She looked…

Almost regal. Even her posture was different, wearing silk instead of muslin. There was something about her, a confidence he had never seen before. Perhaps it was just how she held herself. Whatever it was, it made her even more beautiful. Even more intoxicating.

Anne smiled, evidently pleased with his reaction. "Will I do, do you think?"

A strange strangling noise was heard in the room, and only after a moment did Timothy realize that it was himself. *Bloody hell, man, get a grip on yourself!*

Anne twirled, the pleats of the gown allowing it to blossom around her. Timothy could not take his eyes away—until he realized the footman, Holt, who had stepped into the room behind her was also goggling at her appreciatively.

Timothy straightened up. He was not going to make a fool of himself like a mere footman. He would control himself.

Clearing his throat with a pointed look, the footman caught his eye and immediately dropped his gaze to the floor, ears flaming red.

"Have…have I done anything wrong?" Anne had stopped twirling and was looking between the two men with a look of concern.

Heat flushed across his chest. "No, not at all. Come, sit here."

Anne obeyed, and the footman had the good sense to step forward and pull out the chair. Seating herself at the head of the table, she smiled as Timothy sat beside her.

He was close to her. *Very close.* Closer than he had expected, and now every inch of him was crying out to reach his hand out and—

"I had not expected the dining table to be so attired," Anne said with a smile. "Will it really be this impressive on the night itself?"

"More so," said Timothy, fighting the temptation over-whelming him. "There will be flowers upon it, of course, and candles. I wished to give the footmen a good practice."

Anne's eyes met his. "Yes, I see."

And she did, Timothy realized. She saw right through his lies to the truth. It was all for her, all to impress her, to beguile her.

He swallowed. Having a woman about the place who could so easily see right through him was disconcerting. It had been difficult enough with Louise, but she had a streak of cruelty within her, entirely missing from the woman before him.

The idea which had come to him in the carriage from London had certainly taken on a life of its own. Dinners, dancing, music… Was he making a mistake?

Wouldn't it have been easier to just lie at the ball and say that his countess was still away? She had been 'away,' that wonderful word which seemed to say much but revealed little, for years now. For all he knew, there may not have been any questions about her at all…

The last ball he had attended had been in London, and even there, the rumors had followed him. He had been introduced to woman after woman—all Galcrest's fault, of course—and he had barely had five minutes in the card room.

No, he would not suffer through that again. No more young ladies wondering whether he was secretly divorced, no more mamas attempting to beguile him with their daughters.

He would bring out his countess, and that would be an end to it.

"This should be a good learning experience for you," he said aloud into the silence.

Anne raised an eyebrow. "Oh, I don't know. You may be surprised."

Timothy smiled. "Few people believe they cannot navigate a fish knife, but I think you would find the complexities of fine dining are as numerous as they are opaque."

It required just a quick glance at the footman for the servant to tap gently on the door behind him, carefully concealed with the red velvet wallpaper on the walls. At once, the door opened, and the first course was brought out—a steaming pile of snails.

Timothy tried not to smile. He had instructed Cook to challenge the governess of the house, and it appeared she had taken the challenge rather to heart. Even he had not expected something as complex as...

"Now," he said, full of anticipation. "How would you go about..."

His jaw fell open as his voice trailed away. Without so much as a hesitation, Anne had reached out for the escargot fork, turned it the correct way in her hand, popped a snail out of its shell, and—

"Delicious," she said with a smile.

That smile became laughter as Timothy's mouth remained open.

"My dear Timothy," she said, causing a ripple of delight through his body. "I am a governess! I have been for years, to the sons and daughters of noblemen!"

"B-But..." he stammered, purposefully not looking at the footman who was, he was sure, laughing. "But you ate that like a Parisienne!"

Anne raised an eyebrow. *Ah, au Français? Mais oui, c'est possible.*

She cleverly released another snail from its shell and popped it into her mouth.

"You speak French as well as one of them!"

Anne shrugged, placing the escargot fork carefully onto her plate. "I lived in Paris for just under a year when Lady Maria was at finishing school. The entire family moved there, except for the winter Season. It was considered better for her, you see, to be close to her parents."

Timothy could not understand it. The woman ate in a more refined manner than half the duchesses he had ever encountered!

Was there anything Anne Gilbert could not do?

"You said you did not know how to eat at a fine dining table," he said, unable to keep the accusatory tone from his voice.

Anne met his gaze with one as steely as his own. "No, you assumed. You never actually asked."

Timothy thought back but found she was perfectly correct. He had assumed. He had thought a woman like her, no title, no family of note, would be overcome at such a table.

He laughed ruefully. "Anne Gilbert, you minx!"

Ye gods, he was in trouble now. Her fiery red hair shone in the candlelight, and there was a teasing smile on her lips, and Timothy wanted her. He wanted her badly.

Worse still, the physical desire was now starting to be matched by an equally strong desire for her company. *For her.*

No one surprised him like she did. No one had made him laugh like she did in a long time. In fact, he could not remember anyone making him laugh like that.

"I will have to learn not to underestimate you," he said sheepishly.

Anne nodded with a smile. "Yes, you will."

Her blue eyes met his, and Timothy's breath caught in his throat. She was beautiful, sensual, clever, witty. She was everything a countess should be. He had almost nothing to teach her, and the temptation to reach out and take her hand was growing.

It was only then he realized Holt was looking at Anne with quite the same adoration he assumed was on his own face.

Clearing his throat, Timothy placed his hands in his lap—out of harm's way. He would have to learn to control himself.

"Tell me," he said, nodding at the footman to bring through more courses. "Tell me about becoming a governess. Did you always wish to join the profession?"

Anne shook her head as she looked with interest at the tureen of soup and the basket of rolls that were brought through. "No, to tell the truth. I had not considered any profession while my father was alive. He had a number of investments that kept us to a lifestyle that was quite pleasant—though nothing like this, of course."

Timothy nodded. "But then you lost your father."

"We did," said Anne shortly. It was clear speaking of him was painful. "And that left me with little choice. He had no siblings living, and my brother took on the mantle of the family with disastrous consequences. *Never* give a fifteen-year-old boy access to the family wealth."

The last was said sourly, and Timothy shook his head. "Better men than he have been sorely tempted, believe me."

"Oh, I do not blame him—not really," said Anne, nodding her thanks to the footman as he helped her to soup.

"More, my lady?"

Timothy glared at the footman who colored.

"No, thank you, Holt."

The footman did not move over to Timothy to serve him. "Well, if you change your mind, I will only be—"

"Thank you, Holt," said Anne firmly.

Timothy tried not to smile. It was clear that while the footman's affections were engaged, hers certainly were not. *Why did that fill him with such pleasure?"*

"But it was hard, I admit," Anne continued. "My mother's sister lived in the town, but as a widow and with children of her own, she could do little to help. It became necessitous I go out into the world and earn my keep."

Timothy nodded, though much of what she had said was alien to him. Working for money; it was a bizarre concept he had never given much thought to. He had land, investments, tenants. Money went in, money went out. How much there was did not really matter.

All that mattered was that Clarcton continued.

"I know what you mean," he said. "I, too, work hard to ensure—"

But he did not continue. His words, if they had been spoken, would not have been audible over Anne's laughter.

"What is so funny?" Timothy said defensively.

Anne shook her head. "I do not mean to insult you, Timothy," and he saw the footman's eyes widen, "but...here. Give me your hands."

Unsure why she wished for them, and conscious he was about to do what he had been desperately attempting *not* to do since they had sat down, Timothy offered her his hands.

Anne examined them closely, then turned them over and did the same thing. Timothy swallowed. It was such an intimate act, her fingers brushing over his palms. Only when she had looked closely at both sides of them did she nod decisively.

"'Tis as I thought," she said with a smile. "You have never done a hard day's work in your life. Now, see here."

Releasing his hands, Anne showed him her own. Timothy saw callouses, pinprick scars, and what appeared to be a burn scar on the inside of one wrist.

"How on earth did you get those?" he asked. "Governessing is a dangerous business, from the look of it!"

They laughed together as Anne placed her hands back in her lap.

"Not quite," she said, eyes twinkling. "But I was not a governess at first. You can see the pinpricks from embroidery, and that's where I burnt myself on a tray of cakes when I was helping our local baker." She must have seen the surprise on his face. "Few families would take on a twelve-year-old governess, Timothy. No, I had to take what work I could get."

Pity rushed through him. It was only in moments like these that he realized how privileged he really was. He could not imagine working like that, let alone at such a tender age.

"But...but then you joined the Governess Bureau," he managed to say.

Anne nodded. Their food lay before them, entirely forgotten. "Yes, which was a stroke of luck. The Bureau is very highly regarded. One must be outstanding to join."

"A place such as that must have many rules."

Timothy had not intended his words to be inflammatory, but Anne's cheeks colored.

"Yes," she said, her gaze dropping to her lap. "And, of course,

I follow them all."

There was something so intriguing about her countenance that he could not help but ask. "All of them?"

Was it his imagination, or did she hesitate? "Yes. Well, there are only three which guide us entirely."

Timothy waited. "And they are?"

"Firstly, you must have an impeccable record."

He nodded. "Well, that makes sense. If one is to have the charge of the next generation of nobility, one can hardly be followed by scandal."

Anne smiled. "Not if one hopes to retain one's position for long. Second, you must bring a special skill to the table."

Timothy raised an eyebrow at that. "My word."

Was it the mere insinuation that made her color? "A talent. Languages, music, botany, that sort of thing. And thirdly, you…you must never fall in love."

Now his cheeks were coloring, too. Anne had lifted her gaze and was now looking half fearful, half…

Timothy could not tell. *Was she attempting to convey to him that her feelings, too, were deepening in a way she knew was against these rules?*

How could he halt the feelings soaring through him, unfettered by rules, restrictions, and restraint?

"We…" he swallowed. "We should continue through the courses. Your countess classes are not over yet."

"Why, do you not trust me with the fish knife?" Anne teased.

It was a meal, Timothy realized in hindsight, that could have lasted three hours, and he would not have found himself bored at any moment. Anne Gilbert, governess extraordinaire, laughed, jested, and talked with him as though they were…

As though they were equals. As though they dined together every evening, which was something Timothy was starting to consider.

Because that was what he wanted. To dine with her every evening before he took her to his bed.

Just how far could this charade go?

CHAPTER ELEVEN

November 26, 1812

"B-B-But I don't—I don't want to!"

Frances's sobs were heart-wrenching. If Anne had not heard the same old story before, from at least two other children, she would not have been able to remain firm.

As it was...

"You will enjoy it," she said calmly, buttoning the gown Frances was just as vigorously attempting to unbutton. "I promise you, Frances, you—"

Frances's voice trembled, tears flowing. "I don't want to, please don't make me!"

Anne's heart fluttered. It was never pleasant to see a child in tears, particularly one this young. Frances's cheeks were flushed, her nose red, and tears had poured from her red-rimmed eyes for at least twenty minutes.

Then the child dropped to the floor. "I won't go! I won't go!"

Her cries grew in volume, and it was all Anne could do to stay calm. She should have expected this. This was not a small change for Frances. This nursery, these habits, they had been her way for her entire life.

Frances was sobbing, a pathetic figure who would touch even the hardest of hearts.

Anne sat on the floor beside her charge. "Frances, come now. Come here."

The child went willingly into her arms, only too eager to be held and comforted. Anne's heart twisted. *The poor child*. She never had much in the way of love.

It was a lesson taught far too early for children in the nobility and one they were probably not conscious of being taught. *Don't get too attached to anyone.*

Servants came and went. Even friends of the family could change over time, new alliances, new dalliances, changes in fortune.

One learned not to get too attached. One could not miss something never valued.

Frances had already learned this. Anne sighed heavily. *She had to get this girl into the schoolroom.*

"You will enjoy it when you are there," she said softly, arms still around the snuffling child. "Everyone does. This is exciting, and it shows you are growing older."

It was the wrong thing to say. Tears appeared once more in Frances's eyes.

"But I do not want to do lessons and difficult things," she snuffled. "I want to stay here and play."

Anne allowed the child to pull herself free. There was no point in attempting to keep her there if she did not want to be.

"I will n-not go."

Anne considered her. She was not about to enter into a battle of wills with a four-year-old. Not when one of them was the daughter of an earl. There was no knowing where the balance of power was in that scenario, and she did not want to be the first to admit it.

Besides, this was to be expected. Of course, it was difficult for Frances to comprehend what her life would be like once she stepped, irrevocably, out of the nursery.

She had been treated as a baby for so long. Nothing had changed, it seemed, since her mother had left. The nurserymaid considered her an infant, unable to think or make choices.

Of course, the irony was that the first choice Frances seemed to be making was a refusal to grow up. What would Frances's mother do in this situation?

Anne pushed away the thought. She could not allow herself to think that way; she had done more than enough stepping into the countess's shoes since she had arrived here at Clarcton Castle. Frances was not her daughter, and she should not consider her in that way.

Not that it is stopping you treating her husband like your own, a cruel little voice whispered in her head.

Anne swallowed. Nothing about her encounters with the earl had felt wrong, not while they were happening. Oh, such joy as she had never known before, such intensity of feeling.

But now, in this moment, she had to think of Frances—a Frances lying in a ball on the floor, tears pouring down her cheeks.

There were few things governesses were not taught at the Bureau. Though there was rigorous training, discipline and comfort were two items not on the curriculum.

When she had asked why, she had received a rather stern look from Miss Clarke, who had considered if the question was worth responding to.

"Because," the proprietress had said eventually, *"every child is so different, Miss Gilbert. How do you expect me to instruct you on the potential future charges you will care for? Am I a fortune teller, Miss Gilbert?"*

The entire room had tittered, and Anne had vowed not to ask a single question again in Miss Clarke's training. A part of her regretted that cavalier attitude. Now she had a very real problem before her.

Miss Clarke had been right, of course. Every child was different. Still, any pointers on how to make a crying child stop sobbing would have been valuable.

Anne took a deep breath. All she had to do was stay calm. Frances was not crying because of the schoolroom; she was upset because of change. She was looking for reassurance, and that was something Anne could give her.

She could stay calm. Even if Frances could not.

Kneeling onto the floor to get closer to the sobbing girl, Anne said quietly, "Frances. What is it that so upsets you?"

Whether it was the calm voice, hearing her name, or being asked rather than commanded, Anne was not sure. Whatever it was, Frances sniffed.

"I-I am Papa's baby," she said, eyes wide as she looked at her governess. "When I go to the schoolroom, I won't be a baby anymore."

Her voice was so pitiful, her demeanor so devastated, Anne had to work hard to prevent a smile from creeping over her lips.

It was as simple as that. When had any adult last asked Frances what she wanted or how she was feeling? It was evidently a rare occurrence, with Frances grasping at it so. It was easy to see why the little girl had worked herself into such a state.

The thought of losing the affection of the one parent which remained to her...

Yes, Frances had a right to cry if that had really been the case.

Anne smiled gently. "Well, Frances, I understand. I want you to know that you will always be your father's baby."

Frances's lip trembled. "Really?"

"Really," Anne said softly. "Why, I am still my father's baby, and I am all grown up!"

The child looked up with curious eyes. "Are you?"

Anne nodded. It was not the time to mention her father had died when her youngest brother was not much older than Frances was now. That was a conversation for a different day, years in the future.

"Now, I have an idea," she said conspiratorially. "I know you don't want to do lessons, so I think we should go to the schoolroom," Frances's mouth opened, "and play games."

Frances's mouth closed. She examined her governess for a moment, then burst into tears. "That's just lessons! I am not stupid. I don't want to do lessons!"

Anne's shoulders drooped. *She had been so close, too.* She had at least made some progress. The next step would be to—

"Anne Gilbert, what are you doing to that child!"

Anne whirled around to see Mrs. Seton, arms crossed, scowling in the doorway.

"I am not doing anything," Anne began defensively as Frances's cries grew.

"You should have a greater handle on your charge," said the housekeeper sternly. "I heard the child all the way from the servants' hall, so you can be sure the master heard it, too!"

Anne strove to keep a straight face. "And yet I have received no complaint from him, so I will continue with—"

"Continue? Continue! You shall do no such thing. I have no wish for this ruckus to continue," snapped Mrs. Seton, glaring at the bedraggled child. "If you were any sort of governess, *Miss Anne*, you would not permit such behavior. You can swan about playing the countess all you like, but I advise you to pay a little more attention to your actual duties!"

Anne's mouth fell open. That such words were to be spoken to her, and within earshot of Frances, too!

The poor child may have the advantages a titled father could bring, but she had received nothing but inattention and negligence in her entire life. Frances did not need to be described as a bother to everyone else, not when she was the daughter of their master!

She could not respond immediately, however. Not if she was going to get her temper under control. Red hair or not, she *would* be mistress of herself. She would not give Mrs. Seton the tongue lashing she so desperately deserved.

"Frances and I are discussing her lessons," she said, voice stilted but gaze affixed firmly on the housekeeper. "I am sorry if our conversation disturbs you. I am sure a few closed doors will remedy the situation."

Frances had ceased her sobs and was looking nervously between the two adults.

"I am sorry," she mumbled.

The housekeeper was not, however, pacified. "*Discussing* with the child? Lord above, Miss Anne, but you are a strange sort of governess. Give the child a choice? It's not up to the child to decide!"

Anne was very close to counting silently to ten, which she had not been pushed to since the Earl of Allun had refused to pay her for several months. The earl, at the very least, had the excuse of ignorance in these matters.

"When I have any questions on how to care for a child, Mrs. Seton," said Anne stiffly, "I will come to you. In the meantime, I suggest you return to your tasks and leave me to mine."

It was a measure of how much respect Anne had evidently had from the rest of the household that Mrs. Seton hesitated. The governess, it seemed, was not someone she wished to make a true enemy of.

"When I was young," she snapped, "young ladies were seen and not heard!"

"And so it was when I was young, Mrs. Seton," said Anne stiffly. "But every child is different. We are getting there. Slowly."

The last word was spoken with a glance to Frances, brushing wetness from her face.

The housekeeper shook her head, arms still tightly crossed. "I don't know. Sometimes I look at that child and wonder whether she'll have the worst of her father and the worst of her moth—"

Anne's ears pricked up. This was no time to permit herself to be distracted, of course, but it was so rare that anyone in the Clarcton household mentioned the countess.

Stepping away from Frances and lowering her voice, she said, "Her mother. Tell me about her, Mrs. Seton. You never know, it may help me in my management of the child."

It was not a wheedling tone precisely, but there was more softness in her voice than Anne typically employed when speaking to the irate housekeeper.

To absolutely no surprise, the housekeeper did not relent. "Mind your own business and do your job. That's what you're here for, not to swan about in fancy silks, asking questions, poking your nose in where it's not—"

"And if I am to do the best job I can, the more I know of the mother, the better," said Anne doggedly, dropping her voice even further. *The last thing Frances needed was to hear this.* "The child needs all the support I can give her, Mrs. Seton. You would not begrudge the little information I require to perform my duties?"

Mrs. Seton's steely eyes met hers. Anne could almost see cogs whirring in her mind.

She spoke the truth. The temperament, the nature of the mother, was often a great indicator of the character of her child. With no information, how was Anne meant to guide the child?

"For example," Anne gently prodded, "the painting of the countess. Where is it? And why is there no sign of her anywhere in this house, no suggestion of a feminine touch, no items of hers in my lord's bedcham...in his rooms."

"It's...'tis not my place to say," the older woman muttered, gaze dropping to her arms.

Anne pushed home the small advantage she possessed. "Yet you do know, don't you, Mrs. Seton? You could point me in the right direction, help me to understand how—"

"No. You just keep that child quiet," said the housekeeper firmly, slamming the door.

Anne sighed, her head drooping. This day was not going her way, and if she was any judge of the matter, it would not be getting much better.

But she was a governess of the Bureau. She could not just give up, for that would be easy. No, she had to persevere. That was what Miss Clarke would do.

Anne said matter-of-factly, "Frances, I think you are right."

The girl scrambled to her feet. "I...I am?"

Anne nodded. "I think you may not be old enough for lessons. Lessons are for big girls, and if you are not ready, we should get you back into baby clothes, and you can stay here."

A war of emotions fought across the child's face, and Anne was careful to keep her own expression neutral. If there was one thing she remembered about being four, that she saw time and time again, it was that a contrary nature was at its peak.

A frown puckered Frances's forehead. "I...I think I am old enough."

Anne permitted herself a small smile. It was always the way with children around that age, and some people never grew out of it. Why, her cousin was one such person—never happier than when disagreeing with all around her.

As soon as one suggests the opposite of the intended outcome, they were quick to find themselves desiring the thing they had said no to in the first place.

"Excellent," she said briskly, not waiting for Frances to change her mind. "In that case, up we go. I assume you will wish to inspect the place before we begin?"

Frances was holding herself straighter but still reached for Anne's hand as she approached the door. "Yes, I will."

It was with a great sense of relief that Anne stepped into the schoolroom, laid out with two desks facing each other and a blackboard on the wall, and shut the door behind her.

Well, she had managed the most challenging part of her day, at least. Get Frances into the schoolroom. Anything else was merely a bonus, even further progress than expected.

"Right," she said briskly. "While you are inspecting the room, Frances, I thought we could sing a little song. A, B, C, D..."

It was a simple enough trick. Anne had found Miss Clarke, at the very least, a mistress of manipulation when it came to extracting insight into your future pupils.

"Always make it a game, a song—or a competition," Miss Clarke had said, just a hint of a smile playing about her lips. "Children love to

play games. They consider them the opposite of school and so will snap up any opportunity to escape what they perceive to be a lesson."

Anne lowered her voice as they continued through the alphabet and saw with pleasure that Frances knew the entire thing by heart.

"Well," Anne said as they reached the end of the song, and Frances reached her desk. "Does the room meet with your approval?"

"It's got a pretty view of the gardens," said Frances, shyly. There was something different, speaking to a governess in a schoolroom, Anne knew. It was so very definitely her domain, whereas in the nursery, Frances was the queen.

"It does indeed," she said with a smile. "Now, before we even think about doing lessons, I would like to play a game. Why don't you sit here?"

Frances obeyed eagerly, clambering onto the chair behind her desk and looking up with eager excitement.

Anne scattered a handful of coins, mainly pennies, with a few ha'pennies and sixpences mixed in, onto the desk.

"Here we go," she said. "The game is grouping the coins into tens the fastest! Ready?"

Frances nodded eagerly but took a little time to pick up the coins and examine them. Her face was so aglow with curiosity that Anne, for a moment, could not understand the pause, but then the realization hit her.

Of course. Frances was the daughter of an earl. When did she ever see money?

Anne almost laughed. No earl ever carried something as tradesman-like as coins, and his four-year-old daughter had likely as not never left this castle.

"See, these are worth one," she said, turning over one of the coins. "This is a tuppence, which is two. And this one is a sixpence, which is worth six pennies."

Frances did not take to the coin game as quickly as she had taken to the alphabet song. Anne was careful to watch her, brow furrowed and excited noises coming from the child as she started to gain a greater understanding of the coins.

Already Anne could see tiredness tugging at Frances's eyes. When was the last time the child had concentrated this long?

Time to slow down. Time enough to learn to walk before she could run.

"Now, there is one last song I'd like to sing before we return to the nursery," said Anne quietly, scooping all the coins off the desk and back into her purse. It would not do for someone on her salary to lose almost a pound in change.

"Just one?" Frances looked more disappointed than Anne had expected.

Anne nodded. "And it might be one you know. Thirty days hath September..."

It was a song her mother had taught her. As Anne sang it to Frances, who obviously had never heard it before, she was visited by memories of her own mother, singing to her when she had been small, then to her siblings as they had arrived, one after another.

Her mother had always beamed at the end, and Anne found herself doing the same.

"It's pretty," said Frances.

Anne smiled. "Well, why don't you sing it with me? Thirty days hath September..."

The little girl was a fast learner. Whether or not she was like her mother, and she certainly did not inherit her blonde hair from her father, she had her father's quick wits. After just one serenade, Frances was able to join in with the tune and most of the words.

Anne could not help but smile. She would get there, she and Frances together. Frances would receive the education that befit a lady of such a noble family, and it would be much easier if she was engaged and interested in her lessons.

If only Anne was just as engaged. Every minute that passed was a minute during which she fought to maintain her concentration. Every moment was a second that could be filled with thoughts of

Timothy.

Her master. Anne tried to remind herself, as she sang through the ditty a third time, of her place within the household.

It was here in the schoolroom. There was no earl here, just a girl and her servant. No matter what they were sharing, it was not real. Dinners, dancing, looks across a room…she was the only one who considered them moments of affection.

"Hurray! I did not know lessons could be so fun!" exclaimed Frances, clapping her hands at the end of the song.

"Well, I will always do what I can to make your lessons fun, and I think in time you will enjoy them," said Anne, pulled back to the present with a jolt.

"And will you promise never to go away?"

Anne turned to see Frances's innocent face. She wanted to respond immediately, to comfort her and promise that she would never be going anywhere.

Yet she could not. How could she offer such insincere promises? No matter her intentions, she was not a countess to dictate her own comings and goings in the world. She moved at the beck and call of others.

While Frances clearly was desperate for some reassurance, it was not she who could give it to her. Her mother may have left her, and the details of that removal were murky, to say the least, but that did not mean Anne could lie to her.

Anne swallowed. "I cannot promise that, child."

Frances's face immediately fell.

"I have no wish to go anywhere," Anne added hastily, "but as I do not know what the future holds. I would never lie to you, Frances."

For a child of such young years, she seemed wise beyond her years. "I understand."

Anne was afraid she did. Thank goodness she had planned for such an eventuality.

From her desk, she pulled the toys which she had secreted there that very morning. "Here, I think you deserve some playtime."

It had been difficult to know what to take, as there were so many toys and playthings in the Lexington nursery. Eventually, Anne had chosen two of the current favorites: Maryanne and a toy soldier.

"Here," she said, holding out the doll with as blonde hair as her owner and a toy soldier in a rather ragged red uniform.

Frances smiled as she slipped off her chair and reached eagerly for the soldier. Ignoring the doll entirely, she scampered to the window and started muttering to the soldier about what she could see through the window.

Anne smiled as she sat at her desk. Unusual for a girl, perhaps, but why not? Soldiers were much like dolls, and Frances spoke to the little man like a playmate. Like a sibling. Like they were family.

The very thought wrenched at Anne's heart. *A family.* She should not get into the habit of seeing herself and the earl in that light.

And yet...

Yet she had slotted into this castle, this home, so easily. Her charade as the countess was giving her a taste of what her life could be, if only she demanded it—but no. Whenever her eyes met Timothy's, she thought there might be something there, simmering beneath the surface, she was quickly recalled to herself.

She was the governess. He was the earl. This charade was supposed to be for the world's benefit, not her own.

Frances was chatting away, and Anne rose to look out of the window. The girl had been right; there was a splendid view from here over the kitchen gardens, all delicate rows of beans, carrots, the orchard further on with beautiful, gnarled trees of—

Anne took a step back, out of view of the window, heart racing and stomach lurching.

Timothy. He was out there, walking along a path with a gardener.

How was it possible that he could have such an impact on her, even from a distance, through glass?

Her mouth was dry. Even yards away, he had such an effect on her.

There was something about living in the same house as a man like Timothy. She could never escape him. Every room seemed permeated with his presence. It was intoxicating, like a fine wine that one found in one's glass.

But no, she was being foolish. She would be his countess for one day, one evening really, then the whole thing would be over. She would return to being his governess.

Just one of the household.

Anne smiled slowly as she watched Timothy meander down the path, looking carefully at whatever it was that the gardener was showing him.

She had spent so much of her life considering what other people would think. Her father, her mother, her brothers, society, the ton, Miss Clarke, the Earl and Countess of Allun...

What did she think?

It was not a question she asked herself often, and now that she did, Anne found the answer was simple.

She thought Timothy was by far the most incredible gentleman she had ever met; and she loved him.

CHAPTER TWELVE

November 27, 1812

H E SHOULD GO to bed. Timothy knew it, yet he made no movement to rise from the armchair he had dropped into more than two hours ago—other than to refresh his glass and retrieve a new cigar from the rapidly depleting box on his desk.

Timothy sighed, smoke blowing across the room. His study. A place of sanctuary, a place not even Mrs. Seton was permitted to enter alone. One of the oldest parts of the castle, his domain and no one else's.

Old Critchley had said it had been a chapel on the grounds of an old monastery.

Timothy could well believe it. The arched windows, the vaulted ceiling now painted in the most fashionable color, still had that sense of heightened power and spirituality.

At times, he could forget he was in his own home, as though he had retreated from the world like a hermit.

Timothy took another sip of whiskey. *Damned good stuff, the forty-six.* He should know; he was the only one who ever drank it. The trouble was, with every sip, his mind seemed to drift slowly but inexorably back to…

Anne Gilbert. The countess he had never expected. A shiver crept down the back of his neck as he recalled their dinner together.

"Christ alive," he muttered aloud, taking another draw from his cigar.

So beautiful, so tantalizing. God, he had never imagined having a governess in the place would drive him wild. He had imagined…well, a variation on Mrs. Seton, if he was honest. A solid, older woman who accepted no nonsense and would keep Frances in line.

Instead, Anne had arrived at Clarcton Castle and made Frances come alive. There was something different about that child, and he had spent so little time with her before Anne had arrived that he could not put his finger on what it was.

He knew what he'd like to put his fingers on.

"Damnit, man," Timothy murmured to himself, fire in the grate and smoke drifting from the cigar in his hand. "Can't you leave her alone for five minutes together?"

It did not appear he could. *Anne Gilbert.* It was becoming painful to be around her. A painful concentration not to permit his manhood to jump up as she entered a room, painful not to reach out for her and pull her into his arms, giving her the kiss he knew she wanted.

Timothy swallowed, gaze drifting to the fire. It was late. He should go upstairs, but he could not bring himself to. The bedchamber he had shared with Louise had been empty even when she had been here, and it had been a relief, for a time, to have it all to himself.

Until he wanted Anne in it.

He took another sip of whiskey. Had he made a mistake, inviting her into his home?

Timothy placed his whiskey glass on the fireplace hearth with a sigh. God's teeth, but he had managed to get himself into a tangle. He should be concentrating on more important things— Frances, for example, and what he was going to do with her. The

Christmas ball. It was but seven days away.

But all his thoughts were trained in one direction, like a vine, determined to reach a patch of sun on a wall. Anne Gilbert.

How had she intoxicated him so? Three glasses of whiskey, and his mind was barely touched, but weeks with her in the house, and he was obsessed.

It was not even as though he knew much about her—but had he known much more about Louise before he had married her and shackled himself to a miserable existence?

Timothy brought his cigar to his lips and breathed out the hot, heady smoke. When was the last time he had truly thought about Louise? A week ago? Longer than that?

Slowly but surely, Anne had entirely taken over his mind. Louise had been pushed out, beaten back by a superior woman.

Had he ever loved her? Louise had been…intoxicating, yes, but in a different way. More an infatuation, perhaps.

Impossible to tell, in hindsight. All he could do was try to understand what in God's name he was going to do about the woman before him.

Reaching instinctively to pick up his whiskey glass, Timothy saw to his surprise that the damned thing was empty.

It was only when he rose that he felt the effects of the liquor. He was not too far gone, but perhaps it was best to halt there. He was not a drinker, not like some in his acquaintance from his London club, but he had got into the habit of a whiskey every evening when…

He stood, irresolute, for what must have been a full minute when the door opened.

"No one comes in here," he barked as he turned. "Anne."

The governess stood in the doorway, evidently unsure. "I…well, I thought you would be interested in an update on your daughter."

The last two words made Timothy flinch, but, as ever, he was careful to hide it. *That was a truth not yet ready to be shared.*

"An update," he repeated. *Damnit, if only he had not drunk that last glass.* His mind had entirely gone, his tongue unable to form new words!

Anne smiled nervously. "Yes, an update. It has, after all, been the first few days of school for Frances, and I thought you would...but I can see you are busy."

Her gaze drifted to the cigar in one hand and the empty whiskey glass in the other.

Timothy almost swore aloud. Here he was, wondering what he was going to do with all the confusing emotions for Anne, and he had shouted at her for opening a door!

"Come in," he said hurriedly, pointing to the sofa. "Make yourself at home."

Anne did not immediately obey. "Are you...well, are you sure? I was under the impression from Mrs. Seton that no one was—"

"No one is," interrupted Timothy with a smile. Somehow, it had become very important she enter. It was his, the only part of the castle truly his own.

Now he wanted to share it.

Anne smiled. "Well, then, I do not understand."

Timothy swallowed. "I...I would like you to come in, Anne."

Why was his heart playing such a heavy beat against his ribcage? Surely she would be able to hear it, though Anne made no mention of it as she stepped inside and closed the door behind her, stepping across the room and seating herself in the armchair he had just vacated.

"This room is beautiful," she said softly, sinking into the green leather. "I had no idea the castle was this old."

"Far older than me," Timothy said with a dry laugh.

For older than me? What sort of terrible joke was that? If he could not manage his tongue, then he did not deserve to be here!

Anne smiled but did not laugh for his benefit—something he appreciated. "You were getting a drink?"

Timothy looked blankly at her, then at the glass in his hand. "Oh. Yes, I was."

With Anne now in the room, a whiskey did not feel necessary. The flaring warmth and sense of contentment the liquor brought was already here.

What was happening to him?

"I have just put Frances to bed," said Anne. "She is exhausted."

Timothy laughed as he sat on the sofa. "I can imagine you are just as exhausted. How goes the first few days of school?"

Anne made a face. "It will get much easier over time, I believe, but I would not say we are there yet."

Timothy raised an eyebrow.

"A tantrum every morning," explained Anne with a wry smile. "And that's just the governess."

He could not help but laugh. "So Mrs. Seton tells me!"

She joined his laughter. "Of course she does! I should have known the information would wend its way back to you in one form or another. I hope it came with the additional information that no matter the tantrum, I am always able to encourage Frances into the schoolroom, and within five minutes, she is as happy as anything."

Timothy shook his head with a dry smile. "You think too highly of Mrs. Seton if you think so."

She shook her head ruefully as he chuckled. *By God, this was so easy.* Was this what conversation between a gentleman and a lady was supposed to be? Each word simply rolled off the tongue, nothing was discomforting; they could just converse as two people.

Two souls.

Timothy waited for Anne to tell him more about Frances's exploits in the schoolroom, but nothing was forthcoming. She simply looked at him, those piercing blue eyes looking far deeper than mere skin.

Perhaps she had come to ask something of him. It was a heady thought, and he had to remind himself if that indeed was the case, it was surely something pedestrian, not personal.

New chalk for the board. Books, perhaps.

Nothing to do with the growing burgeoning passion.

"And..." he said finally. "And was there anything in particular you wished to tell me?"

Why was it now he could not catch her eye? Anne's gaze slipped from his.

"This room is beautiful," she said. "Ancient and beautiful. And lonely."

Her blue eyes met his, and Timothy found he could not look away.

"I thought you might wish for some company," Anne said softly. "Even if Mrs. Seton says you are never to be disturbed here."

Timothy spoke without guile, without the censorship he had self-imposed for so long. "Anne, I have been without good company for years. Until you arrived."

It felt strange, saying the words out loud. They seemed to echo in the room, surrounding him with their sadness, the loneliness they betrayed.

The weakness.

But Anne did not look at him as though he was weak. There was kindness in her expression, kindness which had been lacking when he had ever looked at Louise.

Timothy smiled awkwardly. He could not remember the last time he had ever been in this study with another person. Once or twice, perhaps, when he had inadvertently stumbled across someone cleaning in here, and that had been an uncomfortable interaction indeed.

But Anne...somehow the study felt complete with her presence. As if she belonged here. As if the place would be lacking once she stepped outside it.

Timothy shook his head, as though trying to rid water from his ears. *It must be the whiskey, why he was thinking this way.*

"And how are you settling in?" he said bracingly.

It was the first question he could think of, but he regretted the words as soon as they were out of his mouth.

Settling in? The woman was about to be paraded about as your wife, and you cannot stop thinking of taking her to your bed!

Anne, however, did not look surprised by his question. "To tell the truth, I…it's a bit overwhelming. I am comfortable with Frances, and her studies will pick up apace once we have ironed out the tantrums, but…"

Her voice trailed away, her gaze still unwilling to meet his own.

"But what?"

Anne took a deep breath and met his eyes. "I admit myself overwhelmed. Pretending to be your wife…'tis a strange occurrence, I am sure you would agree."

Timothy nodded. "I feel it, too, and yet…Anne, I could have asked a thousand women, and none of them would have risen to the occasion as you have. You belong here at…at Clarcton Castle. I would not have you anywhere else."

It felt strange to bare his soul like this, strange to speak the truths of his heart. The last time he had done this, Louise had just laughed. Laughed in his face.

"You truly think she is yours?"

Timothy swallowed, pushing the memory aside. He had to concentrate on the woman before him.

"The Christmas ball is but one evening," he said bracingly. "You do not have anything to fear, not for one evening."

"That is precisely what I am afraid of."

He waited for her to continue, the silence elongating between them, but somehow there was no awkwardness to it. The fire crackled in the grate, and the warmth that was overwhelming him was not just from the fire but from somewhere deep within him.

"One evening," Anne continued quietly, "might not be enough."

Timothy swallowed. They were getting into dangerous territory here. Whatever this was, beyond the façade itself, had to be halted. This was a path they could not go down.

Should not go down.

"The thing is," Timothy said, breaking the silence because the words simply wouldn't remain in his heart, "I like you, Anne. Christ, I…and I don't know where this is going. Where it could go."

Did she understand? There was no simple way for this to unfold, he knew that, but could she tell what she was doing to him? Could she see how he trembled just to be close to her?

"It cannot go anywhere, Timothy—I should not even be calling you that, really. My lord."

The two words were like daggers to his heart. *My lord?* "I thought we were beyond titles."

"Perhaps we should not be," Anne countered. "I am a servant here. I am nothing, should be nothing but the governess to your daughter."

Your daughter. Timothy could not bear to disillusion her, not in this moment. He had to keep some secrets, after all.

"I may find myself so accustomed to having you by my side, I have no wish to continue without you," he said unguardedly. "I mean—I am not saying," he added hastily. "I did not mean—look, perhaps you should not listen to me right now. I have had three glasses of the strong stuff."

He smiled weakly, trying to show her he was still in control of most of his faculties, but perhaps his tongue was not to be trusted.

Perhaps *he* was not. *What had he been thinking?*

Anne smiled. "I always thought drink would make one more honest, not less."

Timothy opened his mouth, but then closed it again. Perhaps she was right. Perhaps passing thoughts he had forced down were flowing from his lips thanks to the drink.

Truth had been guarded after Louise. The worst arguments were when they were most honest with each other, sharing their mutual hatred and frustrations, and then finding themselves in bed together, angrily taking whatever pleasure they could from each other.

"I think you have excellent intentions," said Anne quietly, stirring Timothy from his reverie. "I...like you, you know that. I just do not think I wish to have my heart broken because of an impossibility."

It was difficult not to feel guilty. He had lied to her, coerced her to pretend to be his wife, wished to take her into his bed—and he was still lying to her. Anne did not have the full truth of the matter with Louise, and she must feel it, the hidden truth below the surface.

"Everyone has secrets," Anne said softly. "Everyone has a past. The question is, what is the future?"

He did not think. Thinking was beyond him at this point anyway. She was just out of his reach, and it would be so easy to...

The distance he had to close between her lips and his was very slight, and he made it in a moment. God's teeth, she was so sweet, so warm, so willing. Anne's hands moved to his neck, pulling him closer, and Timothy lost himself in a kiss that was both passionate and tender until his body quivered with desire.

And then it was over.

"I...I do not think we should get into the habit of that," said Anne, her eyes filled with the same desire Timothy felt. "However much we might want to."

Timothy nodded, unable to speak. God, his entire mind was perplexed. He wanted to breathe her in, touch her, explore the pleasure he knew he could give her.

"That was the best kiss..." his voice trailed off.

She smiled. "You make my top three."

"I—I what?" Timothy stared, utterly lost. Top three? Who on earth had she—

But Anne was laughing. "I am just teasing you, Timothy. Has no one ever teased you before?"

He swallowed. "No, I don't think so. No lady has, anyway."

Anne took his hand. "No, I can see they have not. You will have to get accustomed to it, I'm afraid. The longer I am here, the more it will occur."

Timothy nodded, unable to speak, all of his consciousness concentrating on the warm fingers making his own hand burn.

Christ, Anne slotted into his life so well. How would he ever find someone like her? How could he bring another woman into this household with Anne in it? Siring an heir was nothing to this kind of happiness.

"Well, it comes of being an only child, I suppose," he said bracingly.

"No siblings at all?"

"Oh, I think my parents desperately wanted another child," Timothy said. *Had he ever told the story of his family to anyone before?* "Yet none came. I have the impression that I was rather a miracle, my parents being married almost a decade before I arrived."

He was smiling. His parents had been good people. Far better than he was.

Anne squeezed his hand. "Tell me about them."

Timothy hardly knew where to begin. "Well, they were wonderful parents, but very strict. I think, being the only child and a son, too, they were worried I would grow sick and fade away. I was kept safe, protected—over-protected, in truth."

She did not say anything but nodded silently. Timothy found it a rather strange sensation. The art of true listening. Had anyone ever truly listened to him in his entire life?

Not like this. Not how Anne made him feel so safe.

"Suffocated was, I think, the term I used in the last row I had with them," he said bitterly. "As soon as I reached my majority, I was out of here and into…well, less than reputable company."

There was a wry smile on Anne's face. "I can imagine."

It was a mercy she could not, Timothy thought privately, and a good thing, too. He did not wish to demean himself in her eyes, however much he probably deserved it.

God, he had never told anyone this before. He had never been this open before.

"It sounds as though they loved you very much," she said softly.

Timothy swallowed. "They did. I hurt them very badly, and it is something I have never quite forgiven myself for."

"Forgiven yourself?"

If only he hadn't drunk so much damned whiskey. Why else were these secrets spilling from his lips?

"My father received news I had..." Timothy hesitated. "Well, it does not matter. It was an entirely false report, of course, but the letter from a well-meaning acquaintance—the Merriweathers, you will meet them at the ball—informed him of my death."

Anne raised an eyebrow. "Reports of your death were evidently exaggerated."

He had to laugh at that. "Indeed. But it did not prevent my father from falling into a sickness from which he did not recover. My mother swiftly followed before I could reach them, present myself to them as literal living proof. Broken heart."

The pain of that moment had never truly left him. It was a miracle he was able to speak of it at all.

Anne placed a hand on his arm. Warm, comforting. "You did nothing wrong."

"If I had not left, no false rumors could have so injured them," said Timothy resentfully. "I often think how much they would have doted on Frances. They would have liked you."

His eyes met hers. Damn, but he was meandering into dangerous territory.

"I think," he said quietly. "I should go to bed."

Anne glanced at her pocket watch. "I, too. Good evening, my lord."

She had slipped through his fingers and out of the room before Timothy could say another word, though what it would have been, he could not tell.

He did not trust himself in her presence. He never would now. Not now, he was starting to fall in love with her. *Blast it.*

CHAPTER THIRTEEN

November 28, 1812

"YOU'RE ABSOLUTELY SURE?" Each syllable was dripping with concern.

Anne was not usually this anxious. She was not usually so attached to her charge. Her gaze moved from the bright-eyed child excited about the coming adventure and her supremely confident father.

"Oh, I was already doing it when I was her age," he said calmly, the wintery wind tugging at his hair. "Do not worry."

Anne bit her lip. His words were comforting yet did nothing to quell her concern. Surely this was too soon. Frances was but a child. Why was she so sure she could do this?

"I said, do not worry," added Timothy with a brief smile. "When I was her age, I could already ride. There will be nothing to it."

Anne nodded. It was impossible not to compare the size of the child to the size of the pony; power in every inch of its muscles, shaking its head fretfully.

A pony like that may be nothing compared to her—Anne was not even sure whether her feet would be lifted off the ground if she mounted it—but Frances?

The child did not even come up to its shoulder. What if the beast did not take to Frances? What if the pony should bolt— what if Frances fell to the ground?

"Oooohh," murmured Frances, raising an unquivering hand to pat the pony.

Anne's heart softened, despite her fear. There was no such emotion on the child's face. She did not seem even aware the animal could hurt her.

There was something about being a child. An innocence Anne had forgotten, no matter how clearly she thought she could remember her own childhood.

"Look, Papa, I'm stroking it!" Frances squealed.

The pony snorted and shook its neck, but that did nothing more than please the child, who clapped her hands.

It was, Anne had to admit, a rather wonderful thing for a child with no playmates, who had relied entirely on her own imagination for animal and human playfellows, to find oneself standing before a real-life animal.

"Good girl," said Timothy briefly, catching Anne's eye and grinning.

Anne smiled weakly. Yes, Frances was being remarkably good—although if she was any judge, it was more the excitement of spending more than five minutes with her father that was giving her the most amount of joy.

Her gaze slipped back to the pony. It looked docile enough, but she was hardly an expert. She could ride, just about, but when her father had died, many horses had to be sold. Working beasts had remained. As she looked at the pony, it appeared to grow larger.

Anne swallowed. Timothy seemed content, moving around it and putting on the bridle and saddle and all the accouterments Frances would need.

She should trust him. He knew what was best for his daughter. He was not likely to put the child in danger just to prove a point to her.

She could not shake the worry. There was something about Frances; she had wormed her way into Anne's heart, and she had not even noticed. Almost like her own daughter.

Whatever it was, it was clouding her judgment, and Miss Clarke would never approve.

"'Tis quite easy to find oneself attached," Miss Clarke had said stiffly, as though she had never been attached to anything in her life. "Especially if there is but one child in the house, and even more so if that child is young."

At the time, Anne had just returned from her first-ever assignment: six children, all under the age of ten. The idea of being attached to a child had seemed incomprehensible.

"It is easy I say to get attached, and I do not blame the sentiment," Miss Clarke had continued, her entire demeanor suggesting the contrary. "While you should care about the wellbeing of the child, one cannot consider the child your own. You are a servant. You will leave one day, and they will never remember your name."

Anne swallowed, watching as Frances was encouraged by her father to gently pet the creature on the nose.

They will never remember your name.

Well, while that might be true—though the thought seared her heart—she still had a duty. She could not permit this to go forward if it put the child in danger.

She took a deep breath. It was vital she remained calm and sounded neutral when she expressed her concerns. She would get nowhere if—

"Whoops! Careful, girl," Timothy said briskly, pulling the pony's head up to, Anne was sure, prevent it from taking a bite out of the child. "Gentle strokes, like this."

To her horror, Anne saw that instead of immediately removing the child and returning the pony to the stables, he encouraged Frances to reach out once more to pet the nose of the pony.

"Are you..." Anne swallowed. *She must not permit her voice to waver.* "Are you sure, Frances, that you would like to go riding?"

Frances turned a face of absolute contentment to her governess. "I'm going to ride the pony, Miss Anne, with my Papa!"

Anne smiled, despite herself. *Ah, to be a child again, when the worst thing that could possibly happen was a slap on the wrist or a stern word.*

"You have been looking forward to this all day, haven't you?" said Timothy, catching Anne's eye and grinning.

She rolled her eyes. *The last thing he should be doing is putting words in the child's mouth!*

But it was too late. Frances was nodding eagerly. "Papa will look after me!"

She did not exactly have the authority to forbid such an exercise. In a way, he was right. Many children of her birth had been in and around stables from the moment they could toddle without falling over.

Frances was behind in this part of her education, true, but not for long. The pony was accepting her rather indelicate pats with good grace, and her squeals did not disturb it.

"Anne."

Anne jumped. Timothy must have walked around the pony without her noticing, for now, he stood before her and had taken her hands in his.

"Anne, I promise you, she is quite safe," he said in a low, gentle voice, his blue eyes meeting hers. "Besides, you work too hard. Why not take an hour or two for yourself? Go back to the house, sit down and do nothing, or whatever it is that you governesses do to relax."

Anne smiled wistfully. "Plan more lessons and write reports for Miss Clarke?"

Timothy chuckled softly. "Whatever it is that you choose. I will ensure you are sent for when Frances is ready to be governed again."

It was impossible not to be reassured. She could not entirely put her finger on why, the sense of calm his voice brought, the searing touch of his hand, having him close to her...

Perhaps it was a medley of all three. Whatever it was, the

combination calmed her in a way that mere words would never have achieved.

She almost wished to stay, to see Frances discover the joys and adventures that riding could bring. It would be a crucial part of her childhood. With luck, she would have this memory for all her life.

But Timothy was right. She was tired. Looking after a four-year-old day and night was not for the fainthearted.

"When was the last time you took a day off?" Timothy asked, as though able to read her thoughts.

Anne sighed. "I do not think I have had a day off since I arrived."

There was a very slight widening of Timothy's eyes as she spoke. "Dear God, am I that tyrannical?"

"Yes," said Anne with a smile. "Very."

They laughed together, quiet, soft laughter. Anne wanted to reach for him, to release her hands from his, only so she could draw him closer.

Thankfully, she was able to restrain herself. *He was not hers to claim.* He did not even know what he wanted from her, and no words of affection had, at any time, passed his lips.

And they never would. She knew her place, and it was not by his side.

"Well, if you need me," she began, pulling her hands away.

Timothy shook his head with a wry smile. "I say this with respect, but we won't need you! I have been with horses, man and boy, for almost thirty years—your entire lifetime, I'll be bound."

Anne smiled. Perhaps she had inherited it from her father, but Frances looked calm, unconcerned with the power of the beast and far more interested in stroking its nose.

"Still," she said, unable to shake the feeling that she was leaving a child in danger. "If you want me."

Something changed in Timothy's face. Where there had been merriment, there was now a look of intensity, a serious look that captured her attention so utterly it took her breath away.

"I always want you," murmured Timothy, quietly so Frances could not hear.

Anne's cheeks flushed. There was something so magnetic about this man, something that drew her to him even when her better judgment told her it was foolishness to do so.

How could she stay away? How, even if she wanted to, could she explain to him that her feelings were not just desire for his touch, but to join him in his life—to be his partner, his wife?

Besides, the want she could see in his eyes did not appear to be for her personality or character. No, the Earl of Clarcton wanted her body. He wanted to bed her, and she wanted to let him.

But that could not be. She had to be resolute if she was ever to capture his heart.

"Have a good time, Frances," Anne managed to say as she stepped out of Timothy's burning gaze and toward the house.

There was a shock of heat as she closed the door behind her. She had almost forgotten how chilly it was outside as she removed her bonnet, gloves, and pelisse.

Anne took a deep breath as she laid them down. *An hour, maybe two.* That was all she had, not exactly a day off, but it was something.

She had not been entirely truthful with Timothy, as it turned out. She had her lessons planned for the next month, and Miss Clarke only expected a report once a month. Her first had already been sent, though her December report had been neglected.

A bell rang somewhere in the house. She was close to the servants' hall from this side of the house, and there was an answering clatter as a door opened and someone moved down a corridor.

A door opened before her—a door where there had only been a wall.

"Oh! Miss Anne!" Holt beamed. "How pleasant to see you!"

Anne smiled weakly as her heart sank. She had managed to

avoid the over-enthusiastic footman ever since the discomforting attention he had given her while dining with Timothy. Eager though he was for her company, Anne had not considered forming an attachment with anyone in the Clarcton household.

It was just her bad luck that the man she had fallen in love with was the master.

"Ah, Holt," she said in a detached tone. "Are you going somewhere?"

Unfortunately, Holt shook his head with a wide smile. "No, not really. What are you doing? Why don't I show you around the kitchen gardens, we have time to—"

"No," said Anne hurriedly, face flushing. She was no fool. She had heard what the maids got up to when they thought no one realized. *Walk around the kitchen gardens indeed!*

She knew what that meant. What better place in the entire estate to hide away, where no one else could see?

Holt looked profoundly disappointed. "No?"

"No," said Anne firmly. *Poor man, she did not intend to be cruel, but she had to put a stop to this.* "Thank you, Holt, but I am not interested."

The smile flickered, and a look of more intense concentration appeared on Holt's face. "You are not better than me, you know."

Anne's heart flickered. "I-I know that. I did not say—"

"You may look down on me because you are a governess," interrupted the footman, taking a step toward her. Anne took a step back and quickly found herself against the side door. "But I am trusted here, and you are not, Miss Anne. You should be careful."

She could not permit such a statement. "Careful? What are you implying, Holt?"

She had spoken boldly, but she felt no such thing. Only now did Anne realize just how tall Holt was. He was but a foot from her, towering over her, shoulders broad and lips in a thin unflinching line.

Holt leaned toward her, and Anne shrank back against the

door, painfully aware she had nowhere to go. No one knew she was here. No one was coming to her rescue, and—

"Not so sure of yourself now, are you?" breathed Holt, smiling with no warmth. "Now, maybe you want to reconsider. Do you want a walk in the kitchen gardens with—"

"Thomas Holt, the door!"

Holt whirled around, and Anne silently thanked her savior—only to see Mrs. Seton standing behind him, arms as usual crossed.

"Door?" he said blankly, quickly stepping away from the governess.

Mrs. Seton's glare was terrible to behold. "Yes, Holt, the front door! Did I not ask you minutes ago to attend to it?"

Anne watched Holt swallow, then nod. "Yes, Mrs. Seton."

Her entire body sagged as the footman hastened down the corridor.

Never before had she endured such an experience. Her rank was usually enough to protect her—it always had been in the households she had served in before.

"Do not permit him to do that again." Mrs. Seton was not exactly encouraging a confidence, but her voice was softer, and she was no longer glaring.

"I beg your pardon?"

"You know precisely what I mean," said the housekeeper quietly. "Holt. Do not permit him to address you when alone again."

Anne opened her mouth but then closed it again. Only after swallowed did she find her voice. "You…you knew he would—"

"I'm only guessing," said Mrs. Seton swiftly. "I'm assuming, based on…I wouldn't ruin a man's reputation based on an assumption."

Their eyes met, and Anne could see Mrs. Seton knew full well how Holt had spoken to her.

What was it the gardener had said?

"I can't think of no one who has ever been asked to leave."

Anne swallowed. "Thank you, Mrs. Seton."

The housekeeper nodded and stepped through the door Anne only now realized was cleverly hidden in the wall. It snapped shut behind her and left Anne in silence.

Anne took a deep breath. She had never considered herself an easily shakable woman, but what had just occurred had rocked her to her very core.

What had Holt wanted?

No, that was foolish. She knew precisely what Holt had wanted, had seen it in his eyes. The question was, would he have just taken it if she had not given it to him willingly?

Anne pushed aside the thoughts. She would not dwell on them. She would not give him the satisfaction of knowing, in any way, that he had affected her.

Reading a good book in the privacy and calm of her bed-chamber was surely the best way to spend the next hour or two while Timothy was trotting Anne about on that pony. If she was fortunate, she might just catch a glimpse of him through the window.

CHAPTER FOURTEEN

November 30, 1812

"—AND THEN, OF course, there is the harvest next year, also. The ground must be repaired differently, is that what you said?"

Timothy looked up from the sheaf of papers in his hands, wintery gray clouds scudding across the sky, giving no light nor joy to the drawing room where he was seated.

His steward, an able man by the name of Erskine, was standing before him. "Yes, my lord. The trouble is, we've used that field for grain too often these last few years. It takes the very essence of the land out from it. I recommend we lay it fallow."

Timothy nodded. All he had to do was concentrate on the man before him and not look at the woman just out of his periphery view. It had been a mistake, inviting Anne to sit and read here while he met with Erskine—but how could he resist her presence?

"Fallow, of course, means profitless," he said. "We will make nothing from it, and in fact, require cattle to graze there, to keep it under control."

"Yet it will return to profit far quicker if we do so," said Mr. Erskine evenly. He was not cowed by his master's tone and met his gaze confidently as he said, "Which I think is what we both desire. Healthy land."

It was difficult to argue with such a statement. "Indeed. What else would you do then, Mr. Erskine?"

Mr. Henderson, who had come before Erskine, had been the Clarcton steward for…what, thirty years? Maybe more?

Big boots to fill.

As the man began speaking again, Timothy found himself surreptitiously looking down to see if Mr. Erskine wore the same boots as his predecessor.

"We have good cattle and good breeders for next year, but I think within five years, we will find the stock too limited. I would speak to the steward at the Duchy of Axwick. He has a specialism in…"

Timothy nodded, making notes on the papers before him. He had done well—or at least, he had chosen well. Half the trouble of being an earl was finding the right people.

Like Anne. By God, she was perfection. Precisely what he had needed, though he hadn't known it. As the Christmas ball drew closer, it was hard to recall himself to the fact that after it was over, she would return to the schoolroom.

He was so accustomed to having her by his side. Timothy glanced over and saw she was lost in a book, brow slightly furrowed.

The steward cleared his throat, and Timothy turned back to his notes. Mr. Erskine had been his first appointment after the untimely death of his father, and it had been one which filled him with trepidation.

And yet, Mr. Erskine impressed, time and time again.

"And what do you need from me?"

A slight change in the light of the room; a darker cloud swept across the large bay windows, and the pitter-patter of rain started to drench the glass.

"Only your permission to write to the Duke of Axwick's steward," said Mr. Erskine confidently. "I know of him, and with your authority, I can begin correspondence and negotiations."

It was difficult not to smile. "Negotiations."

The steward nodded fervently. "The exchange or sale of best breeders? I should say so, my lord. You could disrupt the entirety of a family line with one bad breeder."

Timothy nodded, his throat dry. *Well, the man was not to know*. There was no possibility anyone would know if he was careful. Frances's true parentage was something he would take to his grave, whenever that was, and the girl would always be provided for.

Once again, Timothy was thinking of Anne. Confound that woman. He was utterly in her power, though she sat there silently.

How could a man be expected to put up with such torture?

"You could disrupt the entirety of a family line with one bad breeder."

What was stopping him from offering the woman his hand? Most matches were made with significantly less acquaintance, especially anyone of his birth. Why, many of his friends—the Duke of Orrinshire sprung to mind—had an arranged marriage. Even if the damned thing was not entirely pleasant, it was at least done.

But Anne…

She was a no one, a commoner, a governess. Yet his heart yearned in a way he had never experienced before.

He wanted her. Wanted more than just—

"My lord?"

Timothy jumped.

Mr. Erskine looked concerned. "Are you feeling quite well?"

"What? Oh, quite well," said Timothy hastily. Was that a giggle coming from the other side of the room? "Right. Land, cattle, both discussed. Anything else?"

There evidently was, if Timothy was any judge, but it did not appear to be a comfortable subject.

"Out with it, man," he said easily. "I doubt I will have any real opposition, whatever it is."

"It's..." The steward coughed before he continued. "It's about the mining, my lord."

That old story again.

"I know you are not particularly minded to consider it," said Mr. Erskine quickly. "And I think if I was in your position and did not know all the circumstances of such a thing, then perhaps I would agree with you. But the potential is huge, my lord, and would adequately fill the coffers of the estate to withstand any changes in..."

Timothy had never been very favorable of the idea.

"The potential to earn thousands, and all from land we are sitting on," he had said, eyes ablaze. "Just think, my lord..."

And he had thought—his father had, and now Timothy did. In this very moment, his mind was full of Anne.

Timothy had never known such intoxication from the presence of another. Louise had been one thing, all feminine wiles and tantalizing touches—but Anne? There was something more there, something of great substance.

He had taken her into his home and offered her lies upon lies and not yet revealed any part of the truth. And after asking what he had considered a damned cheeky request, what did she do?

Perform the act of a goddess. Timothy could feel his body stiffening—the dancing, the conversation, the way she looked at him...

Christ, he needed to concentrate. He could not say he cared for the people and land under his jurisdiction and then not concentrate!

"Erskine," he said, interrupting the man's flow. "Tell me this. Would we need to sell the land or rent it out?"

It was unusual for Timothy to receive approval from any of his servants, and so it was a rare surprise to see the steward looking with such admiration.

"That is precisely the question I asked, my lord," said Mr. Erskine. "Of course, there is never one simple answer. If we were to rent the land…"

Timothy tried to follow the numbers, but they spanned out into the air into all directions as he tried to affix them to his mind, the proximity of the governess not helping.

Rentals, capital expenditure, money upfront or in advance dependent on deposits discovered…

Good grief. Timothy watched the man become animated as he started to go into detail. He needed to give the man more power, more control. It was clear he knew what he was talking about.

"Erskine, tell me," he said. "You do a fine job caring for the estate. What would you do?"

The steward looked taken aback. "Me, my lord?"

Timothy nodded. "I have been impressed with everything you have done to date. What would you do here?"

"B-But…" stammered the steward. "But it's your land!"

"Well, go away and think about it. Make a recommendation," said Timothy easily. "Tell me what you would do, and we shall see—say, in a week."

Mr. Erskine was looking wide-eyed, as though he had been handed the keys to the castle and told to redecorate the guest bedrooms. "A week?"

Timothy smiled. "I trust you, Erskine. I know you will do an outstanding job, so I am interested to see what you would make it all. Consider it carefully, however. I may not be handing over the deed itself, but I wish you to treat it that way."

A smile crept over the man's face. "Th-Thank you, my lord. I will think on it."

"Excellent," said Timothy, laying down the sheaf of papers. "That will be all."

The man floated out of the room, and Timothy almost laughed as the door closed behind him.

"You are a very good master," came a teasing voice.

Timothy grinned as he turned to the speaker. "Is that a personal recommendation?"

"Perhaps," said Anne, lowering the book to her lap. "I suppose I shall have to observe your behavior at the ball, to ensure you are just as charming to your neighbors as you are to us."

He pulled a face. "Lord, I like my servants far better than my neighbors."

She laughed at that. "I think you are the first man of nobility I have met who thinks that way!"

"Then I am fortunate indeed in my household, especially in one," he said.

Did she understand? Christ, if only there was not such a gap between them. He wished to bridge that gap, to be within kissing distance. The memory of that heady moment in the study had teased his dreams too long. If only he could repeat it. If only she would—

"The Reverend Critchley, my lord," said Dewey smoothly as he opened the door and ushered in the local vicar.

Timothy sank back into his chair and tried to hide his disappointment, an emotion that was significant twice fold. Firstly, because it would mean he would have to delay kissing Anne with all the passion he had fought the last few days. And secondly...

"Ah, my lord," smiled the man dressed in his surplice. "How nice of you to see me."

It was on the tip of Timothy's tongue to say he had absolutely no say in the matter, but instead, he unleashed his frustration by glaring at his butler.

This was all Dewey's fault. The man had been giving delicate hints for months that he should return to the church.

As though the church would truly accept him after all he had done...

"Ah, Reverend," he said aloud, indicating that the visitor should take a seat by the gently roaring fire. "How unexpected."

Dewey at least had the good graces to look sheepish at that remark. It was rather uncouth of the man to simply usher in a guest to the Earl of Clarcton's drawing room, after all, particularly when everyone in the household knew Timothy's opinion of the church.

"You know my wife, of course?"

The vicar bowed as Anne inclined her head. "Of course, my lady, how wonderful to see you."

Timothy swallowed as Anne sat. Damn and blast it, what terrible luck. With no forewarning of the man...Mr. Erskine had been one thing; he was a servant. The reverend, on the other hand, was no such man.

It would be another test of Anne's mettle, but she had survived the first minute at least. If only she had not been wearing such a plain gown!

"You will have to forgive my casual attire," she said smoothly. "I have been in the garden most of the morning and thought it was not worth changing so close to dinner."

The reverend bowed his head. "I quite understand, my lady. So much to do in the garden this time of year, despite the inclement weather!"

Anne smiled briefly, then disappeared behind her book.

Timothy let out a slow breath. She was magnificent. How had he even considered that she would be unable to meet the challenge?

While all he wished was to be alone with her, he had no opportunity to politely ask the man to leave, and so the Reverend Critchley sat with a smile.

"What a wonderful luxury, a fire in the middle of the day," he said comfortably. "For my Mabel and I, 'tis a rare treat."

Timothy smiled mechanically. "Then I will ensure a bushel of logs is sent down every week until Easter. No, no, 'tis my pleasure. Anything to serve Mrs. Critchley."

The vicar uttered gratitude and thanks in abundance as Dewey brought in a tea tray and a series of cakes that, to Timothy's mind, looked too impressive for a Monday.

Ah. So Cook was in on this as well.

"Now then, my lord," said the Reverend Critchley as he accepted a cup of tea poured by the butler. "I have come to ask you why you are not attending church."

Timothy raised his eyes to his butler.

"I think I am needed below in the servants' hall," said Dewey hastily. "Please do excuse me, my lord, my lady, Reverend."

The door closed quicker behind him than Timothy thought was possible, leaving him unprotected from the well-meaning ministrations from the man of the cloth.

It was difficult not to allow the hackles on the back of his neck to rise. *Attend church?* How could he go back there, after all he had seen of the world, of human nature?

If that was God's creation, then he wanted no part of it.

"I lost my faith," Timothy said bluntly, reaching for a cup of tea himself and wishing it had something stronger in it. "In God and in people. A long time ago."

He had attempted to speak calmly, but there was repressed emotion in his voice that he realized, to his dismay, Anne would now hear. Christ alive, he hadn't expected to bear his soul to anyone today.

The Reverend Critchley was nodding with…was that sympathy? "Ah. A loss of faith."

He did not appear to have any more to say, sipping his tea and taking a large bite of the cake as though he had never eaten before.

Timothy blinked, waiting for the onslaught. *Wasn't that what happened when one irritated a vicar?* Where was the fire and brimstone?

"It is not that I have any disrespect for you," he added into the silence.

The Reverend Critchley, on the other hand, seemed perfectly serene. "Of course, my lord."

Again, Timothy waited for more, but there appeared to be none forthcoming.

It was all Louise's fault. She was why he had stopped believing in the power of good within people. They had been married in that church. When he stepped across the threshold, it was as though God was laughing at him.

Anne was so different, though her appearance was so similar. Chalk and cheese. She was different. She was his. Even though he would never possess her in the way he wanted, which was a damned shame, he wanted her near him. *Permanently.*

"More tea?"

The reverend raised a hand to indicate he was quite well served in the tea department and took another bite of cake.

Timothy's jaw tightened. *Well, he was no Catholic and did not believe in any of this confession nonsense.* He was not going to start pouring out all his thoughts and feelings.

"Everyone has their moments of doubt." The Reverend Critchley had an expression of benign interest, as though he was an interesting passage in the Bible he had to work out.

"Even you?"

It was a damned cheeky thing to say, and if Timothy's mind had not been primarily distracted by a certain woman, he would never have spoken so.

He cleared his throat. "I mean…"

The vicar was spluttering, although that may have been a badly timed gulp of tea.

"I-I beg your par-pardon?"

Timothy swallowed. "Look, may I be totally frank with you, Reverend?"

The older man smiled faintly. "By God, I wish you would."

"I have no bone to pick with you," said Timothy heavily. "I shall keep paying my tithes, which are not inconsiderable. I'll sponsor the harvest festival, Easter. I'll keep sending baskets to the poor of Clarcton. All of that. None of that will change."

A small part of him, a shameful part, knew he had only spelled it out for Anne's benefit. Why was he so desperate to impress her?

Reverend Critchley's smile had not faded. "But?"

Why did men of the cloth have to be so damned insightful? "But I will not attend church and profess a faith that I cannot, in all honesty, adhere to."

It could not be clearer the man expected more. "But my lord, you are a symbol to the village, to the entirety of Clarcton. If you do not attend—"

"That is their business," interrupted Timothy. *No matter how well-meaning the man, he would not be lectured on his own faith.* "I will not tell my people how to spend their money, nor who to marry. I consider faith a private matter, Reverend, and I leave it at that."

"And that is all?" he said stiffly. "You will not reconsider?"

Timothy thought of all the times he had turned this over in his mind, those long evenings alone, when darkness came at four o'clock, and there was no respite until the dawn.

He had cried out in those moments, and no one had answered.

"I have reconsidered," he said firmly. "And that is my final word."

"And what do you think of this, my lady?" asked the vicar, turning around to look at Anne. "I notice I have not seen you in our church these last two years either!"

Anne lowered her book slowly and affixed such a long stare on the reverend that Timothy was astonished he did not cower. It was majestic; it was the sort of look a goddess would have given a mortal.

"My faith," she said icily, "is between myself and my God. Until you can claim to be either of those personages, sir, I would ask you to leave it alone."

Timothy snorted, and the Reverend Critchley rose, leaving his unfinished slice of cake on his plate.

"I see," said the vicar. "Well, in that case, we have nothing more to discuss, my lord."

Timothy rose, too. It was the least he could do in the circumstances. "I am sorry I could not give you a different answer."

A sniff was the only reply he received, and the reverend had left the drawing room before Timothy had time to pull the bell.

"Make sure the reverend is seen out safely, will you, Dewey?"

said Timothy quietly as the servant opened the door. "Send him off with a bottle of the '74 and the '89. And organize the bushel of logs. And cake. Send him cake."

Dewey nodded. "Guilty conscience, my lord?"

The look that Timothy shot him was quite vicious as he closed the door.

Damn and blast. It was a filthy can of worms he had just opened by allowing himself to be so honest with the Reverend, but he could not keep lying all the time.

Lies, lies, and hints of truth that made the lies glitter as though they were gold.

"It says here that you are a governess of discretion."

Timothy turned to look at the woman who had heard the entire encounter. "You have not been to church either, then?"

Anne smiled wistfully. "I wish to go, but…well. I was too tired the first Sunday after I arrived here, and by the time the next one arrived, you had already asked me to be your countess."

Her cheeks flamed. Timothy had heard it, too: the longing in her voice. *Damn.*

"It seemed rather reckless to attend church after that," she said quietly. "I did not wish anyone to mistake me for being a governess. Or a countess. You know what I mean."

Timothy returned to his seat. Though he wished to be closer to her, that was not a good idea.

It was terrible to wish someone dead. Oh God, the number of times he had wished it when Louise had been here. It was a curse on him, retribution for the terrible thoughts he had harbored when Louise had…

Punishment from on high.

"I will not attend church and profess a faith that I cannot, in all honesty, adhere to."

Timothy smiled. He had never said he had stopped believing in a God. He just wasn't sure whether God believed in him anymore.

"I think you explained yourself well to the reverend," said

Anne quietly.

Lies, lies, lies. Perhaps it was time to tell the truth. Perhaps after all this secrecy, it would be a relief to finally let go of his grip of the narrative, and tell the story for what it was.

Timothy swallowed. "Thank you."

Visions swept through his mind of what Anne would say if she knew what had really happened. If she heard the full story, knew the strange truth of what had happened to the countess she would be mimicking soon.

Would she forgive him? Would she still look at him with that mixture of devotion and desire?

"Anne," he began.

She was already lost in her book once more, but she smiled. "Yes, Timothy?"

Anne, Timothy...this was too much. He should never have started along this path, but now they had started walking down it together, he could not turn back. He would not turn back.

"It does not matter," Timothy said gently. "Go back to your book."

And he could go back to reminding himself just how off-limits a governess was.

CHAPTER FIFTEEN

December 3, 1812

ONE MORE NIGHT and Anne would find herself on the arm of the earl before all his friends, neighbors, and by the sound of it, scores of anxious mamas desperate to hook the man in for their daughters.

The sun had set hours ago, and it was high time the little girl was heading toward slumberland.

Frances, however, had other ideas.

"I cannot go to bed yet. I am still building my castle!" The child pointed to the heap of cushions around which her soldiers were lying. "If I don't, where will they sleep?"

Anne had never been one for rules for rules' sake. That was what men did.

No, she was always attempting to ensure that when she gave an order, especially to a child, there was some rhyme or reason behind it. There was nothing so galling as being told to do something when the order itself made no sense.

Anne looked into the determined eyes of Frances, then at the clock.

"I am giving you five minutes," she said sternly. "I am going to sit here, Frances—Frances!—and in five minutes, we are going to go upstairs. Do you agree?"

The child nodded and immediately scampered back to her cushions.

Anne tried not to smile as she sank into the armchair in the corner of the room. Well could she remember playing in such a way, only a little older than Frances was now. It did not seem that long ago, in a way. It was easy to forget, but the memories swiftly returned.

She had never been a castle builder. That was one of her sisters. No, she had…

A wry smile crept over her face. She had played with dolls and sent them to balls.

Here she was, on the verge of a ball that would irrevocably change her life. Once she stepped into that ballroom, dressed in finery she did not deserve, nothing would be the same.

Frances chatted away to her soldiers, showing them the different rooms she was building in her castle, but Anne's mind was spinning.

Everything she had learned, names, relationships, piano music, expectation upon expectation which had rained down from Timothy like a storm onto a lake.

Every time she learned something new—a person she should cut down, a family which was no longer friendly to the house of Clarcton—it threatened to force out something else: a piece on the piano, the knowledge of just how she felt about Timothy Lexington…

Anne swallowed, and kept a close eye on her charge. What really consumed her in this moment, though she would not admit it to a single soul, was fear. Fear of letting him down.

He expected much, and she had been so sure she could rise to the challenge. She came from the Governess Bureau. There was rarely anything she could not do—and she was certain she could do this.

If not for him. His intoxicating presence, the way every

movement sparked something in her, something primal.

And at the foundation of it all, the promise she had given him.

"I...I will do it."

It was just a ball, she told herself as Frances proudly informed her dolls this was the Great Hall. Just one evening. She could remain as aloof as she wanted, no one would suspect anything was amiss. She was a countess. A pretend one, true, but still, a countess.

He was depending on her. Timothy had told her numerous times how often he was hounded by ladies, both of the marriageable and the motherly persuasion, whenever in society.

Anne could believe it. To have Timothy as one's husband...

Well, it fired her body in a way no other man ever had.

But this was quite a gamble to play on one evening merely because he did not wish to be propositioned by eager mamas. Surely there was another reason, or else he could simply procure the real countess and reveal her as the true reason he could not wed.

Anne swallowed. Wherever the real countess was, she was either unwilling or unable to come to her husband's side, to ward away any potential suitors attempting to make their mark on the earl's heart.

"So...can I call you Mama?"

It was the dearest thing a child had ever said to her, yet it revealed far more about the absence of the Countess of Clarcton than anything else. Her child missed her.

"Right, Frances," she said as she rose, trying not to smile at the look of horror on the child's face. "I promised you five minutes, and you have had ten. Come on. Bedtime."

Frances was not a child habitually given to the temper tantrum. Any child with a temper was difficult to manage, but at four, a child had control over their tantrums.

Just as Frances screwed up her face and opened her mouth, Anne added, "And as we go, let's talk about the ball."

It was a stroke of genius. Frances closed her mouth and considered her for a moment, looking just as imperious as her father, then nodded and stretched out her hand. They were walking into the Great Hall before she really seemed aware what was happening.

"You will have to tell me all about it," said the child petulantly, tiredness pulling at her eyes. "The dancing and the music and the—"

"I will certainly tell you all about it after the ball when I know every single detail," said Anne as they walked one by one up the staircase. "But there will be peacocks on the dining table and musicians playing in every corridor so that when the guests move about the house…"

Carefully speaking in a low and steady voice, Anne saw to her relief that Frances was yawning by the time they reached the top step.

"…and feathers all in their hair," she continued as she opened the door to Frances's bedchamber. "And diamonds shimmering in the candlelight as every gentleman tries to decide who he will dance with first. And as the music begins—"

"And you will dance with Papa, won't you?"

Frances's interruption came just as Anne was trying to pull her gown over her head, so she was spared the embarrassment of the child seeing her flush.

"Yes," she said briefly. "Now, into your nightgown—there we go—"

"And who will be invited? You have to tell me every single name, please," said Frances as she got under the covers and curled up, eyes tired but expectant.

"I will tell you after the ball," she said, stroking back Frances's blonde curls. "When I know whether everyone who said they would come actually arrives."

"And," said Frances with a yawn, "can I go to the ball?"

Anne shook her head, keeping her voice low. "No, not yet."

"When can I?"

"Not until you are older," said Anne wearily. *Goodness, she had almost forgotten how repetitive children could be.* When she had lived at home, her mother had gone around in circles answering some of the questions of the smallest Gilberts.

"How much older?" Frances persisted.

Anne shook her head. "Frances, you need to go to sleep. Come on, eyes shut and lights out. I will see you in the morning."

"And…and then will you tell me?"

It was hard to resist such a child. "Perhaps. Now, close your eyes."

Frances obediently closed her eyes. Anne stifled a laugh. She should not complain. She was a delightful child, and thankfully the only one. A governess of the Bureau never had much choice where she was sent, nor the children she cared for.

Rising from the bed, Anne reached for the lamp but halted as a small voice spoke.

"My…my mama used to sing to me when she put me to bed," said Frances, eyes open again. "Well, a few times, she did. I cannot really remember."

It was her foolish curiosity. Anne knew she shouldn't be asking a child such questions—but no one else was willing to speak about the countess. She did not even know her name.

She sat back on the bed. "Tell me about your mother, Frances."

Frances hesitated. "I…I am not allowed to talk about it."

Anne was not surprised. No one seemed permitted to talk about it—but the only person who could have given such an edict was the earl.

"Who…who told you not to talk about it?" she asked softly.

Frances did not appear to understand. "Everyone, I think. I thought you knew her."

Anne shook her head. "No, I never knew your mother. She was gone before I arrived."

"Yes, but you look so alike."

It was a response so unexpected that for a moment, Anne was

not sure whether she had heard correctly.

Look alike? It did not make sense. No one had mentioned a similarity between her and the countess, and surely they would have done if…

Perhaps not. Any mention of the Countess of Clarcton, and the household shut their mouths and went on their way. Everyone knew she was impersonating the countess at the ball—and only now did Anne wonder why she had not asked more questions.

Surely the world would notice a difference between her and the countess; but if Frances was correct, and they looked similar, perhaps that was why the earl had suggested it.

Anne took a deep breath. There was a mystery here, one she did not understand. Though there was the chance this was merely garbled memories from a child, misremembering one woman in her life due to the new presence of another.

Or was there something seriously wrong at Clarcton Castle?

"Are you going to stay forever?"

Anne chuckled. "I would like to stay for a long time."

Frances nodded safely. "That's what my mama said, and then she went away."

There was something strange in the way she spoke. Anne supposed it was only natural a child who could barely remember her mother would feel at once sad and detached.

It was difficult to miss something one could not remember.

It was on the tip of her tongue to ask another question, but Frances's eyes had fallen shut, and her breathing had deepened. She had finally got Frances off to sleep.

After waiting a few minutes to ensure Frances really was sleep, Anne gently stood, picked up the lamp, and crept out of the room, closing the door quietly.

She leaned against the wall and bit her lip. This was becoming too much. Tonight, the eve of the Christmas ball, it was natural to feel some nerves; yet this was more. This was doubt, directed at the man who was both master and tantalizingly out of reach.

Was she about to get herself into trouble? Miss Clarke would have expected her second month's report by now, but what with caring for Frances and being taught by Timothy how to be a countess, there had been little time to put pen to paper.

She would not approve. Miss Clarke, that was. Anne would dread to think what the owner of the Governess Bureau would say if she heard one of her governesses was about to parade herself about like a countess.

Was this just a huge mistake? Something she had been swept up in because her feelings for the earl?

Anne sighed heavily and watched the lamp flicker in her hands. Yes, her heart yearned for him, for something more than merely the pretense of being his countess. Perhaps that was why she found it so easy to go along with the façade.

Yet underneath it all, somewhere deep in the heart of this castle, this family, there was a secret. It caused the hair on the back of her neck to prickle, and yet she could not put her finger on what on earth it could be.

If she changed her mind about her agreement with the earl now—worse, if she decided to leave Clarcton Castle altogether—she would never know the truth.

It was late. She was tired, and it would be a long day tomorrow, yet Anne found her feet taking her not toward her bedchamber, but instead toward the drawing room.

Timothy smiled as she opened the door. "Well, good evening."

Anne knew she was in far too deep when her heart began to flutter with just that short welcome. If any other gentleman had said that, she would have felt nothing. If Holt, the overeager footman had said it, she would have been repulsed. It had been a small mercy she had been able to avoid him ever since their…interaction in the side corridor.

But when Timothy spoke to her…oh, the way her body craved him; it was unlike anything she had ever known.

"Unable to sleep?"

"Unwilling," she confessed, stepping inside the room. "At

least for now. I find myself in need of company, if you are willing to provide it."

Anne's stomach swooped painfully as he smiled.

"Of course."

Anne placed the lamp on a table with shaking hands and sat opposite him.

Was this what she had come to? Forbidden emotions for a man far out of reach and far above her in station?

She took a deep breath. She would not allow herself to make the same mistake any old governess would make. The Governess Bureau had rules for a reason. No one would ever hire a governess if they believed the master of the house to be in real danger of seduction.

"I admit I am pleased to see you," said Timothy with a broadening smile. "I…I missed you today."

Was it madness to think he felt something for her, too? She could not be alone in this whirl of emotions, could she? That stolen kiss in the study came back to her. No, she was not alone in this. Whatever she felt, it was at least matched.

"But this is radical of you, Anne," he continued. "What would Miss Clarke say if she knew you were spending your evenings with me instead of carefully drawing up plans for your charge's education?"

If only she had the bravery to kiss him as he had kissed her. But it was wrong to think in such a way. Even if nothing else had ever felt so right.

"I am sure Miss Clarke would consider Frances just ready for schooling," she said aloud. "And until I normalize having her in a schoolroom, there is no point constructing complex lessons. Besides, my mind is altogether too distracted by tomorrow."

Timothy nodded. "The Christmas ball."

"And…and are you excited?"

She certainly was. Every time she thought of it, her pulse quickened, and her hands seemed to shake, drop whatever she was holding, her mind instantly transported back to that moment when they had danced together, her hands in his, his breath—

"Not really," said the earl, stretching in his seat. "I never was to tell the truth."

Only a gentleman with more diversions than he could think of, Anne thought wryly, *would be bored by such a splendid occasion.*

"I suppose you have hosted many balls here," she hazarded.

Timothy nodded. Anne attempted not to look at the curve of his jaw, the way his hair, cut short around his ears and neck, only showed the strength of his shoulders. She loved him. She loved him, and he craved her, but not as she loved him.

"In my parents' time, they were a regular occurrence," he said. "A Christmas ball and a New Year's ball, one or two in the summer, one for my mother's birthday, of course—any excuse would do. They loved dancing, loved people. Games in the summer, hosted for the whole village. Long house parties in the autumn…"

Anne was utterly enchanted. It appeared that during his father's reign as earl, there had been not a single day that went by without some sort of entertainment or diversion.

"Some of the people I have met here," Timothy continued, a smile creeping over his lips. "Beau Brummel—what a man. Most unpleasant, I have to say. Criticized my appearance on my first ever ball."

Anne chuckled. "I hear he was most injudicious with his criticism."

"And his praise," added Timothy with a mischievous laugh. "God, I remember when he faced a tirade from Lady Romeril after making a disparaging comment about her gown. I never forgot that, and I think to this day neither has she."

Anne leaned forward. Beau Brummel, Lady Romeril…these were names of high society she had heard but never met. Yet in a few short hours…

"The balls sound marvelous," she said. "What a precedent to meet."

Timothy nodded. "My parents never lived to see me host, but

I always hope to do their love of entertaining justice. Though, to be honest, it was…the countess dealt with most of the details. The latest fashions, impressive food, that sort of thing."

Anne swallowed. They were so close to the topic of his wife and her mysterious absence, yet she did not know how to take it further. It did not feel possible she was about to take on the mantle of this woman who was beloved by some and clearly loathed by her husband.

"She…she's dead, you know."

It was as though time had stopped. The words spoken by Timothy hung in the air like snow, wafting down to Anne's ears, which could not quite take them in.

"Dead?" she repeated.

Dead. The countess was dead?

The earl was discomforted, yet he said nothing. All words appeared to have failed him.

Anne swallowed. She had to ask. "I…I beg your pardon?"

After all her curiosity, after wondering for weeks where the countess was…

"If you ask me, he did it."

Well, it was no wonder rumors had whirled up in society. After two years completely out of view, why had she not thought there was a possibility the Countess of Clarcton was not just missing, but had ceased to be?

Anne's shoulders were tight, every muscle on edge, but Timothy did not appear concerned. There was sadness in his eyes, yes, but it was not distress but melancholia.

"My wife died," he said heavily. "Suddenly. An accident, two years ago."

Anne could not take in his words. *Dead.* The countess was dead? She was about to impersonate a woman who had died in an accident—an accident which evidently had been hushed up to such an extent that half the staff did not appear to know what had happened, and the other half had never spoken of it for fear of…what? Retribution?

"Frances was upset, as you could imagine," said Timothy, his gaze drifting away from the governess and toward the dying embers in the grate. "I think she has forgotten it now. She was so very young, you see."

Anne nodded wordlessly. She could not speak, had no words to utter.

"I would like to stay for a long time."

"That's what my mama said, and then she went away."

"There would have been scandal, intrigue—no one believes an accident is ever truly an accident when nobility is involved," said Timothy. He was attempting to convince himself, it appeared. "I did not wish to be a bachelor again. To enter the marriage market three years older, a decade wiser, with a two-year-old child...so I lied. I lied, Anne."

She could not believe it. This was the sort of thing one would read in a disreputable newspaper, and it was all nonsense, surely!

But why? Why lie about his wife's death? Why tell such a story unless it was the truth? He gained naught from the admission but her silence, which he had not asked for.

A governess of discretion. That was what he had asked for. By God, she could see now why discretion was the sole character trait he needed from a woman entering this household.

"You..." Her voice was croaky, and she swallowed before attempting to speak again. "You have kept this up, this lie about the countess being away for her health...you have maintained it for two years?"

It did not seem possible.

Timothy nodded. "It was easy for the first year. I told you, ladies are delicate. Many go abroad for their health. For one winter, for a winter and a summer, it did not seem such a difficult pretense to maintain."

Anne could well believe it. How many husbands and wives had she encountered in the upper echelons of society, through her connections with the Alluns, who lived apart for most of the year? Whether for their health or for more personal reasons, it was not uncommon.

But still. They were *seen* in public. Occasionally.

"Then, of course, people started to remember they had not seen my wife in over a year," said Timothy heavily. "I was beginning to be asked impertinent questions. Receive impertinent suggestions. Matchmaking, that sort of thing. I should have thought that there would be a time when someone wondered, eventually," said Timothy with a dark laugh. "Even I had not foreseen it would go this way."

"But what about her family?" Anne found herself saying. "Countesses do not just die, and no one notices! Her friends, her family? Parents, siblings?"

Timothy shrugged in a careless way. "She had no family— none who ever owned her, that is, or perhaps it was the other way around. I do not know. None of them attended our wedding. I know that, and we received no congratulations on the birth of Frances."

The birth of Frances. It was a strange way of saying it. Anne would have expected him to say 'our daughter' or even 'my daughter,' now she knew him to be a widower.

His voice had become stiff when he reached the name of his daughter. Was there another secret there, too? Was this castle merely full of secrets which he was hiding?

"I...I own I struggle to believe it," said Anne into the silence. "I believed myself to be impersonating a woman who was too sick, too unwell to travel here and be by your side. Now I learn I am impersonating a dead woman. A woman you have surely grieved and—"

"My wife was not a great mother nor wife," said Timothy unexpectedly. His voice was harsh but measured, as though he was holding a great deal back. "I tell you that not to dismiss her memory, but to ensure you understand. The woman you will be tomorrow at the Christmas ball was not a pleasant woman. She did not endear herself to my neighbors. She endeared herself to very few. *That* is the woman you will be."

Anne took a deep breath. Well, she had always prided herself on her ability to continue on regardless. *Just keep going.* But this news? The death of a countess in mysterious circumstances, in an accident which never saw the light of day?

"You are trusting me with a great deal of information," she said. "If it is all true."

Timothy waved his hand dismissively. "Of course it's true—why would I lie?"

"She is away. For her health."

"Well," Anne said, "because I have been here now for over almost two months, I will be pretending to be your wife tomorrow—your wife who I now learn has not just gone away but passed on, and it is only now you are telling me this. On the eve of battle, as it were. After...after everything."

Only then did he meet her gaze. Something connected them in that moment which Anne did not understand—a moment of intensity, a moment of trust, of longing. She did not need to spell out what she meant: after the evenings together, the dinners, the walks. The dancing. That kiss.

"I trust you," he said, leaning over the fire and disturbing the embers with a poker. "I am sure you can understand why it has taken me such time to ensure that trust is merited."

Anne twisted her fingers in her lap. Here he was, admitting such wild things to her—and now she had a decision to make. Whether to trust him in the same way he purported to trust her.

"I lost my wife," Timothy said heavily. "More dramatically than you can ever know. Whatever the detail of the matter, I need to protect Frances. She is my priority."

Anne's mind soared upstairs to the child sleeping in the expectation that, one day, her mother would return. "You cannot leave her in ignorance forever."

"She is four," said the earl with a shrug. "She was young when it happened, too young to understand. I doubt she even remembers her mother."

"My...my mama used to sing me a bedtime story when she put me

to bed."

A clock chimed somewhere in the castle, and Anne rose to her feet hastily, grateful for the interruption.

"My goodness, is that the time? I really must be going to bed," she said hastily.

Timothy rose to his feet, too. "I will walk you up. 'Tis probably best I get some rest, too."

Further time in his company was not really what Anne had in mind, but there was no way to politely decline his offer. She needed to think, get away from his intoxicating presence, try to untangle her emotions from her thoughts from what was probably the truth—but there was no time for that.

As they walked across the Great Hall and up the stairs, they remained in silence, for which Anne was grateful.

What could she say to him? Until she managed to untangle the knot of emotions he had sparked by revealing what was presumably the truth about his wife, she should remain silent.

They reached her bedchamber quickly. "And this is where I—"

But she could not continue speaking. Not now one hand had been captured by his.

"Anne," Timothy said in a whisper.

The corridor was dark, and they were alone. Anne's fingers burned with his touch, and yet she could not pull it away. She did not want to.

"Anne, I…I want…"

Anne saw the desire in his eyes. She knew if she permitted it, he would kiss her again; more, if she opened the door to her bedchamber and welcomed him in, there was a very real chance he would take her to bed and—

"You don't know what you're doing," she whispered. "You don't know what you want."

A dark shadow crossed the earl's face. "Oh, don't I?"

The movement was sudden—so sudden she had no time to pull away, even if she had wanted to.

And she did not want to. Here, in Timothy's arms, his lips on hers, passion poured down on her mouth, and she whimpered in his arms. Every inch was alight, as though it had come alive for the first time, and this kiss would be one she would never forget.

And then it was over, as quick as it had begun.

"For-Forgive me," was all Timothy said, releasing her. "Damnit, Anne, you do something to me...something I cannot control. I should not have..."

He looked at her fiercely, as though attempting to show her rather than tell her his feelings.

"I want a great deal from you," he said in a jagged voice. "Far too much then you should give me. I—Christ in his Heaven."

He strode away without a second glance.

Anne stood for a moment in the corridor, heart racing, the sensation of his lips on hers still overwhelming her. Only after a full minute did she realize she was looking into the gloom of the corridor for a man who was not coming back.

Her bedchamber door closed with a dull thud, and Anne leaned against it, desperate for the sensation of reality.

She should not have permitted that. It was a lapse in judgment from them both—one which would not, could not be repeated.

So why did she wish she had invited him in?

CHAPTER SIXTEEN

December 4, 1812

H E WAS NEVER going to host a ball ever again in his damned life.

The tightness of Timothy's cravat was surely causing blood restriction around his neck. That must be why his fingers were tingling painfully, why every breath as he raced through corridors adorned with candles and feathers was so painful.

Why his temper was rising with every passing moment, the closer he stepped to the moment when all would be lost, or the entire endeavor would be proven to have been in vain.

"I said, where are the musicians?" he snapped at a footman hurrying along in his wake. "They were told to be here at six o'clock, and it is almost seven—"

"They arrived fifty minutes ago, my lord, and are in the ballroom," panted the footman. *Burnham? Poll? He could barely tell those two apart.*

"And the punch? Is it ready?"

The footman stumbled as they turned a corner, foot snagging on a rug. "Cook finished it and sent it up with—"

Timothy barely heard him. He had to keep asking these questions, for then his mind and tongue were occupied, and he could not ask the one question he knew he had to ask.

Where was Anne?

"I expect dining to begin at nine o'clock sharp," he said curtly as they entered the Great Hall. "My father had high expectations for this sort of thing, and so do I."

"Yes, my lord," murmured the footman, looking relieved they had halted.

She was not here, and that meant he had to keep asking more questions, for as soon as he started asking where the devil that woman was, he was surely going to lose his temper.

If he had not already.

"I assume," he said icily, catching the eye of the unfortunate footman, "all servants have been instructed that Anne—the governess will be referred to as 'the countess'?"

"All that has been taken care of."

The smooth and calm response had not been uttered by the footman. Dewey had strode into the room, looking completely unrufflable.

"And her?" Timothy snapped.

It was a mark of the butler's experience that he did not need to inquire as to whom his master was referring. "She is being dressed now, with the help of Patrick."

Timothy blinked. "You mean to tell me you have allowed someone into this house, a gentleman, someone who does not know the secret, to—"

"Molly Patrick, the countess's lady's maid, my lord," interrupted Dewey calmly.

Timothy hesitated. Of course, he had forgotten. They had kept her on, of course, and she assisted Mrs. Seton whenever there was fine embroidery or mending required.

Good. Anne was receiving the proper attention due a countess before such an event.

The knowledge did nothing to calm his frantically beating heart, nor soothe the growing feeling he had made a terrible mistake by attempting this ruse. Who did he think he was, to do such a thing? Yes, there was a strong likeness between the two, and most of the guests had only met Louise once or twice...

But surely, they would realize they were not speaking to the same woman? Different hair, though Timothy was certain any amount of society fashion was a reasonable excuse.

It was an awful gamble. He had thought so when the idea had first occurred to him, what felt like years ago now. He had known the risk was great, just as the reward would be.

But now, he thought himself foolish. Here he was, encouraging his entire staff to lie, something he was sure the Reverend Critchley would disapprove, all to convince women to stop throwing themselves at him!

And, said a rather uncomfortable voice in his ear, *to throw anyone off the scent of where his precious wife was.* She was dead and buried, but the world did not need to know that.

The fewer questions asked about Louise, the better.

"Good, good," he said distractedly, his gaze following a pair of footmen carrying a set of candles from one place to another. "Lady's maid. Excellent. Careful with those!"

The last three words were issued as a bark, and the footmen who had been so carefully moving the candles jumped, causing hot wax to slip onto the floor.

The curses which uttered from Timothy's mouth were not to be repeated. "Get this cleared away at once. Guests will be arriving any minute!"

The butler stepped away to oversee such an operation, and Timothy was left in the miserable company of his own thoughts.

Damn. Damn and blast. He swallowed, tasting bile in his throat, knowing his very body was rebelling against this sort of intrigue—but he was too far down this path now. There was no way he could turn back, not after he had entrusted Anne with the truth.

Or near as damned the truth as she was likely to get.

One of the footmen who had been so startled was flapped

away by the butler, and as he stepped past Timothy, the earl heard a little of his muttering.

"—damned good job until he shouted…"

Timothy bit his lip. He could not be offended by such a statement, not one so blatantly true. He knew he was being unreasonable. He was, ironically, not so unreasonable that he could not see that.

But he could not help it. The anxiety rushing through his veins was hot, spiking his temper in a way that it had not been riled for…

Two years. Since his wife's revelation, designed to injure him to his very core. She had succeeded.

"Five minutes," came the severe voice of Mrs. Seton as she blew into the Great Hall like a storm, dark clouds around her forehead. "Five minutes and carriages will arrive, and—what are you doing there, man, go to the ballroom and assist with the punch!"

The second footman who had been so unfortunate to have spilled the candle wax immediately hurried through a door toward the ballroom.

Timothy glanced at the staircase. He had assumed she would be down now. How long did it take to prepare for a ball? Put the gown on, a few jewels, and there you were.

The gamble felt even greater without her by his side, without his ability to inspect her before she presented herself to the world as his countess. Perhaps he should go up there. Ensure she was suitably dressed. Give her a few last instructions which would aid her in her deception? Kiss her. Kiss her so hard the panic of the evening faded away into nothingness…

Just as he took a few steps toward the staircase, Dewey appeared before him.

"I am afraid there is not time to visit the countess," he said smoothly.

Timothy scowled. "And just why would I want—"

"To see her? Perhaps to ensure she was dressed adequately,

perhaps to calm her nerves," said the butler, lowing his voice. "Perhaps to satisfy your own curiosity. You cannot help her now, my lord. She has all the instructions she is to receive. All we can do now is trust."

It was never pleasant to be schooled so by one's servant, but Timothy had known Dewey for many years. There was no malice nor censure in his words. He was attempting to protect his lord from himself. A worthy endeavor. If only he could be so restrained.

Taking a deep breath which only pained his lungs rather than relieve them, it was all he could do not to push past the well-meaning servant and leap up the stairs in twos and threes to make sure he saw Anne before she came downstairs.

She had to get this right. If she did not impress people—worse, if she was suspected, noticed to be significantly different from the impression his neighborhood had of his wife...

He would never live down the ignominy of attempting to parade a governess, a mere servant, out before society as a countess.

Timothy's jaw tightened. Yet she was not just a mere servant, was she? God's teeth, the temptation to follow her into that bedchamber last night had been unbearable. He had earned the title of gentleman in that moment, resisting the charms of a woman who tasted so sweet, who evidently wanted him, even if she did not have the language to express it.

If she was found out, there would not just be questions; there would be an inquiry. It was maddening! All he needed was five minutes with his own thoughts, and—

"Ah, the first of the carriages arrive," said Dewey, stepping away from his master and nodding at a footman who immediately moved to the door. "My lord?"

A clock was chiming somewhere. *Damned people, they were precisely on time. How dare they?*

"Christ and all his saints, it begins then," he said heavily, before adding hastily, "I beg your pardon, Mrs. Seton."

The housekeeper had raised an eyebrow but did not look mortified. "Nothing I have not heard before, my lord. I will return to the kitchen to ensure all is prepared for dinner."

As he moved to stand beside the footman and butler by the door, a timid looking maid hurried down the staircase and stood behind the butler, whispering something urgently.

Timothy's curiosity was piqued. The butler nodded and dismissed the maid before nodding curtly to his master.

"I have been informed," he said in a low voice, "that my lady will be down presently."

Timothy snorted. "I remember what that means from when *she* was here." He did not need to spell out the name. "So, we have at least half an hour to wait until she decides to grace us with her presence, do we?"

Dewey cleared his throat. "I couldn't possibly say, my lord."

It was almost enough to make Timothy laugh, despite the severity of the situation. What did they think they were doing? If high society ever got wind he had attempted this—worse, if someone like Lady Romeril, or the regent, heard of such nonsense…

He could tear up his Almack's vouchers for a start. There would be no invitations for him at St. James's Court, no grand dinners.

He did not care about such things, but Frances… His heart contracted. If he was to lose all honor, Frances would suffer. He had to maintain the family name. Even if—

"Ah, your first guests arrive," said Dewey.

Timothy sighed. Well, he had brought this entire thing upon himself. He was the one who had suggested it, and now he would have to bear the brunt of the damned thing.

"Let the onslaught begin," he said dully.

And it was an onslaught. Timothy knew every face that passed. At least, in theory. When one had lived in a place like Clarcton for one's entire life, one could spot family resemblances that could at least place a face within a surname.

"Ah, Miss Anderson," he said with a stiff smile. Yes, definitely an Anderson nose.

The young lady simpered as she curtseyed lower than was really required. Timothy caught a glance of an ample bosom and quickly averted his eyes, but it was too late.

Miss Anderson's nose was now accompanied by a large smile. "My lord."

He forgot her as soon as she had stepped away, and the next assault of guests arrived. So many things to remember, petty disputes to be aware of. So much to be taken into consideration, and still, the damn woman had not thought it worth her attendance.

Where in God's name was she? Timothy had no wish to stand here like a moron, welcoming every single person who arrived, but—well, it was the way it was done. The way his father had done it. The way he did it. One day, Frances would do it in her own home.

His stomach lurched as the Great Hall warmed up, heated by candles and bodies, their chatter pouring around the room.

The very thought of Frances made his blood boil, but he could not permit himself to think of her now, nor the betrayal she represented. Though his gut may rebel at the very thought, he could not bear to even permit himself to dwell on it.

Frances was his daughter. For all intents and purposes.

"Ah, Clarcton!"

Timothy blinked. The Astors were obviously waiting for him to greet them, and he did so with a genuine smile. It was only his miserable thoughts preventing him from warmth.

"Ah, Lord and Lady Astor," he said, inclining his head. "I hear that your daughter is well?"

Their chatter washed over him like waves on a shore. As so often with married couples, he was not actually required to partake in any of the discussion. It was more that he provided an audience, and that was all that mattered.

Besides, he could not entirely pull his mind away from the

irritation that Anne was causing. She was not just late. She was now absent, absent from a party thrown in her honor.

"And where is the countess?"

Timothy snapped back to attention. "Countess?"

Lord Astor laughed. "I imagine she must be beautiful indeed if you guard her this closely—hosting the Clarcton Christmas ball but not presenting the hostess of the evening!"

Timothy attempted to smile. "I would never dare deprive society of my wife's good graces, but I am afraid the countess is running late."

Lady Astor smiled. "'Tis a lady's right to be late to her own ball if she chooses."

"But not her responsibility," her husband laughed, to Timothy's chagrin. "Who knew a gown was such a complicated thing to get into!"

They laughed as they wandered into the medley of guests, and Timothy bit the inside of his cheek to prevent himself from retorting something most ungentlemanly back.

God's teeth, he'd given Anne much closer instructions as to timings, for though there was an element of gracefulness in her being late, this was getting ridiculous.

This was the first hurdle. Her reentrance into society and she was absent!

As long as he did not say Louise's name, that was the important thing. That was vital. If he said that name—

Anne Gilbert was supposed to be here to help him with the child and play the countess for one evening! She was not supposed to be ensnaring his affections and refusing to make an entrance...

"Well, how rude," he overheard someone say behind him. "I came all the way from Kent to see the countess!"

If those words had been spoken by anyone else, Timothy would probably have turned around and asked them just what business it was of theirs to pass judgment.

As it was...

"Lady Romeril," he said, smiling at society's doyenne. "How pleasant to see you."

There was never anything gained from speaking rashly to Lady Romeril, so Timothy held his tongue. It appeared he had decided well, for the elderly woman was dressed to the nines in her finery and diamonds and a formidable scowl.

"Hmmmph," was her only reply as she leaned on her walking stick.

Timothy licked his lips. Whatever he said here, now, would undoubtedly be all over society in London by the end of the week. He would have to choose his words carefully.

"My dear Lady Romeril," he said sweetly, "who am I to rush a countess?"

"Well, she is your wife, isn't she?" snapped Lady Romeril with a glare. "The last I met your wife, she was damned insolent and had a temper worse than anyone I've ever seen."

There was nothing for Timothy to say to this. Lady Romeril was entirely correct.

"But I see you still have affection for her," she continued haughtily. "Yes, I can see it in your eyes. I suppose she is waiting until we are all here to give herself a better and more impressive entrance?"

It was difficult not to smile. That was precisely what Louise would have done.

"Lady Romeril," he said, ignoring all mention of Louise and the countess, which he considered to be two very different people. "I beg you will ensure to patronize my dining room soon after nine o'clock. There will be rather fine figs in there, to which I know you are partial."

Lady Romeril gave him a stare rather too like the ones Anne gave him when she thought he was being unreasonable, but it appeared the promise of figs in winter was too much to bear.

"Do not think this conversation is over," she said, pointing a finger at him as though at a naughty child. "I will find you when your wife has deigned to gift us with her presence."

The elderly woman strode away with far more purpose than could be expected of anyone of that age, and Timothy shook his head. To have Lady Romeril as one's enemy would surely be a terrible thing indeed—but to have her as your supporter must be truly terrifying.

The Great Hall was almost full now. Timothy could not understand it; the corridors had been decorated most assiduously, and the ballroom was a picture of elegance and taste, yet all his guests were here, milling about and starting undoubtedly to get rather hot.

Timothy's gaze brought over a footman. "My lord?"

"Is there a problem with the ballroom?"

The footman looked confused. "The ballroom?"

"Or is a door jammed?" asked Timothy. "Is there a reason no one has progressed through to the ballroom?"

He had never seen Burnham so discomforted. "'Tis because...well, they all want to see her, don't they?"

Timothy's neck prickled. "Her?"

The footman nodded. "The countess. They are all waiting for the countess."

He sighed heavily. *Of course they were.* One could not hide a woman's existence—or lack thereof—for two years and then expect everyone to act like rational human beings when the promise of her reveal was made.

"Well, they may be waiting some time," he snapped, turning to point at the staircase. "When she bothers to...to come down..."

He could not continue. Speech was not possible, and he was not the only one afflicted.

A hush swept across the Great Hall as heads turned and gasps were heard as a figure appeared at the top of the staircase.

Timothy felt his jaw physically drop. He was no schoolboy, no green youth out in the world. He should be accustomed to visions of beauty, to attractive women.

But this was...she was...

Anne Gilbert was standing at the top of the stairs with her head held high, a coronet around her fiery hair simply dripping with sapphires and a blue silk gown that showed off her complexion and figure in a way that was surely criminal.

Timothy's throat was dry, his arms hanging by his sides like an idiot—but he was not the only one. The entire room took a collective gasp as she stood, absolutely beautiful.

That dress. The way it shaped her—or how she shaped it, Timothy was not entirely sure. She was the very picture of a countess. How had he ever doubted her?

A forceful nudge in his side made Timothy almost cry out.

"My God, Clarcton," said Lord Astor in a whisper. "You look as though you haven't seen her in years!"

Timothy smiled weakly. "I haven't."

He wasn't sure whether the man had heard him. A rush of chatter blossomed as Anne started stately down the stairs, the long train of her gown emphasizing just how lithe she was.

Perhaps they had gone too far. Timothy's heart was pounding. No, it was Anne's mere presence. Damn, she was unlike anyone he had ever met. He had never seen the queen walk through a crowd of people with such an imperious smile, untouched by whispers.

She made straight for him, of course.

"I hope I am not too late," she said with an arched eyebrow and just a hint of a smile.

Timothy's stomach turned over. *Christ, he was in trouble.*

"You are late," he admitted. "We have all been waiting for you. I think you've caused a blockage in the corridors."

Anne smiled. "Perfect. I was waiting for the right moment."

A loud sniff behind them told Timothy Lady Romeril, at least, was not impressed.

Well, blast her, let her sniff. With Anne at his side, Timothy was certain the ball would be a success.

Impulsively kissing her on the cheek, he was reminded of the passionate one they had shared last night. Anne's eyes met his, and he could see she was recalling the same thing.

"Where…where have you been all this time?" he asked, gently folding her arm into his. *Anything to feel a connection with her.*

Anne laughed as though he had told a joke and leaned close, whispering in his ear and making his entire body tingle.

"Mrs. Seton informed me that the countess was always late," she breathed, "and so here I am."

Timothy almost laughed. "You mean to tell me you have been ready all this time but just waiting upstairs?"

"And very boring it was, too," she shot back with a wicked smile.

He really did laugh now. *God, she was so different from Louise.* That playfulness, that artfulness with grace rather than gall. There was no possibility believing she was the countess.

Yet the governess, for that was how he was supposed to consider her, played her part. As he introduced her to people in the Great Hall, now quietening as guests poured through the corridors to the ballroom and card rooms. Timothy saw with surprise just how Anne could treat people with that casual mixture of indifference, politeness, and that vague sort of awareness that they were lower in status than her.

She was perfect.

Timothy watched, amazed at the fact he had this woman by his side and not in his bed. Warm but imperious, looking down on those she should and cutting anyone who had ever cut the Clarcton family, she had an ability of recall to astound even the dons at Oxford.

"And this is Sir David Merriweather, his lady wife, and their daughter," said Timothy comfortably. Thank God he had left these ones until the end. She could not fail him now.

Anne met his eyes. Yes, this is her, his gaze told her, and she nodded imperceptively.

"Miss Merriweather," she said, inclining her head. "My husband tells me you're an excellent rider?"

The woman's cheeks flushed, and her gaze darted to Timothy

before she replied. "I-I am, my lady. Perhaps you will one day favor me with your company?"

Anne considered before replying. "Yes, perhaps. If I ride, which I rarely do, it is usually with my husband."

The silence that followed this pronouncement was uncomfortable indeed. Timothy found, to his surprise, that he felt rather sorry for Miss Merriweather. It was not her fault he was married—at least, he was not married, but she did not know that.

His eyes met those of Anne's.

"Miss Merriweather, walk with me," said Anne with a slightly warmer smile. "Your gown is most exquisite, and I wish to hear your opinion on everyone else's. Come."

Anne took the woman's arm, and they walked toward the ballroom.

"Such beauty, such elegance," murmured Lady Merriweather.

Her husband nodded. "We will follow our daughter in, my lord, and converse later."

The Great Hall was empty now, and with an echo, the front door was closed.

"That is the last of them," said Dewey with a sigh. "Now, my lord, I believe you are opening the dancing?"

"Dancing?" repeated Timothy like the fool he was.

Of course. This was a ball. His ball. He was supposed to be hosting the damned thing.

All eyes moved to him as he entered the ballroom. There was a gaggle of women around Anne, all giggling and smiling, but their faces fell as he approached.

"My dear," he said stiffly, holding out his hand with a sparkle in his eyes.

Anne disentangled herself from Miss Merriweather and took his hand. "Clarcton."

Timothy smiled. There was something about her, something mischievous yet with no malice whatsoever, that he found rather intriguing.

Were all women like this—all women save Louise? Or was this something unique about Anne—the way she captivated a room without decrying someone else, the way she could laugh and giggle without destroying a reputation?

"Well done," he murmured as he took her aside. "Very impressive."

"I hoped you would be pleased," she replied softly.

It was not Timothy's stomach that contracted painfully, but something further down. *God's teeth, he was in trouble.*

Her hand was warm in his as if it belonged there, as though she belonged by his side.

Now they had to suffer hours of dancing, conversation, dining—all when his greatest desire was to take Anne into his arms, carry her upstairs, and—

"But 'tis the dancing I worry about," Anne said.

Timothy smiled and unconsciously raised his free hand, and brushed her cheek. "You will be perfect. You are perfect."

Her blue eyes met his, her mouth slightly parted.

"Besides," he said hastily, dropping his hand and terribly conscious of the hundreds of eyes on them. "Shouldn't you be more concerned about conversation?"

Anne arched an eyebrow again. "Conversation? I am a mistress of conversation."

Timothy would quite happily have spent the entire evening where they stood with no one interfering with them—yet it was not to be.

"Ah, my lord and lady," said Lord Galcrest as he and his wife approached. "The elusive Countess of Clarcton, I presume."

Timothy watched as Anne, evidently unsure who these people were, curtseyed just low enough to be polite.

"Ah, Lord and Lady Galcrest," he said, aiding her. "How pleasant to see you."

Anne understood immediately. These were friends of the House of Clarcton, and so were to be treated as such.

"Indeed, it is a shame I have not yet made your acquaintance," said Anne, her smile warming.

"Ah, but that is your fault and not ours," said Lady Galcrest playfully. "Where on earth have you been, my lady?"

Timothy should not have been worried.

"Oh, all over the place," Anne said nonchalantly. "I believe you know Bath well?"

Lord Galcrest shook his head. "Now, do not tell us you have been in Bath this entire time!"

"Did I say that?" said Anne with a mischievous smile. "Come, sir, a woman must have some secrets, mustn't she?"

They laughed, and Timothy found his concerns melting away. *She was a natural.* She belonged on the stage, not in the schoolroom!

"What, even from your husband?" Lady Galcrest asked.

Anne smiled as her gaze flickered to Timothy and then away again. "Well, I struggle to keep secrets from my husband. Even if he manages to do it from me."

The Galcrests laughed at the joke, but a shiver moved up Timothy's spine. *Yes, well, it was a well-fired shot and no mistake.*

She knew he had not been entirely honest. *Well, she's no fool.* But it was not as though he could explain the full story. She would never believe him. She would never understand.

He was spared the discomfort of further conversation as the musicians started a simple country dance. *Well, no time like the present.*

"Time to dance," he said, catching Anne's eye.

She offered him her hand.

Timothy fought the instinct to just pull her into his arms and kiss her. He must control himself. This was his chance to have his countess by his side, and no one would ever attempt to marry him off to their darling daughters again.

A line of other couples grew around them. Timothy looked at Anne. The music reached a peak, and he stepped forward, eyes on her and hands meeting hers.

Even through the gloves, Timothy could feel the heat in her, the desire. *Christ, if he did not know any better, he would say she wanted him just as he wanted her.*

The dance unfolded, his hand on the small of her back, his breath on her neck.

"Is everyone looking?" she whispered.

Timothy chanced a glance. "Yes."

"Good," she said low so only he could hear as they progressed through the set. "Now you have what you want."

Their hands were entwined, her breasts pressed against him. "I...I do?"

He wanted her, that was what he wanted. Anne, in his bed, crying out his name and—

"Everyone knows I am your countess," Anne whispered, her eyes never leaving his. "I am yours, Timothy."

Timothy almost moaned. *Hearing those words on her lips...*

The dance was over before he knew it. Polite applause echoed around the room, but while other couples disappeared, Timothy and Anne stayed in the center.

"I could..." Timothy swallowed. "I would dance with you forever."

Anne took a step closer to him. "Would you?"

Who knows what nonsense he would have spouted if they had not been interrupted.

"Well, hello again," said Lady Romeril stiffly as she approached them. "Very lovely you are indeed, my lady, but entirely absent from society. Where have you been?"

"Been?" Anne said lightly.

He came to her rescue immediately. "Lady Romeril, let me introduce you to—"

"Yes, yes, very pretty," said Lady Romeril irritably. "Answer the question, my lady."

Anne trotted out the script they had prepared. "All over, Lady Romeril. The world is an exciting place indeed, and I needed to take time. For my health."

The older woman did not look convinced. "Indeed."

"I believe you, too, have traveled," said Anne smoothly. "Tell me about India."

Lady Romeril's frown softened. "Ah, the Empire. I cannot tell you, my lady, just what a place India is. The heat! Oh, it did my old bones so good, as I told Lord Romeril at the time. When one first arrives at Bombay…"

Timothy stared in amazement. Anne had even managed to tame the lioness that was Lady Romeril.

This was a life he could live with no regrets and no pain, a life so unlike that which he experienced with Louise.

Was this ruse perhaps something that could be repeated? *Perhaps…permanent?*

CHAPTER SEVENTEEN

I T WAS AN absolute relief to take the weight off her feet and collapse onto a sofa.

"What a night!" Anne exclaimed, closing her eyes and luxuriating in the softness of the sedan. She could not remember the last time she sat down. It felt not like an evening, but a year had been consumed with conversation, polite inclinations of heads, and dancing with...

It was a good thing her eyes were closed. She could therefore not be accused of any impropriety as her cheeks flushed.

Dancing with Timothy. A gentleman fast becoming the most precious, necessary part of her life.

Yet still her master.

"I am quite exhausted," she said aloud.

There was a chuckle as the drawing room door closed. "And that is the last guest gone. Not too late, either."

Anne opened her eyes and sat up, astonished. "Not too late? Timothy, 'tis three o'clock in the morning!"

The earl looked at the clock in dazed surprise. "Yes, but is it even the same week? I admit, I am not sure what year it is. I believe we were in that dining room at least four months!"

Anne laughed as Timothy dropped onto the sofa beside her. His finely tailored jacket had disappeared, abandoned no doubt in the Great Hall as he had seen the last guest out, and his fingers were moving languidly to loosen his cravat.

"It is difficult to believe people are finally gone," he breathed, closing his eyes.

"Time flies," said Anne, trying to keep her voice strong, "when one is having fun."

He was so close.

"I must say, you should be complimented on your dancing," said Timothy, opening his eyes and grinning.

A ripple of pleasure flowed through Anne. She recalled the feeling of his hands on hers. The way they had leaned closer to each other, ignoring the world around them.

It had been only them. No one else mattered. No one else existed. It had been perfect.

Anne smiled. "You were the one leading, and by the end of the evening, I think we were the only ones still standing!"

"Your stamina amazes me," Timothy said in a teasing manner.

"I think it far more to do with the potent wine you were serving than anything else! Did you hope your guests would drink themselves into a stupor so as not to recognize me?"

Timothy roared with laughter. "You know, it had not occurred to me—but it might have occurred to Mrs. Seton. Clever woman, I shall have to give her a token of my affection."

Anne laughed. It was perfect, sitting here, the rest of the house asleep. The earl sent his servants to bed—the place, as he had said, would not become any more untidy overnight. The clean-up operation could begin in the morning.

So here they were, the only people in the world. Timothy's hand was close to hers, but Anne did not have the bravery to reach out for it. Her gloves had been discarded when she had entered the room, and the intensity of that connection would be unbearable.

Who knew what would happen if she did?

Giddy, that's what she was. Anne could barely believe the

evening had succeeded: everyone had accepted her as the Countess of Clarcton without a second thought.

Being a countess was, on the whole, rather wonderful.

"I believe I could get used to this," she said. "Being a countess. Having everyone bow and scrape—did you see the Duchess of Axwick? She couldn't wait to speak to me!"

"Oh, Tabitha is all right," Timothy said nonchalantly. "I think she was hoping for a friend, more than anything else. It can be lonely, being a duke's wife."

Anne giggled. "And what would you know about such things?"

"I think you'll find I have plenty in my acquaintance who married into nobility rather than been born to it," said Timothy with mock severity. "And quite a challenge it is, too!"

Anne swallowed. It was a taboo topic, marriage into the nobility.

She was not his countess. For all she could parade about and impress those who never knew the original, there was a woman—had been a woman who had truly been married to him.

Had been Timothy's wife.

Though the evening had been magical, it was not her life. Her reality was that of a servant, a governess. Her charge was upstairs, hopefully still asleep, while here…

Here was a man she could not have. Anne's gaze raked over Timothy—his cropped hair, that smile that teased as it praised, his arms, muscles showing through the thin linen shirt.

Here was a man she could love. She *did* love. She was dallying with danger, sitting here, almost as though they were on an equal level.

"You are quiet."

Anne snapped out of her reverie. "I beg your pardon?"

Timothy was looking at her closely, as though he had never seen her before. "You. You are quiet, and though I would never have described you as loud, I have not known you to hold your counsel so before. What are you thinking?"

What was she thinking? Anne almost laughed. The Earl of Clarcton would like to know what his governess, who had paraded for the entire world as his wife, was thinking!

"This whole evening has been magical," she said aloud. "I do not think I could ever have believed I would experience such a thing. It's…it's like stepping into someone's story."

She had no better words to describe the madness, and Timothy appeared to understand.

"In a way," he said delicately, "aren't you?"

Anne's cheeks flushed. Yes, she was. Despite Timothy's revelation that the countess had died, there was a small part of Anne that wondered whether it was the entire truth.

The truth. Something in scarce supply in Clarcton Castle. Timothy had kept this small morsel of information from her and gave her no cause to believe it other than his word.

She wanted to believe him. Anne looked into his eyes and saw integrity, but she had known the man but two months. Despite her feelings, despite the intensity of connection that this charade brought, she was still not sure if she could trust him.

"I apologize, that was…careless of me," Timothy said quietly. "I did not mean—"

"I know what you meant," said Anne.

She swallowed, tiredness seeping through her temples. All she needed to do was sleep.

It was strange, feeling such opposite emotions. A desperation to be near him, and a dull need to be alone and try to ascertain precisely what she felt. What was she supposed to do with all these emotions? How could she return tomorrow to the sedate role of a governess?

She was supposed to be his governess, not his countess.

"I could never have dreamed all this," she said quietly. "Not with all imaginings could I have created such a sight."

Timothy glanced at her. Even a look was enough to heat her body.

"The food, the dancing, the gown," Anne added, drawing his

attention to things other than herself.

It was not working. Timothy's blue eyes were transfixed on her, and Anne found she enjoyed the attention.

If she were honest, she rather liked this make-believe. She liked the smiles from dukes and duchesses, she liked…she liked being the center of every room she was in.

Who would not? It made her special, something she had never been. She did not want it to end. She did not want to stop being important to him. Being his wife, even in name only.

"I need a whiskey," Timothy announced and rose, stepping toward a cabinet.

Anne let her breath out slowly, unaware she had been holding it in. Her gaze followed him as he moved across the room. *Oh God, she loved him.* She could at least admit it here, in her mind. Besides, who would she tell? A housemaid or footman? They would laugh and rightly so, for raising her expectations to such a man.

"I would offer you one," Timothy said, "but I doubt you would like it."

Anne shook her head mutely. Mrs. Seton, Dewey? They would not laugh but would consider her impertinent. Telling Frances was absolutely out of the question, and as for her father…

Anne swallowed all the things she wished to say to Timothy as he sat back beside her and took a gulp of the amber liquid.

He would never consider her as anything more than a very convenient servant. Able to play the countess, yes, but unworthy to actually step into those shoes.

*And even if he did…*Anne smiled at the thought. Even if she was foolish enough to convince herself he felt anything for her more than physical desire, so much stood in their way. Society would never permit it. An earl and a governess?

Meredith might have managed it, but they had kept the news out of the gossips ears and therefore had got away with it. No such fortune here. The Earl of Clarcton was already such gossip fodder, any marriage would be considered the hottest scandal.

"You are very quiet."

Anne looked over at Timothy, the man who had absorbed her thoughts.

"Yes, I am," she said softly.

Timothy did not seem offended that she offered no explanation. "Well, 'tis to be expected. After a night of being my countess, I imagine you have much to think on. Good God, who would have thought it would go so well!"

Anne smiled weakly. It was strange no one had thought to quiz her more precisely on where she had been—but then, who would speak that way to a countess?

"And...and will I get the chance to do that again?"

The words had slipped out of her mouth before she had been able to stop them. It was a desperate wish, a hope rather than an expectation, but now she had spoken...

Timothy's gaze met hers. "What do you mean?"

"You know exactly what I mean," Anne said with a wry smile. "The world knows your countess is alive now, alive and kicking. They are going to expect to see her again."

"Do you think?"

Anne nodded. She could not look away. "How often do you want to trot her out to prove it? She cannot simply disappear out of sight. There will be questions."

Timothy took another gulp of whiskey. "You know, I have no idea. It had not even occurred to me that our success would be so very great—God, the reverend, of course."

Anne waited, but no explanation seemed forthcoming. "The reverend?"

"You met him, the elderly man who—"

"I know who he is," said Anne. "Why did you mention him?"

There was a haziness to Timothy's eyes now, but it was not due to the whiskey. His glass was still full, but the way he was looking at her...it was far more intoxicating.

"Mention him—oh, Reverend Critchley," said Timothy, as

though unable to focus. "Yes, he said how much he looked forward to seeing *us* at church."

Anne stifled a smile. "He grows old. Surely he remembers your rather direct conversation?"

Timothy chuckled. "Well, he was always better at homilies than noticing what was going on under his nose. Still, we may have to trot you out every week or so, prove you still exist. If it gets too much for you, we could always 'send you away.'"

He spoke so calmly, as though discussing the potential merits of a type of carriage. Anne's heart rate quickened. Though she was tired due to the late hour, her mind was sharp.

"Send me away?"

Timothy waved a hand. "Not actually away. The countess. The governess would stay—and we should probably ensure few visitors see you as Miss Gilbert, the governess, though God knows how many people actually come here. Not many."

Anne swallowed. He spoke so nonchalantly, so easily, as though it was a simple case of picking up one type of life and putting another aside, as interchangeable as a pair of gloves.

He was smiling, but Anne could not remain silent. Timothy may treat the whole exercise as though it was all one large reward, but Anne had to say something.

Though she may regret her words, she would regret staying silent far more. When would there be a better time to speak? When they were alone, after such…such an evening?

"So, tell me, Anne," said Timothy. "How do you like being a parttime countess?"

He spoke with a wry smile, that sort of knowing smile Anne had come to love but felt out of place now. He could not possibly know how she felt, or he would speak differently.

Anne swallowed. "I do not like it at all."

Astonishment flashed across his face. "You surprise me. I thought you enjoyed this evening."

It was impossible to know what to say. A blur of words rushed through Anne's mind. *How could one respond to that, spoken by the man she loved?*

"Though I dare say," he added with a smile, "perhaps half the fun is tricking people?"

Anne took a deep breath. There was no going back from this. Miss Clarke would be astonished to have her returned to the Bureau so soon, but she was not one to lie about her feelings, and it was intolerable for this to continue.

"This will surprise you," she said softly, "but I find, Clarcton, that—"

"Timothy."

Anne's breath caught in her throat. "I beg your pardon?"

Timothy placed his glass of whiskey on the floor and turned to her. "I thought we had reached a first name business, Anne— or would you prefer Miss Gilbert?"

Was he purposefully attempting to make this as difficult as possible?

"I prefer Anne, as I well think you know," she said ruefully. His hands were only a few inches from hers... "I think it best I tell you that...oh, you will undoubtedly spot the signs soon enough. I would rather tell you—have it on my own terms, as it were."

A crease appeared between Timothy's eyebrows. "This is serious conversation indeed for...what is it, four o'clock in the morning?"

But Anne could not stop. She loved him, and until he knew...a part of her hoped...

"I know 'tis foolish, but I have to say it," she said in a rush. "I...this whole experience has been..."

He was looking with such interest, such openness, Anne could not bear it.

"I am falling in love with you."

The words echoed around the room, finding a life of their own.

Anne swallowed, her throat dry. "You...you intoxicate me, Timothy. I know 'tis out of place to say such things, let alone feel them, but I cannot help it. I shall pack my bags in the morning and—"

She had intended to say more. Words, whole sentences, designed to indicate how she realized it was inappropriate for her to even look at him—yet not another word was uttered.

His mouth met hers in a deep and passionate kiss. *Timothy was kissing her.* Anne quickly lost herself in the heady sensations that his lips imparted onto hers.

Timothy Lexington, Earl of Clarcton, was kissing her.

More, his arms were around her, pulling her closer, and he broke the kiss only to capture her lips once more and deepen the connection between them. There was no going back from this. She would pack in the morning.

Further thought became impossible as Timothy's hand moved slowly down her back, cupping her buttocks through the silk of her gown, and Anne moaned, unable to help herself.

The kiss was broken. As Anne opened her eyes, it was to see Timothy pulling back to the other side of the sofa.

"Anne, I had not expected such a declaration," he said. "I...I hardly know what to..."

Anne swallowed. "You do not need to speak. I expect no—"

"I want to give you something." Timothy's voice was soft now, but his gaze was no less penetrating. "Something only an earl would give his countess."

Anne's heart fluttered. "I require nothing from you."

"I know," he said softly. "But I want to give it to you. Something that has no price. Something worth far more than words."

Anne gasped as he took her hand in his, his fingers entwining with hers. As she looked down, she saw a future, a future she wanted desperately, but knew she could not have.

He rose, pulling her upward as he started towards the door.

"Where are we going?" Anne lowered her voice as they entered the corridor, though no one was going to hear her. They alone knew what would happen this night.

"You'll see."

Anne took comfort in the strength of his hand, the warmth of his fingers. Her body tingled at the connection. *What was she about to see?*

It was only when they reached the double doors of his bed-chamber that Anne realized what the earl intended.

Her hesitation was not spoken, but Timothy must have felt it. He stopped, looking deep into her eyes. "Anne?"

"This was not the sort of gift I had in mind," she said softly.

It was a wonder she was able to get those words out. *What did Timothy think he was doing?* He knew the rules of society; a lady should never even be kissed before matrimony, though Anne was not so childish to think that all adhered to that rule.

But to take her to his bedchamber…that could only mean one thing.

What would Miss Clarke think? More, what would she think of herself? Once she stepped over this threshold, once she allowed a gentleman to…to make love to her, there was no going back.

She would be ruined, forever, for any other man.

Timothy took her hands in his, and Anne looked into the face of the man for whom she would do anything.

Almost anything.

"Anne, I would never—I will never make you do anything you don't want to do," he said quietly, "but…surely a countess should end her evening of triumph in the bed of her earl?"

If she had never fallen in love with him, then this would be simple. She would merely laugh, throw it off as a bad joke, release her fingers from his intoxicating grip…

And return to her bedchamber. Large. Cold. Empty.

"I can make it safe." Timothy had evidently seen the hesitation on her face. "I can make it safe, so you do not—so we do not conceive a child. You are aware of this?"

Anne nodded mutely. Yes, it was impossible to be a member of the Earl of Allun's household without being aware of it. The French letter.

Her gaze met his; two pairs of blue eyes caught in each other. She trusted him, and walking away would be a mistake she would live to regret.

He had lied about his wife. Perhaps he still did; perhaps she was out there, unable or unpermitted to return. If only that could cancel out her growing passion. Anne knew it could be a step toward her own misery, but she could not say no to him.

"Let me love you, Anne," Timothy whispered.

It was hardly the declaration of love Anne wished for, but it was close enough. Every inch was desperate for his touch. She could not walk away from such temptation.

"Love me," she whispered.

How he managed to kiss her so ardently as he opened the door, Anne did not know. All her senses were lost in the kiss, the way his lips knew what to do to extract every iota of pleasure.

The room faded into the background as Timothy shut the door behind her and brought his arms more tightly around her. Her body was on fire, blazing for him, as his kisses trailed from her lips down her neck.

"Oh, Anne," he murmured.

Anne willingly met his lips when they returned to hers. There was no response possible other than clinging to him and wondering just how she would ever look at him again.

Giving herself up to the passion appeared to be the only thing she could do. Timothy was far more experienced, and Anne found she did not care. She would reap the rewards of a man well-practiced, and trembled as his hands moved to the ties of her gown.

"You are so beautiful," he whispered, breath fluttering on her shoulders as they were freed from the expensive silk. "So beautiful, Anne."

If she had time to think, Anne would have been embarrassed as the silk gown pooled by her feet—but she was not given the time to feel fear. Timothy's quick fingers were already pulling at her corset strings, and within a moment, his fingers stroking and lips kissing her body as he did so, he had entirely stripped her.

Anne swallowed. Here she was, standing before the Earl of Clarcton, utterly naked—and it did not feel wrong. It felt right. It felt like all her life had been leading to this moment, this moment of perfection.

"Anne," Timothy said in a jagged voice. "You are..."

It was only then Anne saw Timothy's expression. His eyes were wide, his mouth open as his fingers fumbled at his buttons in his haste to mirror her nakedness.

Growing in bravery, Anne leaned forward, wrapping her arms around his neck and pressing her body against his.

Timothy groaned, losing himself in the kiss for a full heady minute before pushing her away, fingers pulling off his clothes.

Anne gasped.

Well, she knew the mechanics. She knew where this was leading, knew what in theory was underneath all that linen and cotton.

But seeing the reality...

"Come here," Timothy growled.

Anne did not need another invitation. She stepped into his arms, and Timothy carefully laid her down on the bed, covering her body with his as he kissed her.

And what kisses. The passion was uncontrollable; he could not get enough of her, it seemed, and Anne willingly welcomed each and every one, her body glorying in the pleasure, aching for more yet not knowing how to ask for it.

But he knew. French letter found and secured, as Timothy entered her, Anne gasped at the shock, the pain and yet pleasure mingled together like notes of music that jarred with their sweetness.

Timothy paused. "I am sorry, I know it—"

"Love me," Anne breathed. It was a plea for his heart as well as his body, though he would not know that, but she had to say it. "Love me, Timothy."

His lovemaking was gentle at first, and as Anne found the pleasure grow, her breath quickening and her moans growing, Timothy grew the pace that brought her slowly but inexorably to a peak she did not understand but willingly embraced, her hands on his shoulders and her legs in the air until—

"Oh, Timothy!"

It was unlike anything she had ever known and perhaps would ever know again. As Timothy plunged into her, finding his own release, Anne looked at the man who had completely captured her heart.

"Christ," Timothy moaned as he fell beside her. "That was…that was…"

"I know," breathed Anne, clutching the bedclothes around her and wondering what on earth she had done. "I know."

CHAPTER EIGHTEEN

December 5, 1812

T HERE WAS NOTHING like waking up with a woman in your arms. Timothy had almost forgotten what it was like. The softness, the warmth. The sense that nothing could harm you as long as you had her in your arms.

It was a thin ray of sunlight that awoke him, but Timothy did not open his eyes. Not yet. He wanted to stay in this moment, this sense of peace and calm.

It was only when Louise was in his arms that he felt this good, this safe, this…this sense of belonging. Her shoulder just below his mouth, waiting to be kissed, her back curved into his, her sweet buttocks pressed against his manhood.

It was as though she had been made for him.

They fit together perfectly. If only—

Timothy's eyes opened. His mind, heavy with sleep, had finally caught up. *Louise?*

His gaze focused on the woman, utterly naked, curved into his. She felt different. Softer. More welcoming of his arm around her. The hair was different, too. Red, not blonde.

Heart racing, Timothy's mind flew through the last few

weeks, attempting to bring him up to date with all the nonsense he had poured out to…

Anne Gilbert. The governess. The prim and proper, beautiful, no-nonsense governess.

She was naked in his arms.

Timothy smiled. *My God, what an evening.* She had been startlingly beautiful, even when he had first encountered her in London, but last night…

Last night. The charade had come to completion at the ball—the dancing, the wine…

Timothy closed his eyes, took a deep breath, and opened them. Anne was still there, asleep in his arms, a smile on her lips.

Anne. Timothy swallowed. He had offered her his bed, and she had taken it. Their lovemaking had been tender. His mind still whirling, attempting to piece together the evening, Timothy had absolutely no desire to let go of the beautiful woman in his arms.

The beautiful, naked woman.

God, he could feel himself going hard at the thought of what they had shared last night.

He was in trouble. *Anne Gilbert: the governess!* He had never touched a servant before, never been tempted before—even if he had, he would never have crossed that line.

Never before, until Anne. By God, there was something about her. Something that drove him wilder than he had ever been before. Wilder than Louise, even.

"I am falling in love with you."

Timothy breathed out slowly, hoping it would not wake her from deep sleep.

Anne Gilbert. There was not an inch of her that was not beautiful—something he could never have guessed, even after seeing her in petticoats with Madame Griffon. When had he stopped seeing her as a servant and started seeing her as a woman? When she had appeared at the top of the stairs? When he had stolen that kiss in his study? Or outside her bedchamber when he had craved entrance?

Timothy swallowed. *No, he could not lie to himself.* It was Anne's character that had transfixed him, far earlier than her beauty.

Was it possible that he was forming a genuine attachment?

She was Frances's governess. In all the charade, the training he had given so Anne Gilbert could transform into the Countess of Clarcton, he had lost sight of who she was!

Of what she was. A servant. What did he think he was doing, taking advantage of a servant in this way? There she had been, pouring her heart out to him, and what had he done?

Bedded her.

Timothy closed his eyes. He knew better than this. He was not some foolish boy who had no control over his senses and no desire to do so. He was better than that; wasn't he?

His eyes snapped open. *Christ in his heaven, did he...*

A quick glance around and the tension in his shoulders dissipated. *A spent French letter.* He had, at the very least, been careful in that regard. It was not he who would bear the disgrace if she...if Anne was with child. No, it would be her and her alone.

The last thing he wanted was a permanent reminder of this lapse of judgment. Shame would not find a home here, not with her, and certainly not with him.

As though sensing the intensity of his thoughts, Anne shifted in his arms, still entirely asleep. Timothy watched her, waiting to see if she would awaken.

He hoped she would. It was surely for the best that they did not continue this mistake any longer. He should wake her, really, and send her to her own room to face the day with fortitude and a resolute heart.

He did nothing. *Fool that he was,* Timothy thought wryly, *he could not bring himself to untangle her from his arms.*

She belonged there. He could not explain it. It was...pleasant, having her there. There was something about this woman, something he could not put his finger on.

Timothy had never considered himself to be an aloof person.

He had grown up with his parents at a respectable distance, as all parents of their station, and servants who were respectful but just as distant.

He had thought Louise...

But he had been wrong. He had never felt more alone than with her, and then she was gone, and he had resigned himself to a quiet life.

But Anne? He did not want to be without her. Whatever it was, this burgeoning feeling that had nothing to do with his body, he did not understand it.

"I am falling in love with you."

Something quivered within him, something vulnerable he did not quite understand. Was it possible that despite the detachment he had attempted, the lies he had told, he had formed an attachment?

Timothy swallowed. *Perhaps...* A curl of red hair had become tangled, flowing down her back. He was visited by the intense desire to kiss it, to taste her skin once again, but he refrained with difficulty.

Whatever this was, these feelings he had, could they be controlled? Could he, in fact, play them to both of their advantages? Could this just continue as it was?

A governess for Frances and a lover for himself?

A live-in mistress. A woman always there, ready to please him.

Yet Timothy would not be keeping Anne merely for the benefit of her body, great though that was. No, he liked her. More than that, he admired her. He warmed to her as to no one else. Whatever emotion this was, it was strong.

Besides, Frances liked her. They liked each other.

Was this what he wanted? Could he offer her such a thing—would she understand, or take offense at the suggestion that she was merely to be some sort of...scarlet woman?

Something twisted in his stomach. The last thing he wanted was for harm to come to her. His actions looked rash now in the clear light of day. What if she had been discovered as his false countess?

Anne breathed heavily in her sleep, and Timothy smiled.

Something about her had grabbed hold, but the touch was gentle. Loving.

"I am falling in love with you."

A bizarre desire rose in his heart as a thought occurred to him: *marry her…*

It was madness. Making her position in his home permanent would give him access to her bed, that was true, but he could never marry her. A governess?

Timothy swallowed. Besides, he had hardly been honest, even after the charade she had pulled for him.

One day he would tell her the truth, the whole truth. One day she may find out. He trusted Mrs. Seton and all the staff, but there was no knowing what could slip out during an unguarded moment.

Anne moved in her sleep, turning to face him, and Timothy found himself looking into the face of a woman who had been both lover and anchor for him over the last few weeks.

His body responded as he knew it would. It was impossible to prevent it; he was only human after all, and the gentle curve of her shoulder promised greater delights if he allowed his gaze to move lower.

Timothy's jaw tightened. He could not stay this close to her, not unless he was about to do something he would surely regret.

In the light of the morning, Anne may find herself regretting what had occurred between them. He had made no promises, been careful not to do so, but she had admitted far more of her feelings in her exhausted state than surely she had wished to.

Best she was alone when she awoke. It would give her time to gather her thoughts.

Gently easing himself from her, Timothy slipped out of the bed without waking her. Anne merely pulled the bedcovers closer, feeling the absence of his warmth.

Grabbing his scattered clothes from where they had dropped in the early hours, Timothy stepped silently to his dressing room and closed the door behind him with a quiet click.

"Ah, my lord."

Timothy jumped, heart almost lurching out his chest as his valet smiled.

"I thought you would sleep in a little longer, my lord, and so I took the liberty of tidying some drawers," said Cecil smoothly. "Without disturbing you, I hope."

Timothy nodded, swallowing to rid his mouth of the sudden dryness. He had to speak. By God, he knew it would all come out eventually, but the last thing Anne needed was the entire servants' hall buzzing with the gossip.

"You did not see anything," he said, voice hoarse.

The valet frowned as he handed two waistcoats to his master. "I have no idea what you are talking about, my lord."

And Timothy almost believed him, if not for the knowing smile that creased his servant's face for a fraction of a second.

"May I suggest the blue if you are greeting anyone today?" added Cecil.

Timothy blinked. "The what?"

The valet indicated the waistcoats he had just handed him. "Waistcoats, my lord. Are you visiting today or accepting visitors? Or perhaps, recovering from last night's festivities?"

What he really wanted to do, Timothy realized, *was dismiss the man, turn around, and make passionate love to his daughter's governess.*

Damn and blast, what had she done to him?

"I think I will ride first," he said aloud. "Some fresh air."

Cecil nodded. "In that case…"

It took almost twenty minutes, Timothy would have guessed, for Cecil to dress him in his finest riding habit, and another five for his boots to be pulled on.

"Fresh air," said the valet with a smile. "Always good for the body."

Timothy nodded. "And for the mind, which is what I think

necessary. Good morning, Cecil."

He had stepped toward the door before his servant's words stopped him in his tracks.

"No, my lord."

Timothy turned. "You do not think it is a good morning?"

His valet smiled. "I do not think it is morning, my lord."

The stables were bustling as Timothy reached them, and he was forced to cut a conversation short as servants clamored to receive praise for the successful Christmas ball.

"Yes, as I said, very ably managed," he said to one of the footmen kindly, who was enumerating the great difficulty he and a few others had in organizing the coaches while the dancing was going on. "But I really came down here to ride, Poll, so if you will excuse me..."

Thank God Gordon knew him better than that. The stable master had Admiral already saddled and grinned at the master of the house as he mounted.

"You get out of here, my lord," he said in a low voice. "You look as though you're in need of the best company."

Timothy smiled. "My own, I suppose?"

The old man shook his head with a wry smile. "Why, Mother Nature, m'lord. Best company in the world."

Gordon was not wrong. As Timothy encouraged Admiral into a gallop, wind rushing through his hair, there was something of a renewing in his spirit.

This was his land. He was its earl, and there had been Clarctons here for at least three hundred years. He had a duty to it and the people who lived here, and that meant one thing.

Heirs.

Timothy slowed Admiral to a gentle trot as he approached the pine forests toward the lake. He had seen people's disappointment when Frances had arrived and not been a boy.

He had felt treacherous relief. *Not a son.* Well, at the very least, that would prevent him from compromising his principles when the child came of age. With a son, he would have had to make a terrible decision…

But there were no Clarcton sons. Timothy's fingers tightened on the reins. Louise was dead, and he needed to marry and have sons.

Why not Anne?

The thought had flittered in and out of his head before he could interrogate it, leaving him with a dazed feeling, as though he had been whacked over the head with a cricket ball.

Why not indeed? If one was only looking for a vessel with which to bear children, Anne was as good as the next woman. But he wanted more than that, always had. Anne *was* more than that. She was vivacious, clever, far cleverer than he had initially given her credit for.

And she was a good governess to Frances, wasn't she? *Why not mother?*

Timothy knew he wasn't thinking clearly. As he and Admiral approached the lake, he could still feel Anne's touch on his chest, the way she had reached for him as she met her climax, as the desperate need to be close to him had overwhelmed her.

His own body vibrated with the memory. She was…she was a distraction. He could not permit himself to be so overtaken by the temptation.

A temptation he should have resisted last night.

"Ah, my lord!"

Timothy looked up, lost in his thoughts, and saw Miss Merriweather. Slowing Admiral, he thought bitterly if he had been five minutes quicker—or slower—he would have missed her.

It would be churlish to ignore her now, so he waited for Miss Merriweather to approach.

"I wouldn't have thought you would be out here today," she gave as a greeting, pulling up her mount just a few feet from his own steed.

Timothy smiled mechanically. "Really, Miss Merriweather? Why?"

Miss Merriweather smiled, too, but it was different from

normal. As though all the warmth had been taken from it. "I expected you to be up quite late last night. For the ball."

It was strange indeed, her morose tone under that smile. *What did she mean by it?*

It was only when she spoke again that Timothy understood.

"Now I have met your countess, and…and what a woman she is," said Miss Merriweather in what she evidently thought was a light note. "I can see why you have been so loyal to her, though she was away for so long. She is quite a woman."

Timothy smiled. *Well, it was precisely what he wished to occur, wasn't it?* He wanted the misses of society to leave him alone, consider him off-limits due to his wife.

Anne had played her part to perfection. Perhaps too well.

Miss Merriweather, at least, was evidently convinced. "I saw the way you looked at her, my lord. I am not one to come between two people who love each other."

Timothy's smile faded. He had not been acting. What had Miss Merriweather seen?

"Yes," he said, more for something to say. "My wife is truly remarkable."

Miss Merriweather nodded, her horse stepping to the side out of nervousness and her hand moving down to pat her horse's neck comfortingly. "I still do not quite understand why she was away so long, but now she is back. You must be overjoyed."

Timothy's mind slipped back to his bedchamber, where a naked Anne slept. "Yes."

God, if everyone knew the truth; if they realized the countess they had all been so impressed with was merely a governess, a woman he had picked up in London who bore a remarkable resemblance to the woman they had met once a few years ago…

He would never live it down.

"The countess is a special woman," he said to fill the silence.

It was rather odd, describing her as 'the countess,' and not using her name. *Anne Gilbert.* He had wished for a governess with discretion, and by God, he had got it—and more.

But the secret had to stay with them. There was no possibility that he would ever admit it, and certainly not to Miss Merriweather, who was known throughout Clarcton as a lover of gossip.

"You are extraordinarily loyal, you know."

Timothy's head jerked up. Miss Merriweather had a wry smile, something more akin to what he was accustomed to—yet there was something sad playing about the mouth.

"Loyal?" repeated Timothy.

"I had heard rumors...well, not even rumors. Whispers," said Miss Merriweather, her face pink. "I admit I gave them credence, as she was away so long. Whispers she had been disloyal to you, my lord."

It was all he could do to keep his face straight. *So, only whispers had left the castle about Louise's treachery, then?* That was remarkably good fortune. *If Miss Merriweather knew the truth.*

"I am always loyal to those who are loyal to me," he said aloud, and then despite himself, he added, "and the countess is a woman of discretion."

Well, it was true. Even if it was their private joke that Miss Merriweather could not understand.

Yet, she seemed to understand something he had not intended to communicate.

"You love her," she said simply, a wistful expression on her face. "I will not come between you. May I one day be blessed with such a marriage. Good day, my lord."

Without another word, she had nudged her mare onward.

Timothy expected his ego to be flattered by such a statement, for while Miss Merriweather was irritating, she was a pretty thing. Yet his heart was entirely untouched. When he looked within, when he attempted to decipher the feelings storming in his soul, all he found was...

Anne.

It was a cold, sudden thought, and it rocked him to the core. *Anne.* What was he supposed to do with the realization that his governess—governess!—had claimed his heart?

A desire to be with her overwhelmed him, unbidden but unarguable.

"Come on, Admiral," he said quietly, nudging his stallion forward.

It took half an hour to return to the castle. Gordon was waiting.

"You are back sooner than I had thought, my lord," he said cheerfully.

Timothy nodded. "Yes," he said with no explanation.

His riding boots stamped and echoed in the side hallway as he entered his home. For the first time, he felt like a stranger. *Where was she?* Would she accept his intrusion if she was still in the bedchamber—or was it more likely that she had retreated to her own rooms?

A giggle echoed down the corridor. "But if we are monkeys, then what will we eat?"

"Bananas!" came Frances, as laughter rang out.

A soft smile spread across Timothy's face. His feet took him down the corridor, leaving a trail of mud no doubt for Mrs. Seton to discover, toward the source of all the noise.

There they were. The door was ajar, and he watched as Anne, dressed once again in her simple, plain governess gown, was leaping about the room, waving her arms around like a monkey making the most ridiculous faces.

Timothy smiled, but it was nothing to Frances's response. She giggled wildly as she attempted to follow her governess's movements around the room.

"I'm a monkey!" she cried happily, her eyes bright and affixed on Anne.

Timothy watched them, the two women in his life who had captured his heart in entirely different ways.

This could be your life, a small voice whispered. *Frances happy, Anne with you.*

If you want it, you have to take it.

"And here's Papa Monkey!" he found himself crying, stepping into the room.

Frances squealed with joy and rushed over. "I'm a monkey, Papa!"

"I can see that," said Timothy with a laugh, pulling her into his arms. *By God, she was getting big.* The day would soon come when he would not be able to lift her. She was growing so fast.

"And Anne is a monkey, too!"

Timothy looked at Anne, and her cheeks were seared with color. "Is she indeed?"

Anne swallowed. "Good afternoon, my lord. I must thank you for a lovely day yesterday."

"And the evening?" inquired Timothy with a raised eyebrow. *Why did it do his soul good to see her blush?*

"Yes, the ball was wonderful," she said a little defiantly.

Timothy allowed Frances to slip to the floor, and she continued racing around the room being a monkey.

"And did you enjoy," Timothy asked in a low voice, taking a step closer to the woman setting his body on fire, "the finale?"

Anne's cheeks flushed even darker. Her eyes darted to Frances before responding quietly, "You know I did."

Pleasure rushed through Timothy's heart. *God, he could not remember the last time Louise had ever expressed joy in their lovemaking.* Now he thought about it, he could not remember her expressing joy in anything.

He had never been so lonely as when Louise had been here. *But the moment Anne had stepped across his threshold...*

"It must not happen again, of course."

Timothy snapped back to the woman before him. Her gaze was now truly defiant, her cheeks cooled, and her stance strong.

"Not happen again?" he repeated. "Why not?"

There was an iron-clad certainly in her gaze which Timothy had not seen before.

"You are asking me to be your...your M-I-S-T-R-E-S-S," she spelled out, glancing at Frances. "Aren't you?"

If only the answer would naturally come to his mouth. Timothy stared, unsure how to respond. *What was he asking?* There was no chance of offering matrimony.

"I don't know," he said finally. "'Tis complicated."

"I find it difficult, never knowing when I am to be your countess again."

"I don't know what this is," Timothy confessed. God, he felt so vulnerable saying this to her. How did she have this ability to draw the very best from him?

Anne shook her head. "Neither do I."

Timothy wanted to reach out and take her hand, but he knew it would be a mistake to do that. Once he touched her again...

"I must be honest with you," he said instead—anything to distract him from the growing desire. "Usually, with people of my rank...well, you'd become...that...until I tired of you, and then I'd get rid of you. Pension you off somewhere."

He thought for a moment that she had taken offense at his words, but then she nodded.

"Miss Tilbury."

"Now, come on," protested Timothy, slightly hurt at the comparison. "I would never treat you like old Marnmouth did her! The blaggard didn't—this would be different!"

"So, you are asking me?" Anne stepped closer, raising his blood pressure, and glanced at Frances before she continued. "You are asking me to be your mistress?"

Timothy knew he had gone too far; he felt it in his bones, but in case he hadn't, it was clear on Anne's face.

"Look," Timothy said hastily. He had to say something, ensure she knew he had not meant... "Anne, there are no expectations from me. Just...just hopes."

Why did he so desperately hope she would smile, that she would agree to whatever he wanted? God, he craved her, but not under any circumstances. If she wanted a ring on her finger, then she was going to be disappointed.

"I will have to think," she said quietly. "Do you need—I

mean, how much time do I have to think?"

"I would never…" Timothy took a deep breath. How could he explain this? "Your position in this household, it is separate to any hopes I have."

Anne's piercing gaze affixed him once more, and he found he could not speak. *Damn and blast it, he was an earl!* He should not be so swiftly overwhelmed by this woman, any woman!

"I know," she said softly into the silence. "I trust you, and I know you would not do anything against my will, nor hold my position here as governess over me to exact what you wish for."

Timothy nodded. He did not play those sorts of games. Not after he had been such an unwilling participant.

"You have proven you are a-a good man," Anne said, stumbling over her words.

"I know that," he said instead, "but…well, uneven matches have been made."

As soon as the words were out of his mouth, Timothy knew he had gone too far. Anne gasped, her hand raised to her mouth, and Timothy felt a flush sear his own cheeks—a rare occurrence.

A trip down the aisle for himself and Miss Gilbert, his governess?

No, society would never accept it. He would never accept it; he could do no such thing.

No matter how much he wanted to.

"I did not mean," he began hastily.

Anne's smile flickered then disappeared. "Well, I think you need to decide that before you ask me anything else. *You* were the one who asked for the favor, my lord. I have performed that favor. The ball is very much in your court."

Timothy smiled. "You are right. I am usually quite decisive, you will be pleased to hear. It will not take me long to…I mean, it was mere weeks after I met Louise that I married her."

It was only then he realized he had never spoken her name to Anne before. *Damn and blast, he had been so careful—but that was her beauty, loosening his lips.*

She was smiling.

"What?" he said defensively.

"Oh, nothing," Anne said quietly. "'Tis just strange. My cousin was Louise. It's not a very common name, is it? I mean, I had several sisters and cousins, but the one closest to me in age was Louise."

Timothy nodded vaguely. "Yes, what a strange coincidence."

Frances chattered behind him, playing with some sort of nonsense toy, but he had eyes only for the woman before him.

Anne laughed, shaking her head. "Goodness, I have not thought of Louise in months—years, perhaps. That blonde hair, that petulant air. She always had to have her own way, did Louise, and the tantrums she used to throw if she didn't! She put Frances to shame, for sure."

No.

No, it was not possible. Timothy knew he was too sensitive, too conscious of the name Louise. *It was simply not possible that—*

"And then she disappeared!" Anne said with a wry smile. "Or at least, that was what she wanted us all to think. Louise was always one for the dramatic, and though her mother—my aunt, of course—looked for her, Louise evidently did not wish to be found. Ah well. Just keep going, as we used to say."

An icy chill crept over his heart and could not be staved off by the passion he felt for the woman before him—not when she was confirming his most terrifying fears.

His wife—his late wife—and Anne's cousin were one and the same person.

It was too much of a coincidence. Now he knew why there was such a resemblance between his bride and his governess. *Cousins?*

The blonde hair, the petulance, the tantrums, all of that could be mere coincidence, that was true. But Louise had disappeared from her family's life just as she appeared in his own, with no family in tow and no desire to make them known to him.

Timothy could feel his breath catching in his throat, and though Anne chattered on, he could not take in a single word.

"—sisters and cousins can be so close, but then we did live but five miles from each other…"

Louise and Anne were cousins. She was part of Louise's plan, of course, she was. It was too much of a coincidence…was Anne here on Louise's orders? Did she leave instructions with her family, if she was gone for too long, that this was where they could find her?

Anne was her cousin.

Bloody hell, he had been so easily fooled, so simply duped! He had allowed her into his home, his heart, his bed—and there was no possibility he could trust her now.

Timothy cleared his throat. *He had to get away.*

"Timothy?" Anne's face was pained with concern—*far too pained*, Timothy realized. It was all a trick.

She would never truly care for him. A governess, throwing herself at an earl?

No, it was all a plot—this was Louise, somehow, he did not know how.

"Is something wrong?"

"I-I…I am tired," he lied. Any excuse to get away, he had to make it. "I have something to attend to—I need to…"

He did not even finish his sentence, his voice trailing off as he walked away.

"Think about what I said," Anne called after him. "The ball is in your court, Timothy."

He closed the door behind him. He could not be in her presence a moment longer. Timothy reached the sanctuary of his bedchamber within minutes and did something he had not done in a long time. He locked the door behind him.

Falling onto the bed, he looked at the ceiling and tried to slow his frantic breathing. His shoulders were tight, his heart racing, and his stomach churned as he tried to make sense of all he had just heard.

Anne was Louise's cousin. Was it possible that this was a true happenstance, or was Louise trying to control him even from the grave?

CHAPTER NINETEEN

December 6, 1812

ANNE DREW BACK the curtains of her bedchamber window and looked out over the heavy snow which had appeared overnight. There would be no parkland walk today, and any servants who wished to contradict their master's approach to church would find it a difficult walk.

She did not move from the window. Her gaze was unseeing, her mind too utterly distracted by thoughts she had been unable to ignore.

It was only as the flush of desire had seeped away yesterday that Anne had realized what she had done.

Betrayed herself. Lost her innocence to a man who had heard her declaration of love and yet said nothing in return.

Of course, he did not. Why would an earl say anything of the kind to you?

"You are so beautiful. So beautiful, Anne."

She could not dwell on that now. She would have plenty of time to run over and over that evening, as she had done every evening since.

Timothy had his chance to offer her something, and other than that stilted conversation in the nursery, which had ended rather painfully unresolved, he had said naught of love, or devotion, or affection.

"You are asking me to be your mistress?"

Anne smiled sadly. She had been given a taste, just for one evening, of what it would be to be Timothy's wife—and she had found it so delicious, it was painful to think she would never savor it again.

Being his mistress…it was a proposition she would have found offensive mere months ago, and now here she was, actually considering it!

Such men took mistresses, she knew, but they were harlots, women outside good society. Reputations lost, they had naught but the men they spread their legs for to support them.

What would the servants think? What, and it was a terrifying thought, would Mrs. Seton think? Worse, what would Miss Clarke think?

Her heart ached at such thoughts. It was painful to remember she had forbidden a recurrence of what had been the greatest connection she had ever known.

"It must not happen again, of course."

She could not allow it to happen.

While Timothy had been kind and graciously not mentioned her foolish declaration of affections, which caused heat to rush through Anne's chest once more, he had not returned her affections. He had shown her the ways of love, but he did not love her.

A gaggle of figures appeared in the snow below her window. It appeared that some were venturing to church, then, though Anne had no desire for it. She could not bring herself to risk attending, however. It was too much to hope that no one would recognize her as the Countess of Clarcton.

No, she would spend an hour or two exploring the castle. It would distract her from the last few days, and besides, there was so much of the place that she had never stepped into. Exploring would help her mind to slow, her heart to relax.

Taking a step forward purposefully, Anne had descended the main staircase and walked through the Great Hall before she had any occasion to change her mind. She walked past the ballroom and resisted the temptation to go in there. She would be reminded of such happy and yet confusing memories of being in Timothy's arms. *Better she kept going.*

She had never been down this corridor any further than the ballroom, and when she had passed several doors, she opened one at random. Expecting to see a room, Anne saw to her surprise that it opened into a narrow staircase.

Another servants' staircase! She had believed she had found them all, and yet here was another.

Anne looked around. Well, there was no reason she could not take it. Stepping forward, she went up a floor and discovered a landing she had never seen before.

Did this castle ever truly end? It was starting to feel as though the place was infinite. There was a window, and Anne looked out over the forest, to what was, from what she could make out a lake, glinting in the meager, frosty sunlight.

There was only one door on this landing, and she stepped forward and opened it.

Her mouth fell open. It was a dressing room, and what dresses! Gowns of silk, of satin, of muslin, lace and embroidery and gold thread filled her vision.

The walls were lined with them, shelves open to the elements. Silks and gowns were folded carefully all along them, as though Anne had stepped into a modiste rather than a room in the castle.

She reached out a hand and touched one of the gowns. Now she was closer, she could see a thick layer of dust overlaid the beautiful material.

The place had not been entered in years. There were cobwebs in the corners, and the window was crusted with dirt. Every gown had the same gray sheen of dust.

Something glittered. On a dressing table was a hairbrush and mirror set. Blonde hairs poked out of the brush.

It was as though a woman, and Anne had a fairly good idea who, had stepped out of the room intending to return in a moment—and never had.

Anne's quick eyes saw a set of trunks just to the left of the dressing table, an incomplete set. The largest trunk, from what she could see, was gone.

There was a riding glove on the floor—a single riding glove.

Anne picked it up. The glove was made of beautiful brown leather. It was small, delicate. Definitely made for a woman.

A shiver rushed through her body. *So, Louise left in a hurry then?* She had not packed all her beautiful clothes, just one trunk. She had not even paused to pick up the dropped riding glove.

Anne swallowed. *What had Louise been running from?*

There was a door to another room, and Anne opened it curiously—only for her cheeks to flush.

Ah. Well, she should have expected it. Timothy's bedchamber was evidently the master's, and so this...

This was hers. The room was sumptuous, that was the only word Anne could think of. Silk, velvet. Pink everywhere; jewelry boxes on a dresser with diamonds and pearls pouring out of them; what appeared to be jeweled pins for hair; even face lotions and blush...

Beside the bed, which was large and covered in dusty silk sheets, was a champagne bucket filled with green water. There was a bottle in it, with two glasses by the bed.

Anne swallowed. It was rather like unearthing a forgotten civilization. Like traveling in time. Here she could see the last moments, perhaps, of the countess. She and Timothy had been here, and her stomach turned, drinking champagne in bed as they...

Well. She would be a fool to assume he had never bedded his own wife. *Where else did she think Frances had come from?*

Of all places in the castle, she would have expected a portrait of the countess, Louise, to be here. But the only paintings were landscapes, presumably taken from life in the parkland.

There was, however, a small bookcase full of books—novels. Anne smiled. She and her sisters had always loved novels. Stories to lose oneself in.

Her fingers sought out one of Mrs. Radcliffe's, which had been a perennial favorite. As she pulled it out of the shelf, a creaking noise made her jump.

Anne turned to see a door previously hidden in the wall open, revealing a third room. Her heart was thundering, but she could not help herself. This was an adventure, wasn't it? A part of the castle perhaps no one in living memory had discovered.

Refusing to think what Timothy would say if he found her in such a place, Anne took a hesitant step toward the door.

This was a place of pleasure; she could see that. There was another bed, even more extravagant than the last, and there were paintings of people here. One of them was unmistakably Timothy, and the other…

Anne dropped the novel to the floor.

Louise.

Not Louise, the countess. Louise, her cousin.

Anne sat heavily on the bed, dust rising up in a cloud. *Louise.* What was a painting of her cousin doing here?

They had once been so close. As Louise had grown older, she had become less lovely, more irritating. Always petulant, always demanding her way. Anne had not been the only family member to tire of her demands.

She had lost touch with family five years ago, and now Anne found her portrait here? In the boudoir of the countess?

The countess…

The truth dawned in a fitful start, and she could hardly believe it.

Louise, her cousin…had married the earl?

Anne blinked, but the portrait did not change. There she was—Louise, her blonde hair pinned up, a pink gown subtly showing her beauty.

There was no chance she was mistaken. It was Louise. *How could it be anyone else?*

"'Tis just strange. My cousin was Louise. It's not a very common name, is it?"

Louise had married Timothy—she was the mother of Frances!

Anne's heart had stopped. Here she was, pretending to be a woman she thought she did not know, and all along—it was her cousin?

It was all she could do not to lose sense of her surroundings. Only when Anne placed a hand on the bed to steady herself and another cloud of dust rose did she recall herself and remind her lungs to keep breathing.

Did Timothy know? The very thought chilled her bones. If Timothy knew, why had he insisted he dress her up as her own cousin—a woman she had not heard from in five years?

And Anne saw the entire situation clearly, for the first time.

An earl she had never met had found her in London and brought her back to his home. He had paid her wages not to care for his child but to dress up as his wife—*her cousin*—his dead wife!

Anne shivered. *What had happened to Louise? What was going on?*

Panic soared through her veins, utterly overwhelming any ability to think clearly. How could she trust him, Timothy, now she knew he had brought her here purposefully?

He had not just taken her into his home; he had taken her to his bed! How could she trust him, believe a single word he said?

Everything between them, every good thought, every pleasurable touch…

It was all tainted.

At the time, she had enjoyed dressing as a countess, seeing the world bow and scrape to her…it had seemed like a dream then.

It was a nightmare now.

"My God, look at you."

Anne moved toward the portrait, as though that would somehow make it less Louise. There was the freckle on the side of her nose that mortified her when they had been children.

Her stomach swooped. *What had happened to Louise? Was it at all possible that…that she had displeased Timothy somehow?*

With that thought, Anne halted. She could not think this way—she could not think at all. She had to get out of here. She should not be here.

Her feet took her out of the boudoir, the bedroom, the dressing room, down the servants' staircase, and across the corridor toward the servants' hall.

She did not want to be alone.

As Anne opened the door into the servants' hall, she was greeted by two faces: Mrs. Seton and Holt.

Anne's already frantically beating heart skipped a beat. *Of all the people…*

"Are you quite well, Miss Anne?" said Mrs. Seton. "You look as though you've seen a ghost."

Anne swallowed. *In a way, she had.*

But she was hardly about to admit to such with Holt right there. Her cheeks burned as she met his gaze defiantly. *She would not show him that she was afraid.*

"Nothing of the sort," she said airily. "I merely wanted some hot tea, that was all."

That was it: tea. Tea would make everything feel better.

"The master has not gone to church then?" said Mrs. Seton, who nodded at a maid who quickly went toward the kettle.

Anne nodded, not entirely trusting her voice. She lowered herself into a seat at the large servants' table. Her legs were not to be trusted either.

"I think he has gone for a ride," she said quietly. "With Frances. The girl has taken to it as no other child I have seen."

"Of course," said Holt smoothly. "Her mother loved riding."

Anne's lungs were sharp, full of needles, but she had to keep breathing. She nodded her thanks to the maid who placed a hot cup of sweet tea before her, and the boiling liquid did something that nothing else had done.

It grounded her. Stinging hot though the liquid was, it brought her back to herself.

"Really?" she said nonchalantly. "Louise loved riding?"

It was strange to say her name and know better than anyone here what she meant. *Dear God, Louise had married Timothy…*

Mrs. Seton glared at the footman. "You know it's not to be talked about."

Holt, however, did not seem cowed. "What difference does it make? She's gone, not likely to come back. And Anne's replacing her, isn't she? Aren't you?"

He asked the latter question as he turned his gaze back to the governess.

Anne shook her head. "I am sure I couldn't replace the countess."

She hoped that would be an end to it, but the maid said haltingly, "It is strange though. You do look very like her. I'm sure you've been told that."

Anne's cheeks flushed.

"Hmm," said the housekeeper begrudgingly. "I suppose so."

"You are softer though," added Holt, his eyes glittering. "Our lady was harder. No matter what we did, it could always be better. But then, as the mistress would say, just keep going."

In that moment, Anne knew without a shadow of a doubt. It had been her. Louise. Her cousin. There were coincidences, and then there was this. There was no mistake.

She sipped her tea, now starting to cool, but could not shake off the footman's piercing gaze. He was watching her carefully, as though waiting for her to react.

Anne did nothing but sip her tea, mind whirling. *Did he know?* Had Holt guessed there was more than just a passing resemblance between the countess and the governess?

What in God's name had she managed to get herself into?

CHAPTER TWENTY

December 7, 1812

HAD THERE EVER been so many thoughts rushing through his mind?

Timothy couldn't remember a time this overwhelming. In one moment, he was overcome with desire for the woman who was now holding him out at arm's length, and the next, he was wondering just how this had occurred.

Louise was Anne's cousin.

Timothy twirled a cigar between his fingers. He hadn't even lit it. His concentration was lost; his ability to do anything, nowhere to be found.

A shiver crept down the back of his neck as he recalled her body in all its glory, when she had permitted him to make love to her.

His bed had been warm, a place of joy. Now it was barren without her presence, the bed too large, too empty.

He had been worried at first bedding her would ruin her, cause her to regret the encounter, even though he had taken precautions, but instead...

Timothy's jaw tightened. Instead, it was he who had been

ruined. He who had suffered. He could not bear to be without her, and yet the complexities of those thoughts, of that over-whelming emotion, had not yet been untangled. Was Anne innocent, or had she and Louise conspired against him? Did it matter at this point? His feelings were real, undeniable.

What could he do? He could not offer her his hand, that would be madness. As far as the world knew, he was already married. To her. Anne. His countess.

And just in case it was not complicated enough, the specter of Louise hung over him, taunting him.

Timothy ended up daydreaming about offering her his hand.

It felt foolish now that he had not guessed the connection. Just one look, and you could see Louise in that face. They were the same.

Well, except for the important things. Timothy smiled. Anne was caring, loving. She took no nonsense. She saw through him immediately, had done the moment he had lied to her about the absence of his wife. She was honest. She was daring, pretending to be his countess before all those people.

Caring, loving, honest...all the things Louise had never been. And once he had made the connection between the cousins, he had immediately suspected the worst in Anne, condemned her without seeking the truth first.

Yet still, the question nagged at the back of his mind: did she know?

Timothy looked at the cigar in his hand. Christ, what was he going to do? Whenever he had a moment to himself, the question of Anne returned. What was he going to do with her?

His heart yearned for her. Every moment they were apart was a moment wasted. He had started to long for the Sunday evening dinners where she would sit, tantalizingly out of reach, giving a report of Frances and trying desperately both to catch his eye and to avoid his gaze.

He could not stand to be apart any longer.

Leaving the drawing room, Timothy entered the nursery.

The place was empty. Some soldiers had been left in a heap by the window, causing a brief smile that then faded.

Timothy passed a few servants as he crossed the Great Hall and wandered up the stairs to look for Anne and his daughter. Maids paused and curtseyed, the footman—Holt, was it? he could never remember their names, more's the pity—bowed.

He paid little heed. His mind was several steps ahead, reveling in the joy he would find in the schoolroom: the child he had accepted as his own and the woman who had stolen his heart.

The corridor was unusually quiet, and Timothy wondered just how the governess had managed to keep little Frances so calm. He did not knock on the door. *Why should he?* It was his castle.

When he pushed the door open into the schoolroom, it was to find to his surprise that the room was just as empty as the nursery had been.

There were the desks, books stacked tidily in a corner, the blackboard adorned with a poem.

Mary had a little lamb...

All very well and good, but where was the governess and her pupil? *Where was Anne?*

Timothy took another hesitant step into the room, as though by venturing further in, they would reveal themselves. The room was silent, other than his muffled footsteps.

A curl of concern wove its way around Timothy's heart. He had permitted Anne to take almost any license she required to teach and care for the child. But they were usually in one of two places. To find them in neither was jarring. *Concerning.*

His footsteps quickened in rhythm with his heartbeat as he strode to Anne's bedchamber. As he had once done before, he stepped inside without concerning himself whether his presence would be welcome.

"Timothy," said Anne with a smile. She was seated at the small desk, papers before her and a slight ink smudge on her cheek. "You find me writing a letter to Miss Clarke, though I admit the words do not quite—"

"Where is Frances?" Timothy interrupted. *Letter to Miss Clarke be damned.*

Anne blinked as though uncertain as to the cause of his rudeness. "Frances?"

"My daughter," said Timothy, the words tasting odd in his mouth. "Your charge. Where is she?"

Why did Anne look as though he was deranged?

"Why, in the nursery," she said quietly, turning to face him. "Timothy, what is—"

"She is not there." His words were shot out like bullets, accusatory, panicked. Timothy could not help himself. Why didn't Anne understand just how serious this was?

"I left her there, sleeping," said Anne in a calming voice. "Sleeping, Timothy."

A hot bitter panic was rising from his gut into his throat. "Well, she's not there now! Where could she be? Could she have wandered off, got lost?"

Bloody hell, he should have been less careful with her—taught Frances her way around the castle! What if she had wandered off and got trapped somewhere? What if a door closed behind her and she couldn't get out?

Anne had risen to her feet. "There must be a misunderstanding—did you check the entire room? She sometimes likes to curl up on the armchair behind the door, and—"

"Come see for yourself," said Timothy roughly, grabbing Anne's arm and pulling her into the corridor, ignoring her exclamations of pain. "You'll see!"

He was acting irrationally, knew blaming Anne was uncalled for—but his heart was cracking under the pressure of not knowing where his child was.

For she was his child. No matter her parentage, he had taken Frances in, raised her, and loved her as a father. Frances was his, and he'd be damned if anything happened to her.

"Where is my daughter?" Timothy growled as he half pulled,

half dragged the governess down the corridor. "Where could she be?"

"Timothy, let go of me. You're hurting me," said Anne, pulling her arm away.

He released her, glaring furiously. "How can Frances be safe if the one person who is responsible for her doesn't know where she is?"

Anne's mouth fell open. "How—how dare you suggest that—"

But Timothy could not think rationally. All reason had seeped out of his mind when he had realized neither he nor Anne had a clue where his daughter was.

"You are not taking care of my daughter," he said, words tripping out of his mouth. "You—you accept a salary here, and you are not—"

"I'm not going to listen to this," said Anne just as fiercely, sidestepping him and continuing toward the staircase without him.

Timothy gaped. "And where do you think you are going?"

"You can shout all you want," said Anne over her shoulder, "but we have to find—"

"Why are you shouting?"

Timothy's heart froze. A small voice had come from a doorway further down the corridor, past the staircase. A blonde scrap of a thing was holding onto the doorframe as though it was 'home' in a game of tig.

She blurred. It was only then Timothy realized he was crying.

"Papa?" said Frances.

He said nothing to Anne as he strode past her and scooped the child up into his arms, breathing in her comforting smell.

Frances. *His daughter.* In that moment, it did not matter whether she was his by blood. He would do anything for her, die if needed. The thought she could have come to harm…

"I don't know what I would do if anything happened to you," he said in a ragged voice.

Frances put her arms around his neck. "What is going to happen to me?"

Timothy almost laughed. *Such innocence.* "Nothing. Come on. Time for your nap."

"I just went for a wander," she said timidly as he carried her along to her bedchamber. "Am I in trouble, Papa?"

Timothy swallowed as he placed her on her bed. "No. No, you're not in trouble."

And just like that, all the tension disappeared, and she smiled. All concerns were gone, all worries forgotten.

"In you get," said Timothy in a hoarse voice. "Sleep, now."

He crept out of the room and closed the door behind him, leaning against it and closing his eyes. *It could have been so much worse. It wasn't. But it could have been.*

He needed to take a deep breath and calm himself if he wasn't going to lose his temper—though this was worth losing his temper over. *His daughter. His heir. A child, wandering about the place, anything could have happened to her!*

He had to keep her safe. He had almost failed at that once before. *Never again.*

The corridor was deserted, and when Timothy opened his eyes, he swiftly paced back to Anne's bedchamber.

He wrenched the door open. As he saw Anne, all the passion he felt and the fear for his child became tangled.

"Can't you keep control of one child?" he said, eyes blazing. "One child!"

"Any child can choose to get out of bed and wander," Anne protested.

She was standing by her desk as though about to begin her letter again. *Why? Did the fate of his daughter not concern her?*

Blood rocketed through his veins, heart racing, pulse throbbing in his ears. Timothy had tried to calm down, but he could not. Not when it came to Frances.

"I need to know I can trust you," he said harshly. "Can I trust you, Anne?"

"Trust *me*? How can I trust *you*?" she shot back, knuckles white as she gripped the back of her chair. "You married my Louise, my cousin, and now she is dead!"

CHAPTER TWENTY-ONE

HER VERY NERVES were stretched tight like wire, but Anne could not take back the words she had spoken—and neither would she.

"You married my Louise, my cousin, and now she is dead!"

The words echoed around the spacious room, or was that just her? Was she hearing them over again because she had thought them so many times, forced to confront the thought that he, the man she loved, could have in some way harmed her own flesh and blood?

"You married my Louise, my cousin, and now she is dead!"

The burden to hold the the statement inside had been too much. Now the words were out in the ether, and Timothy was looking at her as though…

Anne gripped the back of the chair tightly, the only thing keeping her affixed to the ground. *How could she continue to live in this house, this castle, grand as it was, with the burden of this suspicion on her heart?*

She could not continue living here, loving him, thinking she knew him, when in the back of her mind was the poisonous whisper she could not ignore.

Did Timothy murder his wife? Did Louise, her own cousin, her flesh and blood, come to a dark end at the hands of this man? A man she had already given herself to?

Was it possible the whole thing was a slip of fate? Anne tried to recall the exact likeness of the woman in the portrait she had stumbled upon. In her mind, the woman had been supplanted with her own memory of Louise.

She should have asked him in a calm, quiet manner whether he could explain any of this to her, but she had been unable to hold back. Not after such accusations; she had to defend herself—and to her shame, her first instinct was not to defend but to attack.

"Your cousin," Timothy repeated the words in a dull voice, with no fire, no spark.

Anne's stomach twisted. *Did he not have anything to say against the very serious accusation which she had leveled at him?*

"How can you accuse me of being a bad governess," she said, her voice shaking, "if you yourself have allowed someone to come to harm?"

She could not say the darkest thoughts. The idea that the man before her, that Timothy could have…

No, it was an accident, wasn't it?

"I would never allow *anything* to harm Frances," Anne continued, compelled to fill the silence. "The thought that I would—it is outrageous for you to think so! You should know me better than that!"

Her words were as heightened as her blood, but there was no escaping the conversation now. It had begun, and if Timothy would speak, they could have it out, one way or the other.

Either she would love him far more than she had ever thought possible, or…

Timothy stared. "Your cousin, Louise. She *was* your cousin, then?"

Anne nodded mutely. Why did he not just tell her what happened? After that fright with Frances which must have lasted—*what, all of five minutes?*—she was entitled to know the truth.

She had been asking about his wife, after all, from the very moment they had met. After all she had done for him; the care she had taken of his child; the lengths she had gone to preparing to feign to be his wife, lying to all who knew him.

Pretending to be the Countess of Clarcton could have gone very badly for him, it was true, but he was not the only one who risked their neck. What would have happened to her if the truth had been discovered?

Anne swallowed. *Was it possible that everyone knew?* That she was the only person in the Clarcton household who did not know the truth of Louise?

And then, only then, did Timothy's response jar.

"Your cousin, Louise. She was *your cousin, then?"*

He knew. Timothy had known she was related to his late wife, if Louise really was dead. Why had he not said anything?

"Yes, I married your cousin," said Timothy heavily.

Anne blinked. No words were possible.

"What a rather strange situation we find ourselves in," he said briskly. "A situation I do not think either of us expected."

The words individually made sense, but Anne's mind could not make sense of them. She had expected him to be astonished, to be amazed there was any connection between her and the countess, but by his response, this was not new information.

Had he known from the beginning?

"Y-You knew?" she spluttered?

Timothy shook his head. "Only when you mentioned her. It was too much of a coincidence that your Louise and my Louise were different people. Though I admit, I did think there was a strange resemblance when we first met."

Anne had thought nothing of mentioning her cousin; it had not even occurred to her to keep any information secret. What a fool she had been.

"And was that," she asked stiffly, "why you hid the painting?"

A frown appeared on Timothy's face. "Painting?"

Anne took a deep breath. "The portrait of Louise. In the pink dress, in the gold frame."

Understanding dawned on his face, and Timothy turned away for a moment before facing her once again. "No, that was nothing to do with you. I moved it when she died."

"Moved it?"

He nodded. "The blasted thing was in my bedchamber, and I had looked on that face too long. I could not bear to look at it—or look at her at all, by the time she…she died."

There was a bitterness in his voice Anne had never heard before. He had been flippant, irritable, and downright rude at times. But the fury pouring from his eyes…it was not the Timothy she knew. His gaze was pointed directly at her. As though it was not just Louise who had angered him, but that in some way, she was tainted by association.

As though she had in some way betrayed him.

"I couldn't look at her at all, by the time she…she died."

Anne shivered. Louise *was* dead, then. A part of her had wondered if she was elsewhere, hidden, preferred to be considered dead by her husband.

Her heart cracked. *Louise was dead.*

The question was, how had the terrible event occurred? Louise had always been a healthy child, a healthy woman. Anne could not recall her enduring much sickness at all, other than the coughs and colds everyone suffered.

Anne's gaze met Timothy's eyes, and the terrible question she knew she must have answered flickered across her mind again.

Could Timothy have been involved in her death?

She shook her head as though that would dislodge the question. She could not think that way. She had no wish to believe such a thing, sensational as it was.

Timothy…she loved him. Imperfect though he was, irascible though he sometimes could be, there was goodness in him.

But how much? How could you love someone if you did not really know them?

She had to know, for if she left this place with the question unanswered, her heart would be broken for the rest of her life.

"How did Louise die?"

"None of your damned business," snapped Timothy. "And if you knew what was good for you, you'd keep out of it!"

Anne saw his hands clench, his knuckles almost as white as her own against the chair.

This was all going wrong. Here they were, arguing over the death of a woman who had meant so much to them at such different times of their lives.

"It is precisely my business," she returned, keeping her voice as tranquil as possible. "Not purely because Louise was my cousin and therefore a blood relative, which any rational person would think is sufficient cause to be told the truth, but because I...because we..."

Her cheeks colored, and heat rushed through her chest to her neck. *Was he really going to make her spell it to him?* How could she articulate her love? Love now accompanied by two other conflicting emotions.

Desire, a longing to be by his side both in life and through his day.

But also fear. Here was a man she could not understand, a riddle she had never understood, and now it was vital she did. Her very soul, nay, her very life could be at stake.

Timothy's eyes met hers and seemed to see her internal struggle. He looked wretched, moving about the room with noises of impatience until finally he stopped and stared.

"'Tis a sorry tale, and sorry I am for the telling of it," Timothy said bleakly. "It will be sufficient to say I was taken in, entirely. Your cousin, and now I know the connection I cannot believe I did not further question the resemblance—well, let us say that she had a propensity for pretending she was well-born and no desire to tell the truth."

Anne swallowed. "We are ladies, my lord, though we were certainly not as high born as you."

"Ladies?" Timothy said scornfully.

"Yes, *ladies*," said Anne fiercely. "Daughters of gentlemen, that is what ladies means."

Timothy did not seem appeased. Waving aside her words, he said, "You know very well what I mean. I thought her the cousin of a duchess or the Right Honorable daughter of a gentleman—it never occurred to me to ask for particulars. One usually did not have to request proof of one's nobility."

Anger flared in Anne's soul, but she attempted to let it pass. This was not the time to lose her temper. Finally, after months in his house, Timothy was about to tell her the truth.

"By the time I married her, it was too late," said Timothy bitterly, rubbing his temple. "Only later did I see her for what she truly was. By then, she had what she wanted. She had me and my purse and the title that permitted her to do whatever she willed."

Anne swallowed. No one was perfect, and Louise had always been rather certain of what she wanted. She could almost remember those conversations from over a decade ago…

"Only a duke will do for me," Louise had giggled as they had walked to church one sunny morning. "Oh, to be a duchess!"

"But you might not meet any dukes that you like, Lou," Anne had said reasonably. "And what will you do then?"

And in the shimmering sunlight of her memory, Louise had winked and giggled. "Why, find one I can endure, and then mold him to my tastes, of course!"

Timothy waited for a response, but Anne was not sure she trusted her voice. How could she say, with any honesty, that Timothy was wrong about her cousin?

Louise had changed so rapidly in the last few years Anne had known her. The softness had gone, the gentleness. All that had been left was a delicate viciousness that almost guaranteed she would receive what she wanted.

"Louise was a sweet child," Anne said hesitantly, knowing she had to fill the silence. "But…but when she was older—"

"Spare me the lecture on her faults. I am all too aware of them," interrupted Timothy with a scowl. "Christ alive, I had to suffer through them for two years!"

And it was then Anne lost her temper. It was madness, and someone would hear raised voices, but in that moment, Anne did not care.

"It is not as though you are perfect, either," she said, leaving the safety of the chair and taking a step toward him, fury racing through her. "I would go as far to say that you are no more perfect than anyone, yet you sit in judgment!"

"Yes, I sit in judgment," said Timothy, taking a step forward in turn. "How else should I treat my wife when she betrayed me so bitterly, time and time again? She was no wife to me, Anne, and though I am a poor husband to her memory, I am a better spouse to her in death than she ever was to me in life!"

Anne gaped. *How could she refute such words when they were spoken with such passion and yet such painful candor?*

She could see on his face the cost that these words drew from him. He had no wish to speak, yet she was demanding the truth—even if it pained them both.

"I-I do not see what Louise could possibly have done," she began.

Timothy sighed heavily. "She took lovers, Anne. Many of them."

Anne halted. *Lovers?* Louise had Timothy in her arms, and she was willing to sacrifice the trust they had together by allowing herself to be seduced by other men?

"I..." she said, voice trailing away. Was there any response to such a statement?

"So many," continued Timothy darkly, "that I was never sure whether Frances was mine. I am still not sure, though I treat her like my own."

It was this, perhaps more than anything else, that made Anne's legs tremble. She took a step to the right and sank onto the bed, its soft, comfortable weight supporting her in a way her limbs could not.

Frances. The girl Timothy clearly doted on, the child he had just berated her about for in a mistaken moment…

The idea that Frances might be more her kin than his was shocking.

Frances was perhaps not a true Clarcton. It was madness. It was impossible. But why would he lie? The truth, if that was what it was, evidently pained him. There were lines of anguish across his face and a dullness in his eyes that told her Timothy was telling no falsehoods.

"You…you do well not to blame her," Anne said lamely.

Timothy laughed bitterly and strode across the room to the windows. The sun had set hours ago, the lamps throwing dark shadows and crimson light across the room.

"Who would blame a child for the circumstances of their birth? No, I do not blame Frances. If anyone, I blame you!"

"Me?" Anne spluttered. "What—what could you possibly blame me for?"

Timothy turned. "My…damn. My apologies. I did not mean you. I meant Louise."

Anne had never liked being compared to her cousin even when a child, but to be mistaken by the man she loved in an argument such as this…

"I am not her," she said coldly.

"Yes, yes," said Timothy, waving aside the words again. "Yet you can understand why the confusion is—"

"I understand no such thing!" Anne did not remember rising to her feet, but she was standing now. "I would never betray you like that! Every action I have taken has demonstrated my desire to support you, to care for you!"

How could she pour out her heart to him when he looked at her so coldly? Anne examined him carefully, desperate to see the kindness she had once enjoyed there.

It was gone. There was nothing there but distrust.

"How could I possibly know that?" Timothy asked bitterly. "Admit it, Anne, in some ways, we are nothing but strangers to each other."

Those words cut far deep. The idea he could look at her and see an acquaintance...

"I have served you," she said quietly. "I have performed a great favor for you, been trotted out as your wife, and you have taken me to your bed. We are strangers to each other?"

Timothy had the good grace to look uncomfortable before he turned back to the window. "I met you but two months ago. That is all."

"Something your kind, if you consider us so very different, is quite accustomed to!" shot back Anne with fire. "How many dukes or earls marry a girl after dancing twice in public and enjoying a private dinner with her parents?"

"This is not the same."

Anne laughed darkly. "Though we are strangers, my lord, since we are reaching not even the rank of acquaintances, I would say we have established I am no liar. Can you say the same?"

She had expected a raging reply at her words, which had coursed through her, desperate to spill from her mouth in a way she could not prevent.

But when Timothy turned to face her, there was a sad smile on his face. "I thought I knew Louise. I thought I knew when she was lying. And yet, right at the end, she lied to my face, and I had no idea. No clue at all. And then she was dead."

Anne swallowed. *It was now or never.* "How did she die?"

For a moment, Anne did not believe Timothy would answer. He stepped away from the window and around the bed, finally throwing himself onto the armchair that matched the embroidery on the bed hangings.

"A riding accident."

"I don't believe you," Anne found herself saying. "Louise was a good rider. A great one, perhaps."

Images flashed through her mind: wild summers and freezing winters during which Louise would go out on horseback and Anne, if there were no other horses to spare from her cousin's stables, was forced to follow on foot.

"No one is a good rider when going out at night, unprepared in a gale," snapped Timothy, blue eyes blazing. "No one is a good ride when running away with one's lover."

Anne gasped. The thought was so scandalous she could barely countenance it—but there was no hint of a lie in Timothy's face. Finally, he was telling the entire truth.

He looked stricken. Agony was etched across his face. "We found her body the next day," he said bleakly. "Broken neck. I hope it was quick. I never wanted her to suffer."

"It...it was you who found her?" Anne was not sure how she found the breath to speak.

Timothy nodded. "At the edge of the park, by the gate. She must have tried to jump it, and in the dark... Well. Her horse was still there, her trunk on the ground and..."

His voice broke, and it took him a moment to regain control before he continued.

"And Frances in her arms."

For the second time in their altercation, Anne sank onto the bed. "No."

Timothy nodded.

Anne tried not to imagine the scene, it was all too horrible, but the thoughts invaded her mind, making it impossible to ignore.

Louise, lying dead on the ground, with Frances in her arms—only two years old.

"She...she was trying to take her?"

Timothy nodded. "I was not her father, I suppose that was her thinking, and perhaps she was reuniting Frances with her true father. God knows how the child survived that night, but she did. I do not believe she has any memory of it."

"I do not have a mother, you know."

Anne swallowed. She may not recall that precise night, but there was no doubt in her mind that the child felt the loss of her mother.

"And then here you are," said Timothy, his voice hard. "Out

of nowhere, ready to be Frances's governess and my countess. You knew Louise had been here, didn't you?"

Anne shook her head, still numb after hearing what had happened to Louise. *Oh God, someone would have to tell her mother.*

"You *knew*. Did she write to you?"

"No," said Anne. "No, I had no idea. I had lost touch with her. She had lost touch with all of us. We did not know what had become of her."

"You want me to believe it is all a coincidence?"

Anne's temper rose. "It was you who selected me at the Bureau," she pointed out.

"For all I know," he shot back, "you had some dirty deal with your Miss Clarke. Was the entire place full of Gilberts that day?"

Laughter was the only recourse for her battered soul. This was all so ridiculous! Timothy had been duped by her cousin, and Louise should never have done it, but for the entire saga to end in death...was there any chance her end had been reached not by a misjudged horse jump but by his hand?

"You must have been angry when she betrayed you," said Anne quietly. "Wanted to leave you."

Timothy chuckled darkly. "Very angry. But not murderous."

Everything within her battled to decide whether she believed him. Timothy, the father. Timothy, the lover. Timothy, the husband to her cousin—her cousin who had died in mysterious circumstances, whose very existence had been hushed up.

She had to think, and she could never do that with Timothy in the room. Her body still ached for him, while her mind ached to be free of his hold, if only to think clearly.

"Please leave me," she said. "I...I need some time to think about all you have told me."

Was that anxiety in his expression as Timothy rose?

"I am not sure what you want from me—to leave, to believe you, to stay as your governess, to stay as your mistress, to stay as your..."

How could she finish that sentence? She could not bring herself to say wife as she stood mere feet away.

His gaze met hers, and a frisson of tension rippled between them. Timothy moved forward and tried to press a kiss upon her mouth—but Anne stepped back.

"I need time to think," she reiterated, unwilling to meet his gaze. "And sleep. I...I will see you in the morning."

Timothy looked as though he wished for more, but he stepped outside her room. "Good night."

Anne did not reply but shut the door behind him before looking around her bedchamber.

She had much to do if she was to away before dawn.

CHAPTER TWENTY-TWO

December 8, 1812

"MY GOODNESS," SAID Dewey with a faint smile. "What did the kipper ever do to you?"

Timothy looked up through irritable eyes. Little sleep and bad dreams when finally entering slumber had done him no favors that morning. The kipper on his plate had been torn apart rather than genteelly sliced.

"Hmmmph," he said in reply.

The butler raised an eyebrow as he poured another cup of tea but said nothing. The breakfast room was otherwise empty. *No one else to see him in this roaring temper.*

His jaw tightened. Well, his manners had always been maintained no matter what had occurred, even when Louise had left. Perhaps it was time his manners descended into madness.

"Will that be all, my lord?"

Timothy waved a hand irascibly, and the servant left him alone.

Alone. Christ alive, he had never felt more alone than last night.

"Admit it, Anne, in some ways we are nothing but strangers to each other."

"I have served you. I have performed a great favor for you, been trotted out as your wife, and you have taken me to your bed. We are strangers to each other?"

Timothy shut his eyes. *God's teeth, he had said some things last night...*

He placed his fork down. He could not eat another bite, not with his mind whirring and his concentration on his talk with Anne. His argument with Anne.

"You must have been angry when she betrayed you. Wanted to leave you."

Head dropping into his hands, Timothy could no longer ignore the fact he had been utterly unreasonable at times in their conversation.

"Very angry. But not murderous."

How had it all gone so wrong? He had only sought her out because he wished to see her, and then with Frances missing...or at least, what he thought was missing.

How could such desire transform into bitterness? Why did he speak to her like that, when he cared so about her? Was this his nature to lash out at those who mattered the most?

What prevented him from being close to those he cared about?

"How can Frances be safe if the one person who is responsible for her doesn't know where she is?"

Fear rushed back through his soul, reminding him just how terrifying it had been, not knowing where Frances was. The idea that she was somewhere alone, hurt...

Timothy shivered. It was a dreadful thought. His desperation to find her, fear clouding his judgment, had tipped him back into the habits he had sworn to leave behind.

He had accused Anne.

Raising his head from his hands, he looked out across the lawn, frosted and icy in the morning sun. *Anne, of all people! What had he been thinking?* That Anne, a woman he had only ever seen act kindly and moderately, would harm a child?

It was Louise. She had broken his ability to trust, had seemed to enter this house again through her cousin.

His discovery that they were related…ice had entered his heart, and only now did he see the consequences. Instead of a rational, calm conversation with the woman he was falling in love with, what had he done?

Timothy shook his head. *Hurled accusations at her.*

He swallowed. For all his efforts to leave behind the memory of the woman who had been first his obsession and then his burden, he had not succeeded.

Louise still had a hold of him all these years later. He was not free. If he had been, he would not have looked at Anne and wondered if she was truly a person to be trusted.

"It was you who selected me at the Bureau."

Timothy's heart twisted. God, he could see how his love for her—for it was love, he knew that now—had been warped by Louise's very memory.

Yet, she did not trust him.

"Why couldn't the damn woman trust me!" Timothy found to his surprise he had spoken aloud, a fist slammed onto the table.

"Did you say something, my lord?"

Holt, he thought it was, had entered the breakfast room with that sycophantic smile Timothy hated. He was an earl, not a prince. Still, the poor man probably couldn't help it.

"No, thank you, Holt," he muttered. "Leave me."

The footman bowed his head, but for a moment, their gazes met.

Timothy gasped. There was loathing there, vicious hatred like he had never seen.

And then it was gone. *Was it a trick of the light?*

"As you wish, my lord," said Holt as he backed out of the room and closed the door behind him, leaving his master in solitude.

The hackles on the back of his neck were raised, and the hand he had banged on the table was still clenched.

EMILY E K MURDOCH

By God, that was strange. *Holt!* He had probably spoken no more than two dozen words to him. He was on edge, and who could blame him? The woman he loved, though he had never expressed that emotion, believed he was capable of a most heinous act...

Though you gave her cause, whispered a bitter voice at the back of his mind.

Timothy sighed. *Probably far too much.* He had shouted, lied, kept the truth from her. Even when he had discovered she had a right to know what had happened, he had lied.

Besides, it was not like he could have done anything with those fiery emotions. His body may crave her, his mind may adore her, but Anne was a governess. He could no sooner marry her than...

Now he thought about it in the cool light of day, Timothy found he was unable to find many reasons to prevent his marriage to Anne.

The whole world believed her to be his countess already, after all. Would it not be a natural continuation of their scheme if she was simply to...well. Take on the role permanently?

The door opened. Timothy turned to snarl at the intruder but restrained himself.

"Ah, I thought you would be finished in here, my lord," said Dewey. "My apologies."

"No, no, you may as well come in and start clearing up if you wish," Timothy said heavily. "One of us should do our duty, at least."

It was impossible to keep the bitterness from his voice.

"If you do not mind my saying," said the butler gently, "you do not sound content."

Timothy barked a dry laugh. *Content.* When was he last content?

No, that was not true. A shimmering memory of Anne in his arms in the center of the ballroom, all eyes on him but his eyes only for her. The softness of her hands, the warmth of her arm as it curled around his neck…

He cleared his throat. "I thank you for your concern, Dewey."

The man nodded. "And what will you be doing today?"

"In all honesty, I am not sure," admitted Timothy, stretching under the table.

He knew what he should do: speak to Anne. He longed to be close to her and yet was unsure just how welcome his presence would be.

Had he burnt all his bridges? Had she taken irrevocably against him? She would be within her right. She had little cause to believe he respected her, and he must put that right.

"With your permission," said Dewey delicately, "I would remind you that you agreed to speak with Mr. Erskine today about the mining. I believe there is also a review of staff salaries that needs to be performed, and—"

"Oh, spare me," said Timothy heavily. "Forgive me, Dewey. I did not mean to be rude. But not today."

There must have been something in his tone, for the man's face softened as he nodded.

"Of course, my lord. Not today." The butler left.

God's teeth, he could not stay here. Timothy rose and left the breakfast room at such a pace that he almost walked straight into Holt.

"My apologies, my lord," said the footman quickly.

"Don't worry about it, Holt. I am still deciding what to do. My mind is elsewhere."

Holt raised his eyes to his master. "If I was you, my lord, I would not lose the second woman who loved you."

He had disappeared into a servant's door before Timothy could speak.

The damned cheek of it! So their argument had been overheard then—very little was ever secret in this place. But to think it was appropriate to bring up with his master…

Well, that man had a lot to learn.

Holt. He had been with the family what, ten years? He's been barely a man when he joined as an under footman. One of the servants most affected by Louise's death, from memory.

Louise. Unsure why, his feet started to take him along the path he had not trodden for two years. The route to Louise's private boudoir.

It did not take long before he was standing before the portrait. Louise smiled at him, head slightly tilted, that knowing smile dancing across those lips he knew so well.

He had loved her so much—or at least, what he believed was love. He had thought her perfect, yet the woman the world had seen and the one he had known had been so different.

Though they were related, she could not be more different to the woman who was now a part of his life, a part of his household. *Anne*.

Whenever he was with her, warmth overwhelmed him. He had forgotten himself, his irritability, his desire for solitude, his bitterness…

All had been washed away.

Timothy swallowed. This old room was nothing but a mausoleum to the memories of a woman he had believed would make him happy. *But had she?*

Perhaps for a time. It was Anne who made him feel whole, made him return to himself. After such bitterness, such pain, she was the one who had healed him.

He had wished for a governess of great discretion because he had so much to conceal. He had gained a woman by his side who was discreet, elegant, loyal. Beautiful.

Timothy sank onto the bed, eyes still on Louise's portrait. All the reasons he had concocted in his mind to forbid him from offering marriage to Anne…they faded away in the certain knowledge that not only did he love her, but she made him a better person by her love.

There was no reason they could not be together.

It was a heady thought, one that dazed him. There was nothing stopping them being together, not once they had resolved this foolish misunderstanding.

For that was all it was, a misunderstanding. All she had to do was consent, and a certainty rose in his stomach, searing his heart. She loved him, she had admitted as much. She had willingly allowed him to take her to his bed.

Besides, who would deny an earl? She had tasted briefly the joys of being a countess, his countess.

He would speak with her, apologize for the misunderstanding last night, and offer her his hand. It would all be resolved. They would be a family: himself, Anne, and Frances.

Frances. A tinge of pain seared his happiness. He had not seen her that morning.

From Louise's boudoir, it was only a few minutes' walk to Frances's nursery if one took the backstairs. To Timothy's relief, he encountered no one and opened the door quietly.

There was no one there.

An all too familiar feeling rose in his chest. Timothy looked around hastily—could he have missed her? *No.* She was not here.

No matter, he told himself, holding back the rush of fear threatening to overwhelm him. *Perhaps she is still in her bedchamber.*

It was with relief that Timothy found his daughter in her bedchamber by the window, soldiers in hand, still in her nightclothes. It was late, to be sure, but perhaps Anne had not slept well. He certainly had not.

"Good morning, Frances," he said with a smile.

Frances turned away. To see his daughter turn away, to re-fuse to acknowledge his presence nor reply to his greeting...it tore at the very fabric of who he was.

"Ah, I see you are playing with the soldiers," he said into the silence, stepping toward her. "We shall have to find you some girl toys to play with. These are for boys."

That gained a reaction. Frances glared, blonde hair tangled down her back.

"How do you know they are boy toys?" asked Frances, evidently unaware her papa had once been small just like her. "You never play with me."

It was such a deep criticism of his fatherhood that Timothy sat beside her, legs unable to hold him.

Bloody hell. She was right. He had ignored her for too long; first because she was so like Louise, then because he was unsure whether he had the right to care about her as a father.

He had to show her that he was her father.

"I know," he said softly. "But that is going to change."

Frances still refused to meet his eyes, gaze focused instead on the little men who would do her bidding.

"Frances," said Timothy quietly. "Tell me what is wrong."

Tears suddenly appeared in the corners of the child's eyes, and she said in a halting voice, "I…I don't want you to be angry with me."

Sweet relief rushed over Timothy. If that was her primary concern, perhaps not all was lost. There was time to repair the damage he had wrought by keeping her at a distance.

"I am not angry with you, Frances," he said solemnly, a gentle smile on his face. "I will only ever be worried about you if you do something wrong, and you have done nothing wrong. I was…I was afraid you were hurt, that's all."

Frances's face lit up. "Promise?"

"Promise," he said, leaning forward and kissing the child on the forehead.

His daughter placed her arms around his neck, and Timothy closed his eyes, struggling against his own tears. *His daughter. His child.* He had so much to do, would not risk losing her as he had done the mother. He would love her. They both would.

"And…" Frances pulled away to look into his face. "Is Miss Anne angry with me? I like her, Papa. I hope she stays forever."

A ripple of joy rocked his heart. "So do I, chit. Now, play with your soldiers. I need to speak with Miss Anne."

Timothy hesitated before he left Frances's bedchamber.

Glancing over his shoulder, he watched her play. So much innocence. Innocence he would do his best to protect without repeating the overbearing enthusiasm of his own parents.

He would make his own mistakes. He already had. But he would do his best by her.

All his confidence drained away as Timothy stood outside Anne's bedchamber.

He swallowed and knocked, quietly at first, but when he received no reply, he knocked for a second time with more force.

There was no response.

"Anne," he said quietly. "Anne, please let me in."

Timothy waited. *Goodness, she must still be furious.* He had allowed the situation yesterday to get out of hand. No wonder she wished to avoid him.

"I suppose I cannot be surprised you do not wish to see me," he said quietly, "after the way I behaved yesterday."

He would have expected a reply at that. He imagined her sitting by the desk, just to the right of the door, waiting for him to go away.

"Look, I spoke out of turn yesterday," Timothy said. *Christ, he could not remember the last time he apologized to anyone. Was it always this difficult?* "I should not have lumped you in with Louise."

Anne did not even deign to reply to that.

"I am sure you understand, though," said Timothy quietly, placing a palm on the door. Only this wood separated them. "You look so similar, so much so that sometimes...I thought I was going mad. To discover you were related—it was almost a relief and made me worry there was something going on I was not aware of."

Was that a noise he heard from inside? Was it possible Anne had risen from the desk and moved to the door? Was she right on the other side, waiting for him to say something that would finally appease her and mend the rift between them?

Timothy smiled. He could almost feel her presence. "You know, I was afraid to bring you here. Not you specifically, I suppose, but anyone. I thought…I thought you would discover all the worst of me, and you have. And yet, I find I do not mind."

He pressed his palm harder against the door. "Being…being open with you, being vulnerable with you…it's different."

Though he desperately wished her to speak, he was glad Anne was permitting him to continue. Getting it out without interruption was surprisingly cathartic.

"Anne, I…I love you." Timothy swallowed. "I think I have from that evening when we first kissed. I knew then, even if I didn't understand it. Did you feel it, too?"

That was the strange thing about silences. They could feel cold, distant—or welcoming and warm. If he was not mistaken, his admission of guilt and love had changed the temperature of the silence between them.

"Look Anne, I want to ask you to marry me. You will marry me, won't you, Anne?"

Timothy waited, but there was nothing. Now the silence grew prickly and uncomfortable; here he was, baring his heart, and Anne did not even have the decency to reply!

"Anne, I'm waiting for an answer," he said desperately. "Anne?"

He had waited long enough, surely. Timothy felt his impatience rise and gave into it immediately, lowering his hand to the door handle and turning it.

He stepped inside the room—the empty room. Not only was Anne entirely absent from the conversation he had believed he was having with her, but her trunk had gone. The bed was made, unslept in, and there was a folded piece of paper on the desk.

Timothy swallowed. He did not need to read it. He knew what it said. It was Louise all over again. Worse.

Anne had not decided to leave because she developed feelings for another. No, he had driven her away with his own pigheadedness and inability to listen. This time, it truly was his own damned fault.

CHAPTER TWENTY-THREE

December 11, 1812

A NNE HAD NEVER been a lady in society.
If her father had lived, perhaps she would have done. Perhaps she and her sister, and Louise now she thought about it, would have attended the Season in London, come out at Almack's if they had been fortunate to gain vouchers.

Perhaps then she would have been accustomed to the staring she was now receiving.

She had only been seated in the waiting room of the Governess Bureau for—*what, ten minutes?* Every one of those minutes had been clouded by the stares of others.

Four other governesses were waiting to see Miss Clarke. Two she recognized—one seated alone, the other with two governesses she did not know. Though they were strangers, they seemed to know her. The three of them were whispering together, not attempting to hide their conversations in muffled tones.

"But why is she here?"

"I thought she had gone to the Earl of Clarcton!"

"That was what I heard," said one of them, casting an eye over at Anne.

She could see them staring in her periphery vision but would not give the satisfaction of looking over. They could be rude if they wished to. She would not lower herself to their level.

If only she was not so tired. The journey here had been—she would not think of it.

"There could be a scandal all of someone else's making," said one of the governesses Anne did not know. "Perhaps the earl found himself in some difficulty and—"

"Oh, come now, you must have heard," said another in a crowing whisper. "You must be the only person in London who has not! His wife, the missing countess?"

"She went missing?"

"She turned up," said the governess who appeared to know all about it.

Anne struggled to keep her gaze forward. She would not look at them. No matter how much she was sorely tempted—the heat of their eyes on her boiled her blood.

"At a ball. The countess was an absolute delight, and everyone wondered why the man had kept her hidden away all this time," came the whisper. "Fishy, eh?"

"I am sure there is a perfectly reasonable explanation," murmured Miss White.

"Mayhaps we have the whole thing backward," whispered one of them. "Perhaps it was Miss Clarke who requested she return."

All members of the Governess Bureau held their proprietress in a mixture of awe and fear. *She was truly a formidable woman*, Anne thought, *and to be respected. Perhaps feared.*

"I don't think so," said one of them quietly. "She would have gone straight in if it was that urgent. No, something went wrong."

Anne's head drooped. *If only they knew.* It had never been her intention to fall in love. She had never expected to use her discretion for what was, in hindsight, a scheme of madness.

And now...

Anne swallowed. She would not permit herself to feel guilt over this. She had done nothing wrong, nothing but attempt to understand her master. But that did not matter. Her good name, her reputation, the only things she had left after a night of pleasure…it was all over.

She had always been a credit to the Bureau, and now it did not matter whether she had done anything wrong or not. The world saw her return to the Bureau and assumed the worst.

"Miss Anne Gilbert was always a fine governess," Miss White said softly.

Anne's heart stirred. It was good to know she had friends in some quarters, at least.

The governess who appeared to know all about it, who Anne could see from the corner of her eye was wearing a vivid plum pelisse, did not look so impressed.

"I heard from my mistress at the time," she said in a lower voice, so low Anne could barely catch it, "that the ball was impressive."

"She was there?"

The plum-attired governess nodded impressively. "Oh yes, and so was Miss Gilbert."

"Well, that is no great surprise," said Miss White reasonably. "I cannot recall the number of balls I have attended to keep an eye on—"

"Not to care for her charge, no," said the smug governess quietly. "As the countess."

There was silence in the waiting room. Anne hoped beyond all hope the conversation would end there; something else would occur, another governess would enter, or Miss Clarke would open her door and disrupt the entire conversation.

Muffled laughter erupted from that corner of the room.

"You cannot be serious!"

"As I live and breathe," whispered the governess impressively. "I swear it! They knew her when guests of the Earl and Countess of Allun. They couldn't believe it when they saw her!"

Anne could not prevent her cheeks from burning.

They had believed themselves so clever, so prepared. They had even practiced on the reverend, and he seemed entirely unaware she was not who she was supposed to be. The idea that anyone at the ball had noticed her trick—their trick.

All that discretion had been for nothing. All that hard work, for naught. Was the entire world laughing at Timothy? She could not bear the thought she'd brought shame upon him.

The scandal would soon break.

If only Miss Clarke would usher her into her office, she could be rid of these gossips. Anne folded her hands in her lap, the gentle movement reminding them that she was there.

They took the hint and fell silent.

She should leave. She must find lodgings for the night, and if Miss Clarke was busy.

"Miss Gilbert!" Miss Clarke stood in all her fury in the doorway. "You are not expected," she said in clipped tones. "You do not have an appointment. You are supposed to be with his lordship in the north."

"I know," said Anne hurriedly, rising to her feet and curtseying. "But I…it was vital that I spoke with you, Miss Clarke."

The owner of the Governess Bureau stared, her eyes narrowed, then glanced at her pocket watch.

"You have twenty minutes," she said, turning around and walking back into her office.

Anne swallowed. She was not a timid woman, never had been. No conversation between herself and Miss Clarke had ever been this fraught, however, and she had been unable to consider her approach on the journey.

Too much had happened. Too much that she was still attempting to understand.

Picking up her trunk, Anne walked past the staring governesses into Miss Clarke's office, closing the door behind her.

There was a strange tension in the air as Miss Clarke sat before bridging her fingers together and looking at Anne, who swallowed.

Had there ever been a Governess Bureau governess who had her contract cut short?

She could not recall any—none who had remained with the Bureau, at least.

"Sit."

Miss Clarke had not moved her fingers as she uttered the syllable, and Anne placed her trunk carefully by the door before seating herself before the proprietress.

All she had to do was keep calm. She had done nothing wrong, nothing in the ordinary way of things, at least. It was only now Anne wondered whether colluding with Timothy—with the earl, she must consider him—was not the first mistake on a very long path.

"Well?" said Miss Clarke raising an eyebrow.

Anne opened her mouth but then closed it again. Her thoughts ran so wild, how was she ever to order them in such a fashion that they could be comprehensible to anyone else?

Miss Clarke was not the most inviting woman to start a confidence with, Anne realized. She had never needed to before, but now she was faced with bearing her soul—and her faults—to Miss Clarke, she found the challenge insurmountable.

How was she supposed to explain *this*, whatever *this* was, to Miss Clarke? She was not exactly young, and any passions of youth were surely vague memories now.

Anne swallowed. Perhaps that was uncharitable. Miss Clarke was not old, but she was...*Miss Clarke.*

The stalwart of the Governess Bureau. The woman they respected and admired, who had built her own business. How could she understand the confusion of passion?

"Perhaps you arrive with a message from your master," said Miss Clarke, filling the silence. "Although I believe that unlikely, given the accoutrements you've brought with you."

Her gaze flickered to the trunk Anne had left by the door.

Anne's stomach twisted. It was worse than admitting a falsehood to one's mother. *How did Miss Clarke have this ability to inspire such discomfort?*

"I have not received your expected monthly report, which is unlike you," added Miss Clarke, finally lowering her hands but not her gaze. "Is that it? The earl is in town, and you believed it more efficient to deliver an oral report?"

Anne took a deep breath. The waiting was surely worse than the telling. Once she began, she would feel better. Where to begin?

"Not...not exactly," she said awkwardly.

Miss Clarke sighed. "In that case, you have no excuse for failing to submit a report. You know my standards, Miss Gilbert. They are considerable, but they are part of the burden and the responsibility of being a governess of this Bureau."

Anne nodded. In all the preparations for the ball, the desperation to keep her emotions in check, and her total failure to prevent herself from being seduced by Timothy...

Writing and sending her next report to Miss Clarke had entirely passed her by.

"I...I forgot." As soon as she spoke, Anne wished she had not been so rash.

Miss Clarke's face turned stormy. "Forgot."

"Not exactly forgot," amended Anne hastily.

"I should think not," said the older woman stiffly. "I do not expect such things from my governesses."

Anne nodded weakly. "I know."

If she lost her position here—worse, if the scandal was to get out... How could she explain she was no longer in the employ of the Earl of Clarcton without giving a reason why?

"Out with it!" snapped Miss Clarke. "I afforded you twenty minutes, and you have already wasted five."

If only there was a simple place to start. If only she had the luxury of a calm journey back to London, but she had been denied that from the moment she had left Clarcton Castle.

Anne closed her eyes for a moment, the better to concentrate, but had to snap them open as the memory of that rogue returned. She should never have trusted him. *If she had known then what she knew now...*

Secrets, that was where this had all started. Timothy had a secret, yes, but he was not the only one in the castle attempting to keep things quiet.

Some darker than others.

Why, three days ago, she had been entirely innocent of all of them. Timothy had revealed the death of his wife, how a scandalous love affair had broken apart his marriage...

Anne had been shocked, true, but she had assumed she had heard the worst.

Yet just a few hours later, when she had crept to the servants' hall with her trunk, it had been Holt who was there.

"Why, Anne," he had said with surprise, throwing down the newspaper he had been reading. "And what are you doing up at such a time of night?"

She had hesitated. She had hoped to find Dewey, or at a push, Mrs. Seton. Holt was not a man she wished to spend any time longer with than was strictly necessary, but she had to leave. Holt, though abhorrent, was the driver of his lordship's carriage.

"I need to return to London, immediately," she had said in a low voice, as though frightened she would be overheard. "Is...is there a way to get to the turnpike, down the road?"

"You could walk it, but it's nigh on five miles, and with that trunk, I don't think you'll get there fast," Holt had said with a wry smile. "Why don't I saddle Captain to the dog-cart, and take you? It'll be but twenty minutes, all told."

Anne had hesitated then. *If she could have gone back and warned herself...*

Things would have been different. But they had happened now. Hindsight was not gifted to those who would make best use of it.

Her mind returned to that terrible moment in the side corridor. Holt had tried to...but Mrs. Seton had given him short shrift, and he would surely not be so rash as to try it again.

"Thank you," she had said with discomfort. "That would be…well, thank you. Now?"

Holt had jumped up. "You wait by the stables, and I'll bring him round."

Captain was one of the oldest horses in the stables, Anne remembered. He was a grand old horse, a gentleman of a horse, and Anne had lifted her own trunk up onto the dogcart without too much trouble. But as she turned to hoist herself—

"Now then, you'll want to be up at the front with me," said Holt.

Anne had gasped. In the darkness of the night, she had not realized he was so close. "No, I am perfectly happy to sit in the—"

"Nonsense," Holt had said comfortably. "You're not baggage, Anne, you're the governess. Come on, we can be there in fifteen if we hurry. You going to wait there all night?"

She was seated beside him with the cart rumbling underneath them before she knew it. Perhaps it was all the pain and emotional confusion after her row with Timothy.

Perhaps that had warped her ability to tell there was something wrong. She should have known, then. *Should not have trusted him.*

"So where are you going?" he said companionably in the darkness.

And Anne had swallowed and said, "Just going."

Holt had laughed at that. "I thought you would."

Though she could barely see him in the darkness, Anne had glanced at him. She had never considered him particularly a gossipy man, but she must have been wrong. Someone must have heard them and told him, or he heard them himself.

Even in the coldness of the wintery night, her cheeks flushed. "What do you mean?"

"'Tis the same with all women," Holt said as though he were an expert. "Women cannot stand him. They cannot bear to suffer his company."

Though no name was spoken, Anne knew precisely who he meant.

"It is not because of him, not at all," she said defensively, untruthfully. "It is because of her. Louise."

He had chuckled as the cart moved off the smooth driveway and onto the public road. "I knew it. You did know her, then? Sister?"

Why, oh, why had she continued on with such a conversation? "Cousin."

"By God, I should have known," Holt had crowed into the darkness. "I should have bedded you just as I bedded her. Would have been nice to get the set—unless you have sisters?"

The next few moments were a blur, now Anne looked back and attempted to recall them. *Horror, that was her primary emotion. Horror and fear.*

"God, you didn't know?" Holt laughed. "Yes, 'twas I cuckolding the earl. I would have thought Mrs. Seton might have told— but there it is."

And Anne had swallowed and wondered whether the items in her trunk were really worth her life. *Was that what was about to happen?* Had Holt agreed to take her only to take her innocence— to ravish her? If she jumped from the dog cart now—

"Now, Anne, don't be offended," Holt had said, his voice losing its merriment. "I thought you had guessed, truly. 'Tis not as though I have been coy for my affection for you."

How had she been so stupid? Of course he had. If Mrs. Seton had not interrupted him, what would have happened? Would he have taken his fill, only to abandon her like Louise?

Or worse. Anne's blood had chilled, despite the warmth of her pelisse. She was seated beside a terrible man, and only now did she realize the danger she was in.

"Come here."

Holt had dropped the reins; he must have done, for Anne found his hands had grasped her arms and pulled her into a disgustingly wet kiss.

A none too gentle shove pushed him back.

"How dare you," she had said coldly. "You may deposit me here, and I shall say no more about it."

If only she had been stronger, wiser.

Holt had just laughed. "Oh, give over, Anne. You're no fine lady, and most find they prefer me rather than the master. The question is, does he know Frances is mine, not his? One day I'll tell him, just to see the look on his—"

She had slapped him then. She had felt glorious after the ringing noise and the heat in her hand, but Holt had turned to her with an expression she hoped she would never see again.

"Get out."

She had not needed telling twice. Swinging her arm around painfully to grasp the handle of her trunk, Anne had half stepped, half fallen off the dog cart.

Even here, now, in the safety and warmth of Miss Clarke's office, Anne found her blood was cold. *To think what might have happened…*

Yet it did not. She had made her way to London, and she was never going back.

"Miss Gilbert, are you quite well?"

Anne jumped. She had scarcely remembered where she was. Miss Clarke sat opposite her, expectantly waiting.

She needed to focus. Though the whole story could never be told, no one would ever hear it from her lips, she could not remain silent.

Anne cleared her throat. "I think you are going to be angry with me."

Miss Clarke leaned back in her chair. "Perhaps, but 'tis difficult to tell with such little information. Why don't you tell me all about it?"

Even then, Anne hesitated. *To tell Miss Clarke even half the truth of what she had experienced at Clarcton Castle could…well, make it rather difficult for Timothy.*

She had no wish to ruin him.

"I am concerned the earl has done something wrong," she said slowly. "I certainly have. I think. It did not feel wrong at the time."

Was it possible Holt had killed Louise? Could the accident have been just that, an accident?

Knowing what to believe, knowing what the truth was, it was not something Anne had ever worried about before. Life had been simple, and when small events occurred that needed never to be spoken of, she never had.

A governess of discretion, that was what the Earl of Clarcton had wanted. Would she be betraying him in a different, though no less powerful way as Louise had done if she revealed the scheme he had asked her to join?

"I—well, I was afraid it would come to this," said Miss Clarke with a heavy sigh.

Anne's heart leapt. "What? You…you know?"

"You make the entire thing sound so sordid, Miss Gilbert," she said distastefully. "Besides, the Earl of Clarcton himself was afraid that this would happen. I believed it could be otherwise."

It was all Anne could do to prevent her mouth falling open in complete astonishment. Timothy was a genius indeed if he could have predicted such a convoluted outcome!

"How on earth did Timothy—did the earl," Anne said, cheeks flushed, "know I would return to you?"

"Well, something of this sort," Miss Clarke said, waving a hand. "That was why he told me all about it before he examined you."

A rather uncomfortable heat was rising up Anne's body. "Told you all what?"

Was it possible for anyone to tell her truth, the whole truth? Was the entire world in on the joke when she had been left outside in the cold?

"Why, the tragic occurrence of the countess's death, of course," said Miss Clarke calmly. She bridged her fingers again, looking at Anne closely. "No man wishes his wife's passing to be the only subject of conversation for the rest of his life, so we agreed we would keep it between us."

Anne nodded, numbness spreading across her heart. It all felt rather convenient. What was to stop Timothy feeding Miss

Clarke the same lies he had fed everyone else—that he had, for a time, fed her?

"Louise Lexington had a reputation," said Miss Clarke suddenly. "You would not know that. She moved in different circles to us, but I keep an ear out. For the Bureau, of course."

Even amongst all this, Anne stifled a smile. "Naturally."

"Her death, running away with another man..." Miss Clarke took a deep breath. "I am rather unconventional, I think. I do not believe every marriage is a success and therefore that everyone should be forced to remain in that marriage. But I do think she went about it a bad way, and it had a bad result. The poor child. The poor man."

Anne nodded but could not help herself saying, "And...and you believe him? You believe Timothy—the earl told you the truth?"

Miss Clarke examined her over her fingertips. "My dear woman, what does he have to gain by lying?"

Anne's gaze dropped to her hands. "It's just...spending time with him, the earl, I mean...I started to think..."

Heat was flushing through her body. *A governess of discretion, indeed.* Here she had been so proud of herself for keeping her mouth shut in the past, and what did she do when presented with a potential secret?

She had gone out of her way to unmask it, of course. She had not respected his privacy, not believed him when he said she knew all she needed to know.

"My dear Miss Gilbert," Miss Clarke said stiffly, dropping her fingers, "I believe you have gained ideas far above your station."

Anne swallowed. *So she had heard about the countess charade, then.*

"If you think your appointment to the Clarctons—was designed by the earl to attract you, you are wrong, my girl," said Miss Clarke. "Spending time with him indeed, you should have been concentrating on your charge! Who do you think you are? No dowry, no title, no name of significance! You have got into your own head, seen shadows where there aren't any."

Anne's gaze dropped to her lap again.

"Really," sniffed Miss Clarke. "Spend time with him, indeed! The earl would never give the impression he was interested in you, I am sure. He would have to really and genuinely care for you for that to happen. An earl and a governess? Only if he truly loved you would he ever give a hint of such a thing!"

A rush of warmth spread across Anne's body.

"An earl and a governess? Only if he truly loved you would he ever give a hint of such a thing!"

He did. Timothy loved her. He had invited her into his bed, into his life, and when they had made love—well, it was more than just lovemaking. He had needed her, craved her, wanted her.

She had tasted it on his skin, felt it in his touch.

Anne found a smile had crept across her face. *Would Miss Clarke ever realize the power of her words?* Just when she had felt so lost, so unsure, Miss Clarke had reminded her of the one thing that truly mattered.

How much they loved each other. *She and Timothy.*

He had already been abandoned by a woman once and had spent the following years trapped in his own home with a child he could not bring himself to love, too embarrassed to tell the truth, too tangled in his lies to come clean.

Anne had turned his world upside down, had fallen in love with him...and then gone.

What had she been thinking?

"Ah," said Miss Clarke with a smile, interrupting Anne's wild thoughts. "I can see you are reconsidering."

"I have to go back," said Anne, rising to her feet. "This moment."

"Excellent," Miss Clarke said as she, in turn, rose. "But not before one thing."

Anne had already lifted her trunk and turned wildly back to the woman who had, until that moment, been her employer. "One thing?"

Miss Clarke glared. "Before you go, leave a report."

CHAPTER TWENTY-FOUR

December 14, 1812

"I T IS JUST…ARE you certain you have thought this through, my lord? The consequences are grave indeed."

Timothy did not look at Mrs. Seton as she spoke, preferring to pace around his study. It was so unusual to have anyone here, it put his teeth on edge, but he had to tell them before they heard it from someone else.

"Mrs. Seton is right, my lord," said Dewey quietly. "I would cancel the visit entirely and take more time—"

"Time? Time is the one thing we have had too much of," snapped Timothy, running his hands through his hair. "Dear God, time! Where have the last two years gone?"

In seeking meaning in solitude, he thought darkly as he paced. His feet were restless, his mind unable to focus on anything except that what he was about to do was the right thing.

The last dregs of sunlight spread across the floor. *He would be here any moment.* He had to see him, and if the darkness lent itself to the depravity of the conversation, so be it.

Mrs. Seton shook her head gravely. "You must be absolutely certain, my lord. Once you do this—you know there is no going back from it. None at all."

Timothy nodded. He knew it and having his housekeeper repeat it did nothing for his nerves.

He had second-guessed himself enough today. Ever since the letter had gone out and the positive response received, he had wondered whether he had been rash.

But it was a decision two years in the making.

His butler clasped his hands together, an uncharacteristic sign of nervousness. "It is just...I did not ever believe you would do this, my lord. It feels unlike you. Are you sure that... Miss Anne's departure was indeed upsetting, but—"

"It has nothing to do with her," Timothy lied curtly.

He stopped at the window and looked into the darkness. The tension in his shoulders would not decrease, no matter how he attempted to convince himself this was the right thing.

He should have done it before; no, that wasn't right. He should have done something different.

"Oh, I wish you would not."

The voice was so gentle, so concerned, that Timothy turned around to check that it was Mrs. Seton still speaking. Tears sparkled in her eyes.

"Yet I think I must, Mrs. Seton," said Timothy heavily. "Lord knows I do not wish it for its own sake, but I do not believe there is another way around it."

What he did not voice to his two most senior servants was that he had considered a myriad of different options, and this was sadly the only one that sat well with his soul.

Morals. They had never troubled him before. He had never needed them. So why did this terrible outcome feel in a strange way the only way he could live with himself?

"But what if you are tried as a murderer!" exclaimed Dewey.

Both Timothy and Mrs. Seton looked at him.

"Not that you are," said the butler hastily, hands clasped behind his back. "Naturally."

"But people may not understand. They may jump to conclusions which they have no right to," added Mrs. Seton, tears glittering but as yet unspilt. "What would happen to Frances if you…if you were taken away?"

The panic Timothy had been fighting reared its head, but he forced it down. He would not permit that. His first act as her father, her true father, no matter what biology might say, would not be to lose her.

"That will not happen," he said firmly. "I…I must do what is right."

Dewey and Mrs. Seton. They had been loyal to him, more loyal than he had any right. He had asked much of them, and had encouraged them to lie, or at least hide the truth.

What had it gained him? Two years of living a lie, always in fear of the truth.

No, it was time. The truth had to be told.

"Besides," he added, a painful thought crossing his mind. "Her family are probably worried about her. Not knowing, I think, is perhaps the most painful waiting of all."

"I had lost touch with her, she had lost touch with all of us. We did not know what had become of her."

The mere memory cracked Timothy's already weary heart. If only he had been honest about this at the time when it had happened. Yes, there would have been a scandal, but it would have been nothing compared to what was about to occur.

The gossips would have a field day when they learned the truth, and a family he had never met would mourn the daughter they had not realized they had lost.

It all could have been so different.

He raised a hand to his head, massaging his temple. He had to make amends, even in this small way.

"I should never have lied," he muttered. "I should never have hidden the truth from the world. Louise died, she died on my land, as my wife, and I did nothing."

Something dark shivered within him. *Had he ever said those words out loud?*

"Frances deserves the truth. Her family deserved the truth years ago," Timothy said with a heavy sigh. "The world should trust me, and I shouldn't have done this foolish thing at the ball with Miss Gilbert…"

Timothy's voice faded. *Christ, how could he put into words the foolishness he felt?* Just when he had convinced the world his countess was alive and well, when Anne had revealed her feelings, when he had taken her to bed and realized he had not been truly alive for years…

She had gone. It had been days since he had seen her.

The color of his soul had been revealed to her, and she had left—and the worst of it was he could not blame her. *Why stay with a monster? A man you believed was a murderer?*

No woman would love that sort of beast.

He trusted her discretion to say nothing to anyone. Anne would never betray him. Yet, the pain of her departure had not faded. Timothy was not sure whether it ever would.

From somewhere far away in the castle, a bell rang out.

"And that would be the front door," Timothy said heavily, glancing at the clock on the mantelpiece. "Right on time, of course."

"I can always say you are not in," said Dewey, taking a step forward. "You could have been called away, forgotten the appointment. It could all be postponed for another day."

Timothy laughed darkly. "Oh, Dewey, you are kind. I was the one who invited him! You think I would arrange a meeting like this and conveniently forget it?"

The butler's eyes were downcast. "I still think you are making a mistake, my lord. I know you value my opinion, and so I give it freely. *Do not meet with him.*"

The temptation was strong, though Timothy would not admit it. *Run away*, the dark voice at the back of his mind whispered. *Run away and never come back. Take Frances with you. Everyone else has run away from you. Isn't it time that you ran away from the world?*

Timothy set his jaw. He was not a coward.

"Speaking with Mr. Sackville is a mistake," said Mrs. Seton. "Reconsider, my lord."

"I have made many mistakes," said Timothy. "I do not think this is one of them."

The bell jangled for a second time, and his servants looked to Timothy with anxious expressions.

"It is all that woman's fault," said Mrs. Seton, an unusually hard look on her face. "*Miss Anne Gilbert.* What right did she have to come here and ruin everything? We were doing perfectly well before—"

"I wasn't." Timothy had not intended to speak, but his thoughts were so strong they poured from his mouth. "I think you know that, Mrs. Seton. I wish no harsh words to be spoken about…about the governess. She told me a few home truths, that was all."

Mrs. Seton opened her mouth, and Timothy raised a hand.

"Enough," he said wearily. "I have great respect for Anne—for Miss Gilbert."

He swallowed and tasted the fear in his throat. Mr. Sackville was waiting, and he should not leave him much longer, but it was vital he made this clear to his most senior servants.

Though they would surely not partake in gossip, they would undoubtedly hear the worst in the servants' hall. *They had to know the truth.*

"Anne made her choice, and her choice was to leave," Timothy said, his voice breaking. "And now I must attend to Mr. Sackville. Alone."

Mrs. Seton's lips were so tightly pursed they had almost disappeared, but as the bell rang again, Dewey shook his head.

"I will string those boys up by their ankles," he said darkly. "Answer the front door. How difficult could it be! I apologize, my lord, I will speak to all the footmen this evening."

Timothy dropped heavily into the chair behind his desk. "Send in Mr. Sackville."

It could not be clearer Mrs. Seton was wondering whether or not to stay in the study to listen to his conversation, but Timothy gave her a warm but firm smile.

"Good evening, Mrs. Seton. I am sure I will see you tomorrow."

He was left alone, and only then did Timothy allow his head to drop into his hands.

He should have waited before requesting Mr. Sackville attend on him. He had not considered precisely what he was going to say to the man.

Mr. Sackville, there has been a slight misunderstanding about my wife.

My wife is dead. No, not the one you met. The real one.

The countess died two years ago, and I have been lying to the world about it.

They all sounded so crass, so rehearsed. What sort of fool would the man take him for? Mr. Sackville would surely think the earl had lost his wits rather than spoke the truth.

Timothy's heart pattered as Mr. Sackville approached.

Was he really going to go through with this? He could still lie. He had not written any specifics in the letter sent to the man. He could merely use the time to update his will or go over some of the annuities the estate was paying out.

Timothy looked across his study. It had been his father's. One day, it could be Frances's. He could not live with himself, not sit in the same place his ancestors had done if he could not look a man in the face and tell him the truth.

His conscience needed to be clear. It had not been for years.

"Mr. Sackville, my lord," said Dewey smoothly as he ushered in the solicitor.

Timothy rose. "Good evening, Sackville. Thank you for coming at such late notice."

"The pleasure is all mine, my lord," said Mr. Sackville, inclining his head as he sat in the opposite chair.

Pulse thundering in his ears, Timothy tried to smile as he,

too, took his seat. *God's teeth, what did one do with one's hands when sitting down?*

"That will be all, Dewey."

Timothy had not intended to start a discussion, but the butler did not move.

"I thought you may require my presence, my lord," he said stiffly.

Timothy fought a smile. The presence of his butler would only raise the suspicions of his solicitor. Already Mr. Sackville's eyebrows had raised.

"I thank you for your offer," Timothy said, "but I will manage. That will be all."

There was no more direct dismissal other than spelling it out to the man, and thankfully the butler took him at his word and left, closing the door quietly behind him.

"What a dedicated servant," said Mr. Sackville in an impressed tone. "I do not think any of mine would be so desirous of being helpful."

Timothy smiled mechanically. "I believe I am most fortunate to have Dewey, as with all my servants."

"And you have such a strange policy for keeping them, too," the solicitor observed. "I have not heard of anything like it. Never letting a servant go, you are quite unique."

Timothy inclined his head. "Thank you, that is high praise indeed. I hope Mrs. Sackville is quite well? And your father?"

Mr. Sackville nodded. "Oh yes, the whole pack of them are likely to live forever if they have any say in the matter. And your daughter, she is well?"

My daughter, thought Timothy. He would grow accustomed to that. It still did not trip off the tongue, even after all these years. He had lost so much time.

The time for pleasantries was over. He needed to get this off his chest, and he could deal with the damned consequences later.

"I enjoyed the Christmas ball this year."

Timothy started. His solicitor was smiling. *He had not dreamt it, then?* The words he had spoken, the reminder of the Christmas ball.

Dear Lord, it was sweet, though the memories were tinged with sadness. In every one of them, there was Anne. Smiling, dazzling, brilliant.

The perfect countess. The countess he could never have.

"Good," he said in a strained voice. "I am glad. We always try to put on a good show for the evening. What I thought we would discuss today was—"

"You know, I cannot remember the last time I had seen your wife," interrupted Mr. Sackville. "Years, probably. She looked well, my lord, though I think a little different."

Tension froze Timothy to his seat, preventing him from speaking.

"The hair, I think," mused Mr. Sackville. "These wigs women wear, the dyes they use, 'tis extraordinary. I never know what my wife is going to look like from one day to the next!"

He laughed comfortably, his hands clutching his round belly.

Timothy smiled weakly. He had thought the truth was about to spill out against his own will, which would have been a difficult situation to navigate.

But Mr. Sackville said no more. *If only he knew...*

Well, he would know in a few minutes. Timothy was not going to prevaricate; he had to speak. This was the moment he had to be honest. He had wanted a governess of discretion, but he should have asked for a blabbermouth. *He needed to speak.*

Speak, man!

"I...I need to tell you something."

As openings went, it was not the best—but it at least started the damned conversation.

Mr. Sackville smiled. "What could you possibly have to tell me, my lord? Something to do with your wife, perhaps?"

When Timothy met the solicitor's eyes, he knew he was done for.

He had thought himself so clever. He had believed he and

Anne had been so witty. All their preparations, the terror he had endured before he knew whether they were successful.

They had applauded themselves, yet it seemed no one was fooled. At least, not Mr. Sackville.

Timothy sighed heavily. "I should never have underestimated you, Sackville. What have you guessed?"

The solicitor chuckled. "My dear man, I am not a fool. I could tell that the woman you paraded out at the ball was not your wife the moment she appeared."

Had the world been laughing at him? Had the news already reached London?

"How…how did you know?" he managed to ask.

Mr. Sackville raised an eyebrow. "Why, I would have thought that was obvious, my lord. She smiled too much as she came down the stairs. I sat near her at the sumptuous dinner you laid out, and I had the pleasure of speaking to her."

Timothy nodded. *Damnit, he should have spent more time working on Anne's conversation.* Of course, a mere governess could not fool a learned man like Sackville.

"She was so polite to me I *knew* it couldn't be her," continued the solicitor with a laugh. "Dear me, no. No health cure could cure one of being so rude—oh, forgive me."

Timothy laughed dryly. "No need to apologize, Sackville. I should have been more careful, should have told Anne to be far ruder. I missed that in our preparations."

"Anne, was it?" asked Mr. Sackville delicately. "Her true name?"

He could do nothing but nod. He had never intended to bring Anne into this. The further he could keep her from his infamy, the better. She did not deserve to be dragged down by his own iniquity.

"I do not wish to speak about her," he said, probably too gruffly. "It was on the subject of my wife that I asked you to come here."

Mr. Sackville examined him closely before saying, "Yes. I

thought it might. I have some guesses there."

Timothy raised an eyebrow. It was a morbid fascination that drew him to ask the question, and he was not entirely sure whether he actually wished to know the answer.

What sort of torrid ideas had the man of the law had about why the Earl of Clarcton had trotted out a false countess to his own Christmas ball?

"You do, do you?"

The solicitor was not cowed by his tone. "Yes, my lord, I do. I believe one of three things must have occurred. Either she abandoned the child and took up with a lover, you divorced her using another solicitor so I would not be aware of the action, or she died of illness, accident, that sort of thing, and you chose not to tell the world."

Having them spelled out that way was rather terrible. Timothy took a deep breath. *This* was the moment. He could not back down now; he had come too far.

"Two out of three, I am afraid."

For the first time in their conversation, Mr. Sackville looked amazed. "Goodness, really? I should have placed a bet on it. I am sure you are game for a wager. Looks like this is going to be far more impressive and dramatic than I thought earlier. Please do tell, my lord."

Timothy leaned forward, but the words did not come. *How could they?* Taken in the wrong light, they would hang him.

But the truth had to be known. He trusted Mr. Sackville, perhaps not with his life but certainly with his death.

"I...I am sorry to tell you that I am responsible for her death."

CHAPTER TWENTY-FIVE

"*I* ...*I am sorry to tell you that I am responsible for her death.*"

Anne's heart was thundering so rapidly she could only just hear over its immense thumping, but she had heard enough. She could not permit this to go any further.

Steeling her nerves, she opened the study door and stepped inside, saying with far more confidence than she felt, "Nonsense."

Now she was inside instead of eavesdropping. She saw a gentleman she vaguely knew. Both men turned in astonishment, and to her satisfaction, Timothy's mouth fell open.

If only she had had time to fix her hair or rest from her journey—but there had been no time. She had rushed back from London, afraid that just such a thing would occur.

He was utterly useless without her, it seemed.

"My lady!" said the man. "At least—I think?"

The frantic beating of her heart made it difficult to think clearly, but Anne had done what she had set out to do. She had made it to Clarcton Castle without having to see...that man.

Even the thought of him made her stomach churn. *She would not even think his name.*

"I thought you were in London," said Timothy blankly.

Anne made a show of carefully taking off her gloves. "I was, and then I realized that I was needed here, and so took the time to return."

And a good thing she had, too, Anne thought. It appeared she was just in time to prevent Timothy from doing something so foolish, she would not have credited it.

What did he think he was doing? She would never have forgiven herself if Timothy had managed to incriminate himself for a crime she was now certain he had not committed.

The man she loved—the man she knew—would never do such a thing. It had been fear and foolishness that had even permitted her to consider it.

"Return?" said Timothy quietly.

Anne did not look at him. *Not yet.* She could not look into his eyes and see the hurt she had caused.

"Yes, return," she said breezily, removing her bonnet and pelisse. "And of course, I must apologize for the interruption, I am sure you were talking about something very important, but at the end of the day, I couldn't allow the earl to say something that simply isn't true."

"Isn't true?" said the man she did not know, turning to Timothy. "I am at a loss to understand, my lord."

"Mr. Sackville ..." Timothy began, looking desperately at Anne.

Anne swallowed. He must have felt abandoned when he discovered her gone. She had flown through fear, and once the fear had receded, it was love that was left. *Love and love only.*

But he did not know that yet.

"It is not true, and I am living proof," she said firmly, discarding her pelisse and bonnet.

Mr. Sackville, *yes, of course, that was his name*, looked between her and Timothy in bewilderment. "My lady, the earl just admitted to your murder!"

It was vital she stayed calm. She'd gain nothing if she did not control her emotions.

"Nothing of the sort," she said aloofly. "One can feel responsible for something without actually doing anything wrong!"

Her eye caught Timothy's, the first time they had truly looked at each since she had entered. Since she had asked him to leave her bedchamber before preparing for her flight.

There was such confusion in his gaze Anne almost smiled. It was pleasant, in a strange way, to have the upper hand for a change. Though there was the possibility he was looking at her that way because she had just stepped off the mail coach and had not freshened up since...

But she had not been able to wait. She had to see him. She had to see Timothy.

"Murder—yet here you are! His lordship called you Anne, and you look...you are not the countess," said Mr. Sackville distractedly. "At least, I think you are not. Now I do not know!"

The man was making little sense, but Anne was not really listening. She had not looked away from Timothy. She could not.

She loved him so very much. Throwing himself to the wolves through guilt was not going to bring Louise back and would do no good for either of them.

"Louise?" said the gabbling man. "But...I was told you had died! What is going on?"

So, she had not been swift enough to prevent that piece of news from being imparted.

She would find a way out of this. *A governess of discretion*, that was what Timothy had called her. Was she now able to live up to that title?

Her smile strengthened. "Not quite, but close. I am the Countess of Clarcton."

Timothy was the one spluttering now, but Anne made sure to speak over him. *He did not appear able to keep his mouth shut long enough to protect himself.*

"I know, Timothy, I know we agreed not to tell anyone," she said lightly, stepping forward and leaning against the windowsill. "I think Mr. Sackville deserves to know, don't you?"

Mr. Sackville's mouth was open, and it was then Anne recognized him. *Of course, the family solicitor.* She had been seated near him at dinner, at the ball.

"How is your father, by the way?" she asked sweetly. "I hope he has quite recovered from that rather unpleasant gout he came down with over the summer."

It was a small victory indeed, but a victory nonetheless. There had been hundreds of guests at the Christmas ball, yet she had remembered this small fact.

The solicitor looked pleased. "Well, he—my word, fancy you remembering that. Yes, he is quite well, thank you, my lady."

Anne risked a glance at Timothy, who looked utterly dumbfounded.

Oh, he was such a precious man. Foolish at times, but she had not yet met a gentleman who did not fall into that category. She could protect him and love him for all of time, and this was just the first step she was taking to do just that.

Yes, it was a small lie; but if she had her way, it would not be a lie for long.

"You are the countess," said Mr. Sackville. "But...Anne, not Louise. You remarried?"

He turned to Timothy with this question, and Anne took the opportunity to wink at the earl, who looked absolutely flabbergasted.

"We wanted to keep the whole thing quiet, didn't we, my love?" she said sweetly as the solicitor stared at Timothy.

"W-We wanted to...I mean to say," he spluttered.

Anne took a deep breath. If Timothy was not to ruin everything, she would have to take matters entirely into her own hands. He was not to be trusted, it appeared, to keep his mouth shut—and after two years of doing nothing but!

"You see, Mr. Sackville," she said serenely, seating herself in the armchair by the fire, "when Louise died two years ago, my husband was absolutely overwhelmed, weren't you?"

Their eyes met, and a look of understanding passed between them.

"I was," said Timothy quietly.

Mr. Sackville nodded. "The grief, I suppose. I wonder you bore it alone, my lord."

"It was recently his lordship and I fell in love," said Anne with a wry smile, "and of course, the last thing we wanted was a fuss. Not with Frances still so young…the *gossip*. You can imagine, Mr. Sackville."

The solicitor nodded more fervently this time. "Yes. Yes, I see."

Anne chanced another look at Timothy. He appeared to be still attempting to understand what she was doing here, let alone feeding the man such wild and adventurous lies.

And yet…were they lies?

Anne did not think so. Timothy had certainly been over-whelmed when Louise had died, not with grief, of course, but by a myriad of other emotions which clearly took their toll.

Bitterness. Anger. Confusion. Rage. Devastation.

They had overwhelmed him indeed.

"I wish you would have told me, my lord," Mr. Sackville said reproachfully, turning back to the earl. "'Tis odd indeed to hear it in this fashion. Why did you not inform me?"

"I-I…I cannot exactly say," began Timothy.

"Mr. Sackville?" said Anne lightly. When the man turned to face her, she smiled. "You are the first to know."

A wide smile spread across Mr. Sackville's face. "Am I really?"

Anne nodded impressively. *Really, it was all too easy.* Most men were exactly the same; play on the ego, and you would have them in the palm of your hand.

Timothy was the only man she had met not like that. He danced to his own tune, even if it was one that would make him miserable.

"Well, I say," said Mr. Sackville looking absolutely delighted. "You know, my lord, my family have always served yours in one capacity or another, and I am honored to be your solicitor for such a momentous event!"

"Right," said Timothy weakly.

Anne stifled another laugh. If she had had the opportunity to forewarn him, then, of course, she would have done.

As it was, Timothy had raced ahead far more swiftly than she had imagined. *Calling in a solicitor? Was the man deranged?* What good did he think it would do, confessing to a crime he did not commit to assuage the guilt he should never have felt?

"I suppose you asked me here to revise your will," Mr. Sackville was saying.

Timothy blinked. "I did?"

Anne could not help but feel sorry for him. Timothy was the sort of man, both by nature and by rank, accustomed to being the one who controlled the conversation. Now he was in the unfortunate situation of navigating one without knowing where they were going.

"Yes, at some point, we will," said Anne quickly. "My husband and I want to ensure all our legal documents are in order, but I wonder now whether this is the best time."

Thankfully, Timothy was able to notice a hint that large. "Yes, now that you have returned from London, perhaps we should consider writing ours together."

"We would need to consult privately," Anne said delicately. "I had not realized you had written *so quickly* to Mr. Sackville."

Their gazes met once more, and this time Anne was certain Timothy understood. She should never have left him, but she did not think he would have done something so rash.

"So I am afraid we have called you away from your warm fire for nothing, Mr. Sackville," said Timothy magnanimously. "And for that, I do apologize."

"But you must come back another time," added Anne quickly. "And until then, you will promise to keep our secret, won't you?"

Mr. Sackville looked between them with a dazed expression, as though he had been asked to fly to the moon and given a magical horse to do so, but no one had given him a saddle.

"Right," he said slowly. "Yes, of course, your secret stays with me…that is," and he spoke in a clearer voice, "anything you say is in complete confidence, and this is no different."

"Lovely," said Anne with a smile, rising to her feet. "In that case, there is nothing left for us to do but wish you a good evening, Mr. Sackville."

It was an abrupt dismissal, Anne knew—but she could not remain here with Timothy for much longer without giving him a full explanation, nor receiving one in return.

"Ah," said Mr. Sackville, stumbling to his feet and bowing. "My lord, my lady—"

"Wonderful," said Anne, walking over to the door. "You know the way out, do you?"

"What?" Mr. Sackville looked utterly flummoxed as he stepped into the corridor.

Anne spotted Poll wandering down the corridor. "Ah, Poll. Poll will see you out, Mr. Sackville, and may I say once again what a pleasure it has been to see you again so soon."

The door was shut. Anne leaned against it, took a deep breath, and blew it slowly out.

The tension that had settled in her shoulders during her long journey back from London, tension which had only heightened when she had overhead Timothy bear the responsibility of Louise's death, was finally starting to dissipate.

Thank God she had got here in time. Thank God Mr. Sackville was so easily impressed, so easily persuadable. If it had been a hardnosed solicitor who required facts, dates of matrimony, explanation…

Well, then she would not have managed the impossible.

Anne could not quite believe she had declared herself to be his wife. Now needed to do the one thing she had dreaded.

Face Timothy.

Her revelation to the solicitor was not precisely the discretion he had undoubtedly wished for, but if she was fortunate, if she had not entirely misjudged his affections, she may…may have won herself a rather wonderful man.

"Well," she said quietly, finally looking at Timothy, still seated behind his desk. "That is the hard bit over."

"Anne Gilbert, what on earth do you think you are doing!" exploded Timothy. "You can't just waltz in here and announce yourself as my wife!"

"You are right," said Anne with a wry smile. "We will have to make it official as soon as possible."

Timothy's brow furrowed. "You are such a whirlwind. I am not entirely sure I know what is happening! You pronounce yourself my wife after running out of this castle in the dead of night, leaving me...leaving all of us!"

Anne could hear the pain in his voice. "I know, and I am sorry for it."

"Sorry!" Timothy blew out his cheeks as he shook his head. "Anne, I do not know what...where can I begin? Everything I thought I knew, everything I was sure I felt...it is exhausting attempting to keep up with you!"

Anne smiled and walked to the desk. "I have announced myself as your wife. That cannot be taken back, not easily."

"And to Sackville, of all people!" Timothy said. "You do realize it is—well, some sort of crime I expect, to lie to a solicitor?"

Yet under all the bluster and the rage, Anne could hear it. The love. The relief she had returned. He had not yet permitted himself to feel these things because they were twinned with other emotions, painful ones. *Fear of loss. Rejection. Betrayal.*

"Are you saying," she said slowly, "you do not wish to be my husband?"

For a terrible moment, Anne thought he would say just that. There was such a look of perplexity across Timothy's face he did not appear to know if he was coming or going.

And then Anne squealed. "Timothy!"

She was not permitted to say anymore. She couldn't have, even if she had wanted to. Timothy had grabbed her waist and pulled her into his lap, his lips crushed against hers, all that rage and passion and fear pouring down in a most divine kiss that took

Anne's breath away.

When the kiss ended, Timothy was smiling. "I have never met anyone like you, you know."

"And you're not likely to either," said Anne. His arms were strong around her, keeping her safe, holding her still. The only place she truly wanted to be. "You can't get rid of me that easily."

This time she lifted her lips to his, taking her pleasure eagerly, greedy for the taste of him. He was hers, the only man for her.

"I love you," she murmured, unable to stop herself. "I love you Timothy—"

"And I love you, you governess minx," came the jagged reply. "God, when I discovered you gone...I had not experienced agony like it. I need you, Anne. Every part of me is dependent on you. A life without you..."

Words once again became impossible. The relief they shared, the desperate need to be closer, overwhelmed them. Anne's senses were just as overwhelmed. Timothy's hands around her buttocks, cupping her to him, the way his lips teased her, his tongue worshipped her...

But a jarring thought cut through her passion, and Anne broke the kiss.

Timothy leaned forward, eyes full of desire, but Anne pulled away.

"What's the matter?"

"It's..." Anne swallowed. She had to say this, could not rest if he was still here. *It would not be a pleasant conversation.* "Holt. Your footman, he also acts as your driver."

Timothy frowned with a hesitant laugh. "You...you want to talk about Holt? Now?"

"You need to get rid of him," said Anne. She did not take her gaze from his and tried to make it clear just how serious she was. "He is a terrible man, Timothy. He...he was the one who seduced Louise. He suggested...well, that her death wasn't an accident."

Timothy's laugh died away, his expression solemn. "And you believe him?"

Anne nodded. "Yes, I do. What would he gain by lying? And he tried to kiss me and...well, he was rather horrible to me, actually. I imagine the maids have similar stories."

Timothy's eyes narrowed. "The blaggard. I should string him up by his ankles, I should call him out at dawn—but no, he's no gentleman. I should flog him! Touch you?"

Seeing him angry, the rage so controlled and restrained, was rather exhilarating. For the first time in her life, Anne saw what a temptation power was when it was just out of reach. To have that authority over another person's life...it was thrilling.

"Send him away," she said quietly. "We have no wish for a scandal, but I would ask that he be kept apart from women. The Navy perhaps."

A slow smile spread across Timothy's face. "I shall purchase him a commission. Everyone will think we are rewarding him for some great service, but he will know he is being dismissed. Let the Navy deal with him."

Timothy kissed her gently on the cheek. "Well, I suppose as my wife, you have the authority to do that! When did we get married, by the way?"

Laughter rang out in the study. To see him happy, to hear him jest; it was all she wanted.

"Not too long ago, actually," she said with a smile. "And we had better make it official quick, before Mr. Sackville lets anything slip to anyone."

"Oh, I think Mr. Sackville can be trusted," Timothy said. "One does not keep a family of solicitors for a few hundred years if they cannot be trusted."

"But can *you* be trusted," Anne teased, "not to bed me until we are officially husband and wife?"

He did not need to answer her in words. Anne received her answer with kisses, a trail of them that started on her lips but slowly moved to her neck and down to her breasts.

"I think that answers that question!"

Timothy halted his devotion and looked into her eyes. Anne's heart skipped a beat. *She had never known it was possible to feel love like this.*

"You cannot just pick up her life, you know," he said softly.

Anne's stomach lurched, but she controlled herself. It was natural for this concern to rise, and she would not simply ignore it because it was uncomfortable.

"I don't intend to," she said quietly. "We're going to make our own life, in new ways, exactly how we want. With Frances, too. Besides, after all the rigmarole you put me through for that Christmas ball, I have earned it. I have earned you."

For a moment, she thought she had gone too far, but Timothy did not censure her nor criticize her words. Instead, he sighed.

"Sometimes I think I didn't deserve the trouble Louise brought me," he said with a sad smile, "but then at other times, I thought I did. It was hard to know. I admit, I probably did not help her ease into this kind of life."

Anne's heart softened. "She was a woman who knew what she wanted, and I am afraid to say that it appeared as well as wanting you, she...well, she wanted Holt. It's just a shame she paid for that with her life."

They sat in silence for a moment before Anne finally spoke the pain weighing on her since the moment she realized she loved him.

"I...I feel guilty for inheriting her happiness."

"You have nothing to feel guilty about," said Timothy fiercely. "No, look at me, Anne. Whatever has happened in the past, we love each other. I love you, all of you, all the clever things you do, the way you look at the world, your heart—all of you. *You*."

Anne placed her arms around his neck and kissed him, unleashing all the passion which had been desperately dammed within her soul. It had to find a way out.

When the kiss finally broke, Timothy smiled weakly. "Christ in his heaven, we had better make this official before I take you upstairs and do something I will very much not regret. We will have to be careful, though. Marry somewhere quiet. I am afraid your family will not be able to attend."

CHAPTER TWENTY-SIX

1 January 1813

T HE HOUSE WAS bustling, and for the first time in two years, Timothy was glad of it.

"Careful now, Burnham!" called Mrs. Seton sharply. "That chandelier is four times your age and just as delicate!"

"Sorry, Mrs. Seton," came the nervous reply of the footman.

The housekeeper shook her head as Timothy passed. "They mean well, my lord."

Timothy smiled. "I am sure they do. Please do not worry, Mrs. Seton—the guests have already arrived and are in the ballroom, there is no need to concern yourself with—"

"If that boy knocks over the Clarcton chandelier because of mere foolishness, there will be plenty to be concerned with," said Mrs. Seton severely.

Timothy smiled. Some things never changed, and Mrs. Seton was one of them.

Besides, she was right. An almighty crash of crystal and gold onto the Great Hall floor would certainly bring an unplanned ruckus to the proceedings—though when it came to hosting balls, he was starting to learn there was nothing that one could entirely predict.

"Well, if you need to adjust the candles there before the night's end, please continue," he said magnanimously. "If it can wait until the guests are gone, and the thing can be lowered, even better. Now, I must continue to the ballroom. You have everything under control here?"

Mrs. Seton glared at the blushing footman. "I certainly do."

Timothy could not help but laugh as he left the Great Hall and started along the corridor. The whole house had come alive in the last few weeks, and he knew the cause. She was waiting for him in the ballroom—though if he knew Anne, she would be busy.

Conversation and excitement would be rife if he were any judge, the place packed with all from the surrounding area and a few from town, probably—all to see the new Countess of Clarcton.

Not that any would own they had not realized she was not Louise at the last ball. Timothy had almost cried with laughter when they started to receive congratulations letters.

Even Lady Romeril—

"Ah, there you are," said Lady Romeril, bearing down on him along the corridor. Evidently, she deigned to wait with the rest of his guests in the ballroom for his entrance. No, she had to be the one to speak with him. "You have been hiding from me."

Timothy inclined his head. "Lady Romeril. I would never dare do such a thing."

"Hmmmph," was the response he received. "And I suppose I should congratulate you on your marriage, though I do not know if you deserve it. You attempted to play a very fine trick on us all, you know, but I was not for one minute taken in."

Timothy raised an eyebrow as guests passed them in the corridor. "You were not?"

Lady Romeril raised herself up impressively. "Goodness, no. I could see it was a different woman, of course. Different nose."

It was all he could do not to laugh. "Different *hair*."

"That's what I said," Lady Romeril said smoothly.

Almost seventy years old, yet she held herself haughty, as though she ran the world.

And of course, in a small way, she did. As one of the matrons of Almack's, displeasing Lady Romeril meant one could find oneself on the wrong side of society for the entire Season. Why, Timothy himself knew of a family of three daughters who had—

"I am still rather unimpressed with you," said Lady Romeril, interrupting his thoughts as she fluttered her fan. "It is a good thing I was so taken by your mother. If you have any of her traits, you will do well."

Timothy inclined his head. "Then you do me great honor. To be anything like either of my parents would make me a fortunate man indeed."

"And I am sure your wife thinks likewise," shot back the matriarch. "Tell me, who are her parents?"

He hesitated before responding. Now they were married, such things did not really matter. The question of her family, her background...he knew these were the questions on everyone's lips. *Questions he would not be answering.*

No one would ever know the truth of the entire affair, and that was how he would keep it. Discretion indeed would be the focus on their marriage, as well as a rather delectable enjoyment of the bed—

"I *said*, Anne is a rather common name," said Lady Romeril severely. "Come now, my lord, there should be no secrets between equals, let alone friends. Just whisper in my ear the name of—"

"I am sorry, Lady Romeril," Timothy cut across her with what he hoped was a charming smile. "Both for disappointing you before with our façade, and disappointing you now with my silence. Good evening."

He had bowed and left her before Lady Romeril could splutter much more than 'my word!' and Timothy took that as a victory. *Not every gentleman was that fortunate.*

He was so hasty to leave his conversation with the matriarch, however, that he almost ran headlong into the Duke of Kilkerth as he rounded a corner.

"God's teeth, watch—oh, it's you," said the duke with a scowl.

Timothy grinned. Old Kilkerth was always bad-tempered, always irritable. Not that he could blame the man. His wife had died what—a year ago?

"Sorry, old man," he said easily. "Dining room or ballroom?"

"Neither, if I can help it," snapped the Duke of Kilkerth. "Is there no quiet in this place?"

Timothy thought back to the Great Hall. "Only the Great Hall. What's wrong?"

The duke swept his long dark hair out of his eyes. "Doesn't matter."

"You should get yourself a drink," said Timothy cheerfully. "I find they make the days and the nights far superior."

The duke met his eyes in a glower. "You talk too much, damn you."

He swallowed. The duke was not a man he knew well, but he had extended the invitation as a courtesy—a courtesy he was now regretting.

"Well, find yourself a quiet nook in the Great Hall. There's no need for you to linger if you have no wish to."

The man stalked away, and Timothy watched him go. *Thank God he had Anne.* The idea of living without her now...it was intolerable.

But he could not dwell on Kilkerth's problems; he was supposed to be hosting the New Year's ball with his new wife. Wherever she was.

On a hunch, he followed the sound of laughter to the dining room and saw her—*his wife*—at one end, surrounded by a gaggle of people.

"—and of course, the hat fell off in the end!" she said triumphantly.

The entire gaggle roared with laughter.

"And you will not tell us who it was?" asked a foppish young gentleman eagerly.

Anne caught Timothy's eye across the room as she said, "La, sir, you think I would be that indiscrete!"

There were murmurs of appreciation and even a few shaking heads of disapproval of the young man, who colored.

Timothy found contentment in every nerve of his body. *His wife.* Entertaining people without offending, laughing without malice; it was a miracle. Something he could never have imagined, not before he had ever met Anne.

"You are very direct, Miss Gilbert."

"I like to be. Were you expecting someone a little more demure?"

Her company was clearly sought. Anne was his wife, but she was also the Countess of Clarcton, and he had no wish for her to feel ostracized in her new role—her new life.

If he was any judge of the matter, the countess would be inundated with invitations from neighboring families, even those unfriendly to the Clarcton house for years.

The conversation moved around Frances, her gaze on her husband. Timothy's heart skipped a beat. *He was her husband.* Warmth spread across his body, emanating from his heart to every extremity.

They had been married a week, seven short days, yet it felt like forever. Would forever be long enough? They had the rest of their lives before them, stretching out across days of happiness and joy and difficulties they would face together.

He wanted to be close to her. Stepping through the crowd, Timothy managed to avoid conversation with at least three people until he was accosted by Mr. Sackville.

"My lord!" said the rotund man with a beaming smile. "I have to say how honored I am to be the first to be officially informed—and what a woman she is!"

Timothy glanced at Anne, giggling with the Duke of Kilerth's sister, Lady Maria Fernsby.

"She is indeed," he said softly. "Now, if you will excuse me—"

"But I must admit myself curious," said Mr. Sackville. "Why did you not announce it at the Christmas ball?"

Timothy had almost reached Anne, which meant she heard the solicitor's question. Her shimmering blue eyes met his, dancing with mischief, and Timothy smiled weakly.

"Ah, a good question. You know, I don't think—"

"I must say, I cannot understand how I did not notice it before," interrupted Lady Maria Fernsby with a smile. "Completely different temperaments, though there is a likeness."

Anne suppressed a smile.

He shrugged. *If he treated it lightly...* "I never called her Louise, you know. I never gave any hint she was the same woman I married five years ago. You all assumed."

It was not the convincing speech he hoped, and Lady Maria Fernsby knew that.

"Hmm," she said. "Indeed."

Timothy smiled weakly. He barely knew the Kilerths, but they were in the neighborhood, and it would have been churlish not to invite them.

"Well, I must say that I knew the moment I laid eyes on her!"

Timothy turned and saw with relief a familiar face, the Duke of Rochdale.

"Rochdale!" he said, stepping forward and grasping him by the hand, partly in pleasure to see him and partly in gratitude for distracting him from Lady Maria Fernsby. "You are very welcome, but only if you can keep your mouth shut!"

Timothy grinned as he whispered the last few words, but he was only half-joking. The pretty Duchess of Rochdale's was, Timothy knew, another member—or previous member—of the Governess Bureau. Both gentlemen had much to lose by announcing the past lives of their wives.

"Oh hush," said the duchess, tapping her husband with her fan. "My lord, you can, of course, depend on our discretion."

Timothy could not help but laugh. *There was that word again, something of a theme to his and Anne's love story.* "Discretion is a very valuable quality, and I thank you."

His memory soared back to that first moment he met Anne. The Governess Bureau had been instructed to find him a governess of discretion, and it had done so. He could never have predicted Anne would bring so much color to a life previously gray.

"I quite agree," said the duke smoothly. "I would say a wife of great talents is always your best choice."

His wife tapped him with her fan again with a laugh. "If you are not able to keep your mouth shut, Rochdale, I will take you straight back home. *Archie* is more discrete than you!"

Timothy laughed, but his heart longed for Anne. He had to be close to her. It had been—what, at least half an hour since he had been by her side?

"Excuse me," he hesitated and kept walking.

The room was packed, something he had not anticipated, but as he caught snatches of conversation, it became clear just why they had all assembled here.

Anne.

"—seen her?" murmured one woman. "I simply had to take another look. I barely looked at her last time."

"—understand how I did not notice it before," a gentleman was saying, shaking his head. "It's the wigs, I tell you. They utterly confuse a man! How is one to tell…"

"Oh, I always knew, I was one of the first his lordship told," said Miss Merriweather impressively, though she flushed as Timothy passed her. "I mean…when I say the first…"

"If his lordship did not choose to inform you, as he informed me, then I am afraid that is not my fault," he heard Mr. Sackville say impressively.

Timothy smiled. *Everyone had to feel important, everyone desperate to prove they had known all along.* No one wanted to be the only person kept out of the secret, and now all of them were convincing themselves they had been a key part from the very beginning.

It was foolish, but there it was. Perhaps it was something about human nature.

By the time Timothy reached Anne's seat, she was gone.

Frustration poured through his body. He looked around, desperate to see that flash of fiery red hair, but she was nowhere to be found.

This was ridiculous! They were the hosts. It was their ball! One would think they would be given time and space to enjoy their own ball at their leisure—but the rules of society said they had to ensure everyone else's enjoyment.

It was maddening!

The ball was Anne's idea, of course.

"Frances is old enough to sit and watch her first ball," she had said firmly as he had pulled her to him in bed. "And I don't want to wait until spring. Besides, I like balls."

He had chuckled at that. "Of course you do. Dancing, food, conversation, what's not to like?"

And she had said, "I want to celebrate life with you, Timothy. Our love. Frances should play a part in that."

As he strode out of the dining room, he immediately saw them, Anne and Frances. They had found a nook behind the musicians, and despite the splendid blue silk gown he had commissioned from Madame Griffon, Anne was paying no heed to it. There she was, seated on the floor, Frances in her arms, pointing out the different musical instruments.

Timothy's heart twisted. It was not a painful feeling but had the potential for pain. He loved them so much, both of them. The idea of anything hurting either of them…he would move heaven and earth to protect them. It was a wonderful, frightening feeling.

He had never experienced it before.

"Happy New Year, my lord!" came a few cheers as people noticed their host had entered, and Timothy acknowledged their best wishes with a smile and a nod.

Finally, Frances had a mother she could depend on. Finally, he had a wife and bride he could trust. That he could love, though discretion played a part in bringing them together, there would be no secrets between them.

Not anymore.

It took a mere five strides across the room, and he scooped Frances into his arms.

"And what are you doing, my little monkey?"

The girl squealed with delight. "Papa!"

Anne rose and kissed his cheek. "Hello, you."

"I hope you have spent the entire evening spreading wild rumors about me," he teased. "The more ridiculous, the better. I have a wager with the d'Allaires that I shall hear the first one at my club within two days of stepping into town."

Anne laughed. "The wilder, the better, I always say, though I am afraid you may not like the most outrageous ones."

Timothy chuckled, allowing the squirming child in his arms onto the floor.

"Careful, Frances," said Anne immediately. "Stay close to the musicians, please."

"What a charming child," said a voice.

Timothy turned to see his friends, the d'Allaires, standing close by, and as he inclined his head, they stepped forward to join them.

"Duc and duchesse d'Allaire, may I introduce my wife, Anne," he said formally.

Anne curtseyed beautifully, and Timothy's heart skipped a beat whenever he said that word. *Wife.* He had never taken pleasure in it before, and now it was the dearest syllable he could utter.

"'Tis a pleasure to make your acquaintance, *madame*," said the duc d'Allaire. "To see you with your *belle fille,* it is a delight to see. One might have almost thought you were mamam and daughter!"

Timothy's stomach lurched. It was one of the quirks of their new family, of course, that Anne was Frances's aunt by blood. The connection between them was strong, stronger than could be explained by mere proximity.

But it was not an explanation he was willing to give, not to anyone. *But what if they guessed—worse, what if they guessed incorrectly and believed Anne had been his mistress, the child's true mother?*

But Anne merely laughed. "Yes, there is a special connection between us, I find. I consider Frances just as much my daughter as if I had birthed her."

"And of course," said the duchesse d'Allaire in the crisp English accent Timothy always found so surprising. He always forgot she was an English woman. "You will have to find a governess soon? I am finding the whole thing rather a chore, myself."

Timothy swallowed. It was too much of a coincidence that the topic of governesses should come up so quickly. The d'Allaires were friends—at least he and the duc d'Allaire had known each other since they were boys. *They would not betray him, would they?*

"Yes, the selection of a governess is a very important decision," Anne said seriously.

The tension in his shoulders disappeared. Perhaps he was overthinking this. He could not avoid all conversations about governesses, after all.

His gaze caught Anne's, and they shared a smile.

"I am sure I have a good governess for Frances," he said lightly.

"Oof, you are indeed *très malheureux*," said the duc d'Allaires with a sigh. "We 'ave found it difficult to find one at all, let alone one we consider to be *bon*. I was telling our friend Galcrest of the difficulties – *très malheureux*."

"I could not agree more," said Timothy with a wry smile.

"Sometimes," said Anne with that mischievous look he loved more every day, "I think the best governesses are the ones that truly become part of the family."

"I could not agree more," said the duchess d'Allaire, though any further words she said were drowned out by Timothy's laughter.

"I do apologize," he said hastily. "I thought of something that was amusing."

One day, perhaps, he would tell them. But not today.

"Come, my love," he added. "Let's open the dancing."

Anne placed her hand in his. "Please do excuse us."

They stepped away from the couple, and Anne drew herself into Timothy's side.

"You should not tease them," he said quietly.

Anne chuckled. "Why not? Everyone here is teasing me, trying to work out how we met, who I really am."

"You do not mind?" Timothy asked anxiously as he caught the musician's eye, and the man raised his baton. "You are happy?"

"More happy than I could ever have imagined," she said.

"And so am I," piped up a voice.

Timothy looked down and saw Frances had appeared on his other side.

He laughed, placing his arm around her. "I don't think I could be happier than this, with my two girls beside me."

"Oh, I don't know," mused Anne as he released her arm to place her in the set. "I think I can think of something."

She had a strange look as she said those words, as though she was holding onto a secret far too exciting to keep to herself.

Timothy was about to ask what she meant, but Frances tugged on his sleeve.

"Can I dance, too?"

"I would be honored," he said, lifting the child and placing her on his feet. "As long as you do not mind, Anne?"

The smile she gave him could have melted snow on the frostiest morning. "Mind? I would prefer it. Ready, Frances?"

The music started, and the three of them stepped together, the three Lexingtons arm in arm, where they belonged.

EPILOGUE

January 8, 1813

Dear Miss Clarke,

I wish to thank you for your timely advice which you gave me before Christmas. As it turns out, I was not mistaken in the Earl of Clarcton's affections for me, and I am pleased to say we are now married.

I admit I did not imagine this is the way it would turn out, and I am conscious this contravenes the third rule of the Governess Bureau.

However, if you could see how content we are with each other's company, the great affection we share, the difference our marriage has made to the both of us...well, I would say even you would give us your blessing.

In fact, I

Anne dipped her pen in the ink well, pondering how to continue her letter to Miss Clarke. She should have written weeks ago, the instant she had returned to Clarcton Castle.

Her pen was dripping ink onto the letter, but Anne was still not entirely sure how to continue. It was a letter she never believed she would write, and it was rather difficult to concentrate with the squeals and whoops of Timothy and Frances behind her.

Still, she would never complain. The perfect family.

> *In fact, I believe you would champion our marriage. I do not see this as a betrayal of yourself nor the Governess Bureau, for was it not yourself who encouraged me to return to the earl? You said yourself, and forgive me if I cannot recall your exact phrasing, that the earl would never give me false hope.*
>
> *He did not. Thank you, Miss Clarke, for prompting my return to the arms of happiness.*

Anne looked at the letter. She was rather relieved she would not be present when Miss Clarke received it. *How angry she would be!* The second governess in as many years to wed their master, something that to her knowledge had never occurred before.

Meredith had been brave. Anne remembered meeting her that fateful day in October. Meredith had actually gone to the Governess Bureau to tell Miss Clarke in person! How she had managed the bravery for such a thing, she did not know.

That was not something Anne had any desire to do. A letter would more than suffice. In a strange way, she felt Miss Clarke had given her the Governess Bureau's blessing.

Had she not told Anne to return?

"Spend time with him, indeed! The earl would never give the impression he was interested in you, I am sure. He would have to really and genuinely care for you for that to happen. An earl and a governess? Only if he truly loved you would he ever give a hint of such a thing!"

Though the proprietress was against matrimony, Miss Clarke had, in her own way, been instrumental in Anne finding her happiness, and for that, she would always be grateful.

"You brute, have at you!"

A giggle erupted behind her, and Anne turned with a smile to watch Timothy pretend to die from a sword wound. It was a good thing, too, that the wooden sword crafted for Frances was blunt, for she wielded it like a demon.

"Sorry, Papa, did I hurt you?" Frances asked with a broad smile on her face, absolutely certain she had not.

"No, no, I am quite well," said Timothy hastily.

Anne smiled. He was still not entirely comfortable with Frances, seeking to reassure her far more often than most parents. But it would come with time. Before long, he would not even have to think about it.

Somehow, she did not know how, she had brought healing to this family and been welcomed into it with open arms.

But this thinking did not complete her letter. Turning back to the desk, Anne considered the latest missive she had received from Miss Clarke and the problem within it the proprietress had described.

Twins! Few governesses, even within the Bureau, could deliver the high quality of care and education Miss Clarke expected with twins.

"Specializing in twins means traveling, and wherever I go, I am assumed not to have reached my majority."

A memory stirred. Anne recalled her face: Miss Elizabeth Fletcher. Their paths had crossed a few times. Had she not said she specialized in twins.

Anne could not precisely recall, but it was the best she could think of.

As to your own problem, Miss Clarke, I have given the matter some thought and would recommend Miss Elizabeth Fletcher for the twins. I believe she has experience in such matters, and that is invaluable, especially when they are young.

"Righty ho, you monster, time for bed," came Timothy's voice. "Come on, rascal!"

"Not before I get a kiss," said Anne with a smile.

Frances scampered over to her giggling and placed a sloppy kiss on Anne's cheek. It was the most precious thing they shared. This connection between them only grew over time.

"Good night, Mama," Frances said, hastening to her father and taking his hand.

Anne swallowed back the tears threatening to overwhelm. *Mama*. It was a special name and title she had known she would have to earn rather than be bestowed—but she had received it so swiftly!

Three months ago, she had no knowledge of who the Clarctons were, and now she was a part of that family.

The Countess of Clarcton.

Anne could hardly believe it. Though such swift engagements and marriages were typical amongst Timothy's kind, she knew it was a remarkable change of fate.

"I won't be long," said Timothy with a smile.

It was difficult to manage her emotions at times like this. Most governesses never had their own family; the ties and responsibilities to their charges took up all their time, and there were few men anxious to wed a woman who would never be available for their own children.

She had resigned herself to a life well lived but alone. She could never have predicted such a family.

Even if, in the eyes of her employer, it utterly betrayed everything the Bureau stood for.

Anne bit her lip. She did not regret the path she had chosen, nor did she believe she had acted wrongly, other than perhaps the charade at the Christmas ball. But that did not change how Miss Clarke would feel upon receiving this letter.

> *Please believe me when I say I have not acted with the aim of hurting you, and I am very grateful for all the support and encouragement you have given me. I know the Governess Bureau will continue on from strength to strength.*
>
> *I know falling in love is against the rules of the Bureau, but I could not help it, Miss Clarke. I love him. And after the Duke and Duchess of Rochdale—well, I am sure you understand.*

Anne looked at the letter. Had she explained sufficiently? If she knew Miss Clarke, there was no sufficient explanation for such an act, but she had done what she could.

Timothy was worth everything. He was…oh, Anne could not imagine there was another man in the world as wonderful as him. After all the pain he had endured, believing himself to have been the orchestrator of such a terrible fate…

For all her discretion, she had managed to get what she wanted in the end: true love.

"Goodness, she is getting heavy," was Timothy's greeting as he closed the door behind him, stretching his shoulders. "That girl insisted I carry her all the way upstairs, and she has broken me!"

"I told you she was old enough for schooling, and you did not believe me."

Timothy rolled his eyes as he threw himself onto the sofa. "Nonsense. Well, maybe. I think we need to consider moving her out of the nursery upstairs into something a little more formal. What do you think?"

Small butterflies were emerging from their cocoons in Anne's stomach, but she kept her face resolute as she answered.

"I agree," she said calmly. "Besides, we may need that chamber for something else."

Would he understand her meaning? She had not considered the right time or place to express such hopes, for hopes they were. Or at least, she could not be entirely sure. *Not yet.*

Timothy, however, did not seem to understand her at all. "Well, I can't think what else we would want to use that room for, situated where it is. There are so many rooms in this place. If you want a room for something, there are plenty of others you could use."

Anne rose, moving across the room to sit opposite her husband. *No, it was not a good enough opening for her news. She was sure she would know when it was, and it was not yet.*

"And what is that smile for, wife?"

Her stomach swooped to hear that word. "Wife. 'Tis a strange word to answer to."

"'Tis even stranger for someone to respond," said Timothy

cheerfully, but then his face fell. "You...you do not find it difficult, knowing for a time I was married to your cousin. You said you were close."

"A long time ago," said Anne. She had considered the situation carefully, and though it was a strange situation, it was not unheard of. "Perhaps if Louise and I had remained close. Perhaps if we had been as sisters to each other as women."

"I suppose you are right," Timothy said heavily. "As long as you are not unhappy."

Anne raised an eyebrow. "With you?"

A cushion was thrown at her for that remark, and she caught it with a chuckle.

"How dare you, and you my wife and all," said Timothy in a mock haughty tone, though he did not hide his smile. "In hindsight, having found happiness myself...I know what it is now, and I know what I lacked, but somehow, I wonder whether she lacked it, too."

Anne was silent. Timothy would heal over time.

"I suppose it hurts," she said gingerly after a few minutes. "You were injured by her."

"I look back now and wonder whether I was too hard on her," Timothy said. "It is not as though I made it easy. She must have been lonely, here in this place, far above her birth, and losing my trust. She must have been lonely, finding affection in a servant's arms."

"Oh, I don't know. You did!"

Timothy shook his head. "So I did! That was because the right woman arrived. You are perfect for me, Anne. You and Frances. Now nothing will change for a time. I don't think I could cope with much else changing. I need a bit of normality before anything else happens!"

He spread out his arms behind him and rested his head on his palms, stifling a yawn.

Anne hesitated. "You might find something changing would be a good thing."

"Christ, I cannot possibly think what," Timothy groaned,

eyes closed. "I am exhausted from all this subterfuge, which I should never have started in the first place!"

It was hard to disagree with this. "The moment you asked me to pretend to be your countess at the Christmas ball, you set off a chain of events which was rather unpredictable."

Her husband chuckled. "I know, God's teeth, I could never have foreseen it all. But there we are. All's well that ends well, as they say."

Anne took a deep breath. If she had thought about it, she would have prepared herself better, but now was the right time to speak. Really, she should be commended for keeping this to herself for weeks. *A governess of discretion? She had more than earned that title.*

"Well…I wouldn't call this the end. Not really."

Timothy opened one eye from his reclined position. "What do you mean?"

"I mean…well," she said slowly. "I am not even one hundred percent certain. It could all be a lot of fuss for nothing, and then I would feel ridiculous calling out the doctor, and—"

Both of Timothy's eyes snapped open, and he sat up straight, all mirth gone from his face. "Doctor? Anne, are you ill? Why didn't you tell me something was amiss?"

Anne smiled. It was a strange sort of secret, this one. It filled her very soul with warmth, and yet the pleasure of keeping it was secondary only to sharing it.

"No, I am not ill," she said softly, "but I am certainly not feeling my best."

Timothy was a picture of concern. "Damn and blast it, Anne, why didn't you say so? Here I've been, blathering on, and you've felt—are you too hot? Too cold? Shall I call for Dewey, have the doctor called?"

"I think the doctor would be a good idea," said Anne firmly, "but let's wait until tomorrow."

Her heart twisted to see the concern on Timothy's face. *He loved her.* He really did, passionately and foolishly, in his own way.

"I do not understand why we would bother waiting when

you are unwell," said Timothy urgently. "Unless—unless you know what is wrong?"

Anne took a deep breath. "I do not know, but I suspect that…Timothy, I think I am pregnant."

As she watched him, she wondered whether she should have prepared him. Timothy had not moved—not an inch. He was still leaning forward on the sofa, still had his eyes wide, and stared at her without speaking.

Anne swallowed. "I mean, I—"

"With child! Oh, Anne, are you sure?"

She was unable to reply immediately, breath entirely knocked from her lungs as Timothy swept her up into his arms. Kisses rained down on her face, and he captured her lips in a passionate yet reverential kiss.

When he finally broke away, Anne looked into a beaming smile.

"Oh, Anne! You are sure?"

"Not entirely," she breathed with a nervous laugh, "but all the signs are there, and I suppose there is always a possibility that the precaution we took—"

"Oh, we shouldn't have even bothered with that," said Timothy, his laughter rocking through Anne's body, it was drawn so close to his own. "A baby! A child, a brother or sister for Frances! Oh, Anne!"

As he kissed her again, it was not just pleasure that rippled through Anne, it was relief, excitement, and something else she could not quite identify.

Their family was going to grow larger, more love, more excitement, more drama. And at the center of it all, her and Timothy.

"Oh Anne, you have made me so happy," said Timothy with shining eyes. "But blast it all. You will have to keep this under your hat! While the world is a little confused about when we married, it certainly isn't long enough for that!"

She laughed. "Do not worry yourself about that. I am a governess of discretion."

About Emily E K Murdoch

If you love falling in love, then you've come to the right place.

I am a historian and writer and have a varied career to date: from examining medieval manuscripts to designing museum exhibitions, to working as a researcher for the BBC to working for the National Trust.

My books range from England 1050 to Texas 1848, and I can't wait for you to fall in love with my heroes and heroines!

Follow me on twitter and instagram @emilyekmurdoch, find me on facebook at facebook.com/theemilyekmurdoch, and read my blog at www.emilyekmurdoch.com.

www.ingramcontent.com/pod-product-compliance
Lightning Source LLC
Chambersburg PA
CBHW070747190726
48292CB00002B/442